CASTRO'S DAUGHTER

DAVID HAGBERG

A TOM DOHERTY ASSOCIATES BOOK
NEW YORK

This is a work of fiction. All of the characters, organizations, and events portrayed in this novel are either products of the author's imagination or are used fictitiously.

CASTRO'S DAUGHTER

Copyright © 2012 by David Hagberg

A Forge Book
Published by Tom Doherty Associates, LLC
175 Fifth Avenue
New York, NY 10010

www.tor-forge.com

Forge® is a registered trademark of Tom Doherty Associates, LLC.

ISBN 978-0-7653-5988-9

Forge books may be purchased for educational, business, or promotional use. For information on bulk purchases, please contact Macmillan Corporate and Premium Sales Department at 1-800-221-7945 extension 5442 or write specialmarkets@macmillan.com.

First Edition: July 2012
First Mass Market Edition: May 2013

Printed in the United States of America

0 9 8 7 6 5 4 3 2 1

WRITING AS DAVID HAGBERG

• • •

NONFICTION WITH BORIS GINDIN

FICTION WITH
SENATOR BYRON L. DORGAN

* Kirk McGarvey adventures

This novel is for Lorrel, as always.

ACKNOWLEDGMENTS

This is a work of fiction, though in many ways I wish it could have happened. Special thanks to Eddie Leon, a neighbor, a friend, and my expert on all things Spanish. The mistakes are all mine.

PART
ONE

ONE

The streets of downtown Havana out to the suburb of Miramar were all but deserted at two of a muggy morning as María León, driving an older 7 Series BMW, pulled up at the security entrance to the compound of Fidel Castro.

She was a slender woman, thirty-six, her flowing dark hair framing a finely defined dusky face of high cheekbones, narrow nose, firm chin, and broad, darkly expressive eyes. She was dressed in an L.A. Rams T-shirt and light-colored shorts that accentuated her long legs.

But she wasn't crying, not yet, if ever she would. She had mixed feelings about her father that very often bordered on hate, even now that he was dying.

A pair of officers in slacks and guayabera shirts, both of them armed, came out of the gatehouse. One of them held back, his hand on the butt of the pistol in his shoulder holster, while the other approached the open driver's-side window. They were not smiling.

Neither of them had pulled their weapon. She could easily have shot both of them with a silenced pistol and gotten into the compound without raising an alarm.

She held up her state credentials card, which identified her as Director of Operations for Cuba's foreign secret service—the DI, Dirección de Inteligencia—and for a moment, the man at her window didn't know what to do.

"Damned sloppy, both of you," María said. Security out here came under the umbrella of operations, and up until now, she'd assumed that Captain Manuel Fuentes, the little mouse of a man who ran the division for her, was doing a good job.

"I'm sorry, señora, but you were expected and we recognized the car."

"Anyone could have been driving. The real María León could be lying dead in a ditch somewhere."

"Yes, ma'am."

"Get out of my way, *puto*," María told him, and as he stepped back, she raced down the one-way driveway that passed through one of the security screens of trees that crisscrossed the compound, the first tears beginning to well up in her eyes.

She was angry, as she'd been for most of her life. She felt as if she could count on one hand the number of times she'd ever been truly happy or in love or not lonely. Since she'd finally stopped asking why she was treated differently from the other children in the KGB-run special school years ago, she'd been so filled with resentment that most of the time—like this morning—the bitterness lit up her insides with a nuclear furnace that powered nearly every aspect of her life and her career.

"You're mad all the time," one of her lovers, a dashing captain in the air force, had told her one night after they made love.

"It's what keeps me going," she remembered telling him.

"That's too bad for you, because it's ugly."

But then, he wasn't an illegitimate daughter of Fidel's, not acknowledged, not once. Never told that she was loved, never held in her father's arms, never seated at his table, never allowed to play with his other children. No aunts or uncles or cousins or grandparents to send her little presents. No vacations to the mountains, or even day trips to the beach.

Only tutors, studying, books, small classes where students were identified only by their first names in schools run by stern, no-nonsense Russians who endlessly drummed into their heads that they were special, that ahead of them lay brilliant futures in service to the state.

Later, the purely academic subjects of mathematics and science and languages—Spanish, of course, but also Russian and especially English, and all the rich literature—were followed by political indoctrination lessons last thing every day, almost like boring sugarless desserts.

And then when she turned thirteen, María joined a small class of boys, dressed like them in camouflaged uniforms, and learned weapons and explosives and hand-to-hand combat, a discipline she enjoyed immensely. A vent for her anger.

The entire compound was lit up, and driving up to her father's house, she saw a lot of people milling around, some of them by the pool, some in the covered walkway and in the living room, spilling out from the open doors. She knew this place, but she'd never been here at the same time as her father, and she hated herself all the more for feeling sad about that it.

Fuentes, speaking on a walkie-talkie, came from the house as María parked behind a line of mostly beat-up old American cars from the 1950s. Dressed in green military fatigues with no name tag or insignia of rank— the same as Fidel and most of the others from the revolution favored—he looked like some idiot outfitted for a costume ball, or one of those dreary Marxist stage productions about the bright Communist world, where every worker was treated the same.

"You're almost too late," he sniveled.

María resisted the sudden urge to take the little man apart here and now, but it would wait. "I want you in my office at eight, Captain," she said sharply.

Fuentes flinched, but he didn't back down. "Is there something wrong with my security arrangements, Madam Director?"

"Plenty," she said. "Now, did El Comandante ask for me specifically?"

"Yes, and he's sent everyone away, except for Dr. Céspedes."

Some of the people on the veranda and just inside the house were looking at her—some of them family, others close personal advisers—but none of them smiled. She was an outsider, the fact that Fidel was her father a closely guarded secret except from a select few, Fidel's brother Raúl among them. None of the leader's children had any idea she was a half sister, and the people gathered here this morning knew her as nothing more than some government functionary. But they were obviously curious about why Fidel had called her to his deathbed.

She glared at them, but then admitted to Fuentes that she didn't know the way.

"I'll show you," Fuentes said coolly, and he took her through the modestly furnished living room to the small master bedroom at the rear corner of the house, knocked once, and went inside.

The room stank of death and decay mingled with the odors of medicines and maybe alcohol, and cigar smoke that was permanently embedded in the walls and ceilings and fabrics. Fidel Castro lay propped up with a couple of pillows in the middle of a queen-sized bed, his doctor taking his blood pressure. His face had sagged, and his beard was poorly shaved, leaving a bluish tinge to his skin.

He turned his head when María approached, and she got the impression that he was minutes if not seconds away from death. His eyes were weeping some thick mucus, and a little blood had seeped from his mouth to stain the front of his pajamas. But when he focused on her, he seemed to revive, pulling himself up out of a near stupor.

"Leave us now," he told the doctor, his voice weak but surprisingly firm and understandable.

The doctor hesitated but then took the blood pressure cuff off Fidel's arm and walked out with Fuentes, leaving María alone with her father, and she realized how frightened she was.

Fidel was nearly a god to most people of Cuba, and to her as well, she had to admit. From the time that, as a teenager, she'd learned who her father was—the reason she was so special to her Russian teachers—she'd been almost in awe of herself, of her genes. That reverence had turned to anger within a few years because of his distance, because he never acknowledged her, and because she was constantly reminded that her relationship to Fidel was an important state secret. Divulging it would be considered an act of treason.

And after a while, she began to understand the reasons for the secrecy—or at least she thought she did—which only increased an anger that was directed inward. She began to hate herself for loving her father, or at least her idealized notion of what a father should be. She wanted to be proud, a vanity that she thought was stupid. She wanted to think about him rescuing her from a dreary life; it would have taken only one stroke of a pen, one word to Raúl, and she would have been properly acknowledged. Loved. Yet she hated that longing, too, because of all the years of her life that had been wasted.

In the end, brainwashed or not, she became the functionary the Russians had trained her to be. An agent for the state, taught spy craft and international diplomacy at the finest schools in Moscow.

And right now, she felt like a child. "Hello, Papá," she said, unable to think of anything else.

"Come closer."

She went next to him, where the smell of death was much stronger. Her heart pounded and her mouth was dry. *Dios mio,* she felt stupid. "I'm here."

Phlegm rattled deep in Fidel's chest. "You're a beautiful child," he said, his voice very soft as he tried to catch his breath. "Retribution," he whispered. His eyes closed.

She leaned closer, half-convinced he had just died. "What did you say?" she asked. She didn't want to touch him.

His eyes opened and María was so startled, she reared back.

"Find Kirk McGarvey," he said. "Bring him here. He'll know."

She knew the name, of course: He was the near legendary former director of the CIA who until recently had gone back to work for the agency from time to time. He'd once even conducted some investigation at Guantánamo Bay, so he was a fixture on the DI's Persons of Interest list. But he had dropped out of sight some months ago, and nothing she'd read in any Daily Report or Weekly Summary hinted at any operation of interest to Cuba that he was currently engaged with.

"He's retired," she told her father. "No longer a threat to us."

"It's what I want," Fidel croaked, half-rising off his pillows, his face turning beet red.

María was truly alarmed now. She didn't want to witness her father's death, and she certainly didn't want to cause it. All her anger was gone. "I'll call the doctor."

"No," Fidel said, his voice strong again for just that one word. "He knows."

"What does he know?"

Fidel started to say something, but then he shook his head and fell back. "Our salvation. Bring him here. Ask him. Promise me. My friend Jong-il told me he could be trusted."

She had no idea what her father was talking about, except that Kim had been the General Secretary of North Korea; maybe this was only the lunatic ravings of a dying old man who'd manipulated practically the entire world for nearly all his life. The U.S. embargoes made Cuba poor while at the same time making Fidel more powerful in the eyes of his people. He was the man who stood up to the United States. The Bay of Pigs was his victory, as was the so-called missile crisis, out of which came the pledge from Washington that Cuba would never be attacked.

"Promise," Fidel said, his voice nearly inaudible now.

But he'd first said *retribución*. For what? Guantánamo? María touched his bony shoulder. "I promise, Papá," she told him.

And he smiled the open yet secret way he did when he went on television and shook his fist at the United States. She'd seen the smile a thousand times; everyone in Cuba had. And everyone knew that he was holding something up his sleeve. "Be careful whom you trust, child."

"I promise," she said softly.

And a moment later, Fidel Castro took his last, shallow breath, his open eyes draining of life.

María looked at the old man. The bastard was up to something, even at the last. It was amazing, and perhaps, she thought, her life to this point had been a better one without his acknowledgment.

TWO

Carlos Gutiérrez, one of the gardeners on the staff, had stepped outside for a smoke on happenstance when the woman driving the BMW showed up, and he lingered in the shadows near the end of the covered walkway until she came out after only a few minutes inside.

He was Cuban born but had escaped to Miami with his sister and parents when he was eight, and after he graduated with an honors law degree from Stetson, the CIA had recruited him. He was whip thin with a dark, narrow boyish face that made him look eighteen when in fact he was twenty-eight. He was dedicated to the Cuban people and the eventual overthrow of the Communist government so that his family and other refugees could return to their homeland in peace.

Making sure that no one could see what he was doing, Carlos pulled out his cell phone and snapped a half dozen photos of the woman, two of them nearly face-on and two of the car, one capturing the government license tag.

Whoever the woman was, she had to be well connected. Only important people drove nearly new luxury cars, because sure as hell she wasn't a rich tourist, not with those government plates. And a tourist would not have been invited to Fidel's deathwatch.

Pocketing his cell phone, Carlos started back to his room around the other side of the swimming pool when Captain Fuentes came from the house and said something to the group on the covered veranda, and a woman screamed out loud.

Another woman shouted, "El Comandante!" and began to sob.

The old bastard had finally died, and Carlos held back a smile. Maybe now they could begin to make some progress, come back from the fifty-year slide into abject poverty.

He turned and slipped away into the shadows at the end of the walkway and hurried around the pool to his quarters, actually just one small room with a bathroom, the same as all the other service personnel, including security, here in the compound. No one was above anyone else, they were constantly told.

He stopped a moment in the darkness to check out the window. But evidently no one had seen him take the pictures and then followed him to find out what he was up to. For now, he was safe.

Leaving the lights out, he went into the bathroom—where, by feel, he removed a small panel from behind the toilet and took out an encrypted sat phone wrapped tightly in a plastic bag. It took less than one minute for the device to power up and automatically find the right satellite so that he could enter his eleven-digit alphanumeric password. The phone connected to only one number at Langley, which was answered in English on the first ring by his handler.

"Yes."

"Fidel is dead."

"When?"

"Just minutes ago," Carlos said. "But there is something else. An important woman I've never seen before showed and was taken inside by Captain Fuentes himself. She stayed only a short time, and she left just before the announcement was made."

"How do you know that she is important?"

"She was driving a BMW, looked fairly new."

"Was she alone?"

"Yes," Carlos said. He'd never met his handler face-to-face and knew the man only by the name John. But he had complete confidence in his colleague. John's was a calm voice; his advice had always been reasonable and steady. "I have photographs."

"Send them now."

In the sat phone's bag was a USB cord, which Carlos used to connect his cell phone to the satellite phone. He brought up the stored pictures file and sent them as a message. The transfer took a couple of seconds.

"I have them," John said. "Stand by."

Suddenly nervous, Carlos went to the window to look outside when the door burst open and one of Captain Fuentes's security officers barged in, pistol drawn.

"What are you up to, you bastard?" the officer demanded.

Carlos feinted as if he were trying to make a run for the bathroom to get to the window there, and the guard switched his aim just far enough left to leave himself wide open. But there could be no gunfire to alert the staff, so Carlos grabbed the officer's gun hand, gripping the hammer so that it could not be triggered, and twisted the weapon out of the man's grasp all in one lightning-fast movement.

The security officer was a large man by Cuban standards, and was slow on his feet, giving Carlos time to ram three fingers into a spot just below the man's Adam's apple, driving him backwards and instantly constricting his windpipe.

After jamming the pistol into the waistband of his trousers and dropping the connected phones on the edge of the bed, Carlos was on the gasping security officer, shoving him to the side and twisting the man's head sharply to the left, snapping his neck, and letting him crumple, dying, to the floor.

John had not disconnected.

"I've been burned," Carlos told him. "But I'm okay for the moment."

"What are your chances of getting out of the compound?"

Carlos looked out the window. No one else was coming. "Fifty–fifty," he said. And the fact that he was now armed meant absolutely nothing. Because once the shooting began, by anybody, he would be cornered.

"Your extraction point is X-ray, copy?"

"Roger, X-ray," Carlos said.

"Good luck."

Glancing out the window again to make sure that he was still in the clear, Carlos shut off the phones, pocketed them, and stepped outside into the warm, humid night. X-ray was Marina Hemingway, about fifteen kilometers west along the coast, where a speedboat and captain would be waiting for him. But even if he managed to get to the motor pool on the other side of the house without being spotted, managed to steal a car and drive away, his chances once he got to the boat were hardly better. The Cuban navy maintained a heavy patrol presence around the entire island, but especially on its north coast. And they were good at intercepting watercraft.

More cars were coming up the driveway, and the crowd at the front of the house had grown appreciably in the last few minutes. He'd never really known these people, even though this was his country. From the moment he'd come back to the island, he felt a disconnect between the Cubans here and the Cuban exiles in Miami and elsewhere. That rift was not only the result of fifty-plus years of separation, but mostly came about because of the vastly different lifestyles between here and the States. The language was the same, but the words had come to have different meanings.

Carlos hesitated for just a moment before he started the opposite way he had come, down a path that led behind the house and away from the growing crowd coming from Havana. By dawn, there would be hundreds of people here from all over the island. And he supposed that heads of state or their representatives from all over the world would be attending the funeral sometime next week, fawning over a dictator and mass murderer who'd once brought the entire western hemisphere to the brink of nuclear war.

Light spilled out from the windows in Fidel's bedroom, and Carlos had to get off the path to stay in the darkness.

"*Alto!*" Halt! someone shouted from behind.

And it was over just like that, just as he knew the day would likely come. He veered to the right, directly away from the house, and sprinted deeper into the darkness, pulling the security officer's 9 mm Glock 17 from his waistband.

"Halt!" someone else shouted from ahead.

And Carlos raised the pistol forward and fired five shots in quick succession, and pulled off five more to the rear.

A bullet slammed hard into the base of his spine, knocking him forward off his feet the instant before he heard the sound of the shot. He felt no pain, except that breathing seemed difficult and he was having trouble moving his gun hand.

Moments, or perhaps minutes, later—time seemed to be distorted—someone kicked the pistol away from his hand and he looked up as Captain Fuentes hunched down next to him.

"It seems we were right to keep an eye on you."

"*Bastardo,*" Carlos managed to croak, amazed that he still felt no pain, but worried that he felt as if he were drowning. And the sinking sensation was getting worse.

"Whom do you work for?" Fuentes asked. "The CIA?"

Three years in place, essentially on a deathwatch, from which almost no hard intelligence had been gained, except for the time and date of El Comandante's passing, and the unexpected appearance of a mystery woman—perhaps Fidel's last visitor. John had the photographs, so maybe something interesting would come of it.

Captain Fuentes was shouting words that Carlos couldn't quite make out, and his last thought was that he would have liked to meet John face-to-face, maybe over a cold cerveza.

THREE

The headquarters of the Dirección de Inteligencia is located in Plaza Havana—across from the Parque de la Fraternidad, in sight of the capitol building, amongst most of Cuba's government buildings—and driving there a couple of hours before dawn, María still wasn't quite sure what she was feeling.

Traffic had begun to pick up, most of it heading down to Miramar, leaving her to wonder if everyone in the country except her had been on a deathwatch this morning, dressed and ready to respond. She was sound asleep at her finca on the beach near the tiny fishing village of Cojimar—about ten kilometers east of La Habana Vieja, old town—after a difficult day, when the call came from Fuentes, and it had taken her a half hour to get her act together.

Raúl, who had officially succeeded his brother in 2008, would be the one to announce El Comandante's death, and the proclamation of a state of national mourning. Out of the public's eye, Cuba's military and intelligence services would be placed on the highest condition of alert against the chance that some nation might try to take advantage of what could be perceived as a weakness in government. At least, that's the stance she was sure Raúl and his generals were taking right now. It was another reason for her to go directly to her office, because things were going to get very busy in the government plaza.

The precautions were paranoia, but that was the state of affairs all of them would be faced with, especially her directorate. Another Bay of Pigs? She didn't think so; there'd been no hints, no odd bits of intelligence from Miami or Washington to suggest such a possibility. But she needed to be ready for the rounds of meetings and staff conferences with every scrap of intel her directorate could produce.

Parking in her slot in the rear, she went inside, showing her ID to the man on duty, whose right eyebrow rose at the sight of her in a T-shirt and shorts. But she was a colonel and he was a sergeant, so he said nothing.

She took the elevator up to her suite of offices on the third floor. In addition to the night-duty officer and his four people manning the watch, which closely monitored the output of the entire sophisticated network of signals intelligence (SIGINT) facilities around the island, her chief of staff, Major Román Ortega-Cowan was also seated at his desk.

He was a career intelligence officer of medium height, with a thick barrel chest, a square-jawed face, and wide, smiling eyes under a high golden tinged forehead and coarse, richly black curly hair. His passion was opera, for which it was rumored he knew by heart the score and libretto for every major work performed in the last two hundred years. He was also a patron of the country's four professional orchestras and one seriously depleted opera company, many of whose members had fled to take jobs, mostly in Spain.

But in María's estimation, he was a conniving, two-faced *hijo de puta* whose smile concealed deeper, darker purposes—almost always for his own personal gain—and who needed to be constantly guarded against. Exactly why she had picked him for her chief of staff three years ago: She wanted a conniver who would get results no matter the obstacles. And he'd done a fine job for her, his training at the hands of the Russian intelligence apparatus in Moscow first-rate.

He looked up when she came to his open door, said something to whomever he was talking to on the phone, hung up, and got to his feet. "I was just about to call you," he said.

"I've already heard. Who was that on the phone?"

"General Muñoz's chief of staff. We're at DEFCON Two, and I was ordered to start the call up." General Ramiro Casas Muñoz was chief of the DI; Defense Condition Two was just one step below the actual military invasion of the island, and all military and intelligence personnel were being called for duty.

"That's stupid. Fidel wasn't murdered."

"We can't be certain."

María had turned to go to her office, where she kept a set of military fatigues with her insignia of rank and the DI badge, when Ortega-Cowan stopped her.

"There was a shooting at the compound a couple of hours ago."

She came back, her stomach suddenly hollow. "What are you talking about?" She'd been out there, of course, but she could not tell that to her chief of staff. She was sure that he didn't know the relationship she had to Fidel.

"I don't have the details, but Captain Fuentes sounded excited. He's on his way right now—it's one of the reasons I was just about to call you."

Nor could she tell him that she'd ordered Fuentes to come here first thing this morning because of sloppy security out there. Neither man knew her entire story, though they were both cut of the same conspiratorial cloth, and both of them thought they knew everything. They wanted her job—that had always been obvious—and she had a feeling that now that Fidel was dead and Fuentes was freed from his compound security position, he might think he had the opening he was waiting for. And of course, Ortega-Cowan was a typical Cuban male, full of machismo, who thought from the beginning that María's post should be filled by a man, not by a woman.

As long as the two of them never got together, she would be safe, and perhaps now was the time for her to get rid of one of them. There would be a lot of confusion in the coming days. Who could tell what might happen?

"I want to talk to Captain Fuentes when he gets here," María said. "Not a word about the shooting to anyone."

"Of course," Ortega-Cowan said. "Shall I sit in with you?"

"I'll handle him myself, probably nonsense. You know how he can get."

Ortega-Cowan nodded. It was unspoken knowledge that Fuentes was a homosexual, but he'd been Fidel's choice for chief of his personal security, and everything had been left at that; speculation was not encouraged. "Staff meeting at ten?"

"Oh-nine-hundred," María said, and she walked back to her office to change, and to ponder not only her father's last request, but also the business of a shooting out there. It must have happened just minutes after she'd left. Curious.

Something wasn't right, and although she'd prefer to think that it was some trick that Fuentes had worked up, she wasn't sure, because there was no motive she could think of. Fidel was dead; there was no one left for the captain to impress.

She changed into her crisp fatigue uniform, ordered up a pot of strong *café con leche* from the cafeteria, and was just going over the first overnights from the watch—and especially the collated data from the dozen and a half signals intelligence ground stations around the island—when Ortega-Cowan showed up at her door two hours later with Fuentes, who carried a canvas shoulder bag.

If they were in any sort of collusion, she couldn't make it out from the expressions on their faces, except that Ortega-Cowan was curious and Fuentes was excited. And maybe smug?

"I'll be in my office if you need anything, Colonel," Ortega-Cowan said, and he turned and walked away.

María waved Fuentes to a seat across the desk from her. "You reported a shooting after I left," she said before he was settled.

"Yes, Colonel. We caught a spy trying to escape. He managed to kill one of my officers, and when he fired on us, we shot him."

María sat back. "A spy in El Comandante's compound is nothing short of incredible. CIA?"

"Presumably," Fuentes said, but he didn't seem concerned, which was bothersome.

"Don't play games with me, Captain," María said harshly. "You have sixty seconds to explain to me why I shouldn't have you arrested and tried for gross dereliction of duty bordering on treason."

Still, Fuentes didn't seem to be bothered. "We've had one of the house staff under investigation for the past year and a half. His name was Carlos Gutiérrez, and he was hired as a gardener about the same time El Comandante retired."

"He's dead?"

"Most unfortunately. But it's not likely, had he survived, that he would have told us anything under interrogation."

"We have the drugs."

"We found a hollow tooth with cyanide."

"I'll want to see the report of your investigation, but what the hell was he doing out there? He could hardly have been gathering anything important, other than Fidel's health. Unless he he'd been put in place as an assassin. Was that what happened this morning?"

"No. Dr. Céspedes is certain El Comandante's death was from natural causes. He's been failing for months now. In any event, the gardener had no direct access. They were never alone together."

"How do you know that he was CIA?"

Fuentes took a satellite phone from his bag and laid it on the desk, and María immediately recognized it for what it was.

"Encrypted?" she asked.

"I think so, and the machine needs passwords. Our

technical department might be able to figure it out. But it's almost certain that he called his report in to Langley that El Comandante was dead and was given instructions for his escape."

It didn't add up for María. "It would have been stupid for him to try to run. He'd done nothing wrong, unless his call had been detected and he became aware of it."

Fuentes took a flip cell phone out of his bag and placed it on the desk. "We've kept him under surveillance, as I've said. And we've been extra alert the past few days because of El Comandante's condition. We searched his quarters, but we couldn't be as thorough as we wanted, lest he become suspicious of us. And it was driving us crazy why he was there. What did he hope to learn?"

"And?"

"One of my officers spotted him taking photographs with this cell phone."

"Of what?" María asked.

"You."

María powered up the phone, careful to make sure her hands did not shake, and brought up the half dozen photographs of her and her car, one of which included the tag number. "Are you sure that he managed to send these to Langley?"

"We found a USB cord in his room, which would certainly suggest that he had the opportunity to do so." Fuentes shrugged.

He was enjoying himself, and it infuriated María. But looking at the photographs again, she couldn't see that any real damage had been done. "Were there any indications that he knew my rank?"

"None that I'm aware of."

"Or why I was out there this morning?"

Fuentes hesitated. "No, but I'm wondering the same myself. Is it anything you can share with me, Colonel? You were the last one to see El Comandante alive. What were his last words?"

María waved the question off. "Minutiae," she said. "He wanted to know what SIGINT we'd gotten from Miami in the last twenty-four hours."

"That makes no sense."

"The final ramblings of a very old man who'd been accustomed all his life to knowing everything."

Fuentes was skeptical.

"He died in the middle of my report," María said. "And that bit of information, Captain, will never leave this office. Am I clear?"

"Perfectly."

She'd been taught by her Russian masters that the secret of keeping a subordinate in line was to keep him forever off balance. She'd become adept at it. "I originally wanted you here this morning to discuss your security procedures, but that has become a moot point. So now let us discuss your next assignment, which will depend on your skills."

Fuentes was clearly distressed, but María held back a smile. She'd never liked the man, and maybe having him here at headquarters, close at hand, would force him into making a mistake that she could use to get rid of him.

"Talk to me, Captain," she said. "Tell me what you want."

FOUR

Emerging from the colonel's office and stalking down the corridor, Fuentes knew damned well what the bitch was trying to do to him, had been trying all along, but it still wasn't straight in his mind why she wanted him out. Uncle Fidel had trusted him, and yet he'd called a nobody director of operations to his deathbed, and the why of that alone was enough to drive a man crazy.

Passing Ortega-Cowan's open door, their eyes met, and Fuentes resisted the urge to step inside and have a little talk. Of all the people with any influence in the DI, María's chief of staff was the only one he had common ground with. But not now; the fact that they could be allies was something best kept from the colonel until it was time for them to strike.

Outside, he got into his battered Gazik, which was one of the jeeps the Russians had left behind, but before he could drive away, Ortega-Cowan came out. The parking lot was at the rear of the building, while the colonel's office was in front. They went to a bench in one of the gardens.

"You didn't look too happy up there, Manuel," Ortega-Cowan said. "Mind sharing with me what's going on?"

"She wants to get rid of me," Fuentes said bitterly. He needed to complain to someone.

"I meant about the shooting."

And Fuentes told him everything, leaving out no detail, including the photographs of María and her car that had presumably been transmitted to Langley, and about her reaction.

Ortega-Cowan was impressed. "This just might be what we need to take her down."

"What are you talking about? She means to use the fact that I let a spy so close to El Comandante to have me demoted, possibly even court-martialed." *And she'd be well within her rights and duties,* the errant thought flashed in his head. But the kid's eyes were enchanting, and Fuentes had seen him a couple of times tending the less prickly of the plants while wearing nothing but brief shorts and sandals. He'd been dazzled.

"Use your head. Until now, the identity of all our directorate chiefs has been kept a secret. Just like in the Mossad. But if the CIA has her photographs, especially in connection with Fidel's compound, on the very morning of his death—within minutes of his death—and pictures of that goddamned fancy car of hers, they'll sit up and take notice."

"So what?"

"If she's identified, she's out," Ortega-Cowan said. "And maybe I can help."

"How?"

"Never mind for now. But what exactly was she doing out there this morning? Who called her?"

"El Comandante asked for her."

"By name, or simply as the director of operations?"

"By name, and he even knew her private number by heart. Told me to tell no one else, just fetch her."

"And no one else was alone with them in the bedroom?"

"No."

"Which, of course, you had not bugged."

Fuentes flared, and for a moment he forgot himself. "He was going to come back and I was going to be his new Minister of Foreign Relations."

Ortega-Cowan smiled, but not derisively. "He told you that?"

"No, but it was obvious he wanted to return to government. And my English is nearly letter perfect."

Ortega-Cowan looked away. They could hear the traffic around the plaza, and already the parking lot was beginning to fill as the call-up continued. The coming days were going to be a frenzy of activities. "That was then and this is now," he finally said.

"But you have something in mind."

"Of course. If I can pry the colonel out of her position, I'd have a good shot at taking over the directorate. No one else is qualified. If that's the case, would you serve as my chief of staff?"

"It's not what I wanted, but I'd take it."

"But I'd have to watch my back, right?"

Fuentes smiled. "Naturally." What he really wanted, what he'd realistically hoped to get, was the directorate. And a promotion to chief of staff would put him only a heartbeat away. "Do you have a plan?"

"Yes, but you'll have to be patient. First we need to get past the funeral, and stand down from the general alert. Could be weeks. And then we can find her weakness."

"Might not be so easy."

"You're wrong," Ortega-Cowan said. "Uncle Fidel didn't call his chief of DI operations to his deathbed to discuss Miami signals intelligence. The question is exactly what they talked about."

Fuentes was at a loss, but Ortega-Cowan was waiting for an answer. "A deathbed confession?"

"You may be close, because what does a person knowing he has only hours, maybe minutes, to live, want to talk about? Want to get off his chest? It's either a confession of some past wrong—an infidelity, maybe?—or some last-minute instruction. One last order?"

"But what?"

"We'll find that out eventually, but first we need to learn why it was Colonel León he called."

And Fuentes had a glimmering of an idea. "Perhaps El Comandante did not call Colonel León to his bedside. Perhaps he called María León. One of his mistresses?"

"Somehow I don't think so. Word would have gotten around, especially because of the difference in their ages. She's young enough to be a daughter."

"*Dios mio,*" Fuentes said softly, not sure if he was being manipulated, and he watched the cars and bicycles streaming into the parking lot.

Ortega-Cowan smiled. "It would explain her schooling and her promotions," he said. "She's one of the only female colonels in the service, and the only woman to be in charge of an entire directorate."

"If that's true, she's just lost her protector. Leaves her wide open."

"That depends on what Raúl knows and how he feels about it," Ortega-Cowan said. "If we're right about this, we might not have to do anything at all, just sit back until she's fired." He smiled again. "Let's just wait and see what happens. And if it needs a little nudge here and there, we'll find a way."

"Yes, we will," Fuentes said. His heart was much lighter than it had been in months, perhaps ever.

PART

TWO

FIVE

In Washington, it was a couple of minutes past seven in the morning when a late-model Cadillac Escalade with heavily tinted windows carrying three DI field officers from Miami operations parked across the street from the Lil' Tots Day Care Center for the third day in a row.

Rodrigo Cruz, driving, was not happy with this assignment, which had been so hastily put together that, in his estimation, it had almost no chance of success—with a high likelihood that the three of them would end up in a federal holding cell before noon. But the highly secret orders came directly from the top, and had he not known better, he would have been certain that the colonel was *loca*. The story they had been given was completely crazy.

"Maybe it's true," Julio Cabrera suggested in Miami before they boarded the plane to get up here.

"Not likely," Cruz had told him, but the more he thought about it, the more it made some kind of sense to him. Only a fantastical story like this one would have any chance of convincing the woman and her husband to cooperate with them. Out of simple curiosity, if for no other reason.

And Esteban Álvarez, perched in the backseat, watching the activities across the street through a pair of binoculars, had doubts. "There've been rumors," he'd said. "We've all heard them even in Miami."

"Especially in Miami," Cruz said. "Those *bastardos* will believe just about anything."

The three men were slightly built, typical of a lot of Cubans, with dark hair and eyes and almost handsome good looks. They'd worked in Miami for the past four years, getting back to Havana for only one week each year. After this crazy assignment, they were due home for their seven days, and they were looking forward to it. Miami had glitter, plenty of good food, and nice cars, but it was far too frenetic a place for them. And this city was worse. They felt off balance.

A steady stream of cars came up the short driveway; the parents, mothers for the most part, took their children inside and came back out and drove away. The first half hour was the busiest, and by seven thirty there was almost no traffic until the next rush around eight.

Louise Horn was the exception; yesterday and the day before, she'd shown up at precisely 7:45. Not much to go on, Cruz thought, but they'd not been given the time to do a proper job of surveillance in order to establish a pattern. If she were late this morning, it would put her at the start of the next rush, which would make snatching her impossible.

The Washington bureau had provided the SUV and the safe house just off Massachusetts Avenue between Lincoln Park and the D.C. General Hospital—less than four miles away, as the crow flies—keeping their exposure to a minimum. Plus their untraceable weapons and a syringe filled with methohexital, a powerful sedative they'd used in several Miami operations over the past couple of years. When methohexital was injected directly into a subject's vein, the victim would be out in less than five seconds. In a muscle, it could take five minutes, during which time the target would put up a struggle. If it were a man, they could have some difficulty. But they'd seen the tall, slender—almost anorexic— woman, and they'd gained a little confidence. Handling her would be fairly easy.

And she was a high-value target. In addition to the weapons, an informational packet had been left for them at the house. The woman was the wife of Otto Rencke, the Director of Special Projects for the CIA, and she herself was a high-ranking satellite image analyst working for the National Geospatial-Intelligence Agency with an office attached to the CIA's Old Headquarters Building. The husband was the primary objective; kidnapping his wife was merely to assure the man's cooperation. But the abduction could also result in a firestorm of federal and local cops coming after them, and despite the propaganda, every DI field officer here in the States understood just how effective, and sometimes ruthless, the FBI functionaries could be.

Cruz glanced in his rearview mirror in time to see the battered dark blue Toyota Land Cruiser come up the street and turn into the day care center's driveway, Louise Horn driving.

"It's her," he said.

"She's early," Cabrera said. "Wait until tomorrow?"

Two women who'd dropped off their children came out of the day care center, waved as Louise got out of her Toyota, got into their cars, and drove away. No one else was arriving at the moment.

"We'll go now," Cruz said, watching nervously in his rearview mirror and out the windshield. They had been given three days for the job. This morning was it, or this afternoon, but then they would have to deal not only with the woman but her two-year-old child as well. Involving the toddler was something he wanted to avoid at all costs; he had two small children of his own in Havana. "No shooting."

Louise unstrapped the child from the car seat and walked her through the gate. The moment they disappeared inside, Cruz drove across the street and backed the wrong way into the driveway so that they were directly in front of the Toyota.

Cabrera and Álvarez got out of the Cadillac and walked back to Louise Horn's SUV just as she came out of the day care center. She was out of the gate, obviously in a hurry when she noticed them, and she pulled up, a look of concern on her narrow features.

Cabrera held up an identification wallet. "Ma'am, I'm Ulises Rodríguez, CIA Security. Mr. Rencke sent us."

Louise was suspicious, but she came the rest of the way toward them. "Is there some trouble?"

"Not at all. We were just ordered to pick you up and bring you to the Campus."

Louise glanced at the ID. "What about Joann?"

"I was told the child's name is Audrey. She'll be fine here."

"I'll just call," Louise said, taking a cell phone out of her pocket. She turned to look back at the day care center.

"That's not possible," Cabrera said. He pulled out a Glock 17 with a suppressor and pointed it at her. "Believe me, I do not want to shoot you. But you are coming with us right now."

"Shit," Louise said, and she started to back up, but Cabrera was close enough to grab her arm, and before she could pull away, Álvarez came around and took her other arm.

One of the teachers appeared in the doorway about ten meters away. "Louise?" she called out. "Are you okay?"

Cabrera turned and, still holding Louise's arm with his left hand, fired two shots, both of them hitting the teacher in her torso and driving her back inside.

"No!" Louise screamed. "Help!" But just at that moment, there was no traffic on R Street, no one to witness the struggle or hear her cries, and they half dragged and half carried her back to the Cadillac.

Cabrera yanked open the rear door, but when he tried to shove her inside, she managed to half turn and brace her hip against the doorframe. For just an instant, she was nearly motionless, though she was still screaming, and Álvarez managed to plunge the needle into her carotid artery and depress the plunger.

Louise yelped as if she had been shot, but almost immediately she began to sag, her legs giving out, and Cabrera was able to roll her onto the backseat, far enough inside so that he could close the door.

Álvarez got in on the other side and shoved Louise to the floor as Cabrera got in the front passenger side, and even before he had shut the door, Cruz had taken off down the driveway and was around the block on

Q Street, merging with traffic heading toward Massachusetts Avenue.

Cruz checked the rearview mirror, but no one seemed to be taking any particular interest in them. And although someone inside the day care center had probably gotten a good look at the car, they couldn't have read the license number, nor could they have known which way the kidnappers had gone.

The first thirty minutes were the most critical in cases like this, but before that, they would have reached the safe house and hidden the Caddy safely out of sight in the garage, where it would remain until the operation was completed.

"How is she?" he asked, looking at Álvarez's image in the mirror.

"She's out, but her heart is steady and her breathing is normal."

"That was damned fast."

"I managed to hit an artery."

Cruz turned back to his driving. "I told you no shooting. "

"The woman at the doorway saw our faces. She would have called the authorities."

"Someone has by now, so keep your eyes open," Cruz said. And already in the distance, he thought he could hear sirens.

SIX

Otto Rencke had lost a lot of weight in the past year, in part because of the diet Louise had put him on—no more heavy cream out of the carton to wash down Twinkies, his favorite food in all the world—and in part because the CIA doc had put him on a loose regimen of exercise: thirty minutes on the treadmill every weekday morning. Now, a few minutes after eight thirty and coming up from the gym to his third-floor office in the OHB, he thought he had looked a little bony in the big mirrors, although he had to admit that he felt pretty good. He still dressed badly—mostly baggy jeans and sweatshirts, plus unlaced sneakers—and his long frizzy red hair was always out of control: like an aura around a spirit medium, one of the kids in the Directorate of Intelligence had quipped. And Otto had actually caught the joke.

He keyed his code into the door reader and entered his suite of offices that were filled nearly to capacity with computer monitors, keyboards, and one horizontal touch screen monitor nearly the size of a conference table. All the equipment ran 24/7, though the screens were usually either blank or showed blinking cursors, which indicated incoming messages or sometimes announced that a search engine had come up with results.

Maps, file folders, books, magazines, and newspapers —most of them from obscure cities and paper archival centers around the globe that had not gone digital yet—were scattered just about everywhere; on tables, the one desk, on chairs, on the floor, and pinned up on walls. Field officers sent him a steady stream of the stuff, based on his shopping lists sent out to the chiefs of stations in places of interest to him.

He touched the encrypted incoming message screen, and sat down as a list of eighty-seven e-mails came up, all of them overnights, except for one just a minute ago. A video from Louise.

He called her number upstairs in Geospatial. One of the clerks picked it up on the third ring. "Louise Horn's desk."

"This is Otto. Is my wife handy?"

"Sorry, Mr. Rencke, she's not here yet."

Rencke brought up Louise's video, the first hint of trouble niggling at the back of his head. "Have her call me when she gets in."

"Yes, sir."

Louise's image appeared on the monitor and Otto nearly dropped the phone before he could hang up. She looked like hell: her face had sagged, her eyes were half-closed, and a line of drool oozed from the side of her mouth.

"I've been kidnapped," she said, the words slow and slurred to the point she was barely understandable.

Otto split the screen, and with his heart hammering, his fingers flew over the keys, opening a program that would search for the source of the message—but almost immediately it came up from somewhere in Venezuela. A remailer, because as of six thirty or so this morning, his wife was here in the city.

"Audie's not been harmed. She's at Lil' Tots."

According to his analysis program, the encryption algorithm was an old one that hadn't been used by any U.S. intelligence agency in at least ten years. He started a search for likely users—certainly not civilians, because although the protocol wasn't so secure as modern ones in use, it was still very sophisticated.

"I was drugged. They told me that it was methohexital, but it'll be completely out of my system very soon. No side effects."

The Russian Federal Security Service had used the same algorithm until eight years ago, before selling it to Libya's Military Intelligence Force and to Cuba's DI.

"No harm will come to me if you do exactly as you are told."

Fidel Castro's death, the photographs of the unknown woman who'd apparently been the last to visit him—sent from one of their sources in Havana last week—and now this kidnapping were not coincidental.

Louise looked up into the camera, her eyes still halfclosed, and she winked. "Three Hispanic males, white Caddy Escalade, shot one of the day care—"

The message abruptly ended, and Otto remained seated staring at the screen, which had gone back to the list of incoming e-mails. The goddamned Cubans because of the photographs of the woman? What sense did that make? And why the hell hadn't they edited out Louise's last words?

Security had to be given the heads-up, as would the Bureau, and Audie would have to be taken somewhere, probably down to the Farm, where she was practically the official mascot. He wished to hell that Mac were here. But he wasn't.

A new incoming message came in from the same Venezuelan remailer, and with the same encryption algorithm, but this one was live, and headed only with his name.

Otto touched the screen. His camera activated, but the monitor remained blank.

"Good morning, Mr. Rencke," a man said. His accent was slight, but definitely Hispanic. "We mean your wife, or you, no harm. Nor will we in any way retaliate for the information she passed to you before we could end the transmission."

"What does the Cuban government want with us?" Otto asked.

"El Comandante's funeral will be held this afternoon at four o'clock. An aircraft from your State Department will leave from Andrews three hours from now. We want you to be on that flight."

"Impossible."

"Nevertheless, it is what you will do. Someone will meet you in Havana with further instructions. If you do not comply with our instructions, your wife will be shot to death and her body dumped in the CIA's driveway."

Otto was on camera, and he kept his expression neutral though he was hemorrhaging inside.

"Do you understand, Mr. Rencke?"

"No," Otto said. One of his search engines was working to pinpoint the Venezuelan remailer, and he needed to keep the kidnappers online as long as possible.

"Five days ago, a CIA operative working as a yard boy at El Comandante's compound in Miramar took a series of photographs of a woman who attended Fidel's deathbed. No doubt, your Directorates of Operations and Intelligence are trying to identify the woman. Her name is María León. She is Colonel León, chief of the DI's Directorate of Operations. She is also an illegitimate daughter of El Comandante."

"His daughter is Alina Fernández, and she lives in Spain."

"This is a second one. Unknown."

"Why me?" Otto demanded.

"In trade for your wife's life, of course."

"I understand that part, but what does Cuban intelligence want from me? I go down there, you take me to some interrogation center, feed me some drugs, and then what? What do you think I know that would be of any use to you?"

"You must know that you are considered a high-value target because of your specialized knowledge of the CIA's computer systems."

"Even if I drew your people pictures, you have nobody with the technical expertise to fully understand what we're doing here."

"Nevertheless, you will come to Havana this afternoon if you wish to see your wife returned to you alive."

Otto held up his hands. "All right, I'll be there. But what am I supposed to tell my people here in the building? Or the FBI? Or, for that matter, the State Department whose delegation you want me to join?"

"I'm sure you will think of the proper things to say."

"That somebody totally out of their gourd inside the DI has ordered a high-ranking CIA officer's wife to be kidnapped in order to lure the officer to Cuba? Christ, do you guys want to start a war? Won't be another Bay of Pigs."

"I understand your confusion, señor. Nevertheless, you will come to Havana."

The instant before the connection was broken, one of his search engines brought up the remailer, which belonged to SEBIN—Servicio Bolivariano de Inteligencia— Venezuela's national intelligence service.

This was a legitimate, well-thought-out intelligence operation, not some harebrained scheme dreamed up by a lunatic.

He was going to Havana—he had to—but the problem was what the hell he was going to say to his boss, the new DCI, Walter Page, that would make any sense.

SEVEN

Louise sat on the edge of a narrow bed in a small room with a tiny attached bathroom, her head still swirling from the drug they'd injected into her neck. She'd been awake enough however, to give Otto a little information that the Bureau might be able to use to track her down.

But her captors hadn't seemed to mind, though they'd pressed the SEND button on the laptop they used to record the message before she could say anything else.

And then nothing—they'd just walked out. They hadn't hit her, or shouted at her, or threatened her, which was in itself ominous. That, and the fact they'd made no effort to hide their faces, led her to believe that when this operation was completed, they would kill her. She was no field officer, but in their shoes, it's what she might think had to be done.

But she had no intention of making it easy for them. For Otto's sake. For Audie's sake.

They hadn't taken her wristwatch. It wasn't nine yet, and the entire kidnapping from the day care center to here had taken a little less than two hours. She turned her head and stared at the window, which was boarded over, and in her mind's eye she saw Joyce Kilburn violently shoved back into the school, surprise on her round face. She was the center's director, and was married with three children of her own. Sweet. Gentle. And tears wanted to well in Louise's eyes.

They needed Otto to do something for them, or tell them something. But they couldn't have any real idea whom they were dealing with. And the enormous risk they had taken to carry out something like this, so incredibly dangerous, with so many unintended consequences for them, and for whoever was directing them, had to mean that whatever they wanted was super important.

Something topical, she figured, because she didn't think whoever they worked for had merely gone on a fishing expedition. Venezuela was the most likely. SEBIN was directly under Chávez's thumb, and he hated the United States with a passion that went beyond reason.

The room was mostly in darkness except for what little light seeped in around the edges of the plywood covering the window, and from a small light over the sink in the bathroom. But it was sufficient for her to take stock of her surroundings.

The narrow bed was covered with a dirty blanket and filthy pillow, and she had to hope that whatever they wanted would happen before nightfall so she wouldn't have to sleep here. The floor was bare plywood, on which someone, probably a child, had drawn stick figures in yellow and green chalk. A mother and father, two children and a dog standing in front of a small house with a one-car garage and a big tree. Another showed a swing set and a picnic table under another large tree: in the backyard?

Louise started to struggle to her feet off the low bed, when someone was at the door unlocking it, and she sat back, tensing. By now Otto had gotten the video, and her captors had probably talked to him about the terms of her release. He almost certainly would have agreed to their demands or he would have stalled them—either way, she figured she still had some time.

The man who'd driven the Caddy came in with a bottle of Evian, which he handed to her. "The drug sometimes makes the mouth dry," he said.

"Thank you," Louise said, and she took a deep drink.

"We mean you no harm, señora."

"Right. It's why you jabbed a needle in my neck, filled me with a sedative that had a fair chance of killing me, and brought me here."

"It was necessary—"

"To kill an innocent woman at the day care center?"

"That was also necessary," Cruz said without apology.

"You could have hit one of the children inside—did your man think about that? Or didn't he give a shit?"

Cruz shrugged.

And Louise suddenly got the feeling that she knew these guys. They weren't Venezuelan intelligence officers; they were nothing more than thugs off the streets of Miami. "What does the DI want with my husband that they were willing to send someone like you to force his hand?"

Cruz showed only a flicker of surprise.

"Fidel is dead, so is this something that Raúl hatched to show that he was in charge?"

"Your husband was more cooperative when we talked to him a few minutes ago. Perhaps you should curb your tongue."

"Or what?" Louise demanded. "You'll beat me up, starve me? Or bore me to death with your sad tales of woe in Cuba, all brought on by us?" She wanted to get him angry, force him to make a mistake and say something he didn't mean to say—reveal something, any little scrap of information that she could use.

But he just gave her a long stare, then shook his head and turned to go.

"You've made a mistake."

Cruz turned back and nodded. *"Qué?"*

"My husband and I have a friend who will find you, if something happens to us. And when he does, he will kill you. *Comprende, señor?"*

Cruz smiled but then left the room, relocking the door behind him, and Louise lowered her head. The effort to goad the man had made her a little dizzy and sick to her stomach. And she had learned nothing from it, except that this was almost certainly a Cuban operation. But for the life of her, she could not think of why they would take such a risk.

The problem was that Kirk McGarvey had gone to ground again—to try to heal his wounds, physical and especially mental—and only Otto knew where he was. Certainly not at his home on the Gulf Coast of Florida. Last year, his wife, Katy; their daughter, Elizabeth; and their son-in-law, Todd Van Buren, had all been assassinated in an effort to keep Mac away from an investigation into a powerful lobbyist group here in Washington with its tendrils in just about every important governmental agency, including the Pentagon and the CIA itself.

A *Washington Post* reporter had uncovered the essential parts of the story and brought the evidence to Todd, who worked for the CIA, because he felt the operation was too big for him. And in part because Todd's father-in-law had once been the director of the agency.

And the killings had started that very day, with Todd's assassination and with murders of the reporter and his wife and their son. In the end, of course, Mac had been a driven man, pushed to his breaking point, and he had taken his revenge, bringing down a security firm second only to Blackwater, and causing the deaths of more than two dozen crooked power brokers and Washington insiders whose actual fantastical aim had been to bring down the government.

When it was over he had disappeared, almost as if he had dropped off the face of the earth, and only Otto knew for sure where he was. Or at least she hoped he did.

She took another drink of water, then struggled to her feet and tottered to the window boarded over with a sheet of thick plywood held in place by a dozen screws. She figured that from the outside, this place probably looked like an abandoned house, or perhaps one that had been foreclosed on. It had to be somewhere in the Washington area, but in the two hours since the kidnapping, they could easily have gone fifty miles or more.

Although some light seeped in from around the edges of the plywood, she couldn't see much of anything outside except for what might have been the color green, perhaps the tree from the chalk drawing, but no indication if this was a room at the front of the house or at the rear.

The bed, actually a metal cot, was the only piece of furniture in the small room. Its legs were attached to the frame by nuts and bolts, none of which were loose enough for her to remove, which was too bad because one of the legs would have made a great weapon.

The bathroom had an old-fashioned claw-foot tub, a toilet, and a sink with a medicine cabinet above it. The cabinet's mirrored door had been removed and the shelves were empty, and the small window had been boarded over as well.

Her head was spinning fast enough for her to nearly be sick to her stomach, and she sat down on the toilet seat and closed her downcast eyes for a moment or two. If she had to fight them by hand, she would do so, because there was no way in hell she was just going to lie back meekly and allow them to kill her.

When she opened her eyes, she saw the edge of a small piece of metal, or something, under the tub, and she reached down and got what turned out to be a small nail file, the kind often found in personal grooming kits. One end was pointed, but the other was nearly flat across.

She got up, went back into the bedroom, and looked at the screws holding the plywood on the window frame.

Nearly as flat across as the blade of a screwdriver.

EIGHT

The kidnappers had given him a three-hour window, which didn't leave much wiggle room and especially no time for fretting—that would come later, on the flight down to Havana. Even so, Otto's hand shook as he called Bob Packwood, the director of the Farm, which was the CIA's training facility at Camp Peary, just south of Richmond.

Todd had been a codirector of the Farm, along with Mac's daughter, Liz. Audrey was their daughter, and had become the camp's darling girl. Everyone down there thought of themselves as aunts and uncles to Audie, whom Otto and Louise had adopted.

"Send somebody up to the day care center to get Audie. Louise and I are going to be busy for the next few days."

"I'll send Mary Beth," Packwood said without a trace of hesitation. Mary Beth Stroble was the camp's shrink. "It'll be good to have her back, even if only for a few days. Let them know we're coming to fetch her."

"My next call. But it'd be best if you sent Mary Beth up as soon as possible. There was a shooting there this morning."

"Was Louise in the middle of it?"

"Three men kidnapped her and shot one of the teachers."

"Shit," Packwood said. "What can we do?"

"Get Audie out of there, and send someone to fetch Louise's car—it's probably still in the driveway."

"What's the Bureau saying?" Packwood asked.

"Nothing yet," Otto said, and he cut Packwood off from asking anything else. "Thanks for your help," he said.

He phoned the day care center, and one of the teachers answered. She sounded nearly hysterical.

"Oh, Mr. Rencke, it's just terrible. They murdered Joyce, and then they took Louise—Mrs. Rencke— away, and the police are here and they want to talk to you. I don't know what to do. All the parents are coming to get the children, but we only had Louise's contact number, not yours."

"Mary Beth Stroble is coming to get Audie. She works for the CIA, and she'll want you to see her credentials, but she will not be giving the police a statement. Let them know I'll contact them later this morning."

"They said that the FBI was coming here, too."

"That's all right, just tell them what you know, and say that I will call."

"Yes, sir. But I just don't know what to do next."

"Let the police handle it," Otto said.

He phoned Walter Page and told the director that he was on the way up, and needed their meeting to include Marty Bambridge, who was the Deputy Director of Operations, and Carleton Patterson, the CIA's general counsel.

"Something important?"

"I need to get down to Havana for Castro's funeral."

Page, a stern-looking man who'd been the CEO of IBM before the president tapped him to run the CIA, was seated on an upholstered chair across a coffee table from Bambridge and Patterson on the couch when Otto walked in.

"Good morning," the DCI said, motioning to an empty chair. "You've piqued our curiosity."

"The State Department flight to Havana leaves from Andrews at noon," Otto said, remaining standing. "I need to be on it. Castro's funeral is tomorrow."

"Not such a good idea," Bambridge said. He was a narrow-shouldered man who wore a perpetual look of surprise on his dark features. "You have the keys to the fortress in your head."

Otto had expected the DDO, who was nominally his boss, would say something like that. "They don't have anyone down there who'd understand even if I drew them a picture. So that's a nonissue."

"What is the issue, then?" Page asked. "Why are you so interested in attending Castro's funeral?"

"The DI kidnapped Louise just after she dropped Audie off at the day care center less than two hours ago."

"My God," Patterson said. He was a pale old man, in his late seventies, who had been called from academia to act as the Company's general counsel several presidents ago. The job was supposed to last through just the one administration, but he'd stayed on and no president or DCI since had found any need to replace him.

"Does the Bureau have this?" Page demanded.

"They're at the day care center now. I've sent someone up from the Farm to get Audie out of harm's way."

"We'll have to get them over here to debrief you," Page said, but Bambridge broke in.

"You said it was the DI that kidnapped her. Have they already contacted you?"

"A few minutes ago. They sent a video of Louise, who told me that she wouldn't be harmed if I cooperated. Soon as I'd seen it, one of the kidnappers contacted me and said that I was to be on the plane to Havana, where someone would meet me."

"Did you trace either ISP?"

"A SEBIN remailer in Caracas, but they were using an old encryption algorithm that only the Libyans and Cubans still use."

"Okay," Patterson said. "Why do they want you in Havana? They might take the risk of kidnapping your wife, but they'd never risk luring a high-ranking CIA officer down there to kidnap or kill him, unless the stakes were very high."

"What'd they offer you?" Bambridge asked.

"My wife's life."

"In exchange for what?"

"Five days ago, one of our people in Castro's compound took photographs of a woman who'd been at the dictator's side when he died. Possibly the only one in the room."

"We haven't come up with an ID yet," Bambridge said. "But one of our people in the city swears he's seen her in Government Square. She's probably a functionary of some sort. Our current thinking is that she might be one of Raúl's aides or maybe a personal secretary. Did they mention her?"

"She's one of Fidel's illegitimate kids."

"Did they give you a name?"

"María León. She's a colonel in the DI, apparently chief of their Directorate of Operations. She wants to meet with me."

"Jesus Christ, that's the dumbest thing I've heard in my twenty years," Bambridge said. "No way in hell are we going to allow you anywhere near Havana."

"Wait a moment," Patterson said. "Could be that this is the overture the administration has been hoping for."

"Not by kidnapping," Bambridge said.

"They gave us an important piece of information, with the woman's name and position."

"No reason to believe that they were telling the truth."

"They're in too deep to have lied to me," Otto said. "They shot and killed the day care center director, who was apparently a witness. Whatever the reason the DI wants me in Havana in such a hurry has to be big."

"You fit the bill," Bambridge said.

"It's more than just what Otto knows," Patterson

disagreed. "If that's all they wanted, they could have kidnapped him instead of his wife, taken him to a safe house somewhere nearby, pumped him full of drugs, and he would have told them everything."

"They killed an innocent bystander!"

"Terribly unfortunate. But the entire incident tells us how serious they are."

"I tend to agree with Carleton, though it goes against my better judgment," Page said. "Otto?"

"I've tried to separate myself from the fact that my wife is being held somewhere by men who've shown they're willing to assassinate whoever gets in their way, with curiosity about why the director of DI operations has gone to these lengths to speak to me face-to-face. But I can't do it."

"Of course not," Page said. "What's the next step? What do you want to do?"

"I'm going down to Havana, all right, and if need be, I'll kill the bitch with my bare hands."

"You're not a field officer," Bambridge objected.

"I'm motivated," Otto said. "But I have to go down there to find out what Fidel told her on his deathbed that caused her to go to these lengths."

"Wars have started for less," Patterson said.

"What about Mac?" Page asked.

Otto had thought about it. "Only if something goes wrong." He handed the director a small flash drive. "It's how to reach him, but it's only a onetime read."

"Is there a password?"

"The nickname of your first girlfriend."

Page was taken aback, and he obviously wanted to

know how Otto could possibly have gotten that kind of information. "I'll phone Chris Morgan," he said. Morgan was the Secretary of State.

"Yes, sir," Otto said, a vision of his wife's image on the monitor plain in his mind's eye, especially her wink, and he turned and left the office.

NINE

It was noon, and after more than two hours of work, Louise had managed to remove only one of the screws holding the plywood against the window frame. In the process, the end of the fingernail file was badly twisted, and the thumb and forefinger of her right hand were bloody.

She looked at the other eleven screws in despair and leaned her forehead against the wooden cover and closed her eyes. She felt so incredibly stupid, letting herself be taken so easily. The moment she'd gone through the gate and seen the car and the two men waiting, she knew something was wrong.

Right then, she should have turned around and run away instead of walking up to them like a dope. And the little trick of calling her daughter by a different name hadn't worked, and yet she'd stood there.

And what was she supposed to say to Joyce's husband and their children? They would know that had she run in the opposite direction, leading the guys *away* from Lil' Tots, no one except her would have gotten shot. She hadn't been thinking straight.

Almost as bad was imagining the look in Otto's eyes when he watched the video. He wasn't tough at all; in fact, inside he was mush, a teddy bear, although when someone he loved was placed in harm's way, he could be formidable. She had seen him in action backstopping Mac. He'd been fearless.

Opening her eyes and looking at the eleven screws, she had no doubt that at this moment, Otto was doing everything within his power at the CIA to find her. And his devotion gave her heart.

She went into the bathroom and washed off her bloody fingers, the cuts only superficial, drying them with a few squares of toilet paper. The file would not stand up to another screw, so the plywood had become a nonissue; there was no way she could remove it.

Stuffing the file in the waistband of her slacks, she went back to the bedroom, where she pulled the cover and pillow off the bed, rolled the thin mattress away in a heap, and turned the bed upside down so that the four metal legs pointed up toward the ceiling.

Each was held to the frame with two nuts and bolts, and all of them were snug, making it impossible for her to loosen them with her bare hands. But the bed was old, the metal rusted in spots.

She shoved the frame up against the wall, and bracing it there with her right foot, she grabbed one of the legs from the head of the bed with both hands and, with every ounce of her strength, tried to bend it down. And it came away a half inch or so from a crease at the lower nut and bolt.

Shoving in the opposite direction, she managed to force the leg nearly back into place, and then immediately pulled it away again, the bend increasing another half inch.

Growing up on a farm in Wisconsin with three brothers, she'd naturally been something of a tomboy who knew her way around tools, and a little something about metal fatigue. Bending the leg back and forth would weaken the metal to the point of failure. It would snap off, and she would have a weapon.

But the going was slow, and she had to stop twice to catch her breath and ease the ache in her arms and wrists. She was still a little light-headed and she suspected that some of the sedative they'd given her was still in her system.

What sounded like a large truck pulled up somewhere near, and Louise cocked her ear to listen. Metal rattled against metal several times, and some sort of machinery rumbled into life for maybe ten or fifteen seconds, and the truck moved on, stopping a little farther on—and then the same metal on metal rattled. And she knew she was hearing a garbage truck collecting trash. This was a residential neighborhood. People were here, neighbors who might notice that something odd was going on in the house with the boarded-up windows.

All she had to do was make noise, and a lot of it.

She started on the leg again, and after a minute or so the first cracks radiated out from the bolt and all of a sudden, the work got a lot easier.

Someone was at the door, and Louise looked up as

a key grated in the lock. She attacked the leg now like a woman possessed, the cracks deepening, until it came free in her hand, and she turned as the door swung open and the guy who'd shot Joyce came in, carrying a tray with lunch.

It took him a moment to realize what he was seeing, time enough for Louise to reach him and swing the metal leg like a club, catching him in the side of the head.

He lurched backwards, his shoulder bumping into the doorframe, the tray clattering to the floor.

A large gash on the side of his head just above his left ear began welling blood, and Louise screamed as loud as she could and swung the leg again, meaning to hit him in the same spot, but he grabbed it from her, tossed it aside, and shoved her across the room.

"What's this, then?" he demanded, coming toward her.

Someone was coming up the stairs in a big hurry, and Cabrera looked like he wanted to take Louise apart. She didn't know what other options she had, but she wasn't going to stop fighting.

She feinted to the left, as if she were trying to get away from him, pulled the fingernail file from her waistband, and stepped into him as he started to raise his fist, and tried to plunge the file into his left eye.

His reflexes were good and he managed to twist his head so that the tip of the file only grazed his cheek, opening up a four-inch gash that instantly began bleeding. He grabbed her wrist and bent it back until she was forced to drop the file and he shoved her backwards again.

"Puta!" Whore! he shouted, and before Louise could attack again, he pulled out his pistol and pointed it at her.

TEN

At José Martí Airport, Otto was the last off the State Department's Gulfstream executive jet, which on landing had been instructed to taxi to an empty hangar across the main runway from the terminal. Palm trees dotted the horizon, and puffy white clouds soared overhead to the west.

Several Cuban army Gaziks, which were the leftover Russian jeeps, along with a half dozen Havana policemen on battered old Indian motorcycles were waiting to escort two Cadillacs, one of them a boxy-looking 1950s-era limousine.

A handful of Cuban dignitaries, a few of them dressed in suits and ties, several in plain olive drab fatigues, waited in a reception line.

Otto stood at the foot of the jet's stairs, his overnight bag in hand, as two dark-complexioned, intense-looking men in khaki slacks and white guayabera shirts drove up in an unmarked Gazik and parked a few feet away, between the aircraft and the group getting into the two Cadillacs. They looked at Otto but they remained in the Gazik.

He'd sat at the rear of the Gulfstream on the four-hour trip down from Andrews, and no one but a fe-male flight attendant had said a word to him. He'd been the first aboard, ten minutes before the group from the State Department had arrived, and she came back to him.

"Good morning, Mr. Rencke. May I get something for you?"

"A Coke if you have it, and maybe something to eat? A sandwich?"

"There'll be box lunches once we're in the air. Quite good, I'm told."

Otto had stowed his small overnight bag in the over-head and, buckling in, used his cell phone—which by-passed the normal Cuban control system—to call the day care center. But after six rings, there was no an-swer and he gave up. He felt so damned alone at this moment, more isolated than he'd been when he lived by himself for a time in France a few years ago. He'd had nothing to work for then, nothing to care for, no one whom he could talk to until Mac showed up at his door with a problem he needed help with. And Otto jumped right into the middle of it without hesitation. And had been doing the same ever since, especially last year when Katy, Liz, and Todd were assassinated.

Twice, he'd almost called Mac's contact number, but both times he'd stopped. Mac had his own full plate, his own troubles to deal with, but Otto knew that he would drop everything and come to help if he were told about Louise. But not yet. Not until he learned the reason the Cubans were taking such a terrible risk, which he figured would be made clear to him as soon as he was brought to Castro's daughter.

The attendant had brought back his Coke, and a half hour after they were in the air, she served him a box lunch with a fresh turkey and Swiss croissant, a light pasta salad, an apple, a chocolate chip cookie, and a split of a very good sauvignon blanc.

And after he ate, he'd laid his head against the window and watched the clouds as he tried to make sense of the why of the thing, and tried to send a telepathic message to Louise that everything would turn out well.

The president had sent Deputy Secretary of State Gladys Faunce; along with William Chapman, who was the assistant legal adviser for Inter-American Affairs; and Ralph Scott, the State Department's Coordinator for Cuban Affairs; plus two bodyguards for Faunce. Other nations had sent either their premiers or presidents, but the White House felt it was conciliatory enough to send a delegation of this rank.

When the Cadillacs and their escorts pulled away and sped across the tarmac, the man riding shotgun in the Gazik waiting for Otto got out and walked over. Otto took him and the driver to be DI officers.

"Señor Rencke?" he asked respectfully.

"Yes."

"Have you brought any weapons into Cuba?"

"No."

"A cell phone or satellite phone?"

Otto took out his phone and handed it over. But they wouldn't learn anything unless they came up with his very complicated password, and if they tried too hard, the phone's SIM card would be erased.

"If you will get in the backseat, sir, it is about a half

hour's drive from here," the officer said, and he took Otto's overnight bag.

The day was warm and humid, but the Gazik was a cabriolet; its canvas top was down and the breeze felt refreshing as they headed away from the airport.

Havana city center and the Plaza de la Revolución were about fifteen miles to the north, as the crow flies, the countryside this far out mostly barren, just the occasional small cattle ranch and clutches here and there of shacks down dirt roads, with very gently rolling hills in the distance to the east and west.

They drove fast until they came to Arroyo Naranjo, one of the bigger population concentrations within the city of Havana, seven miles south of the old city on the Havana–Las Vegas Highway. A lot of old cars and bicycles and even donkey carts clogged the narrow road until they reached the modern divided ring road that circled downtown.

At one point a few miles away, they passed a sign for a turn-off to the Finca Vigía, which had been Hemingway's home, under renovation for the past several years. But money was tight and the work would probably take several more years to complete. So much depended on the American tourist dollar, which up to now was practically nonexistent.

A couple of miles past that, they reached the Autopista Nacional, this one a modern highway that went straight into the city, but instead of turning to the northwest, they continued on the ring road that would eventually end up at the castle on Havana Bay and another way into the city, and the headquarters of the DI, where Otto figured they were taking him.

They were out in the country now, in what was considered Havana's east side, some boxy Soviet-era high-rise apartment buildings mixed with small houses, sometimes hovels, and small factories dotted here and there.

But again, the driver did not head into the city; instead, they got off the main highway and drove roughly northeast, toward the coast.

"I thought we'd be going to DI headquarters," Otto said.

The officer riding shotgun glanced over his shoulder. "No."

"Where, then?"

"I don't know."

Otto was alarmed. They were well off the main highway now, in the middle of what amounted to nowhere. People disappeared in places like this. "You have to know where you're taking me. I came here to meet with Colonel León."

The driver glanced at Otto's reflection in the rearview mirror, and said something to his partner, who turned around.

"You are correct, we are not taking you downtown to headquarters, that would be far too dangerous at this moment. And you are also correct that the colonel wishes to speak to you."

"Why too dangerous downtown?"

The officer said something to the driver that Otto didn't catch, then turned back again. "There is much turmoil since El Comandante died."

"I understand. But isn't Raúl fully in control?"

The officer was extremely nervous. "There are some *facciones,* what you call 'factions,' that may be forming."

"Troubles?"

"*Sí, problemas.*"

"Are you expecting trouble for our delegation at the funeral?"

The DI officer reared back as if he'd been shot. "No, nothing like that, I assure you. This trouble I'm speaking of involves only a certain section."

"A power struggle?"

The officer nodded. "Something like that."

This was not good. "Turn around," Otto said. "Take me back to the airport."

The officer was genuinely alarmed. "That's not possible. The colonel has gone to a lot of trouble to get you here."

"Yes. Including kidnapping my wife and killing an innocent civilian at a day care center, and endangering the lives of the kids there, my child included. Take me back! Now!"

"Ramiro," the driver said urgently, jamming on the brakes as a small canvas-covered troop truck pulled out from a dirt path and blocked the road.

"Do exactly as you are told, Señor Rencke," the man riding shotgun said.

The Gazik came to a complete halt a few yards away from where a half dozen armed soldiers jumped out of the truck and took up defensive positions. Their officer came around from the front.

"Or else what?" Rencke asked.

"Or else you will die here. All of us will."

Their driver got out and walked up to where the officer beckoned, and they walked a few feet down the road away from the troops. The driver appeared a minute later and motioned for his partner.

"We're going the rest of the way in the truck," the officer told Rencke. "Just keep your mouth shut."

They got out of the Gazik and, without saying a thing, walked to the truck and climbed aboard. Moments later, the troops joined them, and immediately the truck lurched forward but only about twenty-five yards, where it stopped again.

One of the troops, armed with a LAWS rocket, jumped down, extended the tube, unfolded the sights, and fired, hitting the Gazik dead center, the Russian jeep going up in a ball of flame, the explosion flat and loud.

"It was necessary to maintain the illusion," the DI officer told Otto as the soldier hurried back and climbed aboard.

"What illusion?"

"That you were killed or kidnapped by insurgents."

ELEVEN

It was early evening, already dark outside, when Louise awoke with a splitting headache. For several beats she was disoriented, not sure at all where she was or what had happened to make her body ache all over. But then it came to her that she'd been in a fight and she had been drugged again.

The bed frame had been taken away and she was lying on the bare mattress on the floor, the filthy pillow that smelled of something sour under her head. She pushed herself up to a sitting position, and then struggled painfully to her bare feet. They'd taken her shoes for some reason, which didn't make any sense to her.

For a long time she stood swaying, her legs trembling, until she could shuffle to the bathroom, where she splashed some cold water on her face and used the toilet.

There'd been a towel bar above the tub, but that had been ripped out of the wall, leaving absolutely nothing she could use as a weapon, except perhaps the wooden toilet seat. But she didn't think she had the strength to take the toilet apart, let alone put up a decent fight. At least not for now. And she was actually glad the mirror had been removed so she didn't have to look at herself; she suspected she was a mess.

It had taken all three kidnappers to finally subdue her and stick her arm with the needle, and then nothing. She suddenly felt her wrist, realizing that they'd taken her watch, too, along with her shoes, which she supposed could have been used as weapons. Maybe like brass knuckles.

She walked back into the bedroom at the same moment someone was at the lock, and the door opened. The driver, a tray in his hand, stood there with a half smile on his narrow features, and she decided that he looked dangerous, like a street hood, which had been her first impression outside the day care center.

"You must be hungry," he said.

She nodded. "And thirsty."

"It's the drug," he said. He tossed her a liter bottle of Evian.

Which she caught and opened with fumbling fingers. Her mouth was dry, the water a relief. "What do I call you?" she asked.

"Rodrigo will do."

"Is that your real name?"

Cruz smiled faintly. "May I come in and give you this tray? Or do you mean to attack again?"

"Set it down on the floor and leave."

"I'll do that, señora, but if you wish to have another meal, you will push the tray under the door when you are finished. No tray, no food."

"Okay," Louise said.

Cruz motioned for her to back up, which she did, and he stepped just inside the doorway and set the tray, which was covered with a napkin, on the floor. "Beans and rice, with some shredded pork. Same as we had for dinner."

It smelled very good to Louise, who had eaten nothing since the piece of toast for breakfast this morning. But her hunger meant little to her, except as a reminder that by now the cops, and probably the feds would be in the middle of the investigation, which left Otto where? Doing what?

"How long do you mean keep me here like this? Or do you plan to kill me?"

"We thought that was a possibility, but the danger has passed because your husband decided to cooperate with us."

Louise forgot her hunger. "The DI's not looking for a ransom. So what is it? What is he doing for you?"

Cruz considered his answer for a long moment, but then he shrugged. "He has gone to Havana for El Comandante's funeral."

Louise was rocked, but just for an instant. "He might have gone to Havana, but it wasn't for the funeral. State would probably send a delegation, but his name would most definitely not be on the list. Has he been kidnapped in exchange for me?"

"I don't know."

"Bullshit."

"Señora, believe me for your own comfort and safety. My orders were to pick you up, bring you here, and communicate our demands to your husband. To this point, he has complied."

"You must be raving lunatics to think the CIA will sit still for the kidnapping of one of its officers."

"He has not been kidnapped," Cruz said. "He flew to Havana with your State Department delegation at noon. I was given word that he arrived safely and no harm will come to him, or you."

"Do you people actually think he's going to give you secrets in exchange for my life?" Louise demanded.

As romantic as the notion was, she knew that Otto wouldn't do such a thing for all the tea in China, for anyone, for any reason.

"I don't know that, either."

"Has to be something else, otherwise he wouldn't have dropped everything at a moment's notice and gone down to Havana, leaving me here. He would have moved heaven and earth to find out who you guys were and where you took me. You have no idea how clever he is."

"I'm following my orders, is all."

"But you must have told him something pretty convincing. What was it?"

"Eat your dinner, señora," Cruz said. "I'll be back for your tray in thirty minutes."

"Wait, please," Louise said before he could leave. "If both of us are going to be murdered, it won't matter what you tell me."

"I've told you that no harm will come to you. Those are not my orders once your husband agreed to travel to Havana."

"Okay, that's fair. How long am I going to be held here?"

"A few days, maybe a little longer."

"My husband?"

"The same."

"He knows the reasons you gave him, and if he's sent home in a few days, he's going to tell his boss what they were. So what's the harm in telling me now?"

"There's no reason for me to tell you anything."

"Yes, there is."

"What?" Cruz asked.

"I promise not to give you any more trouble."

Cruz had to laugh. "What trouble?"

Louise stared him down. "I have no idea, except you should think of a caged animal, a cornered animal, who gives you no choice other than to kill it. In that case, Señor DI Field Officer, you would be in a serious world of shit, because of how bad the fallout would be for Raúl and the government."

Cruz was impressed. "I'll think about it."

"Do that," Louise told him. "Or the next time I see you, I'll shove this tray up your ass."

"No tray outside your door, no more food."

"I'd give up that pleasure for a shot at you," Louise said, and she smiled. "By the way, how's your partner? I found the nail file next to the toilet, maybe he'll get the creeping crud."

Cruz just looked at her before he backed out.

"Say hi to him for me," Louise said, not really knowing why she was pushing so hard, except that it felt good to fight back a little.

TWELVE

It was noon, and Kirk McGarvey was running shirtless along the rocky path above the Aegean Sea on the Greek island of Serifos, pushing himself as he had since coming back to the same island, the same converted lighthouse he'd run to a number of years ago.

That time, John Lyman Trotter, a close friend, had turned out to be a mole within the CIA, and in the end, McGarvey had been forced to kill him, getting seriously wounded himself. He'd found this island, this refuge in the middle of nowhere, and started the healing process.

Now in his early fifties, he was a husky man, built something like a rugby player, a little under two hundred pounds, a little under six feet, with a square, pleasant face and expressive eyes that were sometimes green and sometimes, when he was in the middle of high tradecraft, a slate gray. When his wife, Katy, was alive, she'd thought he was devastatingly handsome, self-assured, with a charisma that sent the message that all was well and safe when he was close.

The Trotter business had been long enough ago that he'd bounced back fairly easily, but this time was different, and this time he was truly alone except for his granddaughter, whom Otto and Louise had brought here six weeks ago for a visit.

And seeing Audie, being with her, was wonderful and sad all at the same time because she was the spitting image of Liz, who'd been the spitting image of Katy. A lot of memories had come to the surface, making it next to impossible to keep smiling and keep it light.

Already she was forgetting her parents. It was something Otto and Louise wanted to correct. They wanted to show her the pictures and the few videos that Todd had made and tell her about them.

"Later, when she's older," McGarvey had told them after they'd put her to bed. The night had been soft, the kind Katy had always loved. "She wouldn't understand. You're her parents now. Just love her, it's all she needs."

Reaching the west side of the island, he came in sight of the white tiled patio at the base of the lighthouse one hundred yards farther and pulled up short. The figure of a man was leaning on the railing, looking down at the sea one hundred feet below.

Apparently he'd walked up from town.

McGarvey had switched back to his Walther PPK, in the 9 mm version, more out of sentimental reasons than any other, and it was holstered at the small of his back. After the operation in Baghdad and finally Washington, D.C., when he'd been briefly jailed because he'd angered the president and a lot of other powerful people on both sides of the Beltway, he never went anywhere without it.

So he started down the path toward the lighthouse, wondering who the unfamiliar man was, and why he had come.

And McGarvey was curious, so his step quickened just a little—a sign, he supposed, that he was beginning to heal after losing his wife, daughter, and son-in-law all in the same operation. Their being so irrevocably gone still wasn't real to him. And all the good, honest Greek food and wine, all the exercises and running and five-mile swims every day, even the shooting practice in the hills, which acted as sort of a relief valve to him, had really helped. Yet all of it had done little except hone his body and steady his aim. But at night he had his dreams—nightmares, actually—that he had to deal with during the days.

Some evenings he would walk down to the island port village and tourist center of Livadi, where he would have a light dinner with a half bottle of retsina, and try to convince himself that all he wanted, really needed for now, was some time and peace to heal. Of course, he was aware of his own failings, his impatience with doing nothing for so long after practically an entire lifetime in dangerous service to his country—for the most part as a field officer with the CIA. But like many spies before him, he also knew in his heart that he had become, had always been, an adrenaline junkie.

The biggest thing he'd learned over the past few months was that it is possible to run away from just about everything—except yourself.

The man at the rail straightened up and turned around as McGarvey came down off the path and stepped onto the patio. A tourist boat was coming around the east side of the island, making for the docks at Livadi, and it's what the visitor had been looking at.

He was a short man, well under six feet, with a thin body, narrow pinched-nosed face, dark eyes, thick dark hair, and he seemed surprised about something. He wore boat shoes, faded jeans, and a lightweight white shirt with the sleeves buttoned up above his elbows. McGarvey figured him to be in his mid to late forties, and in pretty good shape.

He came forward and stuck out his hand. "Mr. Mc-Garvey, I'm happy to finally meet you. Marty Bambridge, I'm the new DDO."

McGarvey's gut tightened. For a CIA directorate chief to come all this way, unannounced and apparently without bodyguards, was not good news. He shook the man's hand. "How did you find me?"

"Otto gave us directions," Bambridge said. He took out his CIA identification and held it up. "We're in something of a hurry, so I'd like you to pack, and I'll explain on the run."

"What sort of trouble?"

"We're not sure, but Otto's wife was kidnapped two days ago, and we need your help."

"What about my granddaughter?"

"The babysitters are taking care of her at the Farm. Otto thought it was for the best to get her out of harm's way."

"Where is he? Why'd he send you?"

Bambridge hesitated. "Well, that's just the point. He flew down to Havana with a delegation from State to attend Fidel Castro's funeral. But he's disappeared and there's been no further word from him or the kidnappers."

"Was that part of their demands, that he was to go the Havana in exchange for Louise's safety?"

"Yes, but there's a lot more," Bambridge said.

"There usually is," McGarvey said, wondering just what insanity had to have gripped the DI to pull off such a stunt, and how the Administration was reacting. "Give me fifteen minutes."

"Make it ten, I have a helicopter standing by for us in town."

His bedroom was three-quarters of the way up the tower, with a 360-degree view of the approaches from the sea and land. After kicking off his running shoes, he went to the windows to see if Bambridge had actually come alone. Or if he had been followed.

Landing a helicopter, even one that took tourists around for a bird's-eye view of the island was a fairly big deal, always attracting a fair amount of attention. But he spotted no one sniffing down the DDO's trail.

He took a two-minute shower, then dressed in a pair of khaki slacks, a white button-up shirt, dark blue blazer, and loafers. Once he'd stuffed his pistol and silencer plus two spare magazines of ammunition into an overnight bag, along with a few pieces of clothing, a couple of spare passports, untraceable credit cards and driver's licenses, about ten thousand in cash—all he had in his go-to-hell-kit—he hesitated at the door and looked back.

The islanders would be sitting up and taking notice of the man who'd leased the old lighthouse, and who one day without notice simply got in a helicopter and flew away. He wasn't coming back here, he decided. Maybe his healing was over and done with. Maybe it was time to go home. He had an apartment in Georgetown, and the house on Florida's west coast, and presumably a teaching post in French philosophers with emphasis on Voltaire, still open at Sarasota's New College.

Time to go back, if for nothing and no one else but Louise and Otto and the baby, he thought, heading downstairs.

And because he had a fair idea now why Louise had been kidnapped, and it had nothing to do with Otto.

"I don't know how long this is going to take, do you need to let someone know you're going to be gone?" Bambridge asked. "A caretaker?"

"I'm not coming back," McGarvey told him. "I assume we're going to Andrews aboard a Company jet?"

"Yes. Are you carrying a weapon?"

"Among other things."

"I was warned," Bambridge said. "But we'll not be bothered by customs."

They didn't talk on the forty-five-minute hike along the rocky path that wound around the hills down to Livadi, where an older French Aérospatiale EC120 helicopter with Aegean Air Tours markings on the side was waiting for them on the landing pad just to the west of the docks. Bambridge was a smoker, he explained, and his wind wasn't as good as McGarvey's.

They stopped within sight of the chopper.

"I'm assuming that the kidnappers contacted Otto and told him to fly to Havana," McGarvey said. "Did they say why?"

"We had an asset in Castro's compound. And the night the old man died, his last visitor was a woman whom the kidnappers identified as María León. Supposedly she's one of his illegitimate children, though we've not been able to verify it. She's also Chief of Operations for the DI, and this op is hers. She had Louise snatched in order to get Otto to Havana."

"And you people let him do it?"

Bambridge was surprised. "You know him better than anybody. Do you honestly think we could have stopped him?"

"Is the Bureau making any progress finding Louise?"

"They're looking for the Caddy the kidnappers used, but it's disappeared. No one at the day care got a tag number."

"Has the White House been informed?"

"No. It was one of Otto's conditions."

"Good, and we're going to keep it that way," McGarvey said. "Because they're not interested in Louise or Otto. It's me the DI wants, and luring Otto to Havana was the only way they could dig me out."

"Why?"

"I don't know, but I'm going to find out."

"Just how do you plan on doing that?" Bambridge asked.

"I'm going to Havana to ask the woman why her dying father's last wish was to make contact with me. And then I'm bringing Otto home."

THIRTEEN

It had been several hours since Otto was picked up at José Martí Airport and finally brought in the back of an army truck to a lovely home on the beach near Cojimar, about eight miles east up the coast from Havana. The grounds were tropically lush, and from where he was seated at a poolside table, the sound of the surf just a hundred feet away was soothing.

But each hour that went by increased his anxiety about Louise a hundredfold because the woman who'd supposedly arranged the elaborate kidnapping had not shown up to explain her purpose, and his imagination, vivid at the calmest times, was running wild.

Except for the drama on the back road where he'd been picked up by the army and the DI Gazik had been destroyed, he'd been treated with a pleasant indifference.

The windows were open throughout the house, no screens or bars, but he was sure there were patrols on the grounds, in addition to the pair of tough-looking armed minders who were never farther than ten feet away.

In any event, he wasn't here to attempt an escape; he'd come to find out what had possessed a high-ranking director of the DI to pull such a crazy stunt. And sitting now, sipping a cup of thick Cuban coffee with natural raw sugar, he was no closer to making sense of it than he had been when he'd first watched Louise's video and talked to her kidnappers, which seemed like a thousand years ago.

Otto looked up as a slender woman, long black hair, oval face, large dark eyes, came from the house, said something to one of his minders, and then came over to him. She was dressed in a white polo shirt and khaki slacks, sandals on her feet. He recognized her from the pictures their asset in Castro's compound had managed to send to Langley, and he got to his feet. "Colonel León," he said.

"*Sí*," María said. "We never counted on someone taking my photograph at my father's compound." She extended her hand, but Otto ignored it.

"Nice spot you have here," he said. "Lots better than the average Cuban will ever see."

"It's the same in the States, and just about everywhere

else," María said. She motioned for Otto to sit down, and she took a seat across from him.

A young boy, maybe in his early teens, dressed in a white jacket came out with a silver tray on which was a bottle of Máximo Extra Añejo fine Cuban rum and two glasses, but no ice. "Good afternoon, Señora Coronel," he said brightly. He set the tray on the table. "You're home early. Shall I pour?"

"No. Leave us now."

"Shall I tell Cook there will be two for dinner?"

"Yes, please," María said, and the boy left.

Otto got the impression that the boy and the two minders—the only ones he'd seen in the house—were happy, not at all oppressed by their boss. Which was confusing, because he'd wanted to believe that the woman was a monster.

María was looking at him, a faint smile on her lips. "I'm not what you expected."

"No. But then I suppose that insanity has a bunch of different faces, not all of them ugly."

"A left-handed compliment, I suppose. But there's nothing insane about this operation, except for its difficulty and, I suppose, improbability."

"Your people kidnapped my wife—you can't expect me to cooperate."

"You're here," María said. "Anyway, you must have figured out that she wasn't the target, even though she probably has some interesting information we could use."

It was what Otto had been telling himself from the start. "Neither am I," he said.

"Actually, no—although I know some people in our Technical Directorate who would like to spend a month or two talking to you."

"I'd love to get at the DI's computer system, but what I have in mind wouldn't take much more than an hour or two, ya know."

María poured a couple of fingers of rum into each glass, and handed Otto one. "This is among our better rums," she said. And she delicately sipped hers. "But I've always been curious about something. With your expertise, I've always assumed that you could hack into our systems just about any time you wanted to do. Why haven't you?"

Otto sipped his rum and nodded. "This is very good," he said. "It's never been worth the effort, at least not on my watch. And a lot of your data is stored the old-fashioned way—on paper in file cabinets—and we would have to run the risk of burning some of our assets to get at them. Again, not worth the risk. The Russians didn't leave you enough for us to worry ourselves."

María looked away for a moment. "It'll have to end one day. The embargo. It's so stupid."

"We never pointed nuclear missiles at you."

She looked back. "We didn't invade your country. And we don't maintain a military base on your soil."

"We were willing to help in the beginning," Otto said. "But your father chose the Russians instead of us."

"Your government supported Batista—"

Otto waved her off. "Save it for the faithful. It's not why I'm here, and frankly, I don't give a shit about your internal politics. If you guys ever straighten out your act, you'd be surprised what we could do for you."

"No thanks," María said bitterly. "We've seen what you've done for Iraq and Afghanistan."

"They have free elections," Otto said. He finished his drink, Louise's sweet face popping up in his mind's eye, and it took everything he had not to jump up and start hopping from foot to foot as he usually did when agitated. The only other alternative was to grab the liquor bottle and try to beat her to death with it.

"I took a great risk getting you here, but it was the only way I could see to get Kirk McGarvey to come to me. I want you to get word to him."

"It's already been done."

"Then you knew before you got on the plane?"

"Of course, just not the why."

An odd look briefly crossed María's eyes. "I haven't an idea. It was my father's deathbed wish that I get him to come here. He said something about retribution, and that McGarvey would know."

"Know what?"

"Our salvation. My father's exact words. And he told me something else that made no sense. He said that Kim Jong-il told him McGarvey could be trusted. Does that mean anything to you?"

Otto shook his head. "Sounds like the ravings of a lunatic to me," he lied.

María bridled. "He was my father."

"That's something else you can save for the faithful," Otto said, but he was intrigued. "Salvation from what? Did he say?"

"No. He made me promise to get McGarvey here and then he died."

"No clue?"

"None."

"What about his personal papers? Maybe a daily journal, something like that."

"I don't know."

"Shit," Otto said angrily. "You pulled off this stunt without doing your homework?"

"It's not so easy here. Especially just now. The entire country is on high alert. Everybody is being closely watched. No one can afford to make a false move."

"You don't seriously think we'll invade."

"No one does. But Raúl and the people around him are afraid of a revolution. They've been paying close attention to what's been going on in the Middle East, especially Egypt, and they don't want something like that to get started here."

"And yet you took the risk to kidnap my wife and bring me here so that you could get at Mac."

"I suspect that he'll come for you, and when he does, your wife will be released unharmed."

"He'll come for me," Otto said. "But maybe not in the way you want." And he was very afraid for Louise.

FOURTEEN

But instead of dinner with the American, Raúl's secretary telephoned to order María back to Government Plaza for an urgent meeting. A military helicopter touched down on the lawn in front of her house and she was whisked into the city, where she was admitted to the president's office, less than fifteen minutes after the call.

Raúl was alone in his office, and María, dressed in military fatigues, approached his desk and saluted. He was a pleasant-looking man in his eighties, though he didn't look that old. His eyes were squinted behind square glasses, his hair gray, and just now the corners of his mouth were turned down, as if he'd been given disappointing news. He was dressed in a rumpled tweed sport coat and open-collared white shirt.

He sketched a tired salute and motioned for her to take a seat. "Thank you for coming at such short notice," he said. "This is a troubled time we all knew was coming. And I'm asking for the cooperation of all my important . . . people."

María thought he'd almost said *friends*. "I'm at your service, Señor Presidente."

"You will attend the funeral tomorrow in civilian clothes, but no one else from your directorate must be there. You understand the necessity in order to avoid any speculation about your true identity."

"Of course."

"You will interact with no one, especially the American delegation," Raúl said, and he looked away for a moment, a sudden expression of sadness, maybe even grief, coming to his face. "It's not what I want. Not what your father would have wanted. Not the way any of us thought that this would turn out. None of it."

María felt a little sorrow for him, though he was a wily old bastard, almost as adept at manipulating people as Fidel had been. He'd been there at the beginning of the revolution and as the youngest of the three Castro boys, he had learned his lessons well from the masters of the game, including Che Guevara and the Soviet spy Nikolai Leonov, whom he'd met in Moscow in the mid-fifties. But he'd lost a brother, and he was now fully faced with the nearly overwhelming task of pulling his country out of its abject poverty without appearing to cave in to Washington's demands for political reform.

"I understand, sir," she said. "I've always understood."

"He loved you, as he did all his children."

María lowered her eyes. The remark was unexpected. But she nodded. "I didn't know it until he called me that night."

"You were the only one with him when he passed?"

"Yes."

"What did he say to you?"

María suppressed a smile. Calling her here tonight had nothing to do with the funeral arrangements. "Nothing that made any sense. He talked about the revolution, and before that Mexico City, and the good friends he'd lost. The Bay of Pigs and the missiles that were almost his."

"And me?"

"He said your name, but I couldn't understand the

rest. He was very weak, but he held my hand and told me that I was a beautiful child."

Raúl looked disappointed. "You know about the spy who took photographs of you and presumably sent them to the CIA?"

"Yes. But so far, there have been no repercussions."

"How would you know something like that?"

"We have assets in Washington and New York, some of them quite effective. Had I been outed, the word would have spread."

"Are you telling me that we have someone inside Langley?"

"No, but we have at least two close connections with people in their headquarters."

"Will you share that information with me?"

Operational details were almost never part of a presidential briefing, and certainly the names of key people were usually kept secret, in case of an inadvertent slip of the tongue. "I will prepare a report first thing in the morning, Señor Presidente."

"No need, if you are sure that your true identity has not been guessed."

Raúl was probing, so the problem was what he knew and where he was getting his information. Only her chief of staff, Ortega-Cowan, and very few of her operational people knew the full extent of the Washington operation that got Rencke here, part of which was telling the CIA who she was. And when this op was over, the three kidnappers would disappear.

"No one knows my true identity," she said, and she watched for a reaction, but there was none, except that Raúl nodded.

"I thought that perhaps your father might have told you something that could be useful," he said. "These are troubled times, and I have a premonition." But he trailed off.

"Sir?"

Raúl shook his head. "Nothing. Go back to your home. Tomorrow will be a fateful day for Cuba."

Downstairs, María headed down the long corridor, most of the offices dark now, to the rear exit, where the helicopter was waiting. Ortega-Cowan came out of the shadows, giving her a start. "What the hell are you doing here?" she demanded.

"I was just leaving the office when I saw you get out of the helicopter. What did the great one have to say?"

"He doesn't know about our little operation, if that's what you mean," María said, and she continued down the corridor.

"It'll only be a matter of time."

"Not if you keep your mouth shut and a tight hand on the operational assets."

"Don't worry about me, Colonel, but Washington could have been a disaster. Still might be if the FBI finds the woman."

They stopped at the doors. "What's this all about, Román? Are you getting cold feet on me?"

"If you would confide in me why El Comandante wanted Kirk McGarvey to come to us, I might be able to come up with another scenario that might not be so dangerous. If Washington falls apart, all our heads will be on the chopping block."

"Make sure that it does not."

"I cannot in all good conscience operate blind," he said, and María almost laughed.

"When have you ever had a good conscience?" she said. "I'll tell you one thing, this is important, but even I don't know the full extent of it, nor will I until I actually get to speak with McGarvey face-to-face."

Ortega-Cowan was still troubled, and it showed. "Is he close enough to Señor Rencke to come here?"

"I think so," María said. "But if not, we'll devise another plan, you and I. Maybe even meet him somewhere on neutral ground."

"Mexico City?"

"It's a possibility we might have to consider. Why don't you work something out and have it on my desk after the funeral?"

"As you wish, Colonel," he said, and he turned and walked away down the corridor toward the front doors and the parking lot in the plaza across the street.

On the way back to her house near Cojimar and her guest there, she had time to think about the question Ortega-Cowan had asked: Was Kirk McGarvey close enough to Otto Rencke to come here? And in time—before Washington unraveled or before someone on General Muñoz's staff became interested in what María's directorate was doing in the aftermath of the shooting last week in El Comandante's compound?

The day after her father's death, she had searched the DGI's archives for everything the service knew about McGarvey. Much of it was little more than gleanings from newspapers—mostly in the United States, but elsewhere around the world as well, including London, Paris, Berlin, Prague, Moscow; but nothing in Tokyo, Beijing, and certainly not in Pyongyang.

A somewhat lengthy report concerned an operation in which McGarvey had taken part, at Guantánamo Bay—but it was mostly speculation, because the DI had no one reliable inside the U.S. Navy base, except that there were at least two night incidents in which gunfire had been reported.

She hadn't waded through all the material—there was no time for it—but she'd read enough, including a few DI-generated reports from Washington and the UN, to notice that almost every time McGarvey's name came up, Otto Rencke's had also been mentioned.

Which had led her to Rencke's file, which was curiously a much larger one than McGarvey's because the DI had a great deal of respect for his computer genius. And a certain amount of fear, which was especially shared by the Venezuelan SEBIN.

"Bring that man here, and you might be letting a hornet's nest into our living room," Ortega-Cowan had warned.

"We'll keep him for just as long as need be," she'd said.

"Nowhere near any of our computers."

"Of course not," she'd agreed.

But Rencke had told her that he could break into Cuba's systems anytime he wanted, except that it wasn't worth the effort.

And she'd believed him.

FIFTEEN

At Langley, Bambridge escorted McGarvey up to the DCI's office on the seventh floor. Page was new to the Agency since Mac had been in the Old Headquarters Building last, and it was he who'd appointed the new Deputy Director of Operations. "Welcome back, Mr. Director," his secretary said.

"I'm not really back for very long," McGarvey said, and he and Bambridge went in.

Page rose from behind his desk and came around to shake hands. "Good to finally meet you, Mr. McGarvey," the DCI said. "I assume that Marty briefed you on the way over."

"Yes, he did. Has the Bureau made any progress finding Louise?"

"Nothing overnight. But we've asked that it be kept low key as long as Otto is in Havana."

"What's the reaction from the White House?"

"I've not briefed Bible yet, so it hasn't gotten to the president," Page said. Madeline Bible was the new Director of National Intelligence, and the word on the street, even as far as Serifos, was that she was probably the last. That layer of bureaucracy created in the aftermath of 9/11 had proved ineffective. "I won't be able to keep this under wraps for much longer, though."

"What about the State Department's delegation to Fidel's funeral?"

"If you mean have they reacted to Otto's disappearance, no, they have not. Officially, he wasn't on the plane, but the aircrew reported that he was met by two men and they drove off once the delegation was gone. And that's the last anyone has seen or heard of him."

"Mr. McGarvey is of the opinion that the real target is him, not Otto," Bambridge said.

Page was startled. "How did you come to that conclusion?"

"Otto doesn't have anything they would understand, and he sure as hell wouldn't cooperate with them by revising their computer systems," McGarvey said. "They grabbed Louise, the easiest target, to force Otto to Havana, knowing I would go after him."

"But why? Have you had any connection with this woman who runs their directorate of operations? Or Castro himself?"

"I was involved with something at Guantánamo Bay a couple of years ago, but this has to be something else, something important enough for them to go to these lengths."

"And you intend on going to Havana?"

"Otto is a friend."

Page didn't seem surprised. "What can we do to help?"

"I need to borrow one of your people in Miami, because I'm going through the back door."

"Of course," the DCI said. "Who is it?"

And McGarvey told him.

After the flight across the Atlantic and the meeting in the DCI's office, McGarvey was dead tired and in need of a shower, but using the Company's travel agency to book him a flight direct to Miami, he cabbed it directly out to Dulles. Louise and Otto were in harm's way, and he would catch up on his sleep later.

He was traveling on his Federal Air Marshal Service credentials, so he had no trouble bringing his weapon through security, and the pilot and copilot nodded but said nothing when he boarded. Crews on every commercial flight were more than happy to have an air marshal aboard, but they were to be given no special attention. They were to be anonymous to the passengers.

The two-and-a-half-hour flight got him to Miami International Airport a few minutes after three, where he was met by Raúl Martínez, the CIA's chief of deep-cover operations in the Little Havana section of the city, centered around the Calle Ocho. It was a job the slender, dark-complexioned man had held for a number of years. He and McGarvey had worked together more than once, and they'd built up a mutual trust.

Martínez was dressed in dark slacks and a white guayabera shirt with intricate embroidery around the pockets and along the button line; he didn't smile when he and McGarvey left the terminal and got in his Cadillac Coupe de Ville parked illegally out front. He nodded to one of the cops, who looked the other way, and they took off south toward the Dolphin Expressway.

"Okay, Mr. M, you're not here for a vacation, though it looks like you could use one," Martínez said. "Must be about Otto."

"What have you heard?"

"Nothing official from the Building, if that's what you mean, except that you were on your way down and I was supposed to cooperate. But I saw the squib in the *Washington Post* about the shooting at the day care center your granddaughter attends, and a friend of mine up at the Farm told me that she was there and Otto was in a big rush to get out of town."

"The DI kidnapped Louise and told Otto that he needed to get down to Castro's funeral."

"That's about an hour from now, but I don't think he's going to make it."

"What are you talking about?"

"Word on the street in Havana is that an American who flew in aboard a State Department plane was picked up at the airport by a couple of guys in a Gazik that was found blown to hell on a back road somewhere up around Habana del Este. No bodies. But the American showed up that night at a house on the beach outside Cojimar owned by some government functionary."

"Colonel María León, she runs the DI's Directorate of Operations."

Martínez glanced at him. "No shit," he said. "No one down there knows exactly who the American is, but everyone seems to have the impression that Langley has to be kept out of it for the time being. The American's—Otto's—life depends on it."

"Sounds like DI backspin."

"That's what I thought," Martínez said. He shook his head. "So they grab Otto's wife, but the operation is sloppy and a bystander gets shot to death in the process. Nonetheless, they got her, so Otto can't do anything but get down to Havana, where he's snatched by the deputy director of operations in such a way that his presence is supposed to be a secret. Supposedly, dissidents killed him and the two guys who picked him up. And the DI spreads the rumor that whatever the situation might look like, it has to be kept away from the CIA. And that doesn't sound *loco* to you?"

"*Muy loco*," McGarvey said. "But it's worse than that."

Martínez worked it out in a split second. "*Hijo de puta*. Otto's just the bait. It's you they want."

"That's what I think."

"Why? They can't still be pissed off about the Guantánamo operation. That makes no sense."

"I don't have a clue, but I'm not going in the front door."

"The air force has good radar of the entire strait, and the navy doesn't screw around. The second we take off from Largo or the Matecumbes—by float plane or boat—they'll know we're coming."

"I'm counting on it," McGarvey said. "And if I'm right, they'll wait to pick us up from the beach."

"If you're wrong, you'll find out what the inside of a Cuban prison is like."

"You just need to get me somewhere in the vicinity of Cojimar and then head back. They won't interfere with you."

"And then what?" Martínez said. "At some point, you and Otto will have to get out of there, unless this colonel has something else in mind for you. I mean, it makes no sense. None of it. The risk they've taken is beyond insanity."

"Unless it has something to do with Castro's death," McGarvey said, and he told Martínez the incident with the CIA asset at the compound that night, leaving out the speculation that Colonel León was Castro's daughter.

Martínez was angry. "I know Carlos's family here in Miami," he said. "No one told me, so I could go to them and tell them about their son. They worry about him all the time. They need to know what happened."

"Not yet," McGarvey said. "This is an ongoing op."

"Soon," Martínez said without taking his eyes off the road.

"Soon," McGarvey agreed.

Martínez headed east toward the turnpike, which was the fastest route down to the Keys. "I have a friend who has a float plane on Key Largo. Depending on how long he wants to stay low and follow the Keys west before he turns straight south, could take maybe an hour and a half."

"We'll go tonight," McGarvey said. "Sometime after midnight."

SIXTEEN

Standing alone, one hundred feet from her father's simple mausoleum in the Colón Cemetery, María was also alone with her thoughts and remembrances. A priest was saying something, his words muffled by a huge crowd of several thousand people, most of them Cubans, but many of them from around the world, including the

Americans, so she couldn't make out what he was saying.

But it didn't matter. El Comandante was officially an atheist, and the priest was here only for state decorum, the necessity of which her father would have understood, as he understood just about everything.

Except for his daughter's needs—until the last minutes of his life, when he'd called her a beautiful child. Too little too late.

In the eighth grade, she was the only girl in the special class of thirteen boys who had teased her from the very beginning. But she'd begun to develop that summer, and by midyear she was finally having her periods, her hips had rounded out, and she'd developed breasts, and the boys had began taking her seriously— too seriously. Grabbing at her in the hallways, and outside on the playing fields, and in the swimming pool. Although she had her own tiny section of the dressing room, she'd become aware that peepholes had been drilled and that they watched her in the shower. And she'd wanted to go to someone, a father or mother, to ask for advice, because she truly didn't know what to do.

The situation came to a head in the early spring, when one evening, five of the boys slipped into her sleeping quarters, and before she was fully awake they'd thrown off the covers and pulled off her nightdress. Two of the boys held her down while another dropped his pajama bottoms and started to rape her.

"Wait," she said sharply, but not loudly enough to alert the dorm's night matron, who was asleep at her desk at the front door.

The boys were startled.

"We can do this one at a time and no one will get hurt," she said.

The boy hovering between her legs didn't know what to say or do. She got a hand free, and she reached up and touched his erect penis and he almost jumped out of his skin.

"I'm a virgin, so I don't know what'll happen. But I know that I need privacy. So the rest of you go back outside and wait until we're done."

She had a hold on the boy's penis and she could feel him shivering.

"Go on now," she said.

"Get the fuck out of here," the boy over her ordered. He was one of the class leaders and the school's best soccer player. The others, including most of the teachers, had a lot of respect for him. He was almost certainly the son of someone important in the government or military.

The boys took a last lingering look María's body but then filed out of the room and quietly closed the door.

"Now," María said softly, and she guided the boy's penis inside her, a very sharp pain stabbing at her gut, much worse than her monthly cramps, nearly causing her to cry out.

But it was over nearly before it began, and the boy stiffened and shuddered in her arms, thrust hard one more time, and then pulled away, heaving a deep sigh.

He started to say something, but María rolled over on top of him, clamped her legs around his waist to hold him down, and strangled him, her thumbs crushing his larynx, her fingers cutting off the blood to his brain through his carotid arteries.

The attack had been so sudden, so unexpected, so powerful that the boy only thrashed around for a few seconds before he blacked out, and still María did not release her grip for at least two full minutes, when she was sure he was dead.

Afterwards, she'd walked out without getting dressed, blood running down her legs from her vagina, past the boys who made no move to stop her, and reported the rape and defensive murder to the matron.

And almost nothing came of it, her father more important than the boy's father, other than an examination to make sure she wasn't pregnant, a brief visit with a Russian psychologist on staff, and a long, fatherly talk with the school's KGB headmaster, during which he'd actually used the word *pride*.

No one had bothered her after that incident, which garnered a little respect: *You think you're man enough, go ahead and have a go, see how well you fare.*

Academically she excelled, finishing each form at or near the top of her class. She played soccer and baseball well enough so that she started most games, and she won a gold medal her third year in the South American Swimming Confederation in Buenos Aires.

By the time she'd finished prep school and gone off to university in Moscow, she was considered to be among the KGB's better recruits; she had the rare combination of intelligence, athletic ability, and beauty. But instead of becoming a field officer as had been suggested, her father kept her close to home, in the DI. It was an order she hadn't learned until a couple of years ago. But it was just as well, and she'd accepted the possibility that she might one day run the spy agency.

Until her father died.

El Comandante's coffin was moved into the mausoleum and the crowd began to disperse. Most of the diplomats and government dignitaries were dressed either in uniforms or in black suits. For anonymity's sake, María wore a simple cotton dress and plain shoes much like the vast majority of commoners lining the narrow walkways that honeycombed the cemetery and spilling out of the main gate and into the streets. At least as many as one hundred thousand people, she figured. Despite the islanders' poverty, Fidel was well loved.

She moved back and blended with the crowd as the diplomats moved up the long walk to the waiting limos outside the gate, no one paying her the slightest attention. And twenty minutes later, it was over—just a few people, mostly women, with lit candles staying behind for a last few minutes in the cemetery.

"Nothing will ever be the same," she heard one woman tell another.

On the evening she'd told Ortega-Cowan that she was Fidel's illegitimate daughter, she had the impression that he wasn't surprised. But she had let it go because, of course, she'd needed him to implement the operational details in Washington to get Rencke here. And returning to her office after the funeral, she'd got the impression again that nothing was coming as a surprise to him, and she had to think that he might know a lot more than he was letting on. And it was bothersome.

"How was the service?" he asked, standing in her doorway.

"Boring," she said. She went into her private bathroom and without closing the door she splashed some water on her face. The morning sun had been warm.

"I watched it on television," Ortega-Cowan said. "Quite a crowd."

"Us or them?" she asked.

"Both. But it was too bad that you couldn't have been in uniform in front."

She came out. "What are you getting at?"

"Ibarra called this morning about twenty minutes after you'd left." Julio Prieto Ibarra was Raúl's chief of staff. "He wanted to know how we were involved in the kidnapping yesterday of an American here in Havana. I denied it, of course. But I promised that we'd look into it."

"Evidently he saw the police report. But how did he connect it to us?"

"I didn't ask him," Ortega-Cowan said dryly. "But maybe he has a little bird whispering secrets in his ear."

"Someone here on my staff?"

"Or at Cojimar."

María had worried about this possibility, because no operation was absolutely waterproof. Leaks were common, and the higher the stakes, the greater possibility of a breakdown.

"I don't think McGarvey will wait very long to come to his friend's rescue," she said. "So time is on our side."

"Perhaps not."

"What else did Ibarra say to you?"

"Raúl wanted to talk to you as soon as you returned."

"In person?"

"A phone call will do."

"Any hint?" María asked.

"No, but I'd guess he wants to ask you about the kidnapping," Ortega-Cowan said. "What will you tell him?"

"I'll think of something."

She called on Raúl's private line that only he answered. But it was four rings before he picked up. "Good afternoon, Colonel. Thank you for returning my call so promptly."

"Yes, sir. I only just got back to my desk from the funeral."

"It was a moving ceremony."

She didn't know what to say.

"I want to know what sort of a game you are playing," Raúl said, a harsh edge to his voice. "Your chief of staff is evidently in the dark, which leaves only you to explain why a ranking officer of the American CIA was kidnapped and has disappeared."

"The police report came across my desk this morning. But I wasn't aware that the man worked for the CIA. Was he a spy?"

"Who better to know than you, if you are in complete control of your department."

"There's been no reaction from my contacts in Washington. Maybe he faked his kidnapping so that he could go to ground here. It's a possibility that we shall look into immediately, Señor Presidente. He may have had help from the CL." Which was *Cuba Libre*, "Free Cuba"—the organization, not the drink. "He may even have been killed, for all we know."

"I'm ordering the police to stop their investigation. Your directorate is to take charge, either to find the man and arrest him, or to find his body and return it to Washington."

"Yes, sir," María said. Pulling the police off the case was actually a break.

"There has been no official reaction from Washington because although the man arrived aboard the State Department aircraft, his name was not on the manifest; therefore, he came here unofficially. But before I lodge a formal complaint, you need to find him. Am I clear on this?"

"*Sí.*"

"All eyes are on us," Raúl said. "On you. Your father is dead, so you no longer have his protection."

María flared. "My father has been dead since my conception," she said bitterly, but Raúl had already broken the connection.

When she put the phone down, Ortega-Cowan offered a sympathetic smile. "That should hold him for a day or two, but not much longer," he said.

"Well, the cops are out of it for now, but I think that McGarvey will come either by boat or most likely by seaplane. I want you to coordinate with the navy to alert us when and where he shows up, but he is not to be interfered with."

"What if he's not alone?"

"I want him picked up and brought here undamaged," María said. "There will be no other considerations."

SEVENTEEN

At the Sheraton Key Largo, Martínez got them a room overlooking the Bay of Florida for five days and made a few phone calls before he left, suggesting that McGarvey get a couple hours of sleep before they headed for Cuba.

"This guy who's going to fly us over is cautious," Martínez said. "If the Cubans catch him, he's a dead man, so I'll have to be convincing."

"What's his story?"

"He was a Cuban air force pilot, but his wife apparently was mixing with the wrong people—the anti-Castro crowd—and she was arrested and died on the way to prison. They were coming after him when he took off with his MiG-25 and flew it to Key West."

"Ernesto Ruiz," McGarvey said. "About twenty years ago. I remember it was a big deal because he came in so low and so fast, no one knew he was coming until he'd touched down. And the fighter was loaded with air-to-air and air-to-surface missiles."

"And a new Russian radar jamming system that caught us by surprise. So the DI wants him in a big way. As a result, he's become a careful man."

"There're a lot safer places for him to live than Key Largo."

"That's true, but he changed his name and appearance and runs a nice little charter service for fishermen who want to work the flats in the bay for bonefish. He told me that he likes being this near to home, and that sometimes on a day off when it's clear, he'll fly close enough so that he can catch a glimpse of the island. It's enough for him."

"What makes you think that he'll take the risk to fly me down there?"

"If he thinks doing it will somehow stick it to the regime, he'll jump at the chance," Martínez said, and he smiled. "I'll tell him about Carlos, but just leave that part to me."

McGarvey was sitting in the dark on the balcony, looking at the running lights of a slow-moving boat out in the bay, music drifting down from the Fishtales Lounge on the top floor, people in the pool below, when someone was at the door. He got to his feet, picked up his pistol from the low table beside him, and stepped farther into the shadows.

Martínez was at the door, framed by the lights in the corridor. "It's me," he said softly.

"Are we good to go?" McGarvey asked, showing himself as he holstered the pistol at the small of his back.

Martínez came the rest of the way in and closed the door. "He's gassing up and preflighting the plane right now. Were you expecting trouble?"

"I'm sure the DI would like to catch you at something. They might have followed you back here."

Martínez laughed. "Those *putos* in Miami couldn't find their asses in a lit room with instructions. You going to take your gun with you?"

"They'll expect me to come in armed."

"Might come in handy if something goes south. You can never tell."

McGarvey grabbed his dark blue Windbreaker and, leaving his overnight bag behind, went with Martínez, and they drove down to the tiny village of Rock Harbor, where Bay Flats Air Tours maintained a hangar up a one-hundred-foot concrete ramp from the water's edge on the bay side.

The plane, already on the ramp, was a sturdy short takeoff and landing de Havilland Beaver that had once been used all over the world, but especially up in Alaska, for back country flying. It could carry the pilot and up to six passengers and gear at a cruise speed of a little over 140 miles per hour, its floats equipped with wheels that allowed it to take off and touch down on land or sea. The little aircraft was all but indestructible.

Ruiz was a short slope-shouldered man with a belly, bandy legs, and thinning gray hair over thick black eyebrows and mustache. He was trundling the hangar door closed when they drove up.

"I've read about you in the papers," he said, shaking McGarvey's hand. "Pretty risky for a former DCI to be going into harm's way."

McGarvey instantly liked him. "That's why I get the big bucks."

Ruiz laughed. "They're mostly a bunch of fine people over there saddled by a fucked-up system. But don't think they're incompetent because the Russians are gone and just about every governmental agency is broke. They've got a good coastal navy, and some damned effective radar installations."

"You're taking a bigger risk than I am."

"Acceptable, given the mission."

McGarvey didn't ask what the man understood the mission to be.

Ruiz pulled a chart out of the plane and illuminated it with a small red flashlight. "Raúl says that you need to get somewhere in the vicinity of Cojimar, which is just east of Havana. Not so many people there, but the navy will be active, especially if they have an idea that you're on the way, specifically to that spot on the beach."

"They know I'm coming," McGarvey said. "And the DI knows exactly where."

"In that case, they probably won't start shooting until you're safely ashore."

"Getting out might be a different story," Martínez suggested.

"Might be interesting," Ruiz said without hesitation. He turned back to the chart. "We'll fly down to Big Pine Key, about three quarters of the way to Key West, then head a little west of south, low and fast. Fifty miles to Big Pine and from there a hundred miles to Cojimar."

It was just midnight.

"Should set down just outside the surf line a little before two. You can take the rubber raft, so by the time you're ashore, I'll back in international waters."

"Wait for us at Newfound Harbor," Martínez said. It was south of Big Pine Key. "I'm going ashore with him."

It was about what McGarvey had expected. "You're a high-value target."

"And you're a gringo, so somebody has to hold your hand."

Ruiz laughed out loud. "I think I like crazy people better than sane people, because I feel that I'm among friends."

Heading southwest, they flew at an altitude of about five hundred feet, high enough for them to see twenty-five miles in any direction, the keys an irregular necklace of lights like jewels on a black velvet backdrop. The moon had set, and in the distance they spotted the rotating beacon of an airfield.

"That's the airstrip at Marathon on Key Vaca," Ruiz told them.

· They wore headsets so they wouldn't have to shout. McGarvey and Martínez were in back, where the two middle seats had been removed, leaving space for the small inflatable boat in a bright yellow soft valise.

About fifteen minutes later, they spotted what looked like a barrage balloon, a large Goodyear-type blimp, at a much higher altitude than they were flying, tethered on Cudjoe Key behind the harbor.

"*Fat Albert,*" Ruiz explained. "Aerostat radar system. Watching for illegal traffic coming across the strait."

"Will it cause trouble for you when you fly back?" McGarvey asked.

"They know who I am."

Just past the surveillance blimp, Ruiz banked to the southwest and headed down to fifty feet above the wave tops. The sea was fairly calm, five- to six-foot swells, and after ten minutes he eased the small plane even lower, and looking out the side windows McGarvey got the impression that they were hurtling along like a speedboat, actually leaving a wake behind them. The slightest downdraft, the least little mistake, and they would crash.

Martínez looked at him. "Ernesto has done this before."

"Glad to hear it," McGarvey said. "Now, tell me everything you know about Colonel León's house, and who's likely to be there."

Martínez gave him the general layout of what in effect was a smallish beach house once owned by the daughter of a pre-Castro sugar baron who'd sent her to Cojimar in exile for some indiscretion that no one remembered. The state had given it to María when she returned from Moscow and took up her DI duties as department chief in signals intelligence in the late 1990s. Since then, she'd put a fair amount of money into remodeling and furnishing the house and grounds, adding a west wing, the pool, and a small cabana. But all of the work had been done over a fairly long period of time, in bits and pieces, slowly, so as not to excite much interest. It didn't do to flaunt one's money.

"We have people down there keeping their eyes and ears open," Martínez said.

McGarvey had never remembered seeing such detailed information when he was deputy director of operations or as DCI. "By *we*, do you mean the Company or your exiles in Miami?"

Martínez just shrugged. "Anything important gets to Langley. Nothing is going to change the system until we can go home. Trouble is a lot of people are dying of old age, waiting for the day."

Ruiz had been listening to the exchange, and he glanced over his shoulder. "I won't go back," he said.

"Why?" McGarvey asked.

Apparently Martínez already knew the answer because he said nothing.

"There's a lot of resentment. Years of it. And when the regime finally falls, there'll be a bloodbath in the streets. I don't want to be a part of it, because my hands wouldn't stay clean."

"Nor will mine," Martínez said. "But wild horses couldn't keep me from going back."

"Look," Ruiz said, and McGarvey and Martínez leaned forward to see out the windshield.

A soft glow lit the horizon slightly right of the aircraft's nose.

"Havana," Ruiz said. "You might want to take the raft out of the valise—we'll be landing in about fifteen minutes."

EIGHTEEN

María sat at her desk, alone in the west wing of her house, staring at the images on the computer monitor that were relayed from Coastal Radar Station Guanabacoa and listening to the chatter on the navy's guard channel. A small single-engine aircraft had suddenly popped up on the screen coming from the north, its image breaking up because of its proximity to the water, and the sector commander aboard the Russian-built missile patrol boat *Osa II* was asking for orders to blow the bastard out of the sky.

"Stand by and observe," the squadron's watch officer at Station Santa Cruz del Norte radioed. "Acknowledge."

"Copy," the skipper replied, though it was clear from the strain in his voice he wasn't happy with his orders.

Lieutenant Miguel Vera, the young commander at Santa Cruz, was intimidated by the DI, especially since María had mentioned to him that she knew of his great-uncle's support for the Batista regime back in the late fifties. It was the same sort of power that the Stasi had wielded over the East Germans, and that de facto branch of the KGB had been one of María's major interests of study. Information—didn't matter if it was true or simply implied—was power.

They'd watched for small aircraft in the Keys, looking for the one that would turn south at some point and then disappear in the surface clutter. It was exactly how she figured McGarvey would be coming to her, and she'd called Santa Cruz to keep whatever patrol vessel was in the sector to stand down.

"Pardon me, Colonel, but what happens if the aircraft you say will be coming picks up defectors?"

"Then you would be authorized to blow them out of the sky when they took off," María said. "But I believe this aircraft will be landing someone on the beach."

The squadron commander was impressed. "A spy?"

"We think so, in which case, the matter belongs to the DI."

"What about the aircraft?"

"You would allow it to return to the States, so that they would think their mission was a success."

"I see," the young man said, even more impressed. "I'll have a patrol vessel with night-vision capabilities standing by."

That was earlier this evening. Now her telephone rang, and it was Lieutenant Vera. "A single-engine civilian aircraft has just landed one hundred meters from the beach north of Cojimar."

"Yes, I have a feed from Guanabacoa, and I'm monitoring your radio traffic."

"Stand by, Colonel."

"Base, this is vessel two-zero-niner on station, with a sitrep."

"Roger, two-zero-niner, report."

"I'm seeing two people climbing into a small inflatable. Looks like they mean to come ashore. What are my orders?"

"Did you get that?" Lieutenant Vera asked.

"Yes, I'm still monitoring your radio traffic. Don't interfere with them."

"*Sí, Coronel.*"

"You've done well this evening, Lieutenant. I will not forget," María said, and she hung up.

Moments later, the watch officer at Santa Cruz relayed the orders to the skipper of the missile boat.

"Once they are ashore, this becomes a matter for the DI," the officer said.

"What about the aircraft?"

"Let it go."

As soon as the aircraft had shown up on radar heading south from Big Pine Key and then disappeared from radar, María put Ramiro Toro and Salvador Gonzáles, her two bodyguards, on standby to fetch McGarvey, if that's who had landed. The problem was the second man. She hadn't counted on him. Rencke was safely locked away in a small room here in the west wing, so he couldn't cause any mischief tonight.

She called them over from their quarters and told them what was happening. They'd been shown photographs of McGarvey. "If it's him, bring him here. I don't think he'll give you any resistance."

"What about the second guy?" Toro asked. He was a large man by Cuban standards, over six feet, with a square jaw and mean eyes. He'd been the Cuban All Services boxing champion three years in a row not long ago, and he still had the edge. It's why she'd picked him.

"Kill him, and leave the body in the bush," María said.

"And if neither man is McGarvey?"

"One of them will be."

"*Sí, Coronel,*" Toro said, and he and the much smaller

Gonzáles, one of the DI's better marksmen, turned and left.

María watched the radar feed and listened to the routine radio traffic for a couple of minutes, but then went back to where Otto Rencke was being kept. She opened the door, and Rencke, who'd been lying on his small cot, opened his eyes.

"It would appear that your friend McGarvey has arrived by small float plane a few miles from here," she said. "We'll begin the questioning tomorrow."

"The sooner, the better," Rencke said. "I'm sure Mac has a few questions himself. And he doesn't take to liars."

"Neither do I," María said.

She walked back to the pool, where she heard the Gazik her bodyguards used sputtering off in the night, which became still except for the sounds of the surf thirty meters down the slope on the beach.

Retribution and salvation. It's what her father had said to her on his deathbed, and it made no more sense to her now after questioning Rencke. McGarvey was supposed to have the answers, and her father's unlikely source for this opinion had come from Kim Jong-il, who had possibly been the most unstable government leader in the world.

And she was having some serious second thoughts, even though to this point everything was going according to the plan that she and Ortega-Cowan had worked out last week. But she was terribly unsettled. There were so many things that she didn't know or understand, especially her father's insistence that McGarvey be enticed to come here.

Twenty-four hours, she told herself. Forty-eight at the most, and she would have the answers, though what they might be, she hadn't the faintest idea.

NINETEEN

It was nearly two by the time the small rubber raft, in black Hypalon, pulled up on the beach and McGarvey and Martínez got out. The night was quiet, this spot deserted. They could make out the silhouettes of houses a hundred yards to the east and a little closer to the west, but very few lights were on at this hour. The sky to the west was lit with the glow from Havana, but there seemed to be no life here just now.

"Ruiz picked a good spot," McGarvey said.

"He knows his business," Martínez said. "But that patrol boat out there was waiting for us, you do know that."

"I was counting on it," McGarvey said. The night odors of lush vegetation mixed with the sea smells at the tide line were the same as the beaches of South Florida, except here he was sure that he smelled burning garbage, and maybe the exhaust of a diesel generator or boat somewhere into the sea breeze. Possibly the patrol vessel, though he couldn't hear the sounds of her engines or make out the silhouette of her superstructure.

But it did nothing to explain why the DI colonel

wanted him here, though he was more certain now that they didn't mean to assassinate him. If they'd wanted that, the patrol boat could have blown the plane out of the sky, and been well within its rights to do so. The U.S. would have had absolutely no recourse.

"So what's next, Mac?" Martínez asked. "The colonel's house is less than two miles to the west, so if you want, we can get there on the beach. But she probably has security that we'd have to deal with."

In the very far distance, a stray bit of breeze brought the fading sound of the Beaver heading back to Florida, but then it was gone. Ruiz was safely back in international waters, something else he'd counted on. And something else that made no sense to him. The Cubans would consider Ruiz a high-value target, but they let him fly away.

"We're going to walk up to the highway—our ride should be along any minute now," McGarvey said, and he started toward the line of tall sea oats and grasses that grew just above the high-water line, but Martínez stopped him.

"I'm not coming with you," Martínez said. "The DI wants you tonight, not me."

"You should have gone back with the plane."

"No disrespect, Mac, but I think getting you here was a hell of a lot easier than getting you out will be. So I'm going to stick around until it's time to bail."

"I'll try to get to a radio."

"No need," Martínez said. "You'll know it's time when the shooting starts."

McGarvey had to smile. "It's good to have you around."

McGarvey patted him on the shoulder and headed up to the sea oats, but when he looked back, Martínez had already disappeared, and except for the sounds of the surf, the night was even quieter than before.

The narrow two-lane coast highway was less than one hundred yards from the high-tide line, and when McGarvey made it that far and stepped out onto the pavement, a pair of headlights switched on about that far to the west and slowly came his way.

No other traffic was on the road, and as the Gazik pulled up a few feet away, McGarvey raised his hands over his head.

Two men in civilian clothes got out of the jeep; the smaller of the two armed with what looked like a Soviet-made 5.45 mm AKR compact submachine gun remained behind as the bigger man cautiously approached.

"Señor McGarvey, are you armed?" he demanded.

"Yes."

"Please hand me your weapon, we mean you no harm this morning."

"Why is your partner pointing a weapon at me?"

"Why did you bring a gun into Cuba?" Toro asked reasonably. But he seemed a little uncertain, and his eyes kept darting to the bush along the side of the highway.

"I didn't know what I might be walking into," McGarvey said. He reached with his right hand for his pistol at the small of his back and held it out handle first to the Cuban DI officer, who took it.

"Are you carrying anything else that might harm me?" Toro asked, making sure the Walther's safety lever on the left side was engaged before he stuffed it into his belt.

"No."

"Someone else got off the airplane and came ashore with you. Where is he?"

"I don't know what you're talking about," McGarvey said. "As you can see, I'm alone."

"You were observed from the deck of a patrol vessel."

"Yes, we saw the boat. Perhaps if whoever was watching had been paying attention, he would have seen the pilot help me deploy the raft before he took off."

"He came ashore," Toro said patiently. "And we'll find him. This is our island."

"Maybe not for long if things keep going the way they are," McGarvey said irritably. He was tired of screwing around. "The ball's in your court, gentlemen. Either shoot me or take me to see Colonel León so we can find out what the hell this is all about."

Toro started to say something, but then stepped aside and motioned McGarvey to get in the backseat of the Gazik, and he climbed in beside him.

Martínez crouched in the bush just a few feet from the side of the highway, and less than twenty feet from the Gazik. McGarvey had gotten into the backseat with the larger of the two DI officers.

He almost laughed out loud. Either the two guys were the dumbest security people in the business or they had no real idea whom they were dealing with. It would be like taking candy from babies for Mac to disarm and disable the two men—kill them, if need be—and make his way to the colonel's house, disable or kill her, rescue Otto, and wait on the beach for Ruiz to fly back and pick them up. They could all be back in Key Largo in time for breakfast and Bloody Marys.

But that's not why they'd come down here, and Martínez was just as curious as McGarvey was to find out what this was all about. But in the meantime, he had a bit of work to do himself.

He watched as the Gazik turned around and headed back west before he stepped out on the highway and headed for his contact's fishing shack a couple of klicks in the opposite direction. He wanted to be in Havana before dawn.

No security was evident along the broken seashell road from the highway to the long, low ranch-styled house, very few lights showing. A helicopter pad, empty, its windsock barely fluttering was to the east, while a pair of buildings—one of them McGarvey took to be a garage, the other possibly living quarters for the staff— was off in the copse of trees fifty yards to the west.

They pulled up in front of the main house, and McGarvey was escorted inside to a small windowless room in the west wing that was pleasantly furnished with a comfortable-looking double bed, a dresser, mirror, hand-woven rug on the floor, and some decent Picasso prints on the painted plasterboard walls. A change of clothing, his size, was laid out on the bed, and the small but spotlessly clean bathroom was equipped with a luxury hotel range of toiletries.

The sturdy door and large dead bolt made the purpose of the room clear.

"The colonel is away from the compound tonight and for a part of tomorrow, but she is most anxious to speak to you," Toro said.

"What's wrong with right now?"

"We weren't quite sure exactly when you would be showing up. She asked me to apologize for your inconvenience and to assure you that we mean you no harm."

"I want to see my friend."

"Tomorrow."

McGarvey thought about it for a moment. He could take the security officer down; he had little doubt of that. But such an act would only accelerate the violence. First he wanted to find out what the hell this was all about.

He nodded. "Bring me a couple of Dos Equis lagers, with limes, and a little something to eat."

Toro bristled, but he nodded.

"And I want to take a swim in the morning before breakfast, around six would be fine."

When Toro was gone, McGarvey made a quick tour of his room, looking not only for a way out, but also for a weapon. Behind the plasterboard was cinder block, which could be breached, though it would take time. The mirror in the bathroom was polished stainless steel, and the light fixtures and wall sockets were attached with headless screws.

A lot of thought had gone into this cage, and looking up at the screwheads holding the slow-moving ceiling fan in place, he smiled and nodded.

TWENTY

María's bedroom in the east wing faced the ocean, and the sliders were open, admitting a gentle sea breeze that ruffled the diaphanous gauze drapes. She always had trouble sleeping, or at least she had since the rape at school, but she'd never taken drugs to help. She considered that a sign of weakness.

Standing now at the open window, wearing only a man's T-shirt too big for her, she tried to take her mind off McGarvey for just a minute or two. She'd read his DI file and the press clippings from the *New York Times* and *Washington Post,* but the measure of the man she thought she'd had went completely out the window in the first five minutes of watching him in his room.

It had struck her that he wasn't the caged animal she thought he would become once he realized that his freedom had been taken from him and that he was at the complete mercy of his captors.

He'd looked up directly into the closed-circuit television camera lens concealed in the base of the ceiling fan and smiled patiently, as if he were a man with all the time in the world—but even more important, a man who understood things, a man who'd been around long enough, who'd been through enough, including the assassinations last year of his wife, his daughter, and his son-in-law.

Until her own father's death, such a loss had been meaningless at a gut level. But now, thinking about

McGarvey in his cage, seeing the look in his eyes, the set to his handsome mouth, and the squaring of his shoulders, she did understand, at least a little. And she couldn't help but admire the man for coming to rescue a friend. It was something no one would do for her.

She'd set up a laptop at the foot of her bed to monitor McGarvey, and she sat down cross-legged as Toro went in with two beers and a tray with a bowl of what looked like black bean soup and a couple of bread rolls, plus a spoon. He would have had to heat the soup himself unless he roused the cook, and he'd acted out of loyalty to her rank, not to her personally.

McGarvey said thanks and opened the first beer after Toro left the room.

It was a mistake, of course, feeding him. Now he had weapons—the beer bottles and the spoon—and possibly a means of freeing himself.

But watching him sitting back on the cot while she sat mostly naked on her own bed maybe fifty feet away, she was struck with the totally irrational and erotic thought of going to him, just as she was, to begin their conversation. It had been more than a year since her last partner, an air force lieutenant who'd come back from liaison duty in Caracas, was beaten to death, supposedly by CL dissidents. Actually, she'd killed him herself down south where they'd taken a little vacation halfway up Pico Turquino, Cuba's highest mountain in the Sierra Maestras. He'd told her that they should get married, that she should quit her job, which he believed was as a functionary of some sort in the DI, and settle down and have babies and let a man do the man's work of running a household. She'd said no, he'd insisted, and she'd tossed him off the mountain into a rock-strewn gully three hundred feet below.

He'd just been a kid filled with *machismo Cubano*—unearned machismo—where just looking at McGarvey, she *knew* in her gut that he had earned his chops.

And she lay back and drifted off to sleep, wondering how it would be when she finally met him face-to-face. But not too soon. She wanted him to wonder as well.

TWENTY-ONE

From fifty yards offshore, McGarvey was just able to make out the figure of the smaller of the two men who had picked him up last night sitting on a wooden structure that could have been a lifeguard tower. Standing guard with a Russian-made 7.62 mm Dragunov sniper rifle, any shot at a human-sized target out to 650 yards was a guaranteed no-miss.

After a breakfast of rolls, butter, mango jelly, and strong black coffee, he'd been brought swimming trunks, a beach jacket, and sandals.

"Go for your swim, señor," Toro said. "The *coronel*'s property extends two hundred meters in both directions. Stray farther than that on the beach or in the ocean, and our orders are to kill you."

"What about my friend?"

"Not until the *coronel* returns."

"When will that be?"

"I have not been told," Toro said, and he did not lock the door when he left.

McGarvey had changed, and when he stepped out of his room, Toro was waiting at the end of the corridor. Otto was back here, but he figured that he would wait until nightfall to make a move. If María León had not shown up by tonight to explain what was going on, he would free Otto and kill anyone who got in his way.

And swimming now, he watched the surf breaking another fifty yards offshore, which was about as close in as Ruiz could safely land the float plane. In the meantime, he meant to find out as much about the compound and staff other than Toro and the man on guard duty with the Dragunov as he could this afternoon.

Back onshore, he nodded toward the man on the lifeguard tower as he toweled off and then headed in an easy, loping run down the beach toward the east. He looked back once, and the guard had gotten to his feet and was talking into a handheld radio, but he hadn't raised the rifle yet.

When he got as far as the east end of the main house, he had a clear sight line to the still-empty helipad, the windsock this morning filled out with the light breeze. But a thick line of casuarina Australian pine trees blocked his view of the highway.

About one hundred fifty meters farther, he came to the stump of what looked like a weathered old fence post just above the high-water mark, which he took to be the border of the colonel's property.

He stopped and stretched as he looked back at the tower. The guard was still on his feet, but now it looked as if he had raised the rifle. Ignoring the threat,

McGarvey walked up to the edge of the water line, still keeping well inside the border, and searched the open field all the way to the trees. But if there were motion sensors or infrared detectors or even closed-circuit television cameras, he could not make them out from this distance. Which either meant the colonel relied solely on her house staff to keep the occasional visitor in line, or that the detectors were camouflaged. He expected that for a woman in her position, it was the latter.

Finished stretching, he started back west, running at the same loping pace, scarcely building up a decent sweat even though it was already nearly eighty degrees. As he passed the guard on the tower, who'd lowered the rifle, he smiled and nodded and continued along the beach, gradually building his pace until he was running flat out.

The west wing, which angled away from the main house, was a low concrete block structure that matched the architecture of the rest of the place except that it was windowless, and the roof bristled with three satellite dishes, one of them pointing to the southwest, and several shortwave and UHF antennas. It looked as if she was well connected with the Cuban military and intel operations plus satellite services that the Russians still provided, which included secure connections with the Internet.

The Gazik was parked in front of the building he'd taken as a garage on the way in last night, and the second building—with windows and sliders and a couple of patios with lawn furniture nestled in a copse of casuarinas—was definitely living quarters for the staff, but it was hard to tell for just how many people. Probably the two men who'd picked him up last night and a cook, maybe a houseboy, a yardman, and a communications specialist.

But as he passed, he saw no activity, which could have meant nothing, just routine at this time of the morning, or possibly that the colonel had ordered everyone to remain out of sight as much as possible while their American guests were here.

An old rusted oil drum half buried in the sand just at the high-tide line marked the western edge of the property, and McGarvey stopped a couple of meters short of it, and again did his stretches, sweat pouring off him as he tried to make out the highway, but the line of Australian pines that stretched entirely across the back of the property made an impenetrable screen. Nor could he hear any sounds, though in the distance to the far southwest, he could see a high contrail above the puffy trade wind clouds scudding in from the east.

After a couple of minutes, he headed back to the house and, ignoring the guard, grabbed his towel and beach jacket and went inside to his room, where he took a shower, then changed into a pair of shorts and light T-shirt that had been laid out for him.

Ten minutes later, he came back out and sat down at one of the umbrella tables on the pool deck with a fabulous view of the beach and the electric blue of the same waters that Hemingway had fished eighty or ninety years ago. Cuba had changed, but the ocean hadn't. The guard on the tower was gone.

A young boy dressed in shorts and a white jacket came out of the house with a coffee service plus a bottle of Cuban rum and a pair of glasses on a silver tray, which he laid on the table with a little smile before he hurried away without a word.

McGarvey poured a coffee when María, wearing sunglasses and a white, low-cut, backless bathing suit and gauze beach jacket came out.

"Pour me a cup, please," she said, her English good with just a trace of upper-crust British. English was taught by Brits here and in Moscow.

McGarvey looked up, then got to his feet. The woman was more stunning than beautiful. "Colonel León," he said.

She sat down and crossed her legs as McGarvey poured her coffee, to which she added a dollop of rum. "I trust that your treatment and accommodations last night and this morning were reasonably comfortable."

"The best prison I've been in so far," McGarvey said, sitting.

María smiled faintly. "If I have your word that you won't try anything stupid, your door will not be locked tonight."

"That depends on why I'm here, and what has happened to my friend."

"Otto is just fine," she said. "Quite a brilliant man. Inventive. But he's warned us not to underestimate you, which of course we don't."

"Where is he?"

"Here in the house. I'll have him brought out after we talk."

"What about his wife?"

"We'll talk first," María said sharply.

McGarvey looked at her for several beats, but then

he nodded. "If any harm comes to Otto or to his wife, I'll kill you. Am I clear?"

María started to say something, but she cut herself off. Toro appeared at the open slider for just a moment, but then disappeared back inside the house.

"You went through a lot of trouble to get me here so that you could tell me something," McGarvey said. "You must have known that there would be repercussions, yet you authorized the operation. And coming so close on the heels of your father's death, there must be a connection."

"Yes, there is a connection, as you put it," María said. "I was at my father's deathbed, the only person in the room on his orders, and he made me promise to bring you here. He said that you would know something that could help us."

McGarvey was at a loss, and he told her so. "I have no idea what you're talking about. I never met your father and never had any dealings down here except for a couple of visits to Guantánamo."

"*Sí,* but my father told me that you came highly recommended by Kim Jong-il, who said that you were a man who could be trusted. And that makes no sense to me, unless the CIA is in some sort of collusion with the North Koreans. Or maybe it was just you."

"I was of some assistance a couple years ago."

María said something under her breath. "The Chinese general shot to death outside his embassy in Pyongyang. You had something to do with shifting the blame away from Kim?"

"Something."

"My God, I'd like to hear about it. Must have been amazing."

"Is that why I'm here?"

"Just before he died, my father used the word *retribution,* and when I asked what he meant—because it made no sense to me—he told me to find you. 'Bring him here. He'll know.'"

"Know what?"

"'Our salvation,'" María said. "His exact words. 'Bring him here. Ask him. Promise me. My friend Kim Jong-il told me he could be trusted.'"

"What else?"

"That's it. He made me promise, which I did, and he died. What does that mean to you?"

McGarvey shook his head. "Not a thing."

María flared. "Don't play this game with me. I won't hesitate to kill you and your friend and his wife. Perhaps I could even find a way to get to your granddaughter. Believe me, Señor McGarvey, I am serious."

And frightened, it seemed to McGarvey. "I'm sorry, Colonel, but you've gone through a great deal of trouble, including kidnapping an innocent woman and murdering another for no good reason. I can't help you, because I haven't a clue what your father was talking about."

María jumped up. "We'll see about that!" she shouted. "And we *will* find the man who came ashore with you." She turned and went back to the house.

Toro was there. "Colonel?"

"Kill the bastard if he so much as twitches."

TWENTY-TWO

Lying on his cot in the dark as he had been for twenty-four hours, in his mind Otto was seeing and hearing Puccini's opera *Madama Butterfly* as a break to the master games of chess he'd played through the night and mathematical puzzles he'd set himself to solve.

It was coming to the end of the score: Pinkerton has returned to Japan with his wife, Kate, and they've learned that Butterfly has had a child and that she will probably commit suicide now that she knows her American lover hasn't returned for her in the spring as he'd promised.

Kate tells Butterfly's maid, Suzuki, that she'll care for Butterfly's son as if he were her own.

"*Vi credo,*" I believe you, Suzuki sings. "But I must be quite alone with her . . . quite alone in this hour of crisis! She'll cry so bitterly."

And Otto always cried at this point because he knew that Butterfly had been left with absolutely no hope of being with her true love, and that her son would be raised by another woman, and that in the end there was no choice open for her but seppuku.

Last night for dinner, a metal tray of shredded pork and rice with no utensils had been pushed through a slot in his door, and he'd been forced to eat with his fingers in the absolute darkness. Later, he'd taken a cold shower and lain on the cot to get some rest. But he'd been unable to shut down all night, still awake at a breakfast of bread, butter, and strong coffee, and now at what he took to be late morning or early afternoon, he was exhausted but still awake.

With the last strains of *Butterfly* dying in his head, he sat up and set his mind again to what Fidel's deathbed request to his daughter might mean.

His starting point was the risk/reward ratio. The Cuban government in the person of a DI colonel, and presumably a number of her staff, had taken the extraordinary risk of kidnapping Louise in order to lure him here as bait for McGarvey, who he suspected was already here or certainly on his way.

Such an operation could have gone south in a New York minute, which it had at least partially done with the murder of Joyce Kilburn in front of her day care center in broad daylight, and the fallout when it came would be nothing short of catastrophic for the government.

Yet the risk had been taken, which meant it was either the work of a logical mind, or worst-case scenario, it was an operation designed and ordered by a deeply disturbed person. But he'd not detected insanity lurking around the corners when he spoke with María León. She struck him as a bright, possibly even brilliant woman who'd been faced with a puzzle that she was trying desperately to solve. She was frightened—he'd seen that, too—but he'd been unable to figure out what she was frightened of. Failure, perhaps. Which brought him back to Fidel's final words.

Retribución, the dying man had told his daughter. And there was some sort of sense there; the old man had wanted to somehow get back at the United States, which he blamed for the poor state of his island.

But then he'd used the phrase, *Nuestra salvacion.* "Our salvation," which made less sense to Otto than retribution, and so he'd set himself to remembering every single thing he'd ever heard or read about Castro, the CIA's files unreeling in his mind's eye, page after page, photo after photo, and recorded speech after speech with translations, starting with the base assumption that the promise he'd extracted from his daughter was not simply the ravings of an old man who'd become a lunatic.

The lights in his cell suddenly came on, temporarily blinding him so that he had to cover his eyes until they could adjust.

The door opened and the larger of the two DI officers who'd picked him up from the airport came in and handed Otto a pair of shorts, a shirt, and sandals. "Take a shower and shave. You have ten minutes."

When he was gone, Otto went to the door, which had been left partially ajar, and looked out into the empty hallway. He thought that he could hear music playing somewhere in the house, and he could smell the ocean and perhaps chlorine from the pool and just hint of perfume all mixed together.

He'd counted four doors besides his own when he'd been brought back here yesterday, and hesitating for just a moment to make sure that no one was coming, he stepped out into the hall and tried the three to the left, the first two unlocked and empty, the third at the end of the hall locked, and the fourth just to the right of his own room furnished exactly like his. The cot had been slept in and still-dripping swimming trunks had been hung up in the shower.

Mac was here already.

He went back to his room, shaved, took a quick shower, the water warm this time, and got dressed. Pushing his long frizzy red hair back out of his eyes, he headed down the hall to the main wing of the house, where he pulled up short.

The large DI officer stood at the open sliders, and he looked over his shoulder.

Otto hesitated only a moment before he crossed the broad living room and went out to the pool, where McGarvey, his back to the house, was sitting alone at one of the tables.

"Oh, wow, kemo sabe, you came."

McGarvey turned around and got up, a look of deep concern on his face. "Are you okay?" he demanded.

"I haven't had my lunch, if that's what you mean," Otto said, and he went to his friend and they embraced. "Long time no see," he said.

"You've met the colonel, I expect," McGarvey said. "Did she tell you why she wanted me here?"

"Just her father's deathbed request. What'd you tell Page and Marty?"

"Everything I knew to that point. And that I was coming down here to get you out."

Otto couldn't help but grin. "That must have been some meeting. What'd they say?"

"Said that we were crazy."

They sat down.

Otto turned his head slightly. The same perfume as before was suddenly stronger. "It's Prada, I believe," he said. "Won't you join us, Colonel León?"

TWENTY—THREE

"Not for long unless I get some answers," María said, coming out of the house. She was still dressed in the swimming outfit and beach jacket, and this time neither man rose when she pulled out a chair and sat down.

She'd watched McGarvey's reaction when Rencke had come outside, and Toro had shown himself for just a moment as she'd ordered. And she'd thought that Ramiro was lucky to still be alive, and she also wondered what it must be like to have such a prodigious friend.

"Answers we don't have," McGarvey said.

"I thought that you'd be a more practical man when it came to saving the lives of your friend and his wife."

"The delusions of an old man, Colonel. Are you going to risk Cuba's security over a fantasy? I'm sure that Raúl and the government don't share your tolerance for this kind of meaningless operation; otherwise, we'd be downtown in a holding cell at DI headquarters, or maybe even in a cell at Quivicán Prison, eating boiled beans and chicken broth and having our fingernails pulled out instead of being here, drinking coffee and good *Cubano* rum."

He was an arrogant bastard, just as she had gleaned from his file. But sitting across from him now, measuring the set of his shoulders and the supreme self-confidence in his voice, she was beginning to believe that the files might not have gone far enough. In her estimation, McGarvey was a man among men, and she was impatient with herself for admitting such a thing and, in some respects, even admiring it.

But she refused to look away, and the bastard smiled, her temper spiking.

"I've been thinking," Rencke said. "Your father used the word *salvation*."

It took several beats for what Rencke had just said to register before she could tear her eyes away from McGarvey's. "What?"

"He said something about retribution, but he mentioned that Kim Jong-il had given Mac high marks, which made me think that salvation was more to the point."

"I understand what happened in Pyongyang," María said.

"I don't think you do."

"It was a matter of solving a murder and saving face."

"No," Rencke said. "Mac saved the regime, and by doing so, he averted war not only on the peninsula but in the entire region, Japan included. Nuclear war, because the nut case would have ordered his eight or ten nukes to be launched. Seoul, Tokyo, Beijing. The Chinese would have retaliated—massively—obliterating all of North Korea, killing a lot of innocent people whose only crime is trying to survive."

Something like that was impossible for María to accept. "Our networks picked up nothing."

"Of course not," Rencke said. "Your attention is on this hemisphere. And I doubt Kim Jong-il shared all of the details with your father. But we are talking about salvation. Mac saved the North Korean regime so that he could save innocent lives, and Kim told your father just that."

"I can't imagine that my father thought you would help save our government," María said to McGarvey.

"I see what Otto's getting at, and I don't think he meant saving your father's successors. He meant saving the Cuban people."

"From what?"

"Starvation."

María bridled. She wanted to tell them both that they were wrong. But of course, they were not, and she knew it. Everyone in Cuba knew it. "Anything is possible."

"Maybe I'm just guessing, ya know," Otto said. "But I think you didn't much care about what you probably took as nothing more than the ravings of a dying old man. A father you might have hated."

María held herself in check, but it was hard. Both of them were so smug.

"What changed your mind?" Otto asked. "Why have you gone through all the trouble to get us here?"

"I wasn't going to," she admitted. "Not at first. Not until my photographs from that night were probably transmitted to Langley, which meant it would only be a matter of time before my true identity was no longer a secret."

"For all practical purposes, it still is," McGarvey said. "No one cares that you might be one of Fidel's illegitimate kids."

"They would in Miami."

"Sorry, Colonel, but no one really gives a damn. The regime will either change or it will fall, and if that happens, it'll be a bloodbath, and I think that you and everyone else here knows it."

A blinding rage had been building like an approaching hurricane, and it suddenly struck her what a colossal mistake she had made, mounting this insane operation, risking her career, even her life. Raúl had warned that she no longer had her father's protection. No longer was she anyone special.

Her anger spiked and she jumped up. "Ramiro!" she shouted.

Toro appeared at the open slider. "Colonel?"

"Shoot these bastards and dump their bodies in the sea."

Toro reached for his pistol, and McGarvey was about to shove Otto to the side and upend the table, when Otto laughed.

"It's about money, of course," he said calmly.

Toro had his pistol out and was bringing it up, but María waved him off, not sure exactly what she'd heard. McGarvey was about ready to spring, but Rencke seemed amused. For just a split instant, she wondered if maybe she was a little out of her depth here.

"What?" she asked.

"Money," Otto said. "Cuba is starving. Your only salvation now that Russian doesn't subsidize your sugar and we continue to boycott you, especially the bulk of your tourist trade, is money and a lot of it. Five hundred thousand of your government employees have been laid off, and from what I hear, they're not doing so good."

"We have Caracas."

"How much aid do you get from them? Not much, I think."

"Colonel?" Toro prompted. He still had his pistol pointed at McGarvey.

"As you were," María said, and she sat down, having no idea where this was going, but intrigued nonetheless. Salvation, indeed. "I'm listening."

"Not a loan from the Association of Latin American States or from the IMF, because you'd have no way of repaying it, and in the end, you'd be in bigger trouble than you are right now."

"I'm still listening."

"Not a loan, but from a treasure that your father believed rightly belonged to his people. Something he'd searched for most of his life."

She'd heard talk over the years, not much, but what there was most often was prefaced by craziness. *Muy loco.* "How could you possibly know such a thing?"

"I did some research last night."

"What are you talking about?" María demanded. "Research, how? With what?"

"My memory," Otto replied. "Your father mentioned it once during his trip to the UN in 1960, and again in 1995, celebrating the fiftieth anniversary of his dictatorship."

"Presidency," María said automatically.

"Right," Otto replied dryly.

There'd always been rumors, of course. El Dorado, Cíbola, sunken Spanish treasure ships—some of which had already been found and plundered off the coast of Florida—tantalizingly close. But nothing was concrete.

Nothing that Cuba could lay any legitimate claim to. Nothing easy to find and retrieve. And certainly no fortune large enough to be the salvation for an entire country.

Toro was still at the slider, his pistol still in hand. María could see him out of the corner of her eye. Again, she had to ask herself if luring them here had been a terrible mistake that could eventually cost her everything—her job, even her life.

"I want answers," she told Rencke. "Not fairy tales."

TWENTY-FOUR

Martínez was seated at a table in a small but tidy second-floor apartment on Avenue Jesús María, a few blocks up from La Habana Vieja waterfront, having coffee with his old friends Fidel and Margarita de la Paz.

"By tonight, it will be twenty-four hours since I came ashore with Kirk," he told them. "Plenty of time for his little chat with the *coronel*."

They were in their early sixties—Fidel small and wiry, his muscled arms gnarled with veins and blackened by the sun; his wife just the opposite, buxom, with full broad hips and tree trunks for legs. But no matter how bad things had ever gotten for them— both had spent time at Quivicán, where they'd been starved and beaten—they never lost their sense of humor, their smiles, their good nature, and the basic belief that Cuba would someday be free. And like many Cubans, they knew that their salvation would eventually come from their neighbor to the north. It was the same reason that most Cubans in exile in the United States believed their situations were only temporary. They were on hold until they could return home.

"Then, *niño*, we must help," Margarita said.

Growing up in Havana, Martínez had known Margarita and Fidel—who were close friends and neighbors with his parents—as *tía* and *tío,* aunt and uncle. And from the time they were teenagers, they'd worked underground for the resistance movements in Havana and elsewhere, just lately the militant factions of the Free Expression Solidarity and the Liberty and Democracy movements. Their main pipeline for contacts to the resistance was through a small private restaurant, called a *paladar,* they operated out of the ground-floor apartment just below. It was one of the private enterprises that the government allowed. And there were so many of them in Havana that the DI couldn't watch them all.

"It won't be easy. But I have a plan."

Margarita shrugged. "We can go tonight, if that's what you wish. But once we have them out, where will we take them?"

Martínez told them about the float plane and how they had come ashore without a challenge from the patrol boat less than a kilometer away. "He's standing by at Newfound Harbor for my call."

"Your friend might have been expected to show up, and the back door was left open, but it won't be the same tonight."

"We'll have to take out their communications ability. Antennas and dishes on the roof, and the phone line coming into the property."

"Cell phones?" Fidel asked.

"Jorge will cut power to the Cojimar tower at midnight, and it'll take Cubacel at least until noon to fix it," Martínez said. Jorge Guerra was the man in the fishing shack west of Cojimar, whom he'd gone to after McGarvey had been picked up, and Cubacel was the state-operated company that provided cellular service in the Havana district.

"What about muscle?"

"Jorge spotted two guys out there who were obviously DI. They were the same ones who picked up Otto Rencke at the airport, and probably the two who came for Mac."

"But you can't be sure," Fidel said.

"I was close, but it's impossible to say for sure."

"Then we could be dealing with four guns, maybe more," Margarita said. "How about the house staff?"

"A cook, houseboy, and yardman, plus a DI communications specialist, but apparently he's only on standby in town, coming out when he's called."

"Plus Colonel León," Fidel said. "She could be a factor."

"How do you mean?" Martínez asked.

"If we're going to make sure that you have time enough to get out of there, plus time enough for our people to disappear, we're going to have to take out the DI muscle. That's trouble enough, but what do you want us to do with the *coronel* if she's at the house? If we kill her, this won't blow over so easily, especially if what you tell me is true about her being El Comandante's daughter."

Martínez had given that possibility some thought, and he'd come up with no easy solution. He shrugged. "This is war. We do whatever is necessary."

"It always has been," Fidel said. "What's your plan, exactly?"

"Two cars—four men in each—one from the west and the second from the east, in case she's decided to station someone on the highway at the entrance to her compound. We go in, two guys take out the comms, while the rest of us deal with the DI muscle, however many of them there are out there—two or four or whatever. We'll take out the colonel, free Mac and Otto, and get down to the beach."

"You'll need a boat to get out to the airplane, unless your pilot means to pull right up to the beach."

"He'll stand offshore—it'll be safer for him, quicker takeoff."

"Who is he?" Fidel asked.

"Ernesto Ruiz."

Fidel whistled softly. "He has *cojones grandes*. Offshore will be best. We'll arrange for a fishing boat, something old and slow that won't raise any suspicions. You'll be on it with two men."

Martínez started to object. He wanted to be at the house, the one to take out the *coronel*, if she was there, and there was no reason to think she wouldn't be, but Margarita didn't agree.

"We hear that you are doing good things in Miami,

niño, so your job is to get your Mac and Otto out and return to your work. The time will come soon enough for you to return to us and bring the fight here."

Fidel nodded. "We have plenty of bravery, what we lack are the brains. Someone will have to take over, show us the proper way, once Raúl and his Council of State bunch are gone. You understand the Yanquis and will know how to deal with them when the time comes. A lot of us are afraid of what might happen once they arrive."

Margarita touched Martínez's hand. "We're afraid we might get rid of a dictator only to find ourselves in bed with a well-meaning *elefante.* A very large elephant."

Martínez still wanted to argue, but he knew it was no use because they were right. "It's not easy being a son of Cuba," he said bitterly.

"It never has been," she said.

"We'll arrange everything," Fidel said. "In the meantime, go back to Jorge's. The boat will pick you up there at one."

"I'll call Ernesto."

"Make sure he's on time, or this will all be for naught."

People were going to die tonight, Martínez knew, and there was no way to avoid it.

TWENTY-FIVE

McGarvey estimated the firing angles and distances between Toro at the slider and María seated across the table with her right shoulder toward the house. It would be very close, but if he feinted to the right, placing María in Toro's line—and away from Otto—he might have a chance of grabbing her.

She was staring at him, and as he tensed, ready to move, her eyes widened, understanding what was about to happen, and she started to swing left and raise her hand in a gesture to Toro, who reacted almost instantly, moving to the right and raising his pistol.

It took less than a split second before Otto suddenly leapt to his feet and waved his arms as if he were flagging down a speeding animal. "Oh, wow!" he shouted.

The moment was held in tableau, María looking up in surprise, the muzzle of Toro's pistol wavering somewhere to McGarvey's left, when Otto began hopping from one foot to the other as he often did when he was excited and lost in the moment.

"Maybe not such a big fairy tale after all, ya know!" he shouted, totally wild now, his long red frizzy hair flying in every direction, his eyes flashing as if he were a madman, which in effect, for the moment, he was.

McGarvey was about to move when Gonzáles, the guard who'd sat atop the lifeguard tower on the beach this morning, rounded the corner of the house from the west in a run, a Kalashnikov in his hand.

He shouted something in Spanish.

"No," María ordered. "Stand down! Stand down!"

Otto acted as if he were oblivious of everything, but McGarvey momentarily caught his eye and realized all of a sudden that it was an act meant to bring the situation to a head and then defuse it.

"Fourteen ninety-two!" Otto shouted, and he looked at María as if he expected an answer from her.

Toro and Gonzáles were stopped in their tracks, looking at him.

María spread her hands. "Columbus," she said.

"Exacatamundo," Otto said. He sat down, poured a measure of rum, drank it neat, and then looked again at María as if he'd just told her what she wanted to hear.

She shook her head.

McGarvey had a glimmer of what Otto might be getting at, besides stalling for time, but he let it be.

"Fourteen ninety-two, Columbus sailed the ocean blue," Otto prompted. "Found the New World. Killed most of the natives in the Caribbean with chicken pox, but then did something very bad. Worst thing possible. He found gold. And the floodgates opened. The Old World sat up and took notice when Chris came back from his first trip. He proved the world was round, all right, but he found gold, and there never was anything like it. Every gold rush since has been child's play by comparison to the hordes of Spaniards who showed up here and in Mexico, because those guys sailed up in heavily armed ships, something the natives couldn't even have dreamed of, and landed hundreds of soldiers in armor, along with their horses and their weapons. It would have been like a U.S. aircraft carrier battle group with jets and SEALs showing up off Boston just before the start of the Revolutionary War. It would have been all over except for the shoutin'."

"I know about this," María said. "But what does it have to do with Cuba?"

"Everything, or maybe nothing, depends on who you talk to, and how you follow the money trail, 'cause the first gold the Spaniards found was in Costa Rica and Hispaniola, and after they'd just about killed everyone with disease and overwork, they came to Cuba looking for more slaves. That was in 1511."

"Don't teach me the history of my country," María flared. "Make your point."

"Look, if you added up all the gold the Spaniards mined and just flat-out stole from the Mayans and what was left over from the Aztec civilization all through the sixteenth century, it would only amount to maybe twenty-five tons—not a lot of money even by today's standards. But the next hundred years were a completely different story, because by then the Spanish government was in control of pretty much everything from California, Arizona, New Mexico, Texas, and possibly as far north as parts of Colorado, down through Mexico and Central America to Venezuela. All the while looking for gold. Turning it into ingots, and coins, and sending most of it back home to Madrid, where inflation was killing the government, bleeding it dry. It's why Spain eventually dropped into some serious poverty. It ran out of money."

This was Otto's show, and for the moment McGarvey let it stay that way, waiting for an opening. María was becoming absorbed, but Toro and Gonzáles were focused on what they understood was a dangerous situation.

"Don't you see?" Otto asked.

"No," María said.

"A whole bunch of that gold and silver was sent back to Spain through Havana, where it was loaded aboard fleets of ships, convoys that provided safety in numbers."

"Pirates."

"Right. Everyone wanted some of the action, and they were willing to do whatever it took to climb aboard the gravy train. Including the Spanish governor in Cuba, who took his percentage of everything shipped through Havana. Which was a pretty good deal while it lasted, because he got his share first, before the ships headed out, bunches of them going down in storms. The shipping lanes between Cuba and Spain are carpeted in gold."

"The government in Cuba, as you say, was Spanish," María said. "And if you're trying to tell me that Spain owes us anything, you're crazier than you look."

"That's not the entire story," Otto said. "You're not counting the gold that never got to Havana."

"Are you talking about the gold that pirates or crooked mine operators, or highwaymen in Mexico took?"

"That was nothing but shrinkage—ten or fifteen percent of the total at most. I'm talking about monks."

"The Church?"

"Bingo," Otto said. "By the mid-1700s, serious amounts of gold and silver were coming out of the ground from Costa Rica up to Mexico and into the

States, all of it supposed to be shipped to Mexico City, some of it going to Manila and then China, but a lot of it to Havana by convoy. But the Church figured that its needs for the gold far outweighed the needs of what by then was thought to be one of the most corrupt governments in Europe, so the story goes the monks began siphoning off as much of it as they figured they could get away with."

"How much?"

"Hundreds of tons," Otto said. "At seventeen-hundred-plus dollars per ounce, that's about four and a half billion per hundred tons. Serious money."

María was dazed, and now Toro and Gonzáles were caught up in it.

"But that's just the melted-down value," Otto said. "The historical value could be worth ten times that much."

"If it didn't come through Havana, how did they get it to the Vatican?" María asked.

"That part I don't know, except that the treasure never made it to Madrid, and if it had reached Rome, the Church kept silent. What I really think happened is that the gold never made it out of Mexico."

"You think that it's buried somewhere."

"In the U.S., maybe," Otto said. "I'm guessing about this part, but a big cache of Spanish gold was supposedly found by an American named Milton Noss in a series of caves under a small mountain in southern New Mexico. One of the legends says that a series of donkey caravans manned by hundreds of monks came to the mountain from the south through an area called the Jornada del Muerto—journey of death—dug the caves, and hid their cargo. They also brought their religion and spread the Word amongst the Pueblo Indians that the mountain was holy ground."

"If there is any of this siphoned-off gold, it could be anywhere by now," María said. "In the ground between Mexico and the U.S., maybe at the bottom of the sea somewhere between Mexico and here, or buried in some vault beneath the Vatican. Maybe even spent by the Church for one of its cathedrals."

"If it ended up in Rome, there would be records, in Mexico City or the Vatican," Otto said.

"Or in Madrid."

"Or right here in your father's papers," Otto suggested.

"That would be a starting point," McGarvey said.

Toro and Gonzáles were obviously intrigued, but not so much that they had dropped their guard.

"Maybe," María said. She, too, was distracted. "Even if what you're telling me is true, what claim would Cuba have on the gold? It was taken by force from the natives, most of whom were worked to death as slaves in the mines, but how could a concrete value be placed on that?"

"Some of them were Cuban natives," Otto said.

María waved it off. "An extinct people."

"Retribution, your father told you," McGarvey said. "Maybe he meant *reparations*. Owed to Cuba by the Spanish government."

"What if the gold is in Mexico or the U.S., as you suggest is possible?"

"A case could be made for one third to Spain, one

third to the country wherever it's found, and one third to Cuba. Still a lot of money."

"Craziness," María said after a very long beat, and the afternoon was suddenly very quiet. The wind had died to a whisper and even the surf breaking on the reef seemed to have subsided.

"Colonel?" Toro prompted, breaking her out of her reverie.

She got to her feet and gave them a last lingering look. "Take Mr. Rencke back to his room," she said, and she turned.

"There's no need to separate us," McGarvey said. "You have my word."

She gave him a bleak look, then went back into the house.

"Keep your word, and nothing will happen to your friend," Toro said. "Do you understand?"

"We've told her what she wanted to know, so when do we get out of here?" Otto asked.

"That's up to the *coronel*."

Otto got up. "Well, you might want to tell the *coronel* that if anything happens to my wife, I will personally see to crashing every computer system on this island. Your government networks, your banking and shipping and air traffic control will end up in the Dark Ages. And I can do it from my little room right here. I shit you not."

"And I will kill you and your *coronel*," McGarvey said, no inflection in his voice. "Count on it."

TWENTY-SIX

It was dark again, the evening of what Louise thought might be the third day since she'd been kidnapped, though with the drugs they'd given her, she suspected that she could be off by a full twenty-four hours, maybe longer.

Lying on the dirty mattress, she'd watched the fading light in the crack between the plywood and the windowframe, but she'd been unable to muster the energy to get up and turn on the bathroom light. They'd fed her regularly, she thought, yet she had become weak. Maybe drugs in the food because of her threat yesterday. And she began to truly believe that she was going to die here, and never see Otto or Audie again.

Someone came to the door and Louise struggled to sit up, her head spinning and a sudden wave of nausea making her break out in a cold sweat. When the door opened, the light from the corridor was blinding and she had to shade her eyes. She felt so goddamned helpless, she wanted to scream.

The man who called himself Rodrigo came in with a tray of food and a bottle of Evian. "It's good that you're awake," he said. "You slept through lunch, and we were beginning to get worried about you."

He set the water on the floor next to the mattress and started to put the tray down, when Louise managed to gather some little bit of strength, ball up her fist, and punch him in the face, sending him back, more in surprise than anything, the tray dropping to the floor.

"*Ay, Jesús!*"

"If you bastards are going to kill me, get it over with. But stop drugging my food."

"*Puta,* maybe that's exactly what we'll do. We no longer need you."

Louise kicked the tray away, and rolling over to her hands and knees shoved herself upright and somehow got unsteadily to her feet, her head spinning wildly and bile coming to the back of her throat. She wanted to vomit, but she held it back by sheer force of will. She wasn't going to give the son of a bitch the satisfaction of seeing her sick.

"Come on," she said, holding out her hands. "You want me, let's have it out right now."

Cruz stepped back, an odd, wary expression in his eyes that Louise couldn't read. But she'd gotten his attention. One for the Christians, zip for the lions, as Otto would say.

"Well?" she goaded him.

"We warned you to behave yourself."

"That's not going to happen, 'cause I won't eat this shit anymore, and I get really mean when I'm hungry. Could be next time you come back, I'll take out your eyes, or maybe kick your miserable little balls right up to your armpits."

She stepped forward and Cruz backed up. He was shaking his head. "You're *loca.*"

"You don't know the half of it," Louise said, and all of a sudden, she was so overwhelmed with weariness that her knees began to buckle. "Bring me something decent to eat, and maybe I'll start to behave myself."

"Eat what's on the floor."

Louise bent down, very slowly, her movements those of an old woman, picked up the tray, straightened up, and threw it at him. But it was thrown weakly and he caught it easily.

"If you don't want to feed me, you'd best bring some help the next time you come through that door."

Cruz gave her a last, lingering look—half anger, half grudging respect—and he backed out of the room and closed and locked the door.

Louise sank down on the mattress, her stomach doing slow rolls until she managed to open the bottle of water and take a drink. It was possible that the water, and not the food had been drugged, but she no longer cared. She'd made her point.

TWENTY-SEVEN

"It's on for tonight," Martínez told Ruiz on the encrypted satellite phone. He was calling from a thatched roof porch at the front of the fishing shack right on the beach a few miles to the west of the *coronel*'s compound.

"Same spot?" the pilot asked. He'd been standing by on Little Torch Key near Newfound Harbor ever since he'd flown back last night.

"Yes. I'm shooting for around midnight, give or take a half hour. Can you make it?"

"Of course," Ruiz said. "Have you run into trouble?"

"Nothing so far," Martínez said, and he told Ruiz everything that had happened since he and McGarvey came ashore, including the setup he'd arranged with Fidel and Margarita.

"I've heard good things about them. But take care, Raúl, you're needed here. You could have sent someone else for the rescue."

"Not this time," Martínez said.

Jorge Guerra, his primary contact and longtime friend of the de la Paz's, came around the corner at the same time Martínez heard the low growl of a slow-moving boat just offshore, very close.

"Gotta go, my people are showing up, and they need to be briefed," Martínez said. "Some of them are probably going to die tonight, and they need to know the odds."

"And we're not going to have the protection getting out that we had coming in."

"No. Best you circle low and slow twenty or thirty miles out until it's time for our extraction. I'll call you."

"Go with God," Ruiz said.

"And you," Martínez said, and he broke the connection.

Guerra, a short wiry man in his late fifties whose skin, fried by countless hours of commercial fishing in the sun, made him look seventy, offered a little smile. "They know the odds, not only in the operation but afterwards when the DI comes looking for them and their families."

"Some of them can come with us."

Guerra shook his head. "No."

The boat was very close now, though because it was running without lights, Martínez couldn't make it out until it was a few yards from the rickety dock Guerra sometimes used. When it pulled up, one man jumped down, tied it off, and a moment later when the engine was shut off, the second man jumped down to the dock and the two of them came up to the house, both of them rough looking, weathered like Guerra, who introduced them as Luis Casas and Pedro Requeiro.

"Pedro actually made it to Miami and lived there with his brother-in-law Miguel Sánchez for five years, helping with the dry cleaning business," Ruiz said.

"I'm a fisherman," Requeiro said, laughing. "Anyway, washing clothes is for young mothers and old ladies, not men."

"I know your brother-in-law," Martínez said. "He's a good man."

"He says the same thing about you. It's the only reason we're here tonight."

"It won't be easy."

"What is?" Casas said.

"Come inside, I've made a sketch map I'd like you to look at."

"Is there rum?" Requeiro asked.

"Of course."

TWENTY-EIGHT

At Fidel's compound, where there was already talk about turning it into a museum for El Comandante and the revolution, María was stopped again at the gate by two armed guards. This time, they'd not been warned that she was coming, and they drew their pistols as they approached the car, one of them holding a couple meters back.

It was dark, and she had parked just within the circle of light atop the gatehouse, but the security officer who came over shone his flashlight through her open window.

"Good evening, Colonel," he said. "I'm sorry, but I have orders that no one is to be admitted this evening."

"Whose orders?"

"El Presidente's."

"Call him."

"Colonel?"

"I'm going up to the house, call him and tell him that I'm here."

The security officer was suddenly uncomfortable. "It was Captain Fuentes who actually gave us the orders in the name of El Presidente."

"Then call him."

"Unfortunately, the captain is not in the compound this evening. It's only the security and house staff plus some of the family."

"Fine, then I'll telephone Raúl," María said, and she

took her cell phone out of her shoulder bag. She started to punch in a random number.

"That won't be necessary, Colonel," the security officer said quickly. He stepped away from the car and motioned for the other man to move aside.

María canceled the call and drove into the compound, dousing her lights when she came into the clearing, and pulled up in front of her father's house. The cook, a nervous old woman, met her at the door.

"May I be of assistance, Señora Coronel?"

"No, return to your duties," María said, and she went back to her father's bedroom, hesitating just inside the doorway. The bed had been made up, and she thought that she smelled a cleaning solution of some kind, yet the odor of death mixed with mustiness still hung in the air, and she shivered. She could smell his dying breath.

The room was mostly in darkness, only a single small bulb lit in the bathroom, the door ajar. This place would end up a holy shrine for many Cubans, especially the older ones who remembered firsthand not only the revolution but also the brutalities under Batista, even though her father hated such sentiments. But she could almost feel his spirit here, even though she'd been raised not to believe in ghosts, hobgoblins, spirits, or gods of any sort.

She crossed the room and went through a door opposite the bathroom, which opened into a short corridor, nothing but shutters on the broad windows, to another door, which led to her father's private study. She'd never been in this room, though she knew about it from Fuentes, who liked to brag to Ortega-Cowan how often El Comandante called him here for advice.

It was ludicrous, of course, nevertheless María had counted on the room being left unlocked with no security standing by. More than sloppy, it was criminal.

The study was small, maybe ten by fifteen, with only one small window double-glazed to prevent electromechanical eavesdropping and bulletproof against assassination. Three walls were covered by floor-to-ceiling bookcases, the fourth lined with tall, old-fashioned, eight-drawer steel file cabinets, none of them secured with locks, which was another surprise to María. But then her father might have felt safe here, inviolable.

A small desk sat on a Persian carpet in the middle of the room, with only the one lawyer's chair, a worn cushion on the seat, behind it. Visitors to this room, for whatever reason, were meant to stand in El Comandante's presence like children called before a principal. A floor lamp stood beside the desk.

María closed the wooden blinds over the window and went back and closed the door before she switched on the light. This place, too, smelled like cigars and the hints of a dying old man, though that part she figured was her imagination, as what she felt was a deep chill.

She put her shoulder bag down and started with the desk, not really knowing what she was looking for, but hoping that her father might have kept a diary or some sort of a daily journal that might point her in the right direction. Rencke had talked about Spanish gold, something her father had apparently mentioned twice during his visits to the UN in New York. And if even one tenth of what the American had suggested had a grain of truth to it, the find would be fabulous for cash-strapped Cuba.

An appointment book lay open to a date ten days ago, Fidel's final notation made at nine in the evening: *Arrange for M to be summoned. Soon.* María shivered, the *M* was very possibly her, and *Soon* could have meant that he knew he didn't have long to live.

But there was nothing indicating what he intended to say to her, what he intended asking her to promise on his deathbed. Nor was there anything of interest in the four drawers, other than stationery, a well-thumbed Spanish–English dictionary, a box of cigars, several boxes of wooden matches, and a collection of pencils, erasers, pens, paper clips, a couple of folded maps of Cuba, and of the southeastern section of the United States, along with street maps of Manhattan and down-town Washington, D.C. The only thing that she found odd was a small paper bag filled with what she recognized as votive candles, some partially burned down. But she couldn't wrap her mind around what they might mean, nor did she want to go in that direction.

Next she went to the files, starting with the top drawer of the leftmost cabinet, which contained a series of folders, some of them quite thick, labeled with names in alphabetical order, beginning with ACOSTA, HOMERO, who was the current Minister Secretary of the Council of State, followed by hundreds of names—most of which she did not recognize—for whom her father had kept dossiers.

Under *K,* were three fat folders for the Kennedy brothers, starting with the president, whose dossier actually filled nearly half of one drawer. He'd kept files on a lot of figures before and after the revolution, including Batista and the people in his regime, plus a dozen or more U.S. gangsters, among them Meyer Lansky and Santo Trafficante. A lot of history from Fidel's point of view that would probably never see the light of day.

And in a lower drawer of the second cabinet, she came across a thick file marked LEÓN, MARÍA, which she passed by, not wanting to know what it might contain, her chest tight, her throat constricted. And she felt like a total fool because of her reaction. Stupid, actually.

In the hour and a half it took to go through the files, she'd found no references to Spanish gold or the speeches he'd made at the UN, only names. If there was any mention, she would have to read through every file, which could take weeks, probably months. Time that she didn't have.

After closing the last file drawer, she went to the window, eased one of the wooden slats aside, and looked out. The compound was quiet.

The floor-to-ceiling bookcases held what María guessed had to be at least three thousand books, some of them stacked double deep on the shelves, other larger books lying flat. They weren't arranged in any specific order, and many of them were old and dog-eared, especially the paperbacks, most of which were falling apart. A lot of the books were novels—many of them American Westerns or Mexican and Spanish science fiction. Some were history books, of Cuba and Spain and other countries, including the Soviet Union, with several shelves containing nothing but histories of the United States and its leaders beginning with Washington,

Franklin, and the other revolutionaries, and of Lincoln and Davis and the Civil War.

But she found what she was looking for in less than ten minutes. A series of notebook-sized lined journals—Moleskines, similar to the notebooks that Hemingway had used to jot down his ideas—were stacked behind a full shelf of books on military history and strategy, including von Clausewitz and Sun Tzu. A dozen of them—apparently in chronological order, because the ones toward the bottoms of the stacks were old, the covers tattered, some of them moldy, while the ones near the top were new, even shiny.

María opened one of them, and she recognized her father's distinctive handwriting from documents and drafts of his speeches she'd studied at university. The notebook entries began three months ago, detailing a series of meetings he'd had with his brother and with Darío Delgado, who was the Attorney General, on the advisability of hiring lobbyists to deal directly with the U.S. Congress concerning the trade and tourism embargo. Nothing concrete had come of the meeting, and her father's notes made it seem as if he were vexed, not only by his apparent ineffectiveness in the day-to-day running of his government, but also because of his age and failing health.

> R seemed sympathetic but Gen DD didn't want to listen to anything but his budget concerns. Defense is a must, but whom does he think he's going to war with?

An entry dated two weeks ago was the last, his handwriting nearly illegible.

*Must talk to my people. Much to tell them, much to
suggest, to give them hope.*

She took all twelve of the notebooks off the shelf
and brought them back to the desk, careful to keep
them in the same order. If he'd left any clue to his
search for the Spanish gold, she was sure it would be
somewhere in his journals.

Then she rearranged the military books so that it
wasn't apparent that something had been removed,
and went back to the desk. Some of the notebooks
were held shut by an elastic band attached to the back
cover. Some had a nylon string attached to the spine
that could be used to mark a page.

The journal entry marked in the second book from
the latest took María's breath away. It was under a
date in mid-September last year.

*J-i's letter arrived by secret courier today, and he's
given me much needed detail about the incident in
Pyongyang with the former DCI. Incredible. J-i says
the man is to be trusted, even though he is the enemy—
former DCI and contract assassin. Was involved two
years ago at Guantánamo Bay. J-i promises that KM
is willing to cut through any bureaucracy, including
his own if he believes the truth of a thing. Might be
able to help in your quest. But the right man would
have to approach him, in the right way. Very important. Salvation and especially retribution can be extremely costly. Something I'll have to think about, but
for now there is only one person in all of Cuba I can
trust. . . .*

J-i was Kim Jong-il, and *KM* was Kirk McGarvey, but it was the last four words in that entry that rocked her to the core. Her father had written:

She's not ready yet.

She went to the window again and looked outside, but the compound was still quiet. Evidently the security detail had not been able to reach Fuentes, otherwise he would have been here by now. But the situation would not last, and she didn't want to have to deal with him tonight.

Starting with the first entry in the first journal, dated June 15, 1955, in Mexico City, her father wrote about meeting a very bright and eager medical doctor from Argentina named Ernesto Guevara, known as Che, which was nothing more than a speech filler in Argentine, meaning "hey." The next pages were filled with long discussions he and his brother Raúl had with Che, and with a dozen other people, including Alberto Bayo who'd been a leader of the Republican force in the Spanish Civil War and who agreed to help train the Cuban rebels.

But it was something near the end of the first notebook that caught her attention. Her father was writing about how to come up with the money for arms and ammunition when he met a young Mexican history major studying for his Ph.D., identified only as *Dr. José D,* or sometimes simply as *JD.*

JD has a far-fetched idea that intrigued me last night, though Che and Raúl think very little of him. He talked about gold—as much as tons—buried somewhere in northern Mexico or perhaps even farther north. Not Cíbola, but caves filled with gold, brought by monks from Mexico City that in some cases should have been transshipped to Spain via Havana.

María pulled out the chair and sat down, her heart racing, her mouth dry, and she started thumbing through the notebooks, starting with the first one, looking for any mention of the gold, or of Dr. Jose D or JD. One entry in the middle of the second journal date late in December 1956 briefly mentioned the doctor:

> *Dr. José D wanted to come with us because he wanted to be a part of history instead of merely studying it. But Che was with me in arguing for him to stay in Mexico City, to continue his work. Che later told me JD would be a liability to us, but I thought he would have a better chance of finding Cuba's gold at the National Archives. JD agreed and he agreed to try to keep me informed.*

The next three notebooks were filled mostly with entries from the revolution and the months following when her father was trying to organize the country. But she came across two brief mentions of JD, one of them having to do with the mystery of a place called Victorio Peak in southern New Mexico.

> *. . . Doc Noss deer hunting found a rock that had been worked with tools, beneath which was a hole that led straight into the mountain where he discovered notes and maps and gold.*

In the second entry, her father wrote that JD had promised a full report, but that there was some doubt as to the authenticity of the find. At the end of that entry, her father promised not to give up.

> . . . *clutching at straws. But the gold could solve a serious problem for us—whom to choose as our ally—the US or USSR. Ideology would make it easy to choose. But more importantly we need help to reverse B's destruction of the economy. I will continue.*

Headlights flashed across the drawn blinds, and María heard a car pull up at the front of the house. She hurriedly stuffed the notebooks in her shoulder bag and started for the door, but then turned back to the file cabinets, where she retrieved her file, put it in her purse, then turned off the light and left the room.

Fuentes was charging across the living room when she emerged from the bedroom, and he pulled up short. "What are you doing here?" he demanded harshly. She thought he looked more frightened than angry.

"The real question, Captain, is what you haven't been doing. There is no security here other than your two buffoons at the gate. Anyone could simply walk in and take whatever they wanted to take. Souvenirs, perhaps."

"That's impossible."

"You let an American spy in here, why not a tourist?"

Fuentes had nothing to say.

María arched an eyebrow. "I'm getting tired of calling you to my office to report on mistakes that you have made. But I want you downtown within twenty-four hours with a complete operational directive for security. How exactly you plan on safekeeping the national treasures here while managing what is expected to be a horde of visitors."

Fuentes looked beyond her to the open bedroom door and the door to Fidel's study beyond.

"Am I clear?"

"*Sí, Coronel,*" Fuentes said.

And María could see the cunning in his eyes. He had become a real enemy, but rather than fire him, she wanted to keep him very close so that she would have a reasonable expectation of knowing what he was up to.

TWENTY-NINE

The fishing boat was ancient, even older, Martínez figured, than most of the derelict cars on Havana's streets, but the diesel engine was in perfect tune and very well muffled. "Not very fast or pretty," Luis Casas said, "but she is as reliable as a whore with the scent of money in her nostrils." He was at the wheel, smoking a cigarette, cupping the glowing tip in his hand.

They ran without lights about one hundred yards offshore, and Martínez standing in the back, bracing his hip against the gunwale, looked through a pair of binoculars at a red flashing light a couple of miles inland to the west.

Pedro Requeiro was at his elbow. "Anything yet?"

The red light was atop the cell phone tower, and they were waiting for it to go out, which would indicate that Jorge had managed to cut power to the installation.

"No," Martínez said, but then the light went out. "Okay, he's done it." The time on his watch was five minutes until midnight. He motioned for Luis to head toward the shore.

If the eight men that the de la Pazs had arranged had not run into trouble, the attack on María León's compound would begin any minute, starting with cutting the electricity and taking out the antennas on the roof. As soon as the first shots were fired, he and Pedro would go ashore.

His speed-dialed Ruiz's sat phone number. "It has begun."

"I'm on the deck twenty minutes out."

"Anything on your radar?"

"A couple of fishing boats to the west, and a strong military target about fifty klicks to the east. But I don't think I've been painted yet. Leastways, nobody's heading this way in any big hurry. How did you get word to Mac?"

"I didn't. But he knows I'm here, and soon as he hears the first shots, he'll understand what's happening."

"I'm on my way."

Martínez broke the connection, as Pedro finished attaching the 9.5 horsepower outboard to the four-man inflatable, and he helped ease it over the side of the slow-moving boat. They were headed toward the beach directly below the León compound, the diesel at dead slow, its exhaust noises almost nil.

"Ernesto is on his way?" Pedro asked.

"*Sí.* Twenty minutes." Martínez looked at the man's weathered face, crinkled now in a slight smile. "There's room in the plane to take you back to the States."

"What would I do there? Go back to washing dirty laundry?"

"It's going to get hot after tonight."

Pedro laughed. "This is the tropics. But you know all about that."

"The war won't end tonight. Maybe not in our lifetimes."

"Perhaps not, but you've told us that this battle is worth the effort."

"*Sí.*"

"Then let us take it to them."

THIRTY

María had stormed off just after dark, and hadn't returned yet. The cook and houseboy had retreated to their quarters, leaving McGarvey, who'd been unable to sleep, seated outside at the pool, drinking a Red Stripe beer. Otto had been locked in his room, insurance against McGarvey trying anything, and a second pair of security officers had shown up around nine, one of them manning the radio room.

The sea breeze had died to nothing a couple of hours ago, and the night was hot and humid under an overcast sky, only occasionally lit by distant lighting to the northwest out in Hemingway's Gulf Stream, and McGarvey felt that something was about to go down. Soon. He could almost sense Martínez somewhere close.

He glanced over at Gonzáles leaning against the slider frame just inside the dark living room, a Kalashnikov slung over his shoulder. The only light came from the west wing, where Otto was being kept and where the compound's communications and security center was located.

McGarvey thought that Gonzáles and Toro had seemed nervous all day, and especially since María had taken off and the second pair of muscle had shown up. The entire compound should have been lit up like day, no shadows to provide places to hide. And at the very least, he should have been locked up in his cell, not allowed to have the run of the house.

Except for the beach, which was lit up as if for a party. If something was going to happen tonight, the security staff expected it might be coming from the sea.

In the distance to the north, McGarvey thought he might be hearing the sounds of a diesel engine running at dead idle, and somewhere in the opposite direction, toward the highway, he was sure he could hear something else; something new, a very faint clank of metal against metal.

Gonzáles may have heard something, too, because he turned away for just a moment.

"Señor," McGarvey said, getting up. He started toward the security officer.

Gonzáles snapped around, suddenly alert, wary.

"Do you speak English?" McGarvey asked.

"Yes."

"Will Colonel León be returning tonight? There's something I need to tell her."

"I've not been told."

"Can you find out? It's important. Something she needs to know about the gold we were talking about this afternoon."

"Stop there, please," Gonzáles said, and McGarvey stopped a few feet away as the guard took a cell phone/walkie-talkie out of his pocket and keyed the SEND button. "Ramiro."

The walkie-talkie was silent.

"Ramiro, this is Salvador, come back."

At that moment, the lights on the beach went out, and Gonzáles swung his rifle off his shoulder as he fumbled with the walkie-talkie. Before he could bring it to bear, McGarvey was on him, snatching the weapon and slamming the insole of his foot into the man's left leg, dislocating his kneecap.

Gonzáles cried out as he fell back, grabbing for the rifle, which discharged one shot, catching him under his chin, the back of his skull blowing out.

Someone came running from the west wing at the same time as what sounded like a powerful engine came to life, and the lights on the beach flicked back on.

McGarvey stepped into the living room into the deeper shadows of a corner a couple of feet away from the open slider, when a series of three explosions came in rapid succession outside in front, in the direction of the west wing. The sounds of the engine—which was likely driving the compound's emergency generator—died, and the lights went out again.

"Salvador!" someone shouted from the corridor.

McGarvey got the impression of a hulking dark form emerging into the living room, and a second later, a flashlight came on, the beam finding Gonzáles's body.

"Puto," the man swore. It was Toro.

McGarvey fired two shots from the hip about where he figured the security officer's center mass would be: one to the left of the light beam, the other to the right. Toro grunted and his pistol discharged as he was driven against the wall, and he dropped the flashlight, the beam skittering across the floor.

Someone opened fire from out front in the direction of the highway, what sounded like at least a half dozen guns, the bullets slamming into the front of the house, window glass shattering, and a floor lamp exploding a couple feet from where McGarvey stood.

The two security guards in the west wing began returning fire, the chatter of their Kalashnikovs distinct, as McGarvey, moving fast, made his way across the living room and momentarily held up where Toro's body lay partially blocking the corridor.

More firing started up outside from farther away, up toward the highway. Kalashnikovs, which probably meant Cuban troops catching the rescue party Martínez had organized from behind.

"Otto, down!" McGarvey shouted, and he ducked back around the wall.

"Right," Otto replied from his cell.

One of the security officers fired a long burst down the corridor. When the man's weapon went dry, Mc-Garvey stuck his Kalashnikov around the corner and fired a short, controlled burst. A man cried out in pain, and the firing from inside the house stopped.

Outside, the battle was heating up, the rescuers turning their attention away from the house in an effort to defend themselves from the attack at their rear. It sounded to McGarvey as if they were greatly outnumbered.

McGarvey raced down the corridor into the west wing, where at the open door to the radio room, the guard illuminated by the dim light coming from the front panel of what was a battery-driven portable radio looked over his shoulder, a microphone in his hand.

The man said something urgently as he turned around, a pistol in his other hand, but before he could fire, McGarvey squeezed off a half dozen rounds, two catching the man in his shoulder and driving him to the left, a third catching the side of his head, and at least two slamming into the radio.

The fight outside was intensifying but moving away, back toward the highway. The rescuers were sacrificing themselves to give McGarvey and Otto time to get away.

"Mac!" Martínez shouted from the sliders to the pool.

It was a boat's diesel engine McGarvey had heard. "House is clear!" he shouted. "I'm getting Otto."

"Move it, amigo."

The heavy door to Otto's cell was secured by a thick

steel bolt, which McGarvey pulled back. Otto was there, a deep, troubled scowl on his owlish features, his long red hair flying everywhere.

"If something's happened to Louise, nothing on this planet will stop me from crashing every system in this bastard of a country! I'll drive 'em back to the Dark Ages, kemo sabe, I shit you not!"

"One step at a time," McGarvey said, hustling Otto out of his cell and down the corridor to the living room. "First we have to get out of here in one piece."

Otto suddenly pulled up and turned toward the front door.

Martínez was there at the open sliders. "Mac, *rápido.*"

"They need help," Otto said.

"They're dead!" Martínez shouted bitterly. "Now, move your ass!"

Otto was torn, but McGarvey grabbed his arm and hauled him across the living room, and Martínez led them in a dead run down to the beach, where they clambered aboard the inflatable and headed out toward the dark form of the fishing boat a hundred yards offshore, as the de Havilland touched down fifty yards farther out.

"The dirty bastards," Otto muttered.

"What about the colonel?" Martínez asked.

McGarvey shook his head. "She left about four hours ago."

"Our guys walked into a trap, and she probably set it up."

"I don't think so," McGarvey said. "She wanted more from us."

"Well, someone knew we were coming."

THIRTY-ONE

María had spotted the bright flashes and heard the intense gun battle a couple of kilometers away from her compound, and parked now at the side of the highway behind a pair of troop trucks a few meters from her driveway, her heart hammering, she monitored the unit's tactical frequency.

From what she could gather, they were a small specials ops unit out of the army's Western Command, Seventieth Mechanized Division, based in Havana, but who'd ordered them out here, and whom they were engaged with made almost no sense to her. Unless she was the target.

She tried to use her cell phone to call Ortega-Cowan, but there was no signal. Nor could she reach the OD in the Operational Center.

But it came to her all at once, and suddenly it all did make sense to her. The man who come ashore with McGarvey and disappeared into the bush had mostly likely engineered the attack. It was a rescue mission that had been worked out in advance.

Even now, her people in the compound were most likely dead, and McGarvey and Rencke were on their way out to the same light plane that had landed just offshore the other night. The firefight, which had gradually moved closer to the highway—away from the house and the beach—was starting to die down, lending even more credence to her speculation.

Which left her with a problem that she would have

to solve immediately. Within minutes, because whatever force was driving the special ops troops away from the house probably wouldn't survive much longer. Most of the special ops reports she'd read—the honest ones—generally used the same words to describe the overall efficiency of the two battalions: *ineficaz y inepto,* "inefficient and inept," but each truck she was parked behind held sixteen men—thirty-two plus an officer. Even inept, they couldn't possibly lose against whatever ragtag force McGarvey's people had managed to muster.

Rencke had not lied about the fortune in gold or about her father's interest in finding it to help Cuba's financial recovery—from Batista and from her father's own destructive fascination with socialism. But if he and McGarvey were to be captured and become military prisoners, CIA spies, the trial would be short and sweet. They would be found guilty and executed.

And she would fall with them. Raúl had warned her about involvement with the American who'd arrived aboard the U.S. State Department aircraft and disappeared. Find him and return him or his body. Fast.

Your father is dead, so you no longer have his protection, Raúl had warned her the afternoon of the funeral.

María switched frequencies to the Santa Cruz del Norte surveillance channel and asked for Lieutenant Vera. When he came on, he was just as helpful as usual. If word had begun to circulate that the head of DI's Operations Division was on the way out, which was the way things usually worked, it hadn't filtered down to Santa Cruz.

"*Sí*, Colonel, Station Guanabacoa has reported the landing of another small aircraft near your compound."

"Is there a patrol vessel within reach of that location at this moment?"

"Unfortunately not within fifty kilometers. I was just about to dispatch an air asset from Playa Baracoa." It was home base outside Havana to the 3405 Regiment, which maintained a few MiG-21Bs and Mi6-MFs.

"Don't," María told him. "The aircraft is transporting two of our deep-cover spies back to Miami and then Washington. It's important that they are not interfered with."

"I understand," Lieutenant Vera said, "but there may be a fishing boat involved this time. What shall we do with it?"

"Destroy the boat."

"And the crew?"

"They're traitors who will try to get word to the FBI that we're sending people north. They mustn't be allowed to live to send the message."

"*Sí, Coronel*," the lieutenant said, and he signed off.

Two shots from what sounded like a pistol came from somewhere in the woods to the left, as María switched back to the unit's tactical frequency, and then the battle seemed to be finished. She keyed the microphone.

"Special ops on-scene commander, this is Colonel León standing by on the highway. Report your situation."

The radio was silent for several beats, and she was about to resend her message, when someone came back. "I'll need to confirm your identity," he said. He sounded out of breath.

"You're at my house, you idiot, and apparently somebody wanted to assassinate me tonight. I'm on the highway right now, parked behind your unguarded trucks."

"Stand by."

Still holding the microphone, María got out of the car. The night was quiet; not even the cicadas were chirping.

"This is Lieutenant Abel Cobiella, I'm the unit CO for this operation. If you'll stand by, Colonel, we're making our final sweep."

"Who ordered this operation?"

"Major Ortega-Cowan. He was concerned that he could not reach you and you might be in trouble. As it turns out, if you had been at home we might have been too late."

"Thank you for your concern, Lieutenant. I want to know about my house staff. And I had two body-guards."

"I'm told that your staff is unharmed, but we have found four men so far who've been identified as probable security officers."

"I only have two on permanent staff, so it's likely that Major Ortega-Cowan sent the other two. Have you interviewed them yet?"

"Negative, Colonel. They're all KIAs. But there's something else. It looks as if they were taken down by someone inside the house. We're working on it."

"That won't be necessary, Lieutenant. I know exactly what happened and why."

"Señora?"

"One of the two men Major Ortega-Cowan sent was obviously a traitor," María said. "Did it look as if there was a shoot-out between them?" Once the attack from outside the house had begun, she had little doubt that McGarvey seized the opportunity to take one of them down, disarm him, and kill the other three.

"Stand by," the lieutenant said.

Every minute of delay here and now gave McGarvey and Rencke another minute to get out of Cuban airspace. And then what? she asked herself. What next? What was her next logical move? She didn't think her position would remain stable much longer. But like her father, she could feel gold fever coming over her. Not for personal wealth. For the people. Or that's at least what she wanted to believe.

"One man is down just inside the house from the pool, another on the opposite side of the living room, one in the corridor, and the fourth in the radio room. So you could be correct, Colonel. But I would guess that it's also possible there were one or more other people inside the house, who might have done some of the shooting."

"It's also possible that the attacking force infiltrated my compound, killed the four security officers, and when they realized that I was not home, and that their mission was a failure, they tried to leave, but then ran into your unit. Any survivors among them?"

"No, señora," the lieutenant said. "Give us another hour to make certain that your compound is secured."

And in that moment, María made her decision, one that she suspected would eventually put her head-to-head with Kirk McGarvey. It was a prospect she found strangely disquieting while as the same time exciting.

"Take your time, Lieutenant. I'll spend the night in the city. You can contact me at my office when you're finished, and I'll oblige you to keep some men posted here until I can send out a new security detail."

"Colonel, I'm sorry, but leaving men here is not in my orders."

"It is now," María said.

She got back in her car, switched the radio off, and headed back into the city, where she could find a telephone that worked, so that she could order the immediate release of Otto Rencke's wife. McGarvey was a formidable enemy, but from what she had learned, he was a fair man. But Rencke, if he were motivated, could do much harm to Cuba, devastating harm.

THIRTY—TWO

Louise thought it had to be very late at night when she awoke from a sleep in which she had dreamed Audrey was being taken away from her because she was an unfit mother. And no matter how much she pleaded with the two child welfare officers, she knew nothing was going to work.

Someone was at the door, and she managed to roll off the mattress and get shakily to her feet, when the man who called himself Rodrigo was there with another man who she recognized was the one at the day care center and who had shot Joyce.

They had not brought her food or water, which wasn't a good sign.

"Two against one?" she demanded. "Not a pair of balls between you?" She took a step toward them.

"Our mission has been accomplished," Cruz told her.

Louise's heart sank. Her dream hadn't been so far off the mark after all. She would never see Audie or Otto again because these two were going to kill her tonight. "Goddamn you to hell," she whispered.

"It's not what you think, Mrs. Rencke," Cruz said. "We've been ordered to release you unharmed. We're going to drive you to the Lincoln Memorial this very moment."

"A bullet in the back of my head and then dump my body to freak out the tourists? Is that how you sick bastards think?"

Cabrera said something in Spanish that Louise didn't catch.

"*Sí,* I wasn't exaggerating," Cruz said. "As much as that thought has crossed my mind, because you have been nothing but a royal pain, we have our orders. You are to be set free tonight. Right now. If need be, we'll tie you up and gag you."

She couldn't believe them. She'd seen the man raise his pistol and shoot Joyce, and the teacher was in all likelihood dead. For doing nothing. For simply being in the wrong place at the wrong time.

The third man showed up. "What's the problem?"

"She's crazy," Cruz said. "Thinks we're going to kill her."

Álvarez looked at Louise. "Not such a bad idea. But we don't have time. Tape her hands behind her back and tape her mouth shut. I'll pull the van around front. Be quick."

"Bastards," Louise croaked, and she rushed the men, nearly stumbling and falling down.

Before she could do a thing, they'd easily taped her wrists together, and Cabrera held her head still while Cruz slapped a piece of duct tape across her mouth.

Otto's sweet face swam into her mind's eye. What would he do? What would Mac do?

Before Cruz could step back, Louise lunged forward and with all of her strength head-butted him in the nose.

"*Dios mío!*" he swore, a little blood seeping from his nose. He grabbed Louise's left arm and roughly hauled her out into the narrow corridor. "Maybe we'll say the hell with our orders. Maybe we'll kill you after all."

THIRTY-THREE

Martínez had gotten word to Langley that he would make a try for McGarvey and Rencke around midnight, and Marty Bambridge waited in the long, narrow operations center called the Watch, located down the corridor from the DCI's office on the seventh floor of the Old Headquarters Building, until word came that they were safely out.

It was nearly two in the morning, and he'd been

smoking heavily and drinking black coffee since he'd come in around ten and he felt like hell. Especially now, this late with no news, good or bad.

Tony Battaglia, the Watch officer, walked back to where Bambridge was sitting at a small desk just within the open door from the corridor. He was a slightly built man with a white shirt, tie loose, jacket off. The heels of his loafers were worn down, and like the other five specialists who worked twelve-on, twelve-off—usually for five or six days in a row—he looked like he was sick or used up, not enough sleep, not enough mental rest, but like he was fond of saying, "This is the greatest job in the world because we get to know everything."

The Watch was connected by satellite feeds and highly encrypted computer links to every CIA asset around the world, plus information from the National Geospatial-Intelligence Agency over at Reston, in addition to most of the U.S. intelligence agencies, including the FBI. Flat-panel monitors mounted on the walls displayed just about everything that was going on just about anywhere in the world. It was this room where the raw information to generate the daily National Intelligence Estimate used to brief the president was collated.

"We've finally got a confirmation that what our KH-14 picked up on the coast just east of Havana about an hour and a half ago was a firefight at the DI's ops director's house, just like you thought it might be," Battaglia said.

"How's our confidence?"

"High."

Bambridge glanced up at the clock mounted from

the ceiling halfway down the room. "Anything from our other assets?"

"We're sifting."

A sour burn rose from Bambridge's gut. "We should have heard by now if they got out. Christ."

Battaglia's phone buzzed, and he walked over to his desk and picked it up. After a brief conversation, he held out the phone. "I think you'll want to take this. Line one."

Bambridge answered. "Yes."

"Marty, it's Louise."

Bambridge's head instantly cleared. "Where are you?"

"Lincoln Memorial. A Metro D.C. cop found me about ten minutes ago, where I was dumped on the north side of the building, my hands and ankles and mouth taped." Her words sounded slurred to Bambridge.

"Are you okay?"

"They didn't beat me, but I've been drugged, and I'm still groggy. What about Otto, is he out?"

"We don't know yet," Bambridge said. "Are the cops still there?"

"Yeah, they want to take me to the hospital, but I have to come out to the Campus. Convince them."

A moment later, a MPDC officer came on, and Bambridge identified himself. "I'll have to confirm that, sir."

"Of course. But in the meantime, how does Mrs. Rencke appear to you?"

"A little messed up, but actually not bad."

"Has the FBI been notified?"

"Yes, sir. They're sending someone to debrief her."

"Fine. I want her taken to All Saints Hospital, no matter what she says. It's in Georgetown." The private hospital was used exclusively by U.S. intelligence officers—mostly CIA—hurt in the line of duty. The small staff was among the best anywhere in the world, as was the equipment.

The cop was impressed. "Yes, sir."

"Let me talk to her again," Bambridge said, and when she came back, he explained what would have to happen next. "For now, this has to be the Bureau's case. You don't know why you were kidnapped, except that you and your husband work for us, and you're pretty sure that they were Hispanic. Nothing more than that."

"I want to come in, goddamnit. It's my husband we're talking about."

"Kirk is with him, he'll be okay. But first I want the docs to check you out and as soon as you're cleared, I'll send a car for you. I need you to do this for me."

Louise was silent for a moment. "Okay, I'll do it. Here come the federales."

"This'll all work out," Bambridge said. "All the shooting is over with for now."

"What the hell do you mean by that?" Louise demanded. "What's going on?"

"Anything comes up, I'll let you know. Promise. But for now, you have to keep it together. This is important. Do you understand?"

"Let me know," Louise said.

Bambridge hung up the phone and fished for a cigarette, when Battaglia motioned for him to pick up on two. It was McGarvey.

"Figured you'd be there," McGarvey said, a lot of noise in the background. "But I'm using a nonsecure phone."

"Where are you?"

"Just touching down in the Keys."

Bambridge was relieved but irritated that Rencke, but especially McGarvey, had played it so loose. "I need both of you up here pronto for debriefing."

"As soon as possible," McGarvey said. "Any word about Louise?"

Bambridge wanted to insist, but he knew better. McGarvey was living up to his reputation as a loner, an independent operator, and Rencke would be even more impossible when he got back. "I just talked to her, she's fine. They tied her up and dropped her off at the Lincoln Memorial a couple of hours ago. MPDC found her, and she called me. The Bureau's with her now. When they're done, we're sending her to All Saints."

"Soon as possible, let her know we're back," McGarvey said.

"Will do," Bambridge said. "When can we expect you?"

But McGarvey broke the connection.

Bambridge held the phone in his tight fist for several beats.

You gotta go with the flow, ya know, Rencke had told him a few months ago. Bambridge had come over from operations at the National Security Agency's headquarters in Fort Meade, Page's hire, and it was obvious to everybody from the get-go that he had the NSA mentality—a little aloofness, a sense of superiority.

Fight the battles you can win, and save everything else until later when you've gathered enough ammunition. Otherwise this place will eat you alive. Capisce?

But Bambridge didn't think he'd understood until just this instant. McGarvey and Otto were who they were, odd ducks, dangerous, and there wasn't a damn thing he could do about it, except follow the one other piece of advice he'd been given at the start, this from Page.

They're valuable assets, Marty, but handle them with kid gloves and don't be surprised what they bring back to you. Or how they deliver it.

Bambridge telephoned All Saints to give them the heads-up that Louise Horn was coming in, and asked them to tell her that her husband and Mr. McGarvey were out safely. "She'll understand."

Next he telephoned Walter Page on the DCI's secure line at his home in McLean. "They're back, and Louise has been released apparently unharmed."

"Did Mac tell you what it was all about?"

"No, sir. Said they were just landing in the Keys, but he was calling from a nonsecure phone."

"Did he agree to be debriefed?"

"Soon as possible, his words," Bambridge said. "But it sounded like he was on a mission. Hung up on me."

"Well, we'll find out when the bodies start to pile up," Page said.

"Already started. We tasked one of our birds to take a couple of passes over the island and picked up a firefight at the colonel's compound. No doubt, it was McGarvey's doing."

"No doubt," Page said. "Keep me posted, will you, Marty? No matter the time."

"Yes, sir," Bambridge said, and hung up, and he had to wonder what the hell was coming their way this time.

PART

THREE

THIRTY-FOUR

Martínez went to get something from his car, leaving McGarvey and Otto alone on the ramp with Ruiz for the moment. "There was a gunfight back there," the bandy-legged pilot said. He looked serious, even angry, as if he wanted to break something.

"It was a rescue party Raúl arranged for us," McGarvey said, and he knew what was coming next.

"They're probably all dead by now. Or being interrogated, which amounts to about the same thing. Was it worth it?"

"To get my friend back, yes. Beyond that, I don't know yet, but we're going to work on it."

Ruiz looked at Otto. "You have a good friend, but what the hell were you doing in Cuba?"

"The DI kidnapped my wife in Washington and said they would kill her unless I cooperated. The agency's director of operations wanted to talk to me."

"About what?"

"That part we have to leave out for now," McGarvey said.

Martínez came back with a thick envelope and held it out to the pilot.

"Are you going to hurt the bastards?" Ruiz asked, eyeing the envelope but not taking it.

"We probably won't hurt the government, but if it works out, we just might be able to help the people," Otto said.

"What are your chances?"

Otto shrugged. "Slim at best. But we're gonna try, ya know."

"Fair enough," Ruiz said, and looked at Martínez and shook his head. "If you're wanting to pay me, give it to someone who can use it. I have all I need. And maybe the trip was worth it. I hope so."

"The fight's not over with yet," Martínez said, and the pilot nodded, and some secret knowledge passed between them.

They headed back up the island to the Key Largo Sheraton, where McGarvey had left his bag and his sat phone, traffic nonexistent at this hour of the morning. Martínez took his time driving; he was troubled.

"There'll be reprisals," he said to McGarvey. "What was it all about? What the hell did the DI want with you? And why didn't the air force come after us? We must have shown up on their radar."

"Someone knew your people were going to hit the colonel's compound."

"No shit, Mac. It was Colonel León."

"I don't think so," McGarvey said. "I have a feeling she might have been on her way back, and might have stumbled into the mess. It had to have been her who ordered Louise to be released and let us make our escape."

"Speculation," Martínez said. "Because the timing makes you wonder. But back from where?"

"I don't know," McGarvey admitted.

"From her father's compound," Otto said. "I think she went out there to see if she could find some private files or maybe even a journal or daybook or something before someone else from the government beat her to it."

Otto was sitting in the backseat, and Martínez looked at him in the rearview mirror. "What was she looking for?"

"You're better off staying out of this," McGarvey said. "Because at this point, you're right: All we have is mostly speculation."

"Definitely fringe," Otto agreed.

"When word about the ambush gets back to Miami, which it probably already has, two things are going to happen. First of all, I'm going to get nailed. People are going to want to know what the hell I was doing down there, because from their perspective, it was me who was responsible for the mess. And you know what, I am responsible. And the second is the DI pricks are going to be all over us to find out who was behind it. Me again, which is something I can handle. But people will want to know why. Was it worth it? The same things I want to know."

"Better start from the beginning," Otto told McGarvey. "Okay?"

And he was right. "Colonel León was called to Castro's deathbed because she's one of his illegitimate daughters, and he had a dying wish for her to find me and ask for my help."

"*Dios mío!*" Martínez said softly. "Help with what?"

"She didn't know, and as a matter of fact, it was Otto who made the suggestion about the gold."

"You're not making much sense, Mr. M."

McGarvey had not wanted to head in this direction, because in fact, they actually had very little to go on, but if the word got out, and it would, that there was the possibility of some fabulous treasure, there would be a stampede worse than any gold rush in history. A lot of people would get hurt. And yet Martínez had always been a steady hand, and because of his part last night, a lot of Cuban exiles in Miami would want answers that they deserved.

Starting with what Colonel León told them about her father's dying words to bring McGarvey to Cuba for retribution and salvation, which was a complete mystery to her, to Otto's suggestion about the gold possibly hidden somewhere in Mexico or perhaps the southern United States, McGarvey told Martínez essentially everything they'd learned.

"Apparently, it was an obsession of his," Otto said. "He mentioned it both times he came to the UN."

"If that's what he meant on his deathbed," Martínez said. "It's thin."

"But it fits with why she pulled this stunt," McGarvey said. "And if Otto's right about Fidel's obsession, he might have kept files, or maybe even a diary, which is what I think the colonel was looking for last night. And I think she probably found something; otherwise, we would have been shot down before we'd left Cuban airspace."

"What about the ambush? What makes you think she didn't order it?"

"Her bodyguards who picked me up at the airport said they weren't taking me downtown to DI headquarters, because they were in the middle of some kind of a faction fight," Otto said. "But in order to pull off kidnapping Louise to lure me down to Havana, she must have confided in someone. Maybe her chief of staff. It could have been him who set up the ambush."

"But why?" Martínez asked.

"A simple power play," McGarvey said. "She's a woman in a male chauvinist society, and she no longer has her father's protection. If we'd been killed, she would have taken the fall. Probably the firing squad."

"But they let us fly out of there."

"She has her enemies, but she's a bright, well-connected woman. And right now, we may just be her best hope for survival."

Martínez was silent for the rest of the way until he pulled into the Sheraton's driveway and parked away from the lights. "So let's say, for the sake of argument, that there is this pile of gold buried somewhere. Maybe even somewhere in the Southwest—New Mexico or someplace. How do we find it, and what happens next? Because it sure as hell wouldn't be turned over to Raúl Castro and his cronies, even if they could prove a legitimate claim against a third of it."

"That's what Colonel León wants to happen," Otto said. "Be a feather in her cap. She'd be a star, untouchable, ya know."

"If she lives that long," McGarvey said. "Once it gets

out what she did to get us down there, and then let us fly away, her own people will arrest her, and then it'll just be a matter of time—maybe only a few hours—before they get the entire story."

"That could be easily arranged," Martínez said darkly. "So are you going to try to find the gold, or do you think it's a fantasy?"

"I don't think it's a fantasy," McGarvey said. On the flight across, he'd done a lot of thinking about it, and he'd come to a couple of conclusions, both of which addressed Martínez's, "What next?" Because the treasure would certainly never be shipped to Havana. Not even a tiny portion of it. Washington would be perceived as supporting the regime. The Cuban exiles in Miami and across the rest of the country would in all likelihood rise up en masse, maybe riot like the blacks did in Detroit and L.A. in the seventies. Or at the very least rebel as a voting bloc.

Which had given him an idea. One that would be next to impossible to pull off, but one that had a certain symmetry because of something that Otto had told Colonel León.

"Yeah, we're going to look for it," he said.

"And if you find it?" Martínez asked.

McGarvey told them, and when he was finished, Martínez started to laugh and Otto shook his head.

"Oh, wow, kemo sabe."

THIRTY—FIVE

Martínez had arranged for a CIA C-20G Gulfstream IV jet to meet McGarvey and Otto at Miami International's private aviation terminal and fly them up to Andrews, and it was dawn by the time they touched down, both of them bleary eyed from the events of the past twenty-four hours.

McGarvey drank a couple of brandies neat and managed to close his eyes for a few minutes at a time, but Otto had borrowed a laptop from one of the crew and worked online for the entire two-and-a-half-hour flight until they taxied over to the hangar the Company used, and he broke out into a broad smile.

Louise Horn, looking crumpled in the same faded pair of jeans and tank top she'd been wearing when the kidnappers grabbed her, stood beside her dark blue Toyota SUV, waving at Otto in the window. A pair of Cadillac Escalades bracketed her car, four serious-looking men—dressed in suits, ties snugged up, their heads on swivels—waited with her.

"She looks okay," Otto said, his voice full of emotion.

"That she does," McGarvey said.

They thanked the crew, and as they stepped out of the aircraft, Louise let out a whoop of joy and came running, reaching Otto before he got two feet, nearly knocking him off his feet.

"Oh, wow, kemo sabe," she said when they finally parted. "I was worried about you."

"Did they hurt you?"

"Not as much as I hurt them," she said, and she turned to McGarvey and gave him a long hug. "I told them that because of you, Otto was the last guy they wanted to mess with. Thanks for bringing him back in one piece."

"How's Audie?" McGarvey asked.

"She's at the Farm for now. Until we get whatever this is settled."

"They spoil her rotten," Otto said, beaming, and McGarvey didn't think he'd ever seen his friend more alive and animated and happy. His family was intact, and he had another mission.

One of the four men came over. "Welcome back, Mr. Director. I'm Don Young, and I've been assigned as protective detail supervisor for Ms. Horn."

"Appreciate the help, but you and your people can stand down now."

"Mr. Bambridge asked that we escort you back to the Campus to be debriefed. The FBI is starting to press pretty hard for some answers, and he thought that the operational details might have to be sanitized." Young was being exceedingly careful choosing his words.

"Tell Mr. Bambridge that we'll drive out tomorrow morning. But Otto and I haven't had a decent night's sleep in several days, so we're going to crash until then."

McGarvey started to turn away.

"Sir, I have my orders," Young said.

McGarvey turned back. "I know. But I'm tired and I'm hungry, so don't piss me off by trying to follow us. I'll explain it tomorrow to Marty that I gave you different orders."

Young clearly wanted to argue, but he thought better of it and finally nodded. "Yes, sir. Stay safe."

"Thanks for your help, guys," Louise said, and she and her husband and McGarvey got into the Toyota and drove off.

Otto lowered the front passenger-side window and adjusted the door mirror so that he could watch to the rear until they were out the main gate and on Suitland Parkway into the city. "We're clear," he said, closing the window.

"GPS tracker?"

"Not in this car."

"Okay, so what's all this about?" Louise asked.

"Not now," McGarvey said from the backseat. "They may have bugged your car."

"The Bureau?" she asked.

"Our people," McGarvey said. The Cuba thing was just too big a deal, so out of the ordinary, that if he were in Marty's shoes, it's what he would have done.

"Shit," Louise said, but she held her silence all the way through the city and across to Georgetown, where they maintained a three-story brownstone that Otto had bought and sanitized a year and a half ago to use as a safe house. The Company didn't know about it, nor was it reasonable to think they could discover it, because Otto had been very thorough with the transfer of deed and with the monthly maintenance and utilities fees that were paid from a Paris bank on the account of a doctor with Médecins Sans Frontières who was always out of the country.

She pulled around to the back of the house, where

she parked to the left of the small garden she maintained whenever they were in residence, and they went inside.

Otto motioned for them to keep quiet until he entered a code on a keypad in the mudroom just off the kitchen, and after a few moments, a green light came on.

"We're good here," he said. "No bugs."

Louise put on a pot of coffee for them, then went upstairs to take a shower and change into some clean clothes. She looked beat up, and twice on the ride from Andrews, she had mentioned Joyce Kilburn's death at the preschool. "It made absolutely no sense."

"Could have been you," Otto suggested.

"Or one of the kids, if the bullet had missed."

They could hear the shower running upstairs, and Otto brought a bottle of brandy over and poured some into their coffee. "How much do you want to tell her?" he asked. He leaned against the sink, facing McGarvey, who was seated at the counter.

"Everything."

"Okay. What about tomorrow, how much do we tell Marty? And the Bureau is bound to want some answers."

"We tell them that it was a rogue operation to dig me out in retaliation for what I did at Guantánamo Bay."

"Marty might swallow it, mostly because he won't have much of a choice. He can't send us to Saudi Arabia for interrogation. But Page will suspect that we're being less than honest. He'll press."

"The woman is nuts. Her father was dead, which meant for the first time in her life, she was on her own, so she pulled this crazy stunt to make a big name for herself."

"But it backfired, and the only real casualty was the teacher at Audie's school. We can make them buy it. And then what, because if what you told me in Key Largo wasn't just idle speculation, we could end up in some really serious shit? Not that I'd mind, if we had a chance of pulling it off."

"First we have to find out if there really is any gold buried somewhere on, near, or across the Mexican border."

"There's gold, all right," Otto said. "I did some more research on the flight up here about the mountain in southern New Mexico that I told the colonel about. It's actually a part of Holloman Air Force Base and the White Sands Missile Range, about fifty miles north of the Mexican border, and about the same distance south of Trinity, where the first atomic bomb was tested in '45. Anyway, a lot of gold and other stuff was found buried in some caves dug into the mountain. But nothing much came of it, and so the story goes the air force pulled out the gold and shipped it away. That'd be sometime in the early sixties."

"So it's gone," McGarvey said. "And its information the colonel could have gotten online herself, right?"

"Right. But that's not all. There've been rumors and legends about caches of gold all over the place in the same general area."

"Rumors."

Otto was nodding. "But rumors are all we'll need for the first part of what you want to do, so long as we can find some sort of a paper trail."

"Mexico City," McGarvey said.

"Or Spain."

"And the second part is, what happened to the original gold the air force took away?"

Louise appeared at the kitchen door in fresh sweatpants and a T-shirt, a towel wrapped around her wet hair. "What gold?" she asked.

"Castro's daughter's gold," McGarvey said. "I think she's going to come looking for it, and when she does, she's going to be in for a very nasty surprise."

"Two surprises," Otto corrected. "One of which will come when the deal she'll have to make with one or more of the Mexican drug cartels turns sour."

THIRTY-SIX

In his office in the CIA's Old Headquarters Building, Marty Bambridge brought up the encrypted Skype for Windows on his desktop computer, and in seconds was connected with Raúl Martínez back in Miami.

"Are you someplace where we can talk?" Bambridge asked. It looked as if Martínez was seated at a table in a busy restaurant or coffee shop, using an iPad. It was noisy and people passed behind him.

"Sure."

"You're not alone."

"No one is paying attention, Mr. Bambridge. Believe

me, they're more interested in their dominoes than in someone's phone call."

Bambridge was vexed because Martínez was independent like McGarvey, and a difficult man to deal with. But his presence, watching Cuban dissident movements in Miami and keeping an eye on the DI field officers running around the Calle Ocho was absolutely indispensable. Without him keeping a lid on things in Little Havana by cutting off the right people at the right time, the entire place could erupt in riots. The dissidents had been waiting for a very long time—some of them for their entire lives—to go back to Cuba. Many of them didn't think of themselves as American citizens; they were exiles. Volatile at the best of times.

"What the hell happened down there?"

"Mac asked for my help to get Otto out."

"One of our birds picked up what looked like a pretty fierce firefight just off the beach last night. Make my day and tell me that you weren't involved."

"I had help setting it up, but no, I personally didn't fire a shot."

"Well, thank God for small favors—"

Martínez cut him off. "A lot of very good people lost their lives. Without them, Otto and Mac would still be there."

Bambridge forced himself to calm down. "The ones who survived will talk," he said.

"No."

"They won't be able to help themselves. The DI is pretty good."

"There weren't any survivors."

And Bambridge wanted to ask how Martínez could know for sure, but the look in the man's eyes was cold. "Did they explain what they wanted with McGarvey?"

"You'll have to ask Mac about that," Martínez said. "If he'll talk to you guys."

"He says that he's coming over tomorrow," Bambridge said. "I'd like you here as well, so we can get this mess resolved. I don't want any fallout."

"I don't have the time."

Bambridge was angry. "That's an order, mister."

"The word that some of our people were shot to death outside Havana has already reached the streets, and there are some seriously pissed-off people around here who need calming down. And I expect that within the next twenty-four hours, we'll have some DI goons running around, looking for the same answers you want. So I'm sincerely sorry, Mr. Deputy Director, but I have my hands full at the moment."

Bambridge's monitor went blank, and a moment later he was staring at his own image before he hit the DISCONNECT tab. "Sincerely sorry, my ass," he muttered, and he called to see if Page was in his office.

"The question is why Colonel León pulled off some harebrained stunt like that in the aftermath of her father's death," Bambridge told the DCI.

"Hopefully Mac will shed some light on the matter in the morning," Page said.

They were sitting in the director's office on the seventh floor of the OHB, the big bulletproof and vibration-resistant windows looking over the wooded Virginia countryside. "If he and Rencke actually show up."

"If he says he'll be here, he will. But we're going to take it easy with him. I've had a chat with three of my predecessors who worked with him, and they all said the same thing: Treat the man with respect—after all, he was the DCI, and he's given a lot for his country. But if you lean on him, he'll lean back. Hard. And that, we want to avoid."

Bambridge had also talked to some people who had worked with McGarvey, and they had the opposite opinion. In their view, the man had always been a wild card, totally out of control. And as soon as his name popped up in an ongoing mission or investigation, bodies immediately began to pile up. But he kept his thoughts to himself and nodded. "I understand."

"The thing is, we either trust the man or we don't. Either way, we don't have much choice."

"I don't trust him any farther than I could throw this building," Bambridge said.

"I know," Page replied.

THIRTY-SEVEN

María, in a fatigue uniform with bloused combat boots, entered Raúl Castro's office, came to attention in front of his desk, and saluted crisply. "Colonel León reporting as ordered, Señor Presidente."

The message to report had been on her desk when she arrived a half hour ago, and it did not come as a surprise. There was going to be some serious fallout after last night, and depending on how this went, she figured that she would have to make some tough choices.

Raúl was writing something on a pad, and he let her hang there for several seconds before he looked up. But he did not tell her to stand at ease or to sit down.

"Tell me what progress your department has made investigating the disappearance of the Amercian who showed up for the funeral."

"The investigation is ongoing, sir. And I am happy to report that my department is nearing a successful resolution of the matter."

"I'm told that you made a visit to your father's house last night. Has it anything to do with your investigation?"

"No, sir," María said.

"You are not to go there again without prior permission."

"May I ask why?"

"Because I'm ordering it," Raúl said, raising his voice. A little bird had been whispering in his ear. Either her chief of staff or the little pansy Funetes or both of them. "I'm at a loss, Señor Presidente. What have I done to anger you, or bring my directorate's policies or actions into question?"

"I don't know yet. But I'm going to find out. I think you're involved in something that very nearly cost you your life last night, and it was only through your chief of staff's intervention that you were not assassinated."

"I have not had the chance to thank him, or debrief him," María said, sidestepping the issue. "I had no idea that such an attack was coming, nor did Major Ortega-Cowan say anything to me about it."

"I want a full written report on my desk before the end of the day, including the real reason why you went to your father's house, and what you took, if anything, because a full inventory is taking place at this moment."

"As you wish, sir," María said, and she saluted again, but didn't bother to wait for Raúl to return it before she turned and went to the door.

"What bothers me is the coincidence of the timing," Raúl said to her back. "That and the possibility that a light plane may have landed in the water near your compound. Include an explanation in your report."

"Naturally, Señor Presidente."

At that moment, Ortega-Cowan showed up at Fidel's compound and was allowed to pass the guard post and drive up to the house, which was a beehive of activity this morning. Fuentes met him at the front door, and they walked together around to the pool.

"There were no survivors out there last night?" Fuentes asked.

"We made sure there were none," Ortega-Cowan said. "And we had a bit of luck with the timing, her coming back to her house right in the middle of it. She called off the air strike before I had a chance to do it in her name myself."

"Another nail in the bitch's coffin," Fuentes said with satisfaction. "Raúl will want to ask her about it."

"His office called first thing this morning, and I personally put the message on her desk before coming out here," Ortega-Cowan said, and he glanced over his shoulder. "Have you found out what she was looking for?"

"Fidel kept journals from the days before and during the revolution. We haven't found those yet, so there's a good chance she took them. And we're sure that she went through his personal files."

"How can you be sure?" Ortega-Cowan asked.

"Her file was missing."

"What was in it?"

"I don't know. I just know that the file was there after the funeral, and so far as we can tell, it's the only one missing this morning."

"You had the chance last week, and you didn't read it?" Ortega-Cowan asked. He was astounded.

"I had more important duties to attend to. I didn't think it was going anywhere. Anyway, it probably doesn't contain much of interest for our purposes."

"There's no way of knowing that for sure," Ortega-Cowan said. "What about Fidel's journals? Did you ever get a look at what they contained?"

"He showed them to me once. Just after his second stroke, when he retired. He was sitting in his study, in his pajamas, when I came in to give my daily security report. 'Take a look at this, Manuel,' he told me. And he handed me the notebook, which was just about falling apart. 'We were so young and foolish then.'"

"Did you find anything interesting?"

Fuentes shook his head. "Fascinating but useless.

The usual day-to-day stuff about the revolution and about the early days with Che and the others in Mexico City. And his obsession with the gold. I didn't read much of it."

Some fabulous treasure had been something of a hobby of his, in the early days of the government. Ortega-Cowan remembered reading something about it a number of years back, when he'd worked in the Directorate of Intelligence as a junior officer whose duties had included keeping current files of foreign press clippings about Fidel. He had mentioned something about lost Spanish gold both times he'd been to the UN in New York, but no one had taken him seriously.

A glimmer of an idea came to Ortega-Cowan. "Can you be more specific?"

"About what?"

"The gold."

Fuentes laughed. "Don't be an ass. It's a fairy tale. Right now, we need to concentrate on how to use this situation with the Americans to bring her down."

"The real question is, why did she go to the trouble to arrange the kidnapping in Washington in order to lure the CIA computer expert here in the first place? She didn't share her reasons with me. But they had to be important."

"You're her chief of staff," Fuentes said. "Find out."

"She's staying at one of our safe houses in town until the mess at her compound is cleaned out. She'll need new bodyguards and perhaps some new surveillance equipment."

"And you're just the man to supply them," Fuentes said with admiration. "Keep watch on her—she's bound to make a mistake."

María was at her desk, fabricating a report that would make some sense to Raúl without revealing the actual details of the Rencke–McGarvey operation, when her chief of staff passed her door. She called him back.

"What the hell was that all about last night?" she demanded before he had a chance to sit down.

"Saving your life, Colonel. And it was damned lucky you weren't at home when the attack began, because we might not have been on time."

"They came after McGarvey and Rencke?"

"That's what I was led to believe by my informants, who said the man who'd come ashore with McGarvey was Raúl Martínez, who's been running our Miami operators around in circles for years. It was he who got some Cuba Libre bastards to attack from the highway while he came by boat to ferry the Americans out to the float plane."

"Who are your informants?"

"A couple who run a small *paladar* near the waterfront. We had them in Quivicán a few years ago, where they learned that if they cooperated with us from time to time, we would allow them their freedom."

"Why didn't you tell me?"

"I only just found out last night, and when I tried to reach your cell phone, it was dead, something wrong with one of the towers. At any rate, they're back in the

States now, so can you tell me what the hell it was all about?"

"Not yet, Román," she said. She didn't think that she could trust him. He'd willingly helped set up the kidnapping, but he was a devious man, and it was more than possible that he'd covered his tracks so that when the time came, he would have something on her. And at this moment, she was hanging out in a very stiff breeze.

"Well, at least did you find out whatever it was you wanted to find out?"

"I'll let you know as soon as I can. But for now, my biggest problem is Raúl. I have to write him a detailed report that'll make some sort of sense."

"Raúl may not be your only problem. Fuentes is gunning for you. He said you took something from Fidel's study last night, and he's threatening to make it public, along with the fact that you're one of El Comandante's illegitimate daughters."

Her office was suddenly cold. "He doesn't want to fight with me. He'll lose," she said quietly. "I want him here this afternoon. Six o'clock."

"Now that he thinks he has something to use against you, he might refuse."

"Then arrest him," María said. "Who knows, maybe he'll get shot trying to escape."

THIRTY-EIGHT

Page was waiting in his office with Bambridge and the Company's general counsel, Carleton Patterson, when McGarvey came up with Otto and Louise a few minutes after nine in the morning. They all stood around a grouping of couches and chairs in front of a coffee table.

The DCI gave Louise a chaste hug and a peck on the cheek. "I'm so glad to see that you survived your ordeal. No worse for the wear, I hope?"

"No, sir. None whatsoever."

"I understand that your daughter is doing just fine at the Farm."

"That she is."

"Terrible business, involving an officer's family," Page said, and he directed them to sit down.

A staffer came in and poured everyone coffee from a silver server and then left.

"I thought that it would be more productive if we just had a little chat this morning to try to get to the bottom of this incident," Page said. "Rather than submit you to a formal debriefing."

"The FBI wants to talk to me," Louise said. "It's the no-ransom thing that's driving them crazy. And I'm sure that Joyce Kilburn's husband is wanting some answers."

"She was the unfortunate woman shot to death at the day care center," Patterson explained.

"That's why we're here," Page said. "To find out what

just happened and why, so that we can give the Bureau something to work on."

"The kidnappers were DI operatives here from Havana, either through New York or Miami," Otto said. "And by now, they're back in Cuba. Untouchable. You can count on it."

"Well, what the hell was this all about?" Bambridge demanded. "We're sitting on the edge of our seats here. I mean, one innocent civilian shot to death in Georgetown, and we have no earthly idea yet how many casualties it took to get the two of you home. Martínez won't tell us a thing. He claims to have his hands full in Miami, making sure the pot doesn't boil over."

"It might without him," McGarvey said. "Leave him alone and he'll manage, because it's probably not over with yet."

Bambridge started to say something, but Page motioned him back.

"I think we're agreed that the reason Louise was kidnapped was to force Otto to fly to Cuba, where he was taken, which action precipitated Kirk to become involved," Patterson said. "And from what we've learned so far, the operation was ordered by a colonel in the DI's Directorate of Operations, María León, apparently an illegitimate child of Fidel Castro. And I think it's a fair assumption to guess that all of this had something to do with Fidel's death. Perhaps something he asked his daughter to do for him. A deathbed wish, because we're told that she was the only one with him when he died."

"That was exactly what it was," McGarvey said. "He

apparently told her that Kim Jong-il recommended me. Suggested that if Fidel ever found himself in a situation that even as supreme commander of Cuba he could not resolve, he was to ask for my help."

"Extraordinary," Patterson said. Very few people outside the Operations and Intelligence Directorates knew anything about the operation McGarvey had been on last year, in which he had been of some service to the North Korean leader, but the CIA's general counsel was one of them.

Two police officers in Pyongyang had assassinated a high-ranking Chinese intelligence officer, and China was ready to start a war with North Korea. Kim Jong-il had threatened to launch his nuclear weapons if the Chinese moved against his regime.

North Korean intelligence had contacted McGarvey, and he'd agreed to look into what became, to this point at least, one of the most intense endeavors of his life.

"Fidel was on his deathbed—what did he want you to do?" Bambridge asked.

"Cuba's salvation, he supposedly told his daughter."

"Salvation from what?"

"She didn't know, but she hoped I did, because Fidel told her to contact me. Which she did the only way she knew how, because I'd gone to ground in Greece. But she figured Otto knew, which was actually a pretty astute guess, so she targeted him by grabbing Louise."

"Which was a big mistake," Louise said with some satisfaction, and her remark hung on the air for a long moment.

"You met her face-to-face," Bambridge said. "What did you tell her?"

"That I didn't know what her father was talking about. But my guess was that he might have been talking about his country's salvation from the Soviet economic model that he'd finally admitted wasn't working, and never would. Five hundred thousand of the government's labor force thrown into the private sector has pushed the country into an economic crisis at least as big as Germany's at the end of WWI."

"That's it?" Bambridge pressed. "After killing an innocent bystander here in Washington and ultimately causing the deaths of however many people who came to your rescue, you're sitting there telling us that the woman was merely going on a fishing expedition?"

"Something like that," McGarvey said. "But I wasn't in control of the situation. She initiated it."

"Couldn't have pleased her, your knowing nothing to help," Patterson suggested.

"She threatened to kill us both," Otto said. "She just never had the chance, ya know."

"Extraordinary," Patterson repeated himself. "Is the woman insane, in your estimation?"

"Almost certainly," McGarvey said.

"How should we respond?" Page asked.

"We shouldn't."

Bambridge looked from Page to McGarvey and back, clearly frustrated just about beyond control. "That's it?"

"What would you have us do, Marty?" Page asked.

"For one thing, if she's as nuts as McGarvey thinks she is, we need to expand our presence in Miami. And have the Coast Guard step up its patrols in the strait, maybe send a navy destroyer on an unannounced visit to Gitmo."

"Something like that would be viewed as provocative," Patterson said.

"What are they going to do about it," Bambridge practically shouted.

"We're not suggesting anything quite so drastic just yet," Page said. "What's our operational status on the ground in Havana?"

Bambridge calmed down a little. "We have four assets at the moment: a mechanic at the air regiment in Playa Baracoa; a writer for the political magazine *Carteles,* which was reactivated a couple of years ago, when Raúl began relaxing the state's restrictions on the media; and an old couple who run a little privately owned restaurant near the waterfront. They go back to the revolution as kids, and they apparently know just about everybody."

"Have them keep their eyes and ears open, but stay out of it," McGarvey said. "We're not done with Colonel León."

Bambridge glared at him. "You meant to say that *you're* not done, right?"

"Something like that," McGarvey said.

"Are you going to tell us?"

"Not yet."

THIRTY-NINE

María changed into a print dress and flats around noon and left her office, where she had stayed last night to drive directly over to one of the DI's safe houses, this one on the Avenue Antonio Maceo, commonly known as the Malecón, right on the bay. It was actually a large, nicely furnished apartment in a foreigner's building that was sometimes used on a temporary basis to house visiting VIPs. The entire place was wired, and a listening post had been installed in the attic. She was in civilian clothes so as not to attract any attention.

She was the only one using the apartment now, and she'd made sure that the listening post was not manned before she tossed down her shoulder bag, poured a stiff measure of rum, which she drank down in one piece, then poured a second and went to the French doors that opened to a small balcony.

After her meeting with the president, she needed time to think out her next moves. Away from the office. Away from the prying eyes of her staff, and especially from Ortega-Cowan, who'd reported to the OD that he would be in sometime after lunch.

Her problem as she saw it was twofold. She wanted to find out about this gold business that Rencke had brought up and that she'd found mentioned in several places from what she'd read so far in her father's journals. On his deathbed, he'd asked that she talk to McGarvey for Cuba's salvation. But if it were that simple—that her father meant for her to ask McGarvey to help find the gold and make sure that Cuba somehow got its fair share—then her father had been crazy at the last. Perhaps dementia or some form of Alzheimer's, because even if there was some fortune in Spanish gold buried somewhere in Mexico or the Southern United States, a man like McGarvey would never consent to find it and make sure the Cuban government got a percentage of it. That was beyond fantasy.

The second and most urgent part of her problem was Fuentes, who was making a run at bringing her down, no doubt with Ortega-Cowan's help. Her chief of staff had always played both ends against the middle. Forcing McGarvey down here with his help—the only way it had been possible for her to do so—had left her wide open. Raúl had all but hinted at a charge of treason, which could very well stick without her father's protection.

Traffic was fairly heavy, and the neighborhood stank of car exhaust even with the light breeze coming off the water. All of Havana smelled that way, and most of the time, neither she nor anyone else living here noticed. It was simply a fact of life. But she had become hypersensitive in the past few days; she was noticing just about everything.

Situational awareness, her Russian trainers had drilled her. *Without it, the field agent is as good as dead.*

The two problems—that of the gold and that of Fuentes—were linked, of course. But in order to save herself possibly from jail or a firing squad, she would somehow have to actually find the gold, and then turn the problem over to her government. Whether or not diplomacy—perhaps at the UN or even in the World

Court at The Hague—would result in Cuba's improbable claim being honored would not be her problem. No matter what, she would come out on top: the hero who'd made efforts above and beyond the call of duty for her government.

She could see the smug look on McGarvey's face, and on Rencke's, and it infuriated her. They were arrogant, self-assured men who'd actually pitied her and her country. Rencke had told her that he could hack into Cuba's computer infrastructure any time he wanted to, but that it wasn't worth the effort. She wanted to show them that she was just as good as they were.

But in order to find the gold, or prove that it was nothing but another dream of Cíbola, she would need to remain free to operate. Starting right now, before her situation here became impossible.

After draining the second drink, she left the apartment and went back to her office, where Ortega-Cowan hadn't yet returned.

From her private wall safe, she got a stack of euros and American dollars amounting to ten thousand U.S.; an ID kit, which included a Mexican passport, driving license, and several credit cards in the name of Ines Delgado; along with a cell phone in the same name—all of which she stuffed into her purse. But she left her Russian-made compact 5.45 mm PSM semiautomatic. If she got into a situation in which she had to shoot her way clear, she would already have lost. And taking a weapon across international borders was all but impossible, except for a sky marshal or someone carrying a diplomatic passport.

She had a Cuban passport, too, along with several

others—for Mexico, Venezuela, Colombia, and even Spain. But for now, she needed to go deep. Out of sight. Under the DI's radar.

She'd gathered all the paperwork and other things over the past several years in part because of her Russian adviser, who'd cautioned her to always maintain the means for an escape. It was a cynical thing for him to have told her, but Russia had become a cynical place, as had Cuba. And she'd also followed his advice because in her estimation, just about every high-ranking official in the Cuban government, including her father, was, deeply paranoid. And paranoid people could be counted on to do the unexpected at any moment, especially turning on an insider who they perceived was anything less than absolutely loyal.

She'd told herself that actually, she was practicing sound tradecraft by maintaining alternate identities in case she had to go into the field.

Oretga-Cowan was just getting off the elevator at the end of the corridor to the right, in deep conversation with a pretty young woman who was one of the Directorate's researchers, as María grabbed her fatigue uniform and boots and stepped out of her office. Before he had a chance to look up, she turned the other way and disappeared around the corner and down the stairs to the ground floor.

Someone would mention to him that the colonel had been in her office, but suddenly left again. He was smart; he would begin to sense that something was wrong. And when she hadn't returned for her meeting with Fuentes, he might suspect that she had skipped.

And she was going to lead him to exactly that conclusion.

Back at the safe house, she telephoned Cubana de Aviación, booking a round-trip first-class seat for the morning flight to Mexico City, using the Delgado credit card. Flight 130 left at six thirty, which meant she had to be at the airport no later than five. Which would be easily doable.

Ten minutes later, making absolutely certain that no one had followed her, she left the safe house again and drove over to La Maison, which was a mini complex of upscale shops in an old mansion in Miramar, where she picked up a skirt and white blouse, along with a Hermès knockoff scarf, a pair of faded jeans, decent sneakers, and a few bangles. At another shop, she purchased a nice leather overnight bag and a pair of big glitzy sunglasses with rhinestones, and at a third, some panties and bras.

Her bag would be searched at the airport, and those sorts of items would be expected. Without them, questions might be raised, among them: How could a woman make a trip from Havana to Mexico City without at least a change of underwear?

Once again back at the safe house, still hopeful that Ortega-Cowan hadn't jumped the gun and sent someone looking for her, she changed back into her fatigue uniform and packed her civilian clothes into the bag, including the things she'd just purchased, along with one of the courtesy toiletries kits from the bathroom.

It was nearly three by the time she left the apartment and drove out to the air regiment at Playa Baracoa, where she presented herself to Lieutenant Abeladro, the on-duty operations officer who jumped up from behind his desk and came to attention.

"I need to get to Camagüey in a big hurry," she said. "Do you have any training flights scheduled for this afternoon?"

"No, *Señora Coronel*. As you can see, it is quiet here today."

"Well, schedule one—I'm not going to wait all day. Your pilot is to drop me off and return in twenty-four hours."

"My captain is off base at the moment, but I think I can find him," the nervous lieutenant said, and he reached for the telephone. The only other person in the room that looked out toward the active runway was a clerk typist, who suddenly began typing furiously on an old IBM Selectric.

"This is official DI business, so the need to know is limited. Do you understand?"

The lieutenant wanted to say no, but he nodded. "I'll have to log the flight."

"Routine training mission on my personal request," María said. "I'll sign the flight orders. Now, get on with it, Lieutenant."

María went outside to wait by her car and smoke a small panatela. Timing was everything. She needed to be on the ground and lost as Ines Delgado in Camagüey before Román sat up and took notice that something was wrong. That gave her a little more than two hours before she was supposed to be back in her office to meet with Fuentes.

It might take him a half hour or so to find out that she had cleared out of the safe house apartment, and maybe that much longer to find out where she'd flown to, but by then, she would have dropped out of sight. And in less than eighteen hours, she would be even more lost in Mexico City, from where she would launch her search.

A dark gray Gazik came from a small hangar across the field and drove directly to a much larger hangar, the main doors of which were trundling open, and disappeared inside.

María was just grinding out her cigar when the lieutenant came out and had her sign the flight order on a clipboard. "If you'll give me just a moment, Colonel, I'll drive you over to the ready hangar."

"I'll drive myself. I want to leave my car overnight."

"Sí, Señora," the lieutenant said, and he came to attention and saluted.

After he went back inside, María drove over to the hangar and parked out of the way of the small Czech-made Aero L-39C Albatros that a ground crew was prepping for flight. The aircraft was a two-seat trainer/fighter jet that could do well in excess of five hundred knots. Once they were up, flying time to Camagüey—which was only a little more than 550 kilometers to the southeast—would be about one hour.

The young pilot, whose name tape read MACHADO, looked up when she walked over with her shoulder purse and the leather overnight bag. He came to attention and saluted.

"Pardon me, Señora Coronel, but you should be dressed in a flight suit."

"Not today," María said. "I need you to get me to Camagüey as quickly as possible. So let's get on with it, shall we?"

The pilot seemed uncertain, but he was a young lieutenant and she was a colonel. One of the flight crewmen helped her up the ladder and strapped her in the rear seat. He handed her the purse and leather bag, which she put on her lap, making for cramped seating, but there were no storage compartments in the jet. Finally, he helped her with the flight helmet, which he plugged into a panel at her left.

The pilot checked that she was properly strapped in before he climbed aboard, and within minutes, a towing tractor had pulled them out of the hangar, the engine was started, and they taxied down to the active runway.

"Are you ready, *Señora Coronel?*" his voice came over her helmet comms unit.

"*Sí,*" María said, and suddenly they were hurtling down the runway and lifting off, the city of Havana spreading out behind them, the waters of the Straits of Florida impossibly blue.

Camagüey, a colonial city founded in 1528, was a rat warren of narrow, twisting streets—a good place for someone on the run to get lost in. The pilot taxied over to a commercial hangar that at one time was used by the thirty-first Regimiento de Caza, which flew MiG-21MFs before the air force was downsized to only three bases. A man in white coveralls came over with a ladder and helped María out of the jet.

"I want you back here at sixteen hundred tomorrow," she told the pilot. "Do not be late."

A driver took her across to the civilian terminal, where she entered through the restricted baggage area, none of the employees paying her any attention. She found a bathroom, where she changed into her jeans, a blouse, and the sneakers, and then went into the arrivals hall. It was practically empty at this moment, again no one paying her the slightest attention; she was merely a passenger on her way somewhere.

At the Cubacar counter, she rented a small Hyundai Atos with less than five thousand kilometers on the odometer with her Delgado credit card and driving license. She drove into the city and parked near the train station. Inside, she bought a one-way ticket for tomorrow's noon train to Santiago de Cuba under her real name.

The city was near enough to the American base at Guantánamo that when Ortega-Cowan got this far, he would be convinced that she was a traitor and would have DI officers all over the place, waiting for her to show up.

She walked across the street to the funky old Hotel Plaza just off the broad Avenida Carlos J. Finlay. It was just the sort of place that Ortega-Cowan would never think to look for her.

By five, she had checked in and paid for three days in advance under her real name. After she washed up, she went down to El Dorado, the hotel's main restaurant, where she had chicken cordon bleu with a decent pinot grigio and then went up to her room and lay down for a few hours' sleep.

The highway back to Havana was one of the better in Cuba, but she figured it would take her at least five hours to drive there.

She dreamed about McGarvey. They were having drinks at a sidewalk café in Paris, and he was smiling at her. Although she couldn't quite make out what he was saying, she was certain that it was something nice.

She awoke at eleven, took a shower, and dressed in the blue jeans and sneakers. She folded her uniform and put it in the chest of drawers along with the boots, and bag in hand took the stairs down to the deserted lobby. Five minutes later, she reached the rental car and headed northwest through the outskirts of the city, some neighborhoods still busy, reaching the Santa Clara Highway by eleven thirty, and sped up to a reasonable hundred kilometers per hour, the night overcast, the air thick.

FORTY

McGarvey spent the afternoon catching up on his sleep at the Renckes' brownstone while Otto and Louise worked on the computers, trying to find everything they could about the legends of Spanish gold in the southern United States, especially in southern New Mexico. But by six, he got up and looked in on them.

"Anything?" he asked.

The ground-floor workroom had actually been the

brownstone's sitting room, where in the early 1900s, the owners could receive guests. Now it was filled with electronic equipment. Some of it, including four wide-screen monitors and keyboards, was arrayed on two long tables, while antisurveillance equipment and sophisticated encryption devices sat on the floor or were mounted on racks against the walls. The windows covered with heavy drapes had been fitted with devices that prevented the detection of sounds, including voices by laser beams that could measure microvibrations in the glass, and by a white noise generator that blocked any other sort of mechanical eavesdropping. The entire house, attic to basement, was sheathed in a light copper mesh, most of it simply nailed to the wallboard and painted over. It had taken Rencke nearly two months to finish the job, which resulted in the entire structure being protected by a Faraday cage—totally impervious to electronic snooping.

"Possibly something," Otto said, looking up. "I went back to the Victorio Peak legend I told Colonel León about. The one on Holloman Air Force Base in New Mexico. There was evidently gold there, but it was apparently pulled out by the air force in the sixties and carted off shortly after F. Lee Bailey filed a lawsuit that would have forced the government to allow him to send a search team onto the base. But that died down, and the present whereabouts of the treasure is unknown. Probably in some high-security storage facility somewhere."

"Was there more?" McGarvey asked.

"Milton Noss—his friends called him Doc—was the first one to find the gold, and he may have pulled out a few ingots. Where they are now is anyone's guess. But he also found four leather-covered codices which he supposedly buried somewhere in the desert nearby."

"Also lost?"

"Yup," Louise said. "Lot of that going on."

"But before he buried them, he wrote down what he called a 'cryptic message' he'd found in one of them."

McGarvey moved around behind Otto so he could read what was on the screen.

Seven is the holy number . . . in seven languages, in seven signs . . . look for the seven cities of gold, seventy miles north of El Paso del Norte in the seventh peak, Soledad. These cities have seven sealed doors, three sealed toward the rising of the Sol sun, three sealed toward the setting of the Sol sun, one deep within the Casa de la Cueva de Oro at high noon. Receive health, wealth and honor. . . .

"None of that suggests anything about Spanish gold hidden by Spanish monks from Mexico City, and nothing about transshipment through Havana," McGarvey said.

"No, but if you believe the message in the codices, the cache in Victorio may have been only one of seven. Could be a lot more out there, kemo sabe."

"We'll have to go to Mexico City," McGarvey said.

"The National Archives. The curator there is Dr. José Diaz, and he's agreed to talk to us about early Spanish explorers from New Mexico to Colorado. We're from the Library of Congress Special Research Branch."

"Do you think he believed you?"

"Doesn't matter, we have an appointment with him tomorrow afternoon at six. I've booked us a suite at the Marquis Reforma."

"Fair enough," McGarvey said. "But first I have to get a few things from my place."

"Do you think the Company is watching your apartment?" Louise asked.

"I'd be surprised if they weren't."

McGarvey's third-floor brownstone apartment was located on Twenty-seventh Street just below the end of Dumbarton Avenue N W with a nice view of Rock Creek Park. It was actually less than a mile as the crow flies from Rencke's house near Georgetown University, but he went over to Twenty-ninth Street, where he caught a cab, and had the driver drop him off around the corner from his place.

He'd bought the small, pleasantly furnished place after his wife and daughter were assassinated and before he went to ground in Greece. The house on Casey Key on Florida's Gulf Coast that he'd shared with Katy was still up and running, with a service coming once a week to clean and make any necessary repairs, but he wasn't quite ready to return there yet, nor did he want to sell it. For now, it was tough enough returning to Georgetown. He had a lot of memories here, too.

Coming around the corner, he spotted a plain gray Taurus with government plates parked across the street, one man behind the wheel, but he ignored it and went inside.

No one had been here. In addition to the alarm system,

none of his telltales had apparently been tampered with. Though he supposed that a good second-story man from the Company could have tossed the place, he didn't think Page would have authorized it. There'd been no reason.

From a steel fireproof box with a combination lock he'd kept in plain sight on a closet shelf, he took out a spare 9 mm Walther PPK—a pistol he'd always favored because of its compact size, accuracy, and reliability—a suppressor, a spare passport in the name of Kevin McCarthy, along with a New York driver's license and credit cards in the same name—and five thousand dollars in cash.

He still had the Federal Air Marshal ID he'd used to get down to Miami, which he would use again tomorrow, enabling him to fly to Mexico City armed. The DI's presence was strong down there, and he wouldn't put it past María to have an all-stations alert for him, with orders to shoot on sight. Mexico had become a very dangerous place, so it would be easy to cover up his and Otto's murders as drug related.

He took a quick shower and changed into a pair of faded jeans, a white polo shirt, Top-Siders, and a black blazer, his pistol in a belt holster at the small of his back. His overnight bag with a few items of clean clothes and his shaving gear he'd brought back from Miami were at Otto's, so there was nothing else he needed here.

Outside, McGarvey walked across the street and got in the Taurus on the passenger side. The driver, wearing a khaki sport coat, was of medium build, with a nondescript face and thinning dark hair. He didn't seem surprised.

"May I see some identification?" McGarvey asked pleasantly.

The man was careful to keep his hands on the steering wheel, but he didn't seem particularly nervous that he'd been outed. "All I'm carrying is a Langley driver's license. Mr. Bambridge sent me over to be on the lookout for you."

"Just you?"

"Three of us—four hours on, eight off. My shift started at six."

"Now what?"

"I'll report to Mr. Bambridge that you showed up, stayed around twenty minutes, and left."

"Were you ordered to follow me if and when I showed up?"

"No."

"Trust me, son. Don't."

The agent hesitated for just a moment, but then he nodded. "Yes, sir."

McGarvey got out but turned back before he closed the door. "Doesn't make a lot of sense for Marty simply to want to know if and when I showed up at my apartment."

"I'm just following my orders, sir."

"I've heard that before," McGarvey said, and he shut the door and walked away.

The only explanation he could think of was that Marty figured that if McGarvey was going to make another move, he would have to return to his apartment for clothes, money, papers—exactly what he had done.

Watching his back, he walked around the block—traffic reasonably light at this hour—and at the last corner, he held up and looked down the street. The Taurus was still there, which made even less sense. Unless they were double-or triple-teaming him, in which case, someone on foot would be tailing him, and possibly someone in a van or a car with civilian plates. But he'd spotted no one in his 180.

Still, when he turned around and walked away, he took care with his tradecraft, until two blocks away he entered a small Italian restaurant just beginning to fill up, walked straight back to the kitchen and out the rear door into the alley. He didn't think Marty would have gone to the trouble and fantastic expense to task a satellite, so from this point, he felt that it was reasonable to assume he was out clean. For now.

FORTY-ONE

It was coming up on five in the morning when María pulled into the short-term parking lot at Havana's José Martí International Airport and left the Hyundai, its gas tank nearly on empty, in the middle of a row near the back. She was dead tired from the long drive but hyped up that she was close to getting out of Cuba.

She'd given a great deal of thought last night to what she was about to do, what her father's deathbed order had really meant, and the terrible chance she had taken getting McGarvey down here and then letting him and Rencke escape. At this point, she had no other choice than to move forward. Mexico City first, and then she would have to get help because she couldn't take the next steps on her own.

It was impossible for her to stay in Cuba, and she would never be able to return unless she succeeded in what she felt was most likely a fool's errand. And yet the look in McGarvey's eyes, the set of his shoulders, his arrogance and self-assurance stuck in her mind. She wanted to feel the same thing, and going ahead with this insanely quixotic quest was just about the only way she figured she could not only redeem herself, but also solidify her position and safety now that she no longer had her father's protection.

And when the time came, if it came, she would personally sign the orders of execution for Ortega-Cowan and Fuentes.

She had pinned her hair up and covered it with the Hermès, and she headed across to Terminal 3, where on the upper level—busy at this hour of the morning—she showed her passport and driver's license at the Cubana de Aviación counter to pick up her boarding pass. At the security checkpoint, she had to show her passport again and the boarding pass before her leather bag and purse were scanned and she walked through the arch.

She resisted the urge to look over her shoulder to see if anyone was coming after her until she was all the way through and on her way down the broad corridor past the gift shops, restaurants, and bars all open and crowded. She stopped to buy a bottle of water and glanced back toward the checkpoint, but no one she could identify as DI agents had shown up. To this point, it was still business as usual here; no one paid her the slightest attention.

She found her boarding gate area and sat down near an emergency exit in case she needed to run. It was just before five thirty, and the pilot and his flight crew showed up and the gate agent admitted them through the door to the Jetway. More people were arriving, some of them with children, and a few minutes later the agent announced Cuba Air's flight 130 with nonstop service to Mexico City, first in Spanish then in English, and invited first-class passengers to board.

Still no one paid her the slightest attention as she got up and joined the short line. With luck, Ortega-Cowan had fallen for her ruse in Camagüey, and at this moment had the train station staked out, with men also at Santiago de Cuba, in case she'd given them the slip.

The Airbus A320 was in reasonably good condition, and when she was seated alone in the fourth-row window seat on the right side, the handsome flight attendant brought her a glass of champagne.

"Welcome aboard, señora," he said. "Is there anything else I can get for you?"

"No, I'm fine for now," María said.

"May I stow your bag for you?"

María hesitated for just a moment, but then smiled and nodded. "Please. Is this a full flight?"

"No," the attendant said.

"Then I may spread out here?"

"*Sí*, you'll have this row to yourself this morning."

It took twenty minutes for the boarding to be completed, and many of the people filing past her watched with a little resentment because of where she was seated and the fact she was drinking champagne, and that she was young, good-looking, and obviously rich.

Finally the front hatch was closed, and as the aircraft pushed back away from the gate and trundled down the taxiway to the runway, the attendants gave the seat belt–oxygen mask–emergency water landing drill, and María allowed herself to relax just a little.

She looked out the window, but there were no chase cars coming after them, and minutes later they were turning onto the runway, and immediately began their takeoff roll. She wondered if she would ever see Cuba again. She hoped so, because this was her country, and now that her father was finally dead, a lot of people, including her, had high hopes for the new revolution that was on the verge of unfolding.

But the key was going to be money. It had been about money when the Soviets propped up the sugar industry, but now it was more important than ever. She had seen reports, suppressed by the government, that people were actually starving to death. Not so many as in North Korea, but it was happening, and it made her want to cry. And made her want to try this crazy stunt that had nearly a zero chance of success.

But she'd heard the enthusiasm in Rencke's voice, and the look in McGarvey's eye, and it was enough for her.

An hour later, the island behind them, the Yucatán Channel below, María pulled out the file she'd taken from the cabinet in her father's office, opened it, and began to read. The first pages were copies of her fitness and training reports, some of them in Russian with side-by-side translations into Spanish, many of them from her early schooling by private tutors. A single-page report outlined the rape, and her father's handwritten instructions at the bottom.

> No *immediate disciplinary action will be taken. But the boys involved and all of their family members will be closely monitored for further actions against the state.*

María looked up. The order had been cold, dispassionate. Her rape had been an "action against the state." No father's rage, no concern for a daughter's well-being or continued safety at the school.

And yet from the moment she'd learned that Fidel was her father, she'd hung on every word he spoke in public because it was all she had. Unlike leaders just about everywhere else in the world, in Cuba, Fidel was a private citizen. Very few newspaper or magazine articles were written about his personal life, no streets or plazas were named in his honor, no statues had been erected, and he'd never lived in any grand castle or mansion.

And now he was dead. Gone from her forever.

She flipped to the next page, and for what seemed to be the longest time, she could only stare at the handwritten letter, dated simply *Noviembre,* with no year. But it had to have been fairly recent, because her father's hand had shaken when he wrote it.

But the salutation clutched at her heart, and she had to look away for another longish time, because he had written: *Mi queridisima hija*, My most beloved daughter.

When she was finally able to turn back, she read the short letter in which he sent her apologies for all the years of being a neglectful father, and for all the letters he'd written but never had been able to send.

> *Perhaps we will finally meet and I can hold you in my arms, and smell your sweet perfume and look into your beautiful eyes.*

The next letter was dated in January, again with no year but the same salutation, in which he wrote to her about the isolation he was feeling after the illness that had forced him to step down.

> *I have always loved you, and someday I will tell this to you in person.*

The remainder of the documents in the file were letters to her, dated with months but no years and the same opening, but from the things he wrote about, she could see that they were in reverse chronological order: the Bay of Pigs, the missile crises, defections, and finally one dated on an October thirty-six years ago, when she'd been born.

"*Mi queridisima hija,*" he began, and he wrote about missing her birth in Santiago de Cuba in which her mother had died, but he was out of the country in Moscow and word had not gotten to him until it was too late. Conditions of state meant that their relationship had to be kept secret until someday in the future, but he would make sure that she was well cared for and would never want for a thing.

Except for a father.

She closed the file and looked out the window again. It was the first mention she'd ever heard about her mother, whose name she'd never known. There were times when she was young when she'd dreamed about her mother, being held in her arms, being told about becoming a woman, which was extremely important. Custom dictated that Hispanic females be prim and proper virgins before marriage, but Eves to their Adams afterwards. But no mother had been there to teach her.

She returned the file to her shoulder bag, laid her head back, and fell asleep staring out the window, dreaming again about a mother she'd never known, but only ever imagined. And in her dream, she was happy.

It was a few minutes before nine thirty in the morning local time when María was cleared through passport control at Mexico City's Benito Juárez International Airport. The official welcomed her home and waved her through. At customs, she told the agent she had only her purse and the one carry-on bag, and she was cleared without an inspection.

Two other flights had come in about the same time, and the baggage claims area she had passed through had been busy, crowded with a lot of families and relatives waiting beyond the barriers.

A pair of men in light sport coats wearing hats and

sunglasses were looking toward the people streaming from the baggage pickup area into customs, and María walked right past them. They had the look of cops, possibly even DI, and if the latter were the case, it meant Ortega-Cowan had been faster on his feet than she thought he would be.

Outside on the street, she glanced back as she got into a cab, but no one was coming after her. "Four Seasons Hotel, please," she told the driver in Spanish.

Five minutes away from the airport, she got online with her cell phone and connected with Aeromexico's Web site, where using her Delgado credit card she booked a round-trip first-class ticket to Miami, with no bags to check, on Flight 422, which left in less than three hours.

She had thought hard about this next move and whether she should leave her father's journals and her file behind, but had decided she would almost certainly need them as proof. She would not be welcomed with open arms. Once it was known who she was, just about every tough guy living on and around Calle Ocho would come gunning for her.

"Driver, I've changed my mind. Take me back to Aeromexico. Departures."

FORTY-TWO

It was noon when Delta Flight 363 from Dulles via Atlanta touched down at Benito Juárez International Airport and McGarvey, traveling separately from Otto because of his Federal Air Marshal credentials, was met at passport control by two men who identified themselves as Federal Agency of Investigation agents. He was taken to a small office nearby, where he had to produce his credentials, including his permit to carry a weapon aboard an international flight.

"You might want to let me phone my embassy," McGarvey said.

"That won't be necessary, Mr. McGarvey," the dark, dangerous-looking of the two agents whose credentials identified him as Julio Mejía said. "We merely wanted to confirm your identification, and warn you that because of the increasing gun violence in Mexico, we take a very serious look at anyone carrying a firearm for any reason, no matter who they are, and not declaring it."

"In addition, your reputation precedes you," the other taller agent, whose name was Alberto Gallegos, said. "We know that you are traveling with Mr. Otto Rencke of the CIA. Why have you and your associate come here?"

"To speak with Dr. José Diaz, who is the curator of your National Archives. We have an appointment with him later today."

"In regards to what?"

"Actually, we're on an errand for our Library of Congress."

"Concerning exactly what?" Mejía pressed.

"Electronic data sharing. Mr. Rencke is something of an expert."

"*Sí,* we know this," Gallegos said. "The question remains, why have you come to Mexico armed?"

"As you say, there is increasing gun violence here, and Mr. Rencke is a valuable asset. And a friend. I'm here to protect him."

The agents exchanged a glance. "When will you be leaving?" Mejía said.

"First thing in the morning."

"Take care that you violate none of our laws," Gallegos said. He nodded at McGarvey's overnight bag. "Anything to declare in addition to your weapon?"

"Change of socks and shaving gear."

"May I look?"

McGarvey held out the bag. "Be my guest. And do you want my gun?"

But after a moment the agent shook his head, and McGarvey was allowed to leave. He joined the queue in the customs hall, where he was passed through without question.

Otto was waiting outside at the curb. "Your gun?"

"I still have it, but they wanted to know what we were doing in Mexico City. I told them that I was here to protect you, and you were here to talk to Dr. Diaz about electronic data sharing."

Otto grinned.

They took a cab downtown to the art noveau Hotel

Marquis Reforma, where Otto had booked them into a two-bedroom suite on the seventh floor, the balcony windows of which had a view of the Castillo de Chapultepec. The Company didn't know it yet, but according to Otto, it was paying for this little bit of luxury.

"Anyway, we can charge a finder's fee if we actually come up with the gold," he said.

"Which you don't think is likely."

"Not a chance in hell. But you can't win at lotto unless you put your money down."

"Yet we're here," McGarvey said. "And unless I miss my guess, there were a couple of DI officers just outside customs. Makes you wonder who they were looking for."

"I didn't see them," Otto said. "Do you want to go back and find out what they're up to? I wouldn't put it past Colonel León to put two and two together and show up. She's an inventive woman who's not afraid to take risks."

"That she is," McGarvey said. "But they didn't follow us, so we should be clear unless the Mexican cops are helping out."

After a late lunch in the hotel's La Jolla restaurant, a very good Mexican beefsteak with *mole chichilo,* they took a leisurely walk along the broad Paseo de la Reforma to burn off some time and to see if anyone was taking an interest in them. Traffic was very heavy, and the air stank of diesel and gasoline fumes and something else that could have been burning garbage or something industrial. Surrounded by mountains, which caused air inversions that sometimes lasted for weeks or even longer, the city's air quality was often as bad as Beijing's.

After forty minutes or so, McGarvey was satisfied that they were not being tailed, and he and Otto went back to the hotel, where they cleaned up. Mac left his pistol in the room before they went down to the bar to have a drink. Otto had warned him that they would be required to pass through a security arch before going inside any of the government buildings.

"Lots of paranoid people these days."

"Can't blame them," McGarvey said.

They took a cab over to the Palacio Nacional, the National Palace, located on the Zócalo, which was the largest main square anywhere in Latin America. Also here were a temple and museum dedicated to the Aztecs and the massive Metropolitan Cathedral, which had taken two and a half centuries to complete.

The palace itself, which had been built on the site of Montezuma's home served as the seat of the government and the National Treasury. Also located in the same building were the National Archives, where Dr. Diaz had his offices, that included a smallish research library adjacent to a specialized restoration workroom where only the most delicate projects were brought. Everything else was sent to other restoration centers around the city, including the major one at the National Autonomous University of Mexico, which had been in existence since the mid-sixteenth century.

Checking through one of the entrances on the north side of the massive building that Otto had been instructed for them to use, they were required to pass through a metal detector and afterwards had to surrender their passports.

Dr. José Diaz, a tiny, stoop-shouldered old man with

a shock of snow white hair—unusual for a Hispanic male—nut brown skin, and eyes that were wide, bright, and very much alive, shuffled to his office door and beckoned them inside. He was dressed in a tweed three-piece suit, the bottom button of his vest undone and a plain blue tie properly snugged up.

"The gentlemen from the Library of Congress," he said, smiling furiously as if he were sharing some inside joke.

His inner office was a large room with broad windows that looked toward the Aztec museum. Books, folios, maps, and manuscripts, most of them very old, lay in piles everywhere—on his desk, on a couple of small tables, on the floor—or were stuffed in several overflowing floor-to-ceiling bookcases that appeared as if they were on the verge of tipping over. The place looked like it had not been swept or dusted in years.

He cleared off a couple of chairs that faced his desk, and they all sat down.

"We're not actually from the Library of Congress," Otto said.

"Of course not, though when I talked to Hiram, he said that he thought you might work for the CIA, which is actually quite intriguing for an old revolutionary such as me."

"Hiram Stannard?" Otto asked. Stannard was the Librarian of Congress.

"Yes, we're old friends," Diaz said. "Do you actually work for the CIA?"

Otto nodded. "Were you actually a revolutionary?"

"I was on the edges when Fidel and Che and the Russian were here in the fifties," Diaz said. "Exciting times. But they're all gone now." He turned to Mc-Garvey.

"Kirk McGarvey, I used to run the CIA."

Diaz smiled and nodded. "You must be here to ask about the Spanish gold the monks hid up north. The Jornada del Muerto. Victorio Peak, the seven signs, the seven cities, seventy miles north of El Paso del Norte."

"Then it's not merely a legend?" Otto asked.

"No, of course not. But why are you here now, unless it has something to do with El Comandante's death?"

Otto quickly told him about María León and everything that had happened from the time of Louise's kidnapping and his own research on the Internet.

"He was quite keen on finding the gold. I wanted to take up arms and go back to Cuba with him and the others, but he wanted me to stay here and do my research. Which, of course, didn't yield much more than you apparently know. And in end, his daughter has sent you on the same quest. How odd, how tragic."

"But you think the treasure exists?" McGarvey asked.

"I'm convinced of it," Diaz said. "Six locations in addition to Victorio Peak on the New Mexican desert. Inaccessible now, of course, because your government continues to use the area as a testing range for missiles and other weapons including, of course, the first atomic bomb."

"The treasure inside Victorio Peak has evidently already been removed," Otto said.

"That's common knowledge."

"Which leaves the other six sites."

"So you've come here to ask if I know their locations,"

Diaz said. "If I did, why should I reveal them to agents of the U.S. government?"

"A claim could be made that one third of the gold belongs to Cuba," McGarvey suggested.

Diaz threw his head back and laughed out loud. "The embargo, *el bloqueo,* has been going on since 1960. Don't insult an old man by suggesting the U.S. would lift so much as a finger to help Cuba."

"Not the government," McGarvey said. "But the people. Only the people."

"How?"

"I don't know yet, but if the treasure actually exists as you say it does, and if we can find it, we might be able to make a case in Washington."

Diaz, suddenly serious, looked away in thought for a beat. "My heart has always been with the people of Cuba. Batista was a monster, who was propped up in large measure by your government."

"Fidel was no better."

"At first he was. He was one of the people, he and Che. It was why the revolution succeeded."

"And later?"

"And later," Diaz said. "Moscow got to him before Washington. And after Che was gone, Uncle Fidel maybe went a little crazy."

"Can you help us?" Otto asked.

Diaz looked at them, his mottled face sad, and he shook his head. "I have searched our National Archives, but no such records exist. In any event, it was a situation between the Mother Church and the Spanish government that lasted more than two hundred years. So the legend goes the monks made the trip up into

New Mexico along the Jornada del Muerto many times, perhaps dozens. If there are any written records of those expeditions, they would be located in the Vatican Secret Archives in Rome, certainly not open to treasure hunters. But to my knowledge, the Church has never mounted a search to recover what it believes might be its treasure."

"What about the Spanish government?" Otto asked.

"Now, that's a different story. Records of the losses were undoubtedly kept, and would be in the Archivo General de Indias, where all the documents from the Spanish Empire in the Americas are maintained."

"Madrid?" Otto asked.

"Actually Seville," Diaz said, and he held up a hand before Otto could ask the next question. "I can't help. It's a very long story, but I have had disagreements with the staff ever since illegal notes I'd made were discovered and I was kicked out of Spain."

"But you remember."

Diaz nodded. "The records of the six treasure sites undoubtedly exist, because the Spanish government mounted two military expeditions to the region—the first in the late 1700s, and the second, undercover during the siege of Alamo to the east. Twelve soldiers in civilian clothes rode up into New Mexico along the Jornada del Muerto but only two returned, empty-handed except for expedition maps and journals."

"If you can't help us reach someone in Seville, we're at a dead end," Otto said. "None of that stuff will be digitized."

"But you don't need me."

"No?"

"Not if you represent yourselves as treasure hunters willing to split whatever you find with the Spanish government. It would be something new for them, not having to take every successful American treasure-hunting corporation to court."

Otto was grinning. "Greed," he said.

"It's something just about everyone understands," Diaz said.

FORTY-THREE

Manuel Fuentes got off the elevator on the sixth floor of the Hotel Marquis Reforma and took the stairs up one floor. He hesitated for a moment to make sure the corridor was empty before he hurried down the hall to the suite where McGarvey and Rencke were staying and let himself in with a universal key that had been waiting for him in an envelope, courtesy of the AFI, Agencia Federal de Investigation, when he'd checked in this afternoon.

It was past six, and his DI contact on the ground had phoned to report that the two Americans had taken a cab over to the Palacio Nacional and were inside at this moment. Their purpose for going there was so far unknown.

Donning a pair of rubber gloves, Fuentes quickly went through the contents of the two bedrooms, coming up with a Walther PPK pistol along with a silencer in the overnight bag. These he pocketed, a glimmering of a plan already forming in his head.

In many respects, he felt like a puppet on a chain, his every move directed by Ortega-Cowan, a man he admired and respected and feared and loathed and perhaps even loved a little, all mixed together. But María's chief of staff was a devious son of a bitch who knew exactly what he was doing.

Yesterday, when it seemed likely that the *coronel* had skipped, he'd opened her office safe and discovered that the Ines Delgado identification papers, along with a fair sum of money and a credit card were missing. From there, he'd traced her military flight from Playa Baracoa to Camagüey, where she'd registered at the Hotel Plaza.

At first, the hotel had seemed to be a mistake on her part because it was right across the street from the train station, where a pair of local DI officers discovered that she had booked a train ticket to Santiago de Cuba under her real name. The obvious conclusion was that she was defecting and would try to reach the American base at Guantánamo Bay.

But casting the net a little wider, the agents discovered the Cubacar rental Hyundai in the Delgado name parked near the train station, and Ortega-Cowan had gone searching for airline reservations first from Camagüey and then Havana, coming up with the Delgado reservations for Mexico City.

"Arrest the bitch at the hotel," Fuentes had suggested. "We don't need anything else. Shoot her trying to escape, and we've already won."

"Not yet," Ortega-Cowan had said. "We don't know

why she's going to Mexico City, unless it's to meet with McGarvey or Rencke."

"What do we do, just let her go?"

"For now. But you're leaving for Mexico City this evening, so you'll be there before she does. I want you to organize a couple of teams at the airport to find out where she goes, and another team to watch for the Americans."

"I'll get help from a couple of El Comandante's friends on the AFI."

"Nothing hands on," Ortega-Cowan warned. "We need to keep this completely below the radar. Because of the attempt on her life that very nearly succeeded, and her father's recent death, the good *coronel* is working from seclusion for the time being. I merely want to know what the hell she's up to."

"What about the recording equipment at her house?"

"She switched it off."

"Then she knew that she would be leaving the country and she wanted to leave no trace."

Ortega-Cowan smiled patronizingly. "You'll make a very good chief of staff. But first we need to bring her down."

"Seems to me that she's doing a good job of her on her own," Fuentes said.

There was nothing else of interest in either bedroom, and five minutes after he'd entered the suite, he let himself out and went downstairs to his room, where he used his cell phone to place an encrypted call to Ortega-Cowan.

"Where are you at this moment?"

"In my room," Fuentes said. "But listen, I found a pistol and a silencer in their suite."

"I hope you took them."

"Of course."

"There's been a new development. The *coronel* did not check into the Four Seasons where she had reservations. Instead she came back to the airport about the same time McGarvey and Rencke were arriving from Atlanta."

"We didn't spot her anywhere near them," Fuentes said.

"I had a hunch and did a computer search of all flights leaving about that time—flights to anywhere. Ines Delgado flew out first class on an Aeromexico flight to Miami."

Fuentes's breath was all but taken away by the news. "The bitch is defecting after all."

"I don't think so. If she was, she would have gone to Washington not Miami. If she's recognized on the street, she won't last five minutes before someone puts a bullet in her brain."

"What then?"

"I don't know, but I want you to fly over tonight and take charge of DI operations on the ground. We need to know what she's doing."

"What do you want me to do about McGarvey and Rencke?"

"Where are they at this moment?" Ortega-Cowan asked.

"They were followed to the Palacio Nacional, evidently to meet someone there because they showed up at the north entrance, which at this hour is not usually for the public."

Ortega-Cowan was silent for a long moment.

"Román?" Fuentes prompted.

"Give me a minute, I'm on my computer."

A full minute passed before Ortega-Cowan was back. "It could be the Spanish gold after all," he said, and he almost sounded as if he were out of breath.

"What nonsense are you talking about? It's nothing but a fairy tale."

"Maybe not. Because in addition to the government, the Palacio Nacional is also home to Mexico's National Archives. The curator is Dr. José Diaz."

Fuentes was startled. "I think I know this name from El Comandante's journal. I think he was here in Mexico City with Uncle Fidel and Che and the others."

"And where would men such as McGarvey and Rencke go to find out about Spanish gold in the New World?"

"*Ay, Jesús,*" Fuentes said. "I'll go over there right now."

"I don't want you to interfere with McGarvey or Rencke. Wait until they leave, and then have a little chat with Dr. Diaz and find out what he told them."

By chance, McGarvey and Rencke were just climbing into a cab when Fuentes was paying his taxi driver and getting out, not more than two car lengths away. McGarvey glanced over his shoulder and their eyes met, but if there was any recognition in them, Fuentes couldn't see it. And moments later, they drove off.

Ortega-Cowan had sent a two-year-old photograph

to Fuentes's phone of Dr. Diaz taken from a *National Geographic* article on Aztec ruins, and as it began to get dark, he waited at the corner, where he had a good sight line of the Palacio's north exit. But the plaza across the street, and the sidewalk in front of the building were busy, and as it was, Diaz walked right past him before he recognized the archive's impeccably dressed curator.

Fuentes turned and started to follow the old man, but Diaz walked less than fifty feet to the bus stop. He was frail looking, not more substantial than a scarecrow, but he was carrying a bulging leather briefcase that had to weigh at least ten kilos.

When the bus came, Diaz boarded, told the driver he was going to San Esteban, paid his fare, and sat two rows back. Fuentes got on just ahead of eight or ten others in time to hear the doctor's destination, which he repeated to the driver, paid his fare, and found a seat a few rows farther back.

The small community on Highway 57, which was part of Mexico City's ring road, was located just beyond the Plaza de Toros, less than five miles as the crow flies from the Palacio, but with the heavy work traffic, it took nearly an hour to get there.

Diaz got off the bus with a dozen others and trudged a block and a half to a ten-story apartment building. Fuentes caught up with him just before the curator went inside. No one else was around.

"Dr. Diaz, I have come from El Comandante on a matter of some importance."

Diaz turned, startled, but he was interested. "He's dead."

"Yes, and I was with him when he passed. He asked me to give you an important piece of information. But it had to be done in person not over the telephone or Internet. Is there someplace nearby where we can talk in private?"

"My apartment upstairs."

"I think that the American CIA may have planted microphones sometime earlier today. It's why I'm here to warn you about an American by the name of Kirk McGarvey, who may have been traveling with a partner. You're not to talk to them under any circumstances."

"But they were in my office this afternoon," Diaz said. He was concerned.

"My God," Fuentes said. "We have to talk."

"Across the street, in the park," Diaz said.

It was very dark and the park, though small, had many trees and benches here and there along a meandering path. Fuentes chose a spot that was completely out of sight of the apartment building, and he and the doctor sat down.

"This information was very important to El Comandante. What was it those two men came to see you about?"

"May I see some identification?"

"Of course," Fuentes said, and he handed over his diplomatic passport, which Diaz had to hold up to a stray bit of streetlight filtering through the trees. "El Comandante warned me that the Americans would be looking for information about a treasure in Spanish gold buried somewhere in the U.S."

"That's exactly what they came to ask me about," Diaz said.

"What did you tell them?"

"That I couldn't help."

Fuentes relaxed a little. "Very good, Doctor. You did the right thing."

"You don't understand," Diaz said. "In truth I could not help, because I have no information." He handed the passport back. "What is the Cuban government's interest?"

"Some of that treasure belongs to us."

Diaz smiled. "Fidel had the same thought, and I told him before the revolution that he was dreaming. Spain would never entertain such a claim. At best, you would be tied up in an international court for years."

"Is that what you told the Americans?"

"I advised them that only a treasure hunter would have any possibility of convincing Spain to cooperate. In any event, none of that money would go to the Cuban government."

"I think that you are wrong."

Diaz smiled. "Old men often are."

Fuentes got up and walked a few paces away, where he took out McGarvey's pistol and screwed the silencer on the end of the barrel. He turned back as Diaz was getting to his feet, and shot the old man once in the forehead, killing him instantly.

Wiping the pistol down, he tossed it a few paces away into the bushes and walked through the park, where he found another exit, then went in search of a cab back into the city.

. . .

It was fairly late by the time Fuentes had the cabbie drop him off a couple of blocks from the hotel. He found a small café, where he sat at a sidewalk table, and after he had ordered a coffee, he phoned Ortega-Cowan and told him everything that had happened.

"It is about the gold after all."

"But Diaz said he told them nothing, because he knew nothing. We could still be chasing a fairy tale."

"Men such as McGarvey don't believe in fairy tales," Ortega-Cowan said. "You're flying to Miami tonight, but first I want you to make an anonymous call to the police and tell them that you saw a murder being committed. They'll find the pistol, and if they're in time, they might just delay McGarvey long enough for you to find out what the *coronel* is up to."

"If I find her, I think it would be best I kill her and we can get on with things."

"No," Ortega-Cowan said.

Fuentes had to laugh. "Don't tell me that you believe in fairy tales?"

"El Comandante did. And maybe this isn't such a fairy tale."

FORTY-FOUR

McGarvey had been feeling odd all afternoon, and especially after their talk with Dr. Diaz. And during a light dinner in the hotel's restaurant, Otto had commented on his mood, but he'd not been able to pinpoint any reason except that he was getting twitchy, as if someone were tailing them. Yet when he did a little tradecraft, double backs, feints—entering and immediately leaving buildings—or suddenly crossing against a light, he'd spotted nothing.

But looking in his overnight bag to see his pistol and silencer missing, he was not surprised that someone had traced them this far and had waited until they left the suite to get in and search it. It was a DI operation that obviously had help, possibly from the same Mexican federal cops who'd interviewed him at the airport.

It had been two hours since they left the Palacio, and suddenly this hotel was no longer safe for them, and he had a terrible feeling that Dr. Diaz was involved and that it had something to do with María León. He grabbed his bag and went out into the sitting room.

Otto was at the door to his bedroom. "Hey, I think somebody's been through my stuff."

"Get your things, we need to get out of here," McGarvey said. He opened the door and checked the corridor, which was empty at the moment. It had been dumb to leave his gun in plain sight, but he'd not wanted to create a problem by trying to get into the Palacio with it, so he took a chance that the DI wouldn't catch up with them so soon.

And now he was afraid that his mistake may have cost Dr. Diaz his life.

He and Otto took the elevator down to the hotel's mezzanine level and from there checked out the lobby, where it seemed to be business as usual for this time of the early evening, before taking the stairs down. A handful of people were scattered here and there, and a young couple with two children were at the front desk, but there were no police.

Outside, they headed on foot east on the Paseo de la Reforma, crossed the broad boulevard a block later, and recrossed a block after that, McGarvey reasonably sure that they had not been tailed from the hotel.

"Where are we going?" Otto finally asked.

"Seville, but first we need to get out of Mexico. Whoever got into our rooms took my gun and silencer."

"The DI?"

"That's my guess. But I think they probably have help from the Mexican cops."

"Do you think they traced us to Dr. Diaz?" Otto asked.

"Do you have his phone number?"

Otto got out his cell phone. "I'll try his office first," he said, but after a half a minute, he shook his head and pulled up another programmed number. "He lives in an apartment in San Esteban." But again there was no answer.

"Does he have a cell phone?"

"None that I found," Otto said. "Maybe he's out to dinner somewhere."

"I think he's been shot to death with my gun, and once it's found, probably close to the body, the AFI is going to take a real interest in me. We need to get out of the city and then the country. Let's start with a car."

"I'm on it," Otto said, and he brought up an online air/car/hotel reservations site.

A half block later, they took a table at a sidewalk café, and before their coffee came, Otto showed McGarvey the screen. "Dodge Avenger, Hertz. We pick it up at the airport, is that okay?"

"I don't think they'll expect us back out there, especially not at the arrivals terminal," McGarvey said. He saw that Otto had rented the car in the name of Richard Rank. "Separate passport?"

"Yup, but that's my real name. Richard O. Rank."

"I never knew."

"I got a couple secrets, kemo sabe," Otto said. "Anyway, if they're looking for you to show up, it might take them a while to start looking for me, too."

Their coffee came, and Otto went back to work on the Internet, coming up ten minutes later with a pair of first-class tickets from Miguel Hidalgo International Airport up in Guadalajara direct to Los Angeles. "Leaves at seven tomorrow morning, so we'll have to hole up somewhere 'cause it's less than two hundred fifty miles on a good divided highway."

"We'll chance a hotel up there," McGarvey said. "What airline?"

Otto had to laugh. "You're not going to believe this. We're booked on Alaska Air's 243."

"We're seriously going after a three-hundred-year-old

treasure that probably doesn't exist. So right about now, I'd believe almost anything."

Otto looked away for a moment. "I hear you, Mac. But what about afterwards? What about if we do find it?"

"I have a couple of ideas."

Otto went back online and after two minutes had hacked into the mainframes of the Protection and Transit Directorate, which was Mexico City's largest police force responsible for day-to-day crimes, including murder.

"Two shootings have been reported in San Esteban in the past hour, but there's nothing else except 'Officers en route.' "

"No victim IDs, or probable causes?"

"Drug related is always the first assumption here," Otto says. "But one of them could be Dr. Diaz, and they killed him because he talked to us, on Colonel León's orders."

But McGarvey wasn't all that sure it was her. He'd read something else into the crazy op she'd pulled getting him and Otto to Havana. Something between the lines, maybe something she'd said, or her attitude, or the fact that she allowed them to escape. It wasn't adding up, and he knew that he was missing something.

They cabbed it out to the airport, where Otto rented the car from Hertz, and once they were away, he pulled over and let McGarvey drive. By then, they were heading north on 15D, which was a modern four-lane highway—traffic moderately light—and before they got out of cell phone range, Otto had made reservations with Iberia Airlines for their flight to Spain using a credit card that Louise maintained under her maiden name of Horn.

"We'll get to L.A. tomorrow morning about nine thirty, which gives us a little more than an hour to catch the Continental flight to Newark, and from there Barcelona and finally Seville at five on Monday afternoon."

"Long flight," McGarvey said absently, his mind still on María León.

"First class, so maybe we can get some rest. I know I need it, 'cause I expect that there's a whole lot more coming our way."

McGarvey glanced over at his friend, and an almost overwhelming sense of loneliness for his wife came over him. But then he shrugged. "Always is."

FORTY-FIVE

The Miami River Inn was a funky little Caribbean-style hotel right on the river at the edge of the Little Havana district, and by midnight, the evening was still warm and tropically humid, almost the same as in Havana. Only it was noisier here than at home, and María, alone at the pool, was amazed by the contrast.

She had arrived from Mexico City yesterday, and found this hotel listed in a rack of tourist brochures at the airport that described everything that there was to see and do by day or night in Coral Gables, Miami Beach, and Miami proper—including the neighborhood around the Calle Ocho, which was home to thousands of Cubans. Exiles, they called themselves, but in María's mind they were defectors and traitors.

On the way here, she'd had the cabbie stop at a liquor store, where she'd picked up a couple bottles of Chilean merlot, which she was sipping now, an extra glass on the table beside her. The city was alive with street noises, cars honking, buses and trucks rumbling by, a baby crying somewhere, and in the distance in the general direction of Biscayne Bay, she'd heard what she thought was gunfire. Several shots, then nothing but the city's background noise except until a couple of minutes later a siren and then others in the same general direction.

But the hotel itself, which looked nothing like the pictures in the brochure, was quiet for a Sunday night, in part she suspected because it was summer and the off season. But it was fine with her. Her room was pleasant, the staff at the desk friendly, the pool nice, and the peace good after the past few hectic days.

A perfect getaway, she thought, except she figured that sooner or later she would be recognized and someone would come to kill her. All she had to count on was the likelihood her assassin would be curious and want to know why she had come to Miami.

She was wearing jeans and a light blouse, her sandals off, and she was sitting back on a chaise lounge when something made her look to the right, where a figure stood in the deeper shadows by one of the cottages. Her hand shook for just an instant.

She raised her wineglass. "Won't you join me?" she asked.

A slender man with fine dark hair and a thin mustache, dressed in jeans and a dark short-sleeve pullover, stepped out of the shadows. He was pointing a pistol in her general direction.

When she was able to see his face, she recognized him as the de facto chief of the Cuban dissident community's unofficial intelligence service, and one of the DI's highest-value targets. "Señor Martínez, it's about time you finally showed up," she said. "I didn't know if you liked red wine, but I brought a second glass from my room. Unless you mean to shoot me first."

"Kirk was right. You do have *cojones*."

María was surprised. "It was you who came ashore with McGarvey. And it was you who directed the attack on my house."

"I'm sincerely sorry that you were not at home, *Señora Coronel*."

María's anger flared. "Had I been, the outcome would not have been quite so certain for you."

Martínez chuckled.

"Most of my house staff were gone."

"They were never our targets."

María believed him, and she nodded. "Thank you for that much."

"We are at war with the government, not the people."

"The people are the government—," María said, but it sounded foolish even her ears.

"Spare me."

María shrugged.

"What are you doing here? And give me one good

reason why I shouldn't put a bullet between your eyes."

"I don't know if you'll believe me, but I'll give you two good reasons. Kirk McGarvey and Spanish gold. You wouldn't care about the third."

Martínez stood ten feet away, staring at her. "Are you armed?"

"No. I was on the run through Mexico City, and in the limited time I had, it would have been too difficult to get a weapon through." She nodded toward the wine bottle. "But I suppose if you got close enough and let your guard down, I might beat you to death."

"Stand up."

She put her glass down and stood up, her arms slightly away from her sides, and slowly turned around, until she was facing him again. "No place for me a hide a weapon. Unless you want me to strip so you can make sure."

"The thought is there," Martínez said. "You do it to our people in Quivicán and elsewhere. Full cavity searches, rubber hoses, broomsticks, electric shocks, ice water baths."

"You didn't mention waterboarding," María said. "But then, that's your interrogators' methods."

Martínez nodded. "Sit down, I'll be right back," he said, and he turned and disappeared into the shadows.

María sat down and picked up her glass. She'd made it over the first hurdle, getting this far without being shot to death, but the next part—convincing Martínez and especially McGarvey and Rencke that she was sincere—would be even harder.

She was playing a dangerous game, not so much of

cat and mouse but of balancing a fine line between the complete truth—which would end up with her immediate execution—and a partial truth, enough so that she would come across as credible.

Martínez was back almost immediately, his pistol holstered, and he came across to her, pulled a chair over, and sat down a few feet away. "I have people just outside to make sure that we are not disturbed."

"You're keeping me safe until you find out why I took the risk of coming here."

"Something like that."

"Safe from whom? The DI or your Cuban traitors?"

An expression came across Martínez's face that María couldn't quite read. Interest, perhaps, or maybe puzzlement.

"Are you trying to tell me that you're attempting to defect?"

"No, it won't be that easy. Not for you, not for me, and especially not for Kirk McGarvey and the CIA."

"I'm listening," Martínez said.

"How much have he and Rencke told you about what we discussed at my house, and the reasons I had them brought to Cuba?"

"I'm listening," Martínez repeated.

FORTY-SIX

At the corner of SW Eighth Street, known locally as Calle Ocho, and Twenty-sixth Avenue SW, which turned into a one-way heading east, Fuentes sat in the backseat of an older Chevrolet van with DI operatives Eddie Hernández next to him and Abelando Parilla at the wheel.

"She's here, but we're not sure exactly where she disappeared," Hernández said.

Fuentes was angry. "You saw her passing through customs yesterday but then you lost her? And twenty-four hours later, you're no closer to finding out where she is hiding?"

"There was a problem with traffic at the airport," Parilla said. "We were blocked by a bus and a couple of taxis. By the time we managed to get out of there, she was gone. So we thought it best if we came back to wait for you. And as you have seen, it's almost impossible to get any cooperation out of these people. Every one we manage to turn ends up dead in a day or so, and the ones who say they're helping us can't be trusted."

"Damned sloppy," Fuentes said, fuming. They looked and sounded more like Americans than trained DI officers, and he made a note to have Ortega-Cowan recall them for retraining before they got their heads blown off.

At this time of the night, the streets were busy. This was practically the heart of what the Cuban defectors and traitors who lived here called Little Havana, and all the shops and coffeehouses where men were playing dominoes at sidewalk tables looked very much like what the real Havana looked like. Except that it was busier here—louder, more traffic, newer cars, bustling. And he could almost let himself feel the excitement.

"We have informants looking for her," Hernández said. "Believe me, Captain, if she is anywhere here in the city, we'll find her sooner or later. But if in fact she is trying to defect, as you say, she's probably already on her way to Washington."

"How? According to you she hasn't shown up back at the airport."

"She may have rented a car and driven to the airport at Fort Lauderdale. It's only a half hour, depending on traffic, from here. And from there Washington."

"Do you have people up there?"

"We're stretched thin," Hernández said. "We don't have the manpower to spare."

"If she's still here as you think she is, she's probably lying shot to death in some alley somewhere," Parilla said. "Or perhaps her body was tossed into the Miami River with all the other trash. We'll find her."

"Give me a pistol and silencer—I'll find her myself."

"Not such a good idea, Captain. You won't get two blocks without someone taking an interest."

"I hope it takes only one block."

Parilla gave him a Soviet-made 9 mm Stechkin pistol with a twenty-round magazine and a silencer. It was an old but reliable weapon that in the right hands at medium range was lethal. He checked the load, screwed the silencer on the barrel, and stuffed the pistol in his belt under his shirt.

"What do you want us to do?" Hernández asked.

"Stand by someplace close—I may need to be picked up soon," Fuentes said, and he got out of the car and walked away to the west, deeper into the district.

He was dressed much the same as most of the other men here: slacks, an embroidered guayabera shirt, and leather sandals. He put a little swish into his walk. In the past, he'd learned that if he acted openly gay, most men, not just Hispanics, would underestimate him. It gave him an advantage at the start.

A block later, he figured that he had picked up a tail—two men, both of them as lean and fit-looking as soccer players—and at SW Twenty-seventh, he headed south, picking up the pace. After a couple of blocks he turned again, this time on Eleventh, a much quieter neighborhood of apartment buildings and a few shops, closed for the night.

A dog was barking on someone's balcony near the corner as Fuentes ducked into the deeper shadows of the entrance to a men's clothing shop, roll-down iron security grates covering the windows and doors.

Seconds later, the two men came running, and when they had passed, Fuentes stepped out. "Back here, sweethearts," he said.

They pulled up short and turned around. "A fucking *invertido*," one of them said, and the other laughed.

"You boys want some action?" Fuentes asked sweetly, and he stepped back into the doorway and pulled out the pistol, thumbing off the safety catch.

The first showed up in the doorway, and Fuentes grabbed him by the shirt so that he wouldn't fall backwards and shot him in the forehead at point-blank range, pulling him forward. He crumpled in a heap, dead before he hit the ground.

The second had just enough time to react and start to reach for something at the small of his back when Fuentes showed himself and pointed the Stechkin at the man's face.

There was traffic passing a block away on Eleventh, but for the moment, everything was quiet down here.

"I need information," Fuentes said. "If you lie to me, I will kill you without hesitation. If you tell me the truth, I'll wound you but let you live."

The man shrugged, almost indifferently. "What do you want?"

"Colonel León showed up here yesterday, but I lost her. Where is she at this moment?"

The man started to say something, but Fuentes stepped forward and placed the muzzle of the silencer directly on his forehead.

"Where is she?"

"I don't know, but it doesn't matter anyway."

Fuentes lowered his pistol, as if he had changed his mind, but then shot the man in the right kneecap, knocking him to his left knee with a grunt.

"*Bastardo!*"

"Where is she?"

"Miami River Inn."

"Here in Little Havana?"

"*Sí,* but if the *hija de puta* isn't dead already, she soon will be."

Fuentes grinned. "At least as far as she's concerned,

we're on the same side," he said. "And you're right about me being gay, but I never much liked the word *invertido*. It's vulgar."

The man started to say something, but Fuentes shot him in the top of his head just at his hairline, and blood gushed out of his eyes as he fell over.

The street remained quiet, and Fuentes stuffed the pistol back in his belt, stepped out of the doorway, and as he headed down the street, called his DI operatives to come pick him up.

FORTY-SEVEN

Martínez sat listening to María León with a mixture of incredulity bordering at times on disbelief, and outright disgust. As chief of the DI's Directorate of Operations, she had personally signed extrajudicial death warrants for dozens if not hundreds of Cuban dissidents—traitors, as she called them.

She had directed operations here in Little Havana and up in New York through the UN and in Washington that had resulted in more incidents of torture and death. It was under her direction that Otto's wife, Louise, had been kidnapped, during which an innocent day care teacher had been shot dead.

And it was because of her that Martínez had become involved in a gun battle to free Mac and Otto, losing some good people in the operation.

Yet she had left Havana and come here, of all places, where she was on every Cuban exile's hit list, and had simply checked into a hotel and waited for someone to come for her.

"Assuming you're telling the truth, and you left Cuba to find some Spanish treasure, which even by your own admission probably doesn't exist, or if it does would be unreachable, it's impossible for me to accept that as a reason for you coming here to Miami."

"Nevertheless, here I am, and you'll have to do something about it before my presence touches off a riot."

"I think I'd find it easier to believe if you told me that you were defecting."

María sat forward. "You know the situation right now in Cuba. Since my father's death, no one knows what's coming next. The government is nearly in a shambles, and every other bureaucrat or functionary in just about every department, including the DI, is positioning themselves to make the deal of a lifetime. And without my father's protection, I'm vulnerable."

"According to you, it's why you went to the trouble of getting McGarvey to Havana, some deathbed wish of your father's. Mac told me all about it. But it still doesn't explain why you came here. Why not Washington?"

"I need your help."

"Me specifically?"

"If I'm right, someone from my directorate will trace me here, and probably send someone to kill me."

"Does the name Manuel Fuentes mean anything?" Martínez asked, and he watched for her reaction.

Her left eyebrow rose slightly. "He was chief of my

father's security detail. And he was the one who killed the spy inside the compound."

Martínez had thought as much, but hearing it from the head of the Operations Directorate made him want to take out his pistol and put a bullet between her eyes. He steadied himself. "He's already here, and we're keeping an eye on him."

"Is there any chance he'll find me?"

"He's probably dead by now, but even if he were to get this far, I have two very good people just outside."

"His coming here proves that at least something of what I've told you is the truth," María said.

"Okay, I'll buy that much that someone in the DI is after your scalp, but it still doesn't explain why you left Cuba. Raúl is your uncle, and I would have thought that you'd be in a better position to defend yourself by staying put. Maybe even pushing back."

"I need proof."

"Of what—?" Martínez asked, but then it came to him all of a sudden. "You found something after Mac and Otto were gone. That's why you left your house that night."

"I went back to my father's compound and looked through his personal files and journals. There is Spanish gold buried somewhere in New Mexico, and the proof is in Mexico City or maybe in Rome at the Vatican or in Spain."

"You were in Mexico City?"

"I had no way of protecting myself there, so I came here, hoping to convince you to help."

"Ave María," Martínez said softly. "Did you manage to bring any of the files or his journals out with you?"

"All the journals, dating back to Mexico City, before the *revolución*."

"You have them here?"

"*Sí*," María said. She reached for her bag.

Martínez pulled out his pistol, instantly hyperalert. "Take anything other than a book or a file out of your bag, and I will shoot you."

"I'll keep that in mind," María said, and she very carefully took the first of her father's journals out. "This is his writing from Mexico City, when he was with Che and the Russians, along with an historian by the name of José Diaz who knew about the Spanish gold."

Martínez laid the pistol on his lap and took the notebook. "You have all of them?"

"Yes. He made the last entry days before he died."

Martínez felt as if he couldn't catch his breath. Having Fidel's journal in his hands was akin to a Jew holding something written by Adolf Hitler. Monstrous, was all he could think for just a moment. And he understood that once he opened the journal and began to read, everything he thought he knew would be indelibly stained for everyone to see. There would be no going back once he looked into the mind of someone he'd always believed was a madman, an evil man, because even such men had inner thoughts and hopes and desires that sometimes were very much like any man's.

María read something of that from his expression. "He was one of the people at first. Before the Communists got to him."

Martínez nodded. "Makes what happened to Cuba all the more tragic."

And María agreed with him. "Absolute power corrupts absolutely. It got beyond his control."

"*Macbeth.*"

"Actually, Lord Acton," María said. "I may have been a Communist from a poor country, but it doesn't mean I wasn't educated."

For the first time in his memory, Martínez didn't know what to do. Common sense told him that María León was an enemy to the Cuban people, and she deserved to die here and now. And yet something she hadn't said was deeply troubling to him. If she were dead, he would never know what it was.

"Even if your government had a legitimate claim on some of the treasure, you can't possibly believe that Washington would send a shipload of it to Havana. You're educated, as you say, but are you stupid?"

"Not for the government," replied María.

Martínez wanted to be angry, but again there was that something about her manner, about what she was saying, and the very fact of her presence here that was troublesome. "Save me the promise that the gold would be given to the people. Even if you wanted something like that, it would never happen."

"Not without Kirk McGarvey's help."

"Tell me what you have in mind."

FORTY-EIGHT

The Chevy van drove past the Miami River Inn, and a half block later, Fuentes ordered Parilla to turn down a narrow side street lined with tiny houses and cottages, most of them painted in funky bright colors, stopping at the water's edge less than fifty yards off South River Drive.

A few lights were on back here, and there was some boat traffic on the river, but the tall condos, office buildings, and hotels on the other side dominated the night skyline. A man could get lost over there, Fuentes thought. Anonymous. But it would take money.

"Most likely she has someone with her," he said. "I'll go in first to make sure."

"It'll be Raúl Martínez," Hernández said.

"I know about him."

"Watch yourself, he's a slippery bastard and for something like this operation, he'll have backup muscle somewhere close."

"Turn the van around and be ready to leave on a moment's notice."

"Do you want one of us to come with you?" Hernández asked.

"It's not necessary. But I may be bringing Colonel León with me. Is there someplace secure we can take her?"

"Back to the motel in Hialeah, where you stayed last night. We own it."

The place was a dump, but far enough from Little

Havana to be reasonably safe. "Good enough," Fuentes said.

He got out, went past the last house, took four stairs down to the walk that paralleled the river and gave access to boats tied up alongside the seawall, and headed back about one hundred meters to the hotel property bounded by a tall wooden fence. All his senses were alert for the presence of anyone, and he held his pistol, the silencer still in place, the safety catch off, at his side.

He'd expected that the Cuban traitors would send someone after him, which they had, just as he expected that Martínez would cover his back while he was somewhere inside interviewing the *coronel;* the bastard had the reputation of being very thorough. Not once had any DI operator here in Miami gotten close enough to take a shot with any reasonable expectations of making good an escape. On more than one occasion, Ortega-Cowan had suggested a suicide mission be mounted. A bomb in a café, a drive-by shooting, a poison dart fired from a dark alley. The assassin would pay with their life, but he suspected that any number of young, loyal officers would agree to do the job if they were given assurances that afterwards their families would be well taken care of. But each time, the *coronel* had denied her chief of staff's sensible request.

"We don't know who would replace him," she'd said. "Better the enemy we know than the one we don't."

Fuentes had shared his suspicion with Ortega-Cowan that their DI Miami operatives were inept.

"Hand-picked by the *coronel.*"

"My point exactly," Fuentes had said.

A large cabin cruiser, its salon lights ablaze, loud

music with heavy thumping bass booming across the river, passed by as Fuentes reached the hotel fence and held up in the corner. A man stepped out of the shadows less than ten meters away and watched the boat.

Just behind the fence was a swimming pool, Fuentes could smell the chlorine, but the man was dressed in street clothes, not a swimming suit. And he'd been standing in the shadows, waiting for someone.

Fuentes raised his pistol and walked directly toward the man, who at the last moment sensing someone was approaching started to turn, but it was far too late. Fuentes shot him in the side of the head and he went down with only a grunt; that and the sound of the silenced pistol shot were completely drowned out by the fading noise coming from the cabin cruiser.

The one watchdog back here, if that's what he was, and almost certainly another in front. Still holding his pistol in case someone was coming to investigate, Fuentes searched the body with his left hand, finding a 9 mm Beretta pistol favored by the dissidents because it was standard issue in the U.S. military and easy to come by—almost certainly supplied by the CIA.

He tossed the pistol into the river and went to the rear gate and looked through the gap, and nearly stepped away by instinct.

Raúl Martínez, seated on a chair at the pool, not ten meters away, a cell phone to his ear, was looking directly at the gate. But Fuentes steadied himself, because there was no way the *hijo de puta* could see anything, nor could he have heard anything over the noise the cabin cruiser had made.

But more surprising was María León seated on a

chaise lounge next to him, sipping what looked like red wine as calmly as if she had rendezvoused with a lover or an old friend. The two of them were definitely not antagonists. Made her a traitor after all, just as he had suspected all along.

After a moment, Martínez turned back and the night became still enough for Fuentes to hear what he was saying.

"It was nothing," he spoke into the phone. "What were they doing in Mexico City?"

Martínez could have been talking about anyone, but whoever it was had surprised María and she put down her wineglass.

"Are you talking to McGarvey?" she asked.

"Just a minute," Martínez said into the phone. "This is Louise Horn, Otto Rencke's wife. Mac and Otto were checking out something in Mexico City, but they're on the run from the police now. You father's historian, José Diaz, was shot to death apparently with McGarvey's gun, which he brought into the county on an Air Marshal permit."

"It's the DI," María said.

Martínez turned back to the phone. "Are they heading back to Washington?"

This time it was Martínez's turn to be surprised; Fuentes could hear it in his voice. "What are they looking for in Seville?"

María was watching him closely, but he was quiet for a very long time, until finally he nodded, apparently coming to a decision.

"Colonel León is here in Miami. In fact, I'm with her right now, and she's told me this story about Catholic monks from Mexico City hiding what could amount to billions of dollars in Spanish gold somewhere in southern New Mexico. It's the same thing she told Mac and Otto in Havana, and it sounds like they're taking it seriously and so is the DI, because one of her people has followed her here."

Fuentes was astounded. Fidel had been searching for Cíbola or something like it for most of his life without success, and now his daughter with the help of the CIA was on to it.

"I need to get her out of Little Havana, I can't guarantee her safety here. We have DI operatives running all over the place, and probably even a good number of exiles who are plants. I don't know for sure who I can trust with something this big."

Fuentes was torn between killing them both right now or waiting to find out as much as he could about the treasure. Bringing something like that back to Havana—something he was now sure that had been the *coronel*'s plan all along—would guarantee him her job, completely sidestepping Ortega-Cowan. And with that leap under his belt, he could think of many other possibilities from a more-than-grateful Raúl. With his success here and his command of the language, maybe even Minister of Foreign Relations after all.

"I want to put her in a safe house until Mac gets back. She says that she has a plan, or at least the start of one, that she wants to talk to him about. She wants some of the gold for the Cuban people, not the government."

Fuentes almost laughed out loud. The *coronel* was an ambitious woman—every bit as ruthless as her father had been. The two of them had been cut of the same cloth. The Cuban people indeed.

"I agree," Martínez said. "Send a plane for us, I don't want to risk flying commercial." He suddenly turned around and looked directly at the gate.

Fuentes stepped back, his grip tightening on the Stechkin.

"I'll call you right back," Martínez said. He pocketed his phone and got to his feet, a pistol in his hand. "Roberto?"

Fuentes wanted to kill both of them outright, but knew that he would have to allow the *coronel* to reach the safe house, probably somewhere close to CIA headquarters. Even with the might of the entire DI, he didn't think that he would be able to find the treasure faster than her and McGarvey. But if he let them do the work, he could step in at the last minute, eliminate them, and take the credit.

He headed away from the gate and had just reached the stairs when someone came running behind him. Firing two shots over his shoulder, he made it up to the street and the van parked a couple of meters away.

The side door was open and he clambered aboard just as they took two shots, starring the rear window.

"Move it!" Fuentes shouted, and he snapped off three shots at a figure just at the top of the stairs, his aim spoiled as the van suddenly accelerated.

They took two more hits in the rear, but then they were turning onto South River Drive and heading away from the hotel.

Hernández was slumped forward against the back

of the front passenger seat, blood soaking his neck and shirt.

"What happened, Captain?" Parilla demanded. He sounded shook up.

"I found out what I needed to find out. Have you been hit?"

"No. What about Eddie?"

"He managed to get himself shot to death by an *hijo de puta*," Fuentes said. "We need to dump his body somewhere and then get back up to Hialeah and make this van disappear. I'm sending you home."

"I'm sorry, Captain," Parilla said.

"Don't worry, you did nothing wrong. You're just getting out of Miami for your own good."

"Eddie and I were friends."

"I understand," Fuentes said. But the stupid bastard was dead because of his gross ineptitude, and Parilla would almost certainly not like the firing squad he would face for his own failures over the past twenty-four hours.

FORTY-NINE

Getting out of Mexico through Guadalajara had gone without a hitch, and while they'd waited in Los Angeles for their flight, Otto took another quick look at the Mexico City police network, but the murder of Dr. Diaz still hadn't shown up, which puzzled McGarvey all the way across the Atlantic. It was a loose end, something that usually signaled trouble was coming their way, and Otto agreed.

The Iberia Airlines flight touched down at Seville's San Pablo Airport a few minutes after five, Monday afternoon. They'd already cleared passport control and customs in Madrid, so they were simply able to walk off the airplane and pass through the arrivals hall and baggage claim area to the waiting cabs.

Otto had made reservations for them at the Hotel Alfonso XIII, less than four hundred yards as the crow flies from the ancient Seville Cathedral with its bell tower that had been converted from a minaret in the thirteenth century and across the street from the building that housed the Archives, closed at this hour until ten in the morning.

He had not bothered using the onboard Wi-Fi service on the flight over, because it was too insecure, but even before their cab for the city had pulled away from the curb, he'd powered up his encrypted Nokia, where he found four messages from Louise, each asking him to call back. Urgent.

"Something up?" McGarvey asked.

"Louise wants me," Otto said, and called her work number at the CIA. She answered on the first ring. "Me," he said.

The cabbie, a younger man with long hair tied in a ponytail, looked at them in the rearview mirror.

"He's right here," Otto said, and he handed the phone to McGarvey.

"Are you someplace where you can talk?" Louise asked.

"In a cab heading into the city."

"Okay, careful with what you say for now. You can call back later. There've been some developments. Colonel León was in Mexico City about the same time you and Otto were there. But she showed up in Miami late Saturday night, booked a room at a small hotel right on the edge of Little Havana. No one was expecting her, so Raúl didn't get to her until last night."

It was a surprise to McGarvey, and yet it wasn't, because leaving Cuba, he was sure that they hadn't heard the last of her. "What did she want?"

"To talk to you about the gold. She told Raúl that she has a plan to give it to the people and keep it out of the hands of the government."

"I'll bet she does."

"But there's a lot more," Louise said. "A DI captain by the name of Manuel Fuentes showed up in Miami, killed a couple of Raúl's people who were following him, and somehow found out where María was staying. He managed to take out another of Raúl's soldiers before he was burned. But instead of sticking around to fight it out, he turned tail and took off."

"Could be he and María are pals," McGarvey suggested.

"Not according to her. Raúl wants to stash her someplace up here until you and Otto get back. But he thinks there is a possibility that Fuentes may have overheard some of the conversation that he had with the colonel, and possibly part of a cell phone call he had with me."

"Where's Audie?"

"Still at the Farm. I thought it was for the best until things settle down a bit."

"Keep her there."

"What do you want to do about Raúl and the woman? I'm still holed up at the brownstone. They could come here."

"I don't know if that's such a good idea, but I don't think she'd try anything. What about you, after everything?"

"I can handle her."

"I'll have Otto make that call," McGarvey said. "Just take care of yourself, okay?"

"Will do."

McGarvey handed the phone to Otto and sat back in his seat. That María got out of Cuba and showed up in Mexico City was no real surprise; he had gotten from her that her position in Havana was tenuous at best. But she had taken a very large chance going to Miami. Any number of Cuban expats would love to take someone like her down, and Little Havana had always been a hotbed for DI operations, whose operatives would be gunning for her if she'd defected.

The problem was Captain Fuentes, who was sharp enough to make his way to Little Havana, take out three of Martínez's people, and get presumably within shooting range of María and yet he hadn't taken the shot. It was almost as if the DI operative had managed all of that simply to get close enough to overhear a conversation. But at this moment, with what information McGarvey had to go on, the situation made no sense.

"We're going to play tourists down here and probably up in Madrid for at least a week," Otto said. "Should be home by Sunday, I think."

McGarvey caught the cabdriver glancing in the rear-view mirror again. Otto had evidently realized that the man was interested in what they were saying.

"We'll check in, have some dinner, and get a good night's sleep. Take care, sweetheart. And say hi to our guests for me when they arrive."

The Hotel Alfonso XIII looked like a Moor's dream of a palace of ornate brick arches surrounding a central patio, marble floors, wood-panel ceilings, stained glass, and ceramic tiles—and according to Otto, lots of well-heeled tourists. This was the place in Seville to see and be seen and it was outrageously expensive.

They got connecting suites, ordered up a bottle of fino, the very good local sherry, and while they waited for it to arrive, Otto got back on the Internet, checking first with the Mexican Police and then with Interpol, but still there was nothing about the murder of Dr. Diaz, nor had their names come up as persons of interest.

"Maybe the AFI isn't that sharp," Otto suggested.

McGarvey disagreed. "I registered the gun's serial number on my Air Marshal international entry permit. And when I didn't show up for the return flight, the connection would have become obvious."

"Maybe Dr. Diaz wasn't one of the victims at San Esteban, and maybe whoever took your pistol still has it. Could have been one of the hotel staff, maybe a maid who took it and sold it on the black market."

"You may be right," McGarvey said. But it had been

sloppy on his part, though if it was a pro who'd gotten into his room, hiding the pistol wouldn't have done much good.

"But you don't think so."

"The DI is popping up all over the place."

"They followed the colonel to Miami—do you think they could have followed us here?"

"I think it's a possibility we have to consider," McGarvey said. "And so do you, the way you talked so the cabbie could hear you."

"I guess some of your tradecraft is starting to rub off on me."

"Makes you wonder if we were expected," McGarvey said.

"It'd have to be as an old boy favor, a phone call friend-to-friend, 'cause it's not on the Internet."

"From Mexican Police?"

"And the Cubans. Ever since '07, when Spain and Cuba started talking to each other, their security forces share info. Right now, Spain is Cuba's third-largest trading partner. I'm sure their cops talk to each other."

McGarvey had figured as much. "I'm going down to the concierge to rent a car for one week, with a drop-off in Madrid—we might have to get out of here in a hurry. In the meantime, if we're going to present ourselves as treasure hunters tomorrow, I want you to set up a corporate presence on the Internet. Offices somewhere outside the Beltway."

Otto brightened up. "I set it up before we went to Mexico City," he said. He'd always loved a challenge, even a small one. "The company is Treasure Recovery Specialists, LLC."

"Good. Call Louise back and have her arrange a CIA jet for us first thing in the morning."

"Madrid?"

"No, Gibraltar."

The car was a VW Jetta, which they left in parking lot a half block from the Archives; the morning cool, not a cloud in the sky. It was a Tuesday and the Barrio de Santa Cruz was busy, some of its twisty streets and narrow alleys that had once been the Jewish Quarter were alive with tourists shopping in antiques and souvenir stores, while most were residential and quiet.

McGarvey and Otto made their roundabout way to the museum to make sure that they were not being followed, but no one seemed to be taking any interest in them.

But at the Archives, when they presented themselves to a young woman at the information counter just inside the public entrance, it was a different story.

"Señores McGarvey and Rencke, finally," the pretty dark-haired girl said brightly. "Dr. Vergílio has been expecting you, but we just didn't know when." She made a phone call.

McGarvey was surprised, but he didn't let it show. Adriana Vergílio was the director of the Archives. Otto had looked her up on the Internet. She had spent years in the field as an archeologist in Mexico and the Southwestern United States, researching Spain's early presence in the region. She was considered a leading expert in the field, and eight years ago had naturally taken this position when it was offered.

A young man escorted them upstairs to a second-floor suite of book-lined offices with windows that looked down on a beautiful central courtyard. An extremely short, slightly built older woman, salt-and-pepper hair up in a bun, the skin of her arms and face brown and leathery from too much time in the sun, stood up from behind her desk when they were ushered in. She was smiling more with curiosity, it seemed, than pleasure to see them.

"Good morning, gentlemen," she said, motioning for them to sit down. "Dr. Diaz spoke highly of you, suggesting that we might have a beneficial mutual interest." Her English was good if a little flowery.

Diaz had told them that because of a past indiscretion here, he was all but persona non grata. "And he spoke highly of you, Doctor," McGarvey said. "Did you work with him during your time in Mexico?"

"Yes, we were very close."

"Then you know why we came to visit the Archives?" Otto asked.

"Yes, of course. You're treasure hunters."

"Jornada del Muerto," Otto said. "Two military expeditions were sent to what is now New Mexico, one in the late 1700s, the other in 1836."

"Actually the first was in 1787, under the orders of King Charles III; and the second began in 1835, under the orders of Queen Isabella. The records of the first are scanty because the soldiers never returned. All that remains are copies of their orders, and lists of their personnel, equipment, and provisions, their intended route. But two men from the 1835 trip did make it back: one of them a private, the other a sergeant."

"They brought back the expedition's maps and journals," Otto said. "You have them here?"

"Yes."

"What were they looking for?" McGarvey asked.

Dr. Vergílio smiled faintly. "Why, the same as you. Gold and silver. Hundreds of metric tonnes of it, extremely valuable in itself if it were to be melted down, but of inestimable worth as objects of history. Museums across the world, including ours, would pay just about anything to get their hands on even a part of it."

"But that's not the real issue," McGarvey said. "The gold belongs to Spain."

"Of course."

"But the Catholic Church, whose monks buried it, might consider they, too, had a claim."

"They stole the gold," Dr. Vergílio said sharply.

"As the Spaniards did from the natives all across Central America and the Caribbean."

"But there are no organizations that represent those people."

"The Church might want to take you to court if the treasure were to be found and recovered," McGarvey said. "And so might Cuba," he added, looking for a reaction.

She pursed her lips slightly, and nodded. "They might try. But I doubt they would get far."

"But we're ahead of ourselves," Otto said. "First we need to find the treasure."

"For which you have an idea you think has merit—otherwise, you would not have come this far to see me."

"It's in New Mexico, most likely on White Sands

Missile Range, maybe some of it even as far north as Trinity, the site of the first atomic bomb test."

"You're talking about the Seven Cities of Gold codices supposedly found in the desert. And subsequently lost there."

"We think that the gold removed from Victorio Peak on Holloman Air Force Base was only one of seven caches."

"Your company has access to the Missile Range?"

"We have a limited-time permit," McGarvey said.

Dr. Vergílio started to say something, but then she sat back. "What do you want from me?"

"The records from the two military expeditions," Otto said.

"And then what?"

"We find the gold."

"I meant after that."

"To begin with, we would naturally have a claim," Otto said. "Along with Spain's. After that, your government might be tied up in the courts."

"As you and your company would certainly be," Dr. Vergílio said. "Unless we had first come to an agreement. And we certainly would not consider allowing you to keep half, considering the legal embroglio we would likely find ourselves in."

"One third would be fair," Otto said. "We, too, would face property rights problems with the state of New Mexico and certainly with our federal government."

"Your field work would have to be kept out of the media. Too many complications."

"Of course," Otto said.

Dr. Vergílio handed a five-page document held together with a red ribbon across the desk to McGarvey. "This is an Archives standard finder's agreement in English," she said. "If you sign it, you will be given copies of the expeditions' documents, including the maps and journals."

This was all wrong. In reality, they could have been given permission to view the records and take all the notes they wanted, or ask for copies. Neither the Spanish government nor the Archives would have offered such a document. In fact, no action would have been taken until after a treasure had been found and it origins verified, in which case, there would have been protests, some through diplomatic channels, and finally a court case.

Otto was about to say something, but McGarvey cut him off. "Of course," he said. He untied the document, took a pen from a holder on the director's desk and signed and dated the last page.

"Are you going to read it?" she asked.

"No need, Doctor," he said, handing it back "If we were going to cheat each other, this wouldn't make much difference."

"That's what I told . . . Dr. Diaz. But he suggested this would be for the best."

They got up and went into the anteroom, where the same young man who had escorted them from the lobby was there with a thick accordion file folder, held shut with a brown string.

"I've included a copy of the agreement signed by me," Dr. Vergílio said. "If you have any questions, please call me. And I'd like very much to hear of your progress."

"Naturally," McGarvey said, and he and Otto started to leave, but McGarvey turned back. "When did you and Dr. Diaz speak about us?"

"Yesterday," she said. "Actually last night. Because of the time difference, he reached me at my home."

"It must have been a fascinating conversation," Otto said.

"Oh, it was," Dr. Vergílio said. "Good hunting, gentlemen."

"What was that all about?" Otto asked when they reached the car and headed south out of the city on the A4.

"She sure as hell didn't talk to Dr. Diaz," McGarvey said. "We've been set up."

"By who?"

"I don't know yet. But a few billion dollars or more makes for some strange bedfellows."

"You knew it was coming. That's why we're leaving from Gibraltar and not Madrid."

"I want to get out of Spain without complications."

"Do you think the colonel knows what's going on?"

"I think we should ask her."

Two hours later, they parked the car on the busy street in front of the condo towers right on the bay in the town of La Línea, within fifty yards of the border crossing to Gibraltar.

"Were we followed?" Otto asked as they got out.

"Not unless the Guardia Civil is a lot better than I

think they are," McGarvey said, and carrying only the file folder, they walked to the line at the pedestrian crossing and when it was their turn they showed their passports to the bored officer on the Spanish side and were allowed to pass through the building to the British side.

A Brit in civilian clothes was waiting for them. "Welcome to Gibraltar, gentlemen," she said. "Your aircraft arrived early this morning, I'll take you there."

FIFTY

The CIA jet was an older Gulfstream IV, this one on loan from VR-48, the Marine Air Support Detachment at Andrews. So far as María knew, the Cuban government never had anything quite so nice, not even to transport El Comandante, and she told Martínez as much to cover her nervousness.

They'd boarded in an empty hangar at Homestead AFB just south of Miami. The only crew were the marine pilot, copilot, and an efficient staff sergeant named Anderson, who'd offered them Bloody Marys once they took off, even though it was only a little after eight in the morning.

After the shooting at the motel, Martínez had moved her to a private apartment downtown, and although he didn't say, she suspected it was his, though she'd resisted the urge to poke around and find out when he'd gone out several times over the last twenty-four hours.

"We have a fairly sophisticated operation in the Washington area," she said after they'd reached altitude out over the Atlantic. "Captain Fuentes will put them on alert to watch for me."

"It's a big city, lots of places to go to ground," Martínez said. Since the hotel, he'd looked at her differently, his anger gone, replaced by a hunger as if he were a jungle animal getting ready to pounce. But when he spoke to her, he sounded indifferent.

"It won't do after all of this for them to find me before I can talk to McGarvey."

"I'm not taking you to the Campus or down to the Farm, if that's what you're talking about. But you'll be reasonably safe for the time being, at least from your own people."

"Well, give me a pistol so that I can defend myself if need be."

"You're not worth it," Martínez said with supreme contempt. "As far as I'm concerned, the best possible outcome would be for someone to walk up behind you and put a bullet at point-blank range in the back of your head. Frankly, I'd like to have the job myself."

María refused to look away. "I had a job to do. Just like you. My hands aren't clean, but neither are yours nor McGarvey's."

"We don't kill innocent people."

"Tell that to the Iraqi citizens your army and the contractors you hire have gunned down."

"They were reacting to the threat of suicide bombers."

He was right, of course, though plenty of mistakes

had been made. By everyone, including her own government. She knew the arguments against the *revolución* and the excesses over the past fifty-plus years. Sometimes alone at night, she would awaken from a sound sleep, thinking about things they'd done—the things she'd personally ordered—and wondered how she'd found the justification.

Martínez read something of that from the expression on her face. "You're afraid of a bloodbath when the government fails?" he asked. "You should be. Me and a lot of other people outside of Cuba as well as millions inside are going to rise up, and job one will be opening every prison in the country."

"At lot of them killers, even mass murderers."

"Just like the ones you sent to us during the Mariel boatlift," Martínez said viciously. "Only this time, they're staying inside Cuba and we'll arm them. Who better to do some of the work for us?"

"Insanity," María mumbled, but she could see it happening and she could understand the why of it. The real problem would be the anarchy during the aftermath. Could very well be that the United States would send troops to help stabilize the new government.

Martínez threw his head back and laughed out loud.

But for the moment, it was less about Raúl's government, because he had relaxed many of El Comandante's restrictions, and more about money to feed the people, especially the five hundred thousand who'd been laid off from their government sinecure jobs.

The fortune in gold was for the people, not for Raúl, she kept reminding herself since reading her father's journals and especially his letters to her. But that pipe dream seemed even more utterly unobtainable now than ever before.

María was turning over in her mind what she would have to say and do to convince McGarvey that she was sincere when they landed at Andrews Air Force Base and immediately taxied over to a hangar marked only with a number.

"Where will I be staying?" she asked.

"With a friend, someplace so secure, even the Company doesn't know about it," Martínez said.

Inside the hangar, the engines spooled down and the attendant opened the front hatch. María gathered her purse and overnight bag, and got up.

"I want to read your father's journals," Martínez said.

"As long as they're not out of my sight."

"I could take them."

"Yes, you could," María said.

Martínez nodded after a moment. "Have you read them all?"

"I just glanced through some of them. But so far as I can tell, he was pretty diligent with his entries and we're talking about more than fifty years."

"What about your file?"

"Mostly letters to me that he never posted."

"Your ride is here, sir," Sergeant Anderson said.

"Tell the driver to join us, would you?" Martínez said.

The door to the cockpit was open and the pilot was staring at them; he nodded and the sergeant went down the stairs.

"I'll need a ride back to Homestead, if that's possible," Martínez said.

"When?"

"I'll let you know in fifteen minutes."

"Yes, sir," the pilot said, and he turned and began talking on his radio.

"You're leaving me here?" María asked.

"You'll be safe for the time being," Martínez said. "And Mac is already on his way, so you'd best have your story straight, because he's a man who doesn't take kindly to bullshit."

"I know," María said, and she told herself that she was looking forward to seeing him again and yet afraid of failing because she had no idea what would come next for her. Returning empty-handed to Cuba would mean a death sentence, yet the longer she was away, the greater the chances that Fuentes would find her again and this time kill her. He was a devious bastard, and if he and Ortega-Cowan had formed an alliance, which she was pretty certain they had, the resources of the entire DI would be at their disposal.

"Your coming to Miami the way you did has created a lot of problems. By now, too many people know that I'm helping you and they want to know why. Especially why I didn't kill you myself after three of my people were gunned down, one of them not twenty feet away while I was sitting having a glass of wine with you. Half of Little Havana wants to hold an inquisition for me, while the other half is on the verge of rioting."

"I understand," María said.

"No, you don't, *puta*," Martínez said, keeping a measured tone, though it was obviously difficult. "Because they're right, and it was you and people like you—just following orders—who've created this mess. We want to go home, we're tired of being here, of waiting for a day that a lot of people are beginning to believe will never come."

María didn't know what to say, but she refused to look away or lower her eyes. The situation was what it was.

"Do you know what we did in Miami while your father's funeral was taking place?"

"Celebrate, I imagine."

Martínez glared at her, a deep, deep hatred in his dark eyes. "We were dancing in the streets. All day long, that night and into the next day. The monster was finally dead, finally there was hope, something worth dancing for."

The sergeant came back aboard followed by a tall, slender woman, whom María immediately recognized, and all the air seemed to leave the cabin.

Martínez looked up and managed to smile. "Hi," he said.

"Mrs. Rencke," María said, barely able to get her voice.

"Actually I use my maiden name, Louise Horn. And I've been looking forward to meeting you, and spending some time together."

"Do you want me to stay with you till Mac and Otto get back?" Martínez asked.

Louise shook her head. "You've got fires to put out in Miami. And besides, I'd like to get to know her better. Girl talk, you know." And she smiled, but it was vicious. "We'll be fine."

FIFTY-ONE

Carlos López was a nondescript man of fifty, with black hair that was prematurely gray, wire-rimmed glasses, and a round, pleasant face that pegged him as anything but the Chief of Station for DI activities in Washington. He'd been dead set against the operation to kidnap Otto Rencke's wife, and he was not afraid to repeat himself to Fuentes.

Operations was housed in the upstairs rooms of a well-established Chinese restaurant on M Street not far from Georgetown Park, the Potomac just a couple of blocks south. A half dozen officers worked here, including a couple of communications technicians, but most of the DI's personnel worked under nonofficial cover—as cabdrivers, gardeners, a tailor, and even a Catholic priest who had taught at Georgetown University for the past eighteen years—and they communicated only in code via encrypted telephone, or for more secure operations via letter drops.

"Don't push him," Ortega-Cowan had warned. "He's independent as hell, but he knows how to get things done. Tell him what you want and then step back and let him do his job."

But he'd not been happy when Fuentes had shown up without warning last night and explained what he wanted. Nor was he happy now, perched on the edge of his worktable in the front room, looking down on the busy street.

"D.C. Metro and the Bureau were all over the place

for three days after the kidnapping, but all of a sudden it was as if someone had pulled the pin, and it was business as usual," López said. He was speaking Spanish, but his expressions were irritatingly American.

"I explained all of that," Fuentes said. "Once Señor Rencke and then Señor McGarvey showed up in Havana, the CIA ordered the search called off. All that was left for the police was an apparent drive-by shooting at the day care center."

"Which was still another colossal blunder. If I had been asked to mount the operation, the murder of an innocent woman would not have happened."

"Ortega-Cowan felt, as did the *coronel*, that your overall mission here was too important to jeopardize it by a one-task operation."

"Instead, you sent three idiots from Miami, none of whom had ever been to Washington, to do the job."

"It was a success," Fuentes flared.

López shook his head. "The death of this schoolteacher means nothing to you?"

Fuentes waved it off. "Collateral damage."

"Take care, Captain, that someday you do not become collateral damage yourself."

Technically, the station chief outranked Fuentes, but he was nothing more than a field officer. He'd never served at headquarters in Havana, and he certainly had never enjoyed the trust of El Comandante. Fuentes was about to tell him something of this when López handed him a Post-it note with an address in Georgetown written on it.

"Your coming here to tell me that Colonel León has defected is nothing short of unbelievable," the station chief said. "Until this morning, I did not think it was possible."

"What do you have?" Fuentes demanded.

"I spoke to Major Ortega-Cowan early this morning, who gave me two pieces of information that were vital. Something you should have known about."

"Don't toy with me," Fuentes warned.

"The colonel is at that address."

"Why wasn't I told?"

"She got there less than ten minutes ago, and I needed the time to arrange for someone to accompany you, to make sure that you didn't fly off and make another mess of things. The major told me that she would be arriving at Andrews Air Force Base sometime before noon. I had two teams standing by the main gate, and she was seen leaving the base in the company of a woman driving a blue Toyota SUV."

For a long moment, the significance of what López had just told him didn't sink in, but when it did, he was almost speechless. "Louise Horn, the woman we kidnapped?"

"The same," López said. "But Raúl Martínez was not with them. He apparently flew up merely to deliver the colonel. Which tells us something beyond what I can decipher."

"Your teams were not detected?" Fuentes asked to mask his own uncertainty.

"The two women gave no sign of it. Ms. Horn drove directly over to what turned out to be a brownstone here in Georgetown owned by a French medical doctor. We're still looking for more information—telephone numbers, ISPs, utility records."

"You have someone watching the house?"

"Of course."

It bothered Fuentes that Ortega-Cowan had not given him the same information. "What else did the major tell you?"

"That Señors McGarvey and Rencke will arrive at Andrews from Gibraltar on another military VIP jet within the next two hours."

It was another strike at his ego, and he had to wonder what sort of game Ortega-Cowan was playing at. The man was Colonel León's chief of staff, but he knew too much; he'd had the combination to her safe, he hadn't seemed at all surprised by the possibility that the colonel was El Comandante's daughter, he knew that she'd flown up from Miami apparently on a military jet, just as he knew that McGarvey and Rencke had gone to Spain and for whatever reason were returning to Andrews from Gibraltar.

López was watching him. "What exactly is your mission here, Captain?"

"To find the colonel."

"You've found her, now what? Do you mean to assassinate her?" López was filled with animosity, and it showed. "As you say, my station's mission is too important to jeopardize over a defecting government official, even one so highly placed as Colonel León. Unless there is more to the situation than Major Ortega-Cowan was willing to share with me."

And it suddenly came to Fuentes that Ortega-Cowan didn't really give a damn about some fabled treasure supposedly buried in New Mexico. His only goal was to take over the DI's Operations Directorate, and to do so, he wanted her out of the way and branded a traitor, with Fuentes taking the blame of aiding in her escape. For the moment, López was the key.

"Colonel León is El Comandante's illegitimate daughter."

"So what? His other illegitimate daughter defected to Spain and has even published a book. No one cares. And Uncle Fidel is dead."

"Before he died, her father gave her a deathbed wish."

"To kidnap a CIA officer?" López asked disparagingly.

"That's part of it. But the main reason the woman was kidnapped was to force her husband, Otto Rencke—who is the CIA's leading computer expert—to meet with Colonel León in Havana."

"I know the name—everybody does. But what in God's name did she think she was doing, pulling a crazy stunt like that?"

"Señor Rencke's presence was required to lure Kirk McGarvey to Havana."

"And he actually went down there? And you were a part of it?"

"Only at the edges."

"Well, let me tell you something about Señor Mc-Garvey. If you go up against him, you will die. And that's not a guess, that's fact."

"The *coronel* did, and she not only survived the encounter, she made her way here and, as you say, she was picked up by the woman she ordered kidnapped, and McGarvey and Rencke are on their way as well."

"What does the major want?"

"He wants her brought down so that he can take over the directorate."

"And you, Captain?"

"I want what Colonel León wants, the reason she lured Rencke and McGarvey here, and why they apparently agreed to help."

"You're not here to arrest or assassinate a traitor?"

"Not unless I am given no other choice. But I'll need your station's help getting close enough to her and her new friends to find out what their next moves will be."

"And all of this has to do with Uncle Fidel's deathbed wish to his daughter? Including the apparent duel between you and Major Ortega-Cowan?"

"*Sí.*"

"Tell me," López said.

And Fuentes did just that, leaving out only the possible size and location of the treasure.

"If what you're saying is true, it will be a coup for you."

"And anyone who helps me."

FIFTY-TWO

Carleton Patterson was waiting in the backseat of an armored Cadillac limousine when McGarvey and Rencke showed up at Andrews Air Force Base, and his driver, a beefy man in a baggy suit coat, opened the rear door for them. The CIA's general counsel was on a cell phone.

"They just arrived. We'll be about a half hour."

"Surprised to see you here, Carleton," McGarvey said as he and Otto climbed in and the driver shut the door.

"Page would like to have a word with you. Marty wanted to send someone from security, but considering what's been happening over the past few days, we thought you might have more need of a lawyer than a couple of extra guns."

"Anyway, I'd be more cooperative with you," McGarvey said.

"Something like that."

They were waved through the main gate and got directly on I-495, the Beltway, weekday afternoon traffic heavy.

"Let me guess, there's a warrant for my arrest for the murder of a museum curator in Mexico City, and Interpol in Spain was asked to cooperate."

"It was your pistol, registered as an Air Marshal weapon on your flight to Mexico City."

McGarvey explained how he had come to lose his weapon, because he hadn't counted on the DI being so quick on the uptake. But it was the timing of the thing that bothered him.

"There weren't warrants for our arrests until after we'd gotten out of Dodge through Gibraltar," Otto said, giving voice to McGarvey's thought. "Seems like the Mexican *federales* wanted us to get back here."

"You met this Dr. Diaz?" Patterson asked.

"It's why we went to Mexico City."

"And Seville?"

"To see the curator of the Archivo General de Indias," McGarvey said, and he handed over the copy of the agreement he'd signed with Dr. Virgílio.

"Good heavens," the normally unflappable Patterson said. He quickly read through the five pages, went back to reread a couple of sections, and when he looked up he seemed puzzled. "This is not a standard finder's agreement under any stretch of the imagination. In any event, it would have been in Spanish. So whoever put it together was pulling your leg. But Spanish treasure in the New World? What are you up to this time, and what's it got to do with Cuban intelligence?"

"It's got to do with why Louise was kidnapped and why I went to Havana," Otto said. "And why Mac came to fetch me."

"Louise sent one of our VIP aircraft to pick up you guys in Gibraltar, but she also sent a plane to Florida to pick up Raúl Martínez and an unidentified female, whom Louise met at Andrews a couple of hours ago. Is there any connection? It's important, because of course, both of them have disappeared."

"The woman is Colonel María León."

"Well, three people who worked for Raúl have been gunned down, and little Havana is all but in armed revolt, worse than April 2000, when the boy Elián González was kidnapped by INS agents and returned to his father in Cuba. What's going on, Mac?"

"Plenty, but I'll save it for Page and Marty because you guys won't believe me and I don't want to explain more than once."

Patterson gave both of them the oddest look. "No

one's ever had trouble believing either of you; it's the accepting part that's sometimes a little tough."

At the CIA's Old Headquarters Building, they parked in the underground ramp and took the VIP elevator direct to the seventh floor. As always over the past few years, it seemed strange to McGarvey to be back. He felt out of place, and yet he'd spent the majority of his adult life working for and sometimes with the people here. He knew the tone of the place, he could feel the energy, and very often the uncertainties that could and did eat people alive.

McGarvey, along with Otto and Patterson, was ushered into the director's large office, where Page and Marty Bambridge were waiting for them.

"You two have been busy," Bambridge said, by way of greeting. "Anything you'd care to share with us?"

"That's why we're here," McGarvey said.

"Coffee?" Page asked.

"We had plenty on the way over. And we're not staying long—there's a lot more yet to be done. But I think you deserve an explanation."

"Please," Page said, and when they were settled, McGarvey took them through the entire story, beginning from his arrival in Cuba to the discussions with María León, their escape, and the meeting in Mexico City with Dr. Diaz.

"Who was found shot to death with your Air Marshal weapon," Bambridge said. "The Mexican authorities issued a warrant for your arrest, as has Interpol in Spain."

"After we had safely reached Gibraltar and were already over the Atlantic."

"But you can't be serious about the business with a treasure in Spanish gold," Bambridge said, and for the moment, Page seemed content to let his DDO take the lead. "Sounds like the ravings of a senile old man. Someone with dementia."

"The DI took it seriously enough to send someone to Mexico City to murder Dr. Diaz, and to get the cooperation of some police authority in Spain to keep the pressure on us."

"To do what?"

"To find the gold," McGarvey said. "The same reason Colonel León left Cuba and showed up in Miami."

"Unbelievable," Bambridge blustered. "Then it was her, or people under her direction who killed three of our people?"

"Not her. It's a power struggle inside the DI. Whoever's behind it wanted to get rid of her once she no longer had her father's protection. But then when they realized that there might just be something to this business with the treasure, they changed tactics. Now they're trying to herd us, while giving us enough room to actually succeed."

Bambridge started to bluster again, but this time Page held him off.

"What do you think?" the DCI asked.

What did he think? McGarvey asked himself. "Until we met with Dr. Diaz, who was convinced that a treasure did in fact exist, I thought that it probably was nothing more than a fairy tale. As Marty said, the ravings of a senile old man on his deathbed. But in Seville, we met with the curator of their national museum and document repository dedicated to the Spanish empire in the New World who said that she had personally spoken with Diaz, who urged her to help us. But that was after he'd been killed, so she was lying. In any event, Diaz told us that he was persona non grata at the museum for some past indiscretion."

"But she believed in the existence of this New World treasure?"

"We presented ourselves as treasure hunters, and she had us sign a finder's agreement," McGarvey said.

"I looked at it," Patterson said. "It's a phony, couldn't possibly hold up in any court of law, so this woman apparently has her own agenda, or possibly a deal with the DI."

"And now?" Page prompted.

"I think that there's a very real possibility that something's buried out there, and Castro's daughter has put her life on the line looking for it," McGarvey said.

"Otto?"

"I have to agree with Mac, Mr. Director, although I didn't at first. Not until Spain, and not until we found out that the colonel not only left Cuba and showed up in Miami but also insisted on coming here to talk to us."

Bambridge sat forward. "Good Lord, she's here in Washington?"

"Yes," McGarvey said.

"Well, let's have her, at least for ordering a murder and kidnapping."

"Not yet. Not until we find out why she took the chance of skipping out, and the even bigger risk of showing up in Miami."

"If the DI traced her to Miami as you say it did, then it's likely they'll trace her here."

"I hope so," McGarvey said.

"You want us to sit on it?" Bambridge asked. "Just like that?"

"Just for now."

"You have to be kidding," Bambridge said, but again Page held him off.

"For now, this has nothing to do with national security, so it's not in our brief. But blood has been shed in Miami, and Interpol has listed you as a person of interest, so at the very least, the Bureau is interested in having a word with you and Colonel León. But I think I can hold them off for twenty-four hours."

"Forty-eight," McGarvey said. He'd gotten what he wanted: the CIA's interest and some breathing room.

"I'll see what I can do," Page said.

From the CIA, they took a cab into downtown Washington, getting out at Union Station and walking down to the Hotel George, where they had a drink at the bar. McGarvey was nearly 100 percent sure that they had not picked up a tail, but it had always been suspected that the DI as well as a number of other foreign intelligence agencies kept a lookout in the vicinity of the CIA's main gate, so he had to consider the possibility that he and Otto had been spotted.

Otto phoned Louise to make sure that she'd run into no problems and that Colonel León was behaving herself, while McGarvey phoned Martínez.

"Where are you?"

"Driving up from Homestead. Are you back in Washington?"

"Yes. Page has agreed to give us a little space—forty-eight hours, does that give you enough time to settle your people down and explain what they need to do?"

"I can be pretty convincing when it's necessary. What about Seville?"

"It was a setup, but the curator seems to think the story is plausible. The next step will be to convince Colonel León for the ruse to have any chance of working," McGarvey said.

Martínez laughed. "She came to us this time. I think she's ready for what you have to tell her. But the DI up there will be on your case, so watch your step."

"You, too," McGarvey said.

FIFTY-THREE

María came downstairs to the kitchen from where she'd taken a shower and changed into a pair of jeans and white blouse but nothing on her feet. She'd done her hair up in back, and Louise thought she looked stunning—fresh, pretty in a dark island girl way. But it was just looks, after all; the woman was a killer, or at the very least she'd signed orders for innocent people to be arrested, interrogated, and then executed.

Louise was leaning against the counter. "You found everything okay?"

"Yes, thank you," María said. "Could I have something to drink?"

"Water, coffee, tea, wine, or beer."

"Anything stronger?"

Louise kept her temper in check. Mac wanted her here in one piece, and it was she who had apparently defected from Cuba and come to them. "We have some cognac, but it's for Mac when he shows up."

"He's gotten word that I'm here?"

"He and my husband are on their way."

"Can you tell me what they've been doing?" María asked.

Louise just stared at her for a longish moment, trying to find some measure of the woman, trying to find something in her eyes that would indicate what she was, what she'd done. But only a wariness mixed with weariness and a little hesitancy showed.

María shrugged. "A beer will be fine," she said.

Louise motioned for her to have a seat at the counter, and she opened a couple of Red Stripes and got a couple of glasses.

María raised her glass. "I'm not exactly what you think I am."

"What do I think you are?" Louise asked, holding her temper in check. Her fingers were still beat up from trying to remove the screws from the window where she'd been held.

"A fanatic, a monster."

"The men who kidnapped me did so on your orders."

"To convince your husband to come to Cuba. It was the only way I could get Mr. McGarvey to come talk to me."

"You could have left Cuba and met him on his turf."

"He'd gone to ground—we knew that much, but not where."

Louise wanted to throw the beer bottle at the woman. "Joyce Kilburn was the name of the woman shot to death at the day care center. By your men, operating under your orders."

"It was an accident."

"If I brought her husband and three children here, what would you say to them? Oops?"

"I don't know this word. But I would tell them that I was sorry, and that if it were in my power, I would change everything for them."

"Including my kidnapping?" Louise shot back.

Still María did not look away. "No, that I would not have changed. You were a means to an important end that had to be accomplished as quickly as possible."

"They drugged me."

The faintest of smiles raised the corner of María's mouth. "They were idiots. But you gave a good account of yourself. They were finally very glad to be rid of you. *Pavorosa,* was the word they used. Formidable, dreadful."

"Where are they now?"

María shrugged. "Havana, I suppose. I didn't have the time to deal with them."

"But you let Mac and my husband escape. Why?"

"It was a little more complicated than that. My house was under attack, and had I been there, the same consideration wouldn't have been given to me."

And there it was, the crux of the matter in Louise's mind. A constant, almost an axiom, that people of

María's stripe held dear: The United States was expected to play fair, to play by the rules, while everyone else could do whatever they wanted, including 9/11. They could kidnap anyone and cut off their head. But God forbid we grab them and take them to a place like Guantánamo Bay, clothe them, house them, feed them, supply them with Korans, and find out—by sometimes admittedly harsh means—information needed to save American lives.

Impossible, Louise thought, to argue religion with a believer.

"My questions stand: Why did you let my husband and Mac get away, and why did you give the order to have me released?"

"Because I'd found out what I needed to know, and I found out that my father had been right when he'd promised that Mr. McGarvey was an honorable man who might be persuaded to help if he understood the true nature of what he was being asked."

It sounded like a carefully rehearsed speech. "So you've made it this far, what next? Because if you think that by some twisted sort of logic, you're going to convince him to find a treasure and turn it over to your government, you're deluded. Worse than that, nuts."

"Not to the government, to the people."

"Save it for the gullible, Colonel, because when Mac gets here, he's going to want the truth, not bullshit."

"I am telling the truth," María flared. "I burned my bridges in Cuba to come this far."

"You burned your bridges because you found yourself in the middle of a power struggle. With your father's death, you were vulnerable. It would have been only a matter of time before you found yourself behind bars, probably in front of a firing squad. You ran for your life."

"And the lives of my people!"

"Your people," Louise shot back. "Who the hell are you trying to kid? What did you really come for? Political asylum in trade for secret information from inside the DI? The true skinny on your father's monstrous treatment of *your* people?"

"Mr. McGarvey believes me," María said. "And so does your husband."

"Right."

"Otherwise, why did they go to Mexico City to see Dr. Diaz, the historian my father wrote about in his journals? And why did they go to Seville? It means something."

"It's not the possibility of a Spanish treasure hidden somewhere after several centuries that is under serious question. It's your motivation, Colonel, that nobody believes."

"Well, someone does, because the DI tried to get to me in Miami, and there's little doubt that they'll try to find me here."

"To do what, give you legitimacy?" Louise demanded. She found that she was becoming disturbed, not just by what the woman was saying, but also by what she *wasn't*. No apologies, no defense for her actions. María León was a believer, but of what?

"Maybe just that. Or maybe if the DI succeeds in assassinating me, you'll finally believe that I was telling the truth."

"You're a mass murderer."

"An apparatchik, a functionary," María said weakly.

And Louise laughed. "Delusional. And it would almost be comic if people like you didn't have actual power." Otto had told her that María had almost certainly been trained by the KGB in Moscow. "Is that what you learned in Russia? To blame the system for your excesses—or would you rather call them mistakes?"

A look of genuine anguish made María's face drop. "I was alone for most of my life."

"Save it for the confessional," Louise said harshly.

"I'm here to help."

"To help yourself."

"No," María said. "You have to believe me."

"We'll see," Louise said, and she glanced out the window at the deepening gloom of late afternoon, wishing that Otto and Mac would get here soon. She'd felt competent all the way to this point, even through the ordeal of her kidnapping, But now she felt as if she were in over her head, and she needed help.

FIFTY-FOUR

Fuentes sat in the back of a Capital City Florist windowless van just around the corner from the brownstone where López's operatives had traced the two women. From here, the sophisticated low-lux cameras and surveillance equipment sensors and antennas had clear sight lines to the rear and west sides of the three-story structure. But nothing electronic, mechanical, or infrared was showing up on the scanners. All they had was the dim early-evening visual image on one of the monitors, and although he was disappointed, he wasn't surprised; the woman and her husband were technocrats.

Ariel Garcia in white coveralls with the florist company's logo on the back sat next to Fuentes. He and Hector Vásquez making passes in a Yellow Cab were the only two men López had allowed for the initial stage of the assignment, something else that Fuentes was angry about. But both men were heavily armed with Glock 17 pistols, and the silenced version of the Russian AKS-74U, and both seemed competent.

"If it occurs that we must assassinate her, then we will do it quickly and leave before the authorities arrive," Fuentes had told the chief of station.

"I won't allow more killings," López said angrily.

"The FBI won't care very much if a Cuban defector—one such as Colonel León, who has signed so many death warrants and whose father was El Comandante—is gunned down."

"If McGarvey becomes involved—"

"I will take full responsibility," Fuentes had said, and López reluctantly agreed. Maybe not reluctantly enough, and watching the brownstone from the back of the van, he had to wonder what else the station chief hadn't told him. That Ortega-Cowan was playing some sort of a game was a foregone conclusion: it was the man's nature. But the major had never studied under Uncle Fidel, the master of artifice, and Fuentes found that he was almost beginning to enjoy himself. They were in the middle of a game of chess in which the stakes were the highest. And he possibly had the check-mate move.

He had done a lot of thinking in Mexico City and Miami and on the way up here. The operation hinged on whether or not an accessible gold treasure was a possibility. If it wasn't, the best course would be to as-sassinate the *coronel* as a traitor and return home the avenging hero. If the gold actually did exist, which apparently McGarvey and Rencke believed it did—otherwise, why did they travel to Mexico City and then Seville?—then finding it and reporting back to Havana would make him a hero of a much larger sort.

The problem, of course, was Ortega-Cowan and what designs he'd made to manipulate the situation to suit his own ambitions.

First, then, was to somehow find out if the gold ex-isted, and if it did, eliminate McGarvey, who was the only real physical danger; kill the *coronel*, who would have fulfilled her function by getting them to this point; and finally hold Louise Horn at gunpoint again to ensure her husband's cooperation. Where McGar-vey was a man of action, Rencke was an intellect, a man of the mind, who would find the treasure.

"Base, two." The radio came to life. It was Vásquez in the cab. He was a short, stocky man with a bull's thick neck and a raspy smoker's voice.

Fuentes's headset was on vox. "Go ahead, two."

"Two male subjects on foot just went down the driveway to the rear of the location."

"Can you make a positive ID?"

"A high-probability match."

It was finally coming together. "Get out of there. But don't go far. I may need you."

"*Sí,*" Vásquez came back.

Fuentes pulled off his headset. "Anything from the house?"

"No."

López had supplied all three of them with E71 encrypted Nokia cell phones and Bluetooth headsets. The phone's software, with dual-layered RSA 1024-bit and AES 256-bit military-grade encryption was older generation, but for all practical purposes still unbreakable.

Fuentes speed-dialed Garcia's phone so he would have continuous contact with the van, and when the connection was made, pocketed the phone and hooked the small headset over his left ear. "Keep me posted if you get anything from the house, or if Hector notices anything I need to know about."

Garcia was a little flustered. "Where are you going, Captain?"

"We're getting nothing here, so I'm going in on foot," Fuentes said, and before the DI Washington field officer could object, he jumped out of the van and headed down the block to the corner.

The brownstone was a three story, well kept but anonymous, the blinds on its front windows tightly drawn. A driveway closed by a tall iron gate on the east side of the building led to what looked like a garage in the rear. From the van, they'd seen a tall stone wall at the back, but it had been impossible to see if there was a gate or opening to the adjacent property.

At the end of the block, Fuentes stopped to light a cigarette. This shaded avenue of residences was well enough away from busy M Street NW with its shops and restaurants, so that there was only light traffic at this hour and no pedestrians. The curb was wall-to-wall parked cars, lights showing in many of the houses; people were home from work, their children home from school. Pleasant, established, traditional, rich, and above all tidy. The electric, phone, and cable lines were all underground.

"Anything from the house?" he asked Garcia back at the van.

"Nothing has changed, Captain. What do you want to do?"

"Stand by," Fuentes said. He broke the connection and phoned López, who answered on the first ring.

"Good evening."

"I'll need help, four additional officers," Fuentes said, and he explained what he had in mind.

"So you're going to kill her and McGarvey after all."

"It may be for the best."

"What about the treasure?"

"I think that if we're holding Louise Horn again, it will give her husband incentive to work in our behalf."

"You'll need another safe house to keep her."

"Yes. Will you help?"

"Do I have any choice?" López asked, but it was rhetorical. "I'll send you two men, but it'll take one hour. And you must understand that I am merely complying with your orders, nothing further. It something goes bad, you're on your own, Captain."

"*Sí*," Fuentes said. But when this mission was completed, López would stand in front of a firing squad right next to Ortega-Cowan, if for nothing else than his incorrect attitude.

FIFTY—FIVE

In the brownstone, Mac went directly upstairs to clean up after the trip, and after he'd finished watched from a front window as a man wearing a dark sport coat walked slowly past and at the corner stopped for a minute or so as he spoke on a cell phone before he walked away.

"Looks as if we have company," he'd told Otto on the first-floor landing before they went back to the kitchen, where Louise had nuked a couple of pizzas.

"Want to call for backup?" Otto asked.

"I want to know how they tracked us. And the only way is to ask them."

"I don't want Louise in harm's way again."

"They came for Colonel León, and if it comes to it, we'll offer a trade."

Otto grinned, even though he was concerned for his wife's safety. "But you have no intention of giving her up."

McGarvey shook his head. "We're going to end up needing her just as much as she needs us."

"What about our company?"

"When I ask for a cognac, I want you to turn off

your security systems. But don't say anything to the colonel. We're going to stage a little drama for the DI, and she's going to be the star."

Otto opened a gun safe in the hall closet and took out a Walther PPK, a silencer, and two magazines of ammunition for McGarvey; and a subcompact Glock 29 that fired a 10 mm round, and another silencer, which he pocketed along with two magazines of ten rounds each.

"If this goes down, I want you to take the women out of here. Over the roofs," McGarvey said, as they went back to the kitchen.

"I'll shoot back if need be," Otto said, and he was resolute.

Louise had laid out the plates and glasses, and María was opening a bottle of red wine, and they looked up.

"Home again at last," Louise said. "Did anybody on Campus give you guys trouble?"

"Marty tried to be his usual self, but Walt held him off," Otto said. "At least temporarily. Gave us forty-eight hours."

"To do what?" María asked. "Or did you find out what you went looking for in Seville?"

"Enough to convince us that the gold actually does exist," McGarvey said.

"Well, you better sit down and tell us all about it," Louise said. "Do you want a cognac?"

"A glass a wine will do for now," McGarvey said, and he and Otto sat at the counter, and between them they told Louise and María everything that had happened, beginning in Mexico City and their flight out of the country when Mac's gun had gone missing and they suspected that Dr. Diaz had been assassinated with it.

"It was a DI operation," McGarvey said, and María protested, but it was obvious she didn't believe it herself.

"Román isn't that good, and neither is Manuel," she said.

"They had to have tracked you to Mexico City, where they probably stumbled across us, and from there they followed us to our meeting with Diaz and managed to dig you out in Miami."

"Maybe this is just a big scam," Louise said. "All started by kidnapping me, getting my husband and Mac to come running to your little house by the sea, and then, in a really magnanimous gesture, letting them waltz right out."

"No reason for it."

"Hounds and hares? Is that it? Once they took you at your word, you hopped a plane—just that easy— flew to Mexico City, where you figured they'd follow you, and from there Miami, where you could out Raúl. The point of the entire operation. Right?"

María was shaking her head. "I swear that's not it. I wanted to come here to ask for Mr. McGarvey's help. I wanted to tell him that I believed him about the gold, and I wanted him to believe that I was only interested in the treasure for my people. Not for the government."

"The DI was coming after you in Mexico City and Miami, not Raúl? Is that right?"

"They wanted me dead. Major Ortega-Cowan wants to run operations now that I no longer have my father's protection."

"Then why did they kill Dr. Diaz in Mexico City and not you?" Louise hammered. "And again in Miami, your old pal Manuel had you and Raúl in his sights at the hotel—according to what you told me—why didn't he take the shot? Could have eliminated two big problems, you and Raúl, who's given the DI fits for the past ten years. And the guy was certainly capable of it—he'd already proved that much by taking out three of Raúl's people."

Throughout all of that, McGarvey got the impression that for all her training and experience, María was a little naïve. She'd been sheltered from the real world for most of her life; even though she had risen remarkably fast in the Cuban intelligence service, she'd never wanted for anything, her orders were obeyed, she was treated with a real respect to a measure that most women in the country didn't enjoy, and her future had never been uncertain—at least not in her mind—until her father had died. Yet she had risked everything merely on a speculation that Otto had proposed.

"She could have come straight here from Mexico City," McGarvey said. "But she took a big risk going to Miami first. Lot of people down there would like to have put a bullet in her head. If not to out Raúl, why'd you do it?"

María looked grateful. "It was the only way I thought I could prove my intentions."

"Save us," Louise said, rolling her eyes.

"Just a minute, I want to hear what she has to say," McGarvey interrupted. "What are your intentions?"

"To find the gold—"

"You've already said that. But just how do you envision getting the gold, if we find it, to your people? It's in the U.S., on a military reservation, so just getting to it is the first big hurdle. It has to be dug up, maybe loaded aboard trucks—or were you planning on using helicopters?—and then driven where? Across the border into Mexico, right where it started from a few hundred years ago? All of this would have to be done under cover of darkness, of course, and without the air force or border patrol learning about it—so I guess that would leave out helicopters, unless they flew very low."

María held her silence, as did Otto and Louise.

"So now the gold is in Mexico, maybe several hundred tons of it. The Cuban air force could send some transport aircraft, except even if you had enough airplanes capable of landing in the desert for the job, which I doubt, someone would take notice and want to know what was going on. Our people watch your excursions out into the Gulf pretty closely, and I'm sure that the Mexican air force would be curious about what might look like an invasion or at the very least a smuggling operation."

María managed a faint smile. "Something like that," she said, and McGarvey knew then that he had her. "But it's going to depend on you to not only find the gold, but allow me to bring some of it home, too."

"But not to Havana."

"To a processing and distribution center at Guantánamo Bay at first," she said.

"With my government's cooperation for a piece of the pie."

"I'd need that, too."

McGarvey nodded. "I'll tell you how we're going to

find the gold, and you're going to tell me how you're getting it out of Mexico and across to Guantánamo Bay." He glanced at Louise. "But first I think I'd like that cognac after all."

FIFTY-SIX

After his walk around the block, Fuentes ended up back at the van, where Garcia was about to call him on the phone. The surveillance technician had shoved his headset off one ear and had the Nokia out, ready to dial, and he was excited. Fuentes slipped into the seat next to him.

"Something's finally coming through," Garcia said.

Fuentes snatched a headset, and though he was hearing voices and some other sounds, it took several seconds for him to begin to make some sort of sense of exactly what was coming from the house, and he suddenly recognized María's voice, and that of a man, perhaps McGarvey. "I hope you're recording this," he said.

"It kicked on automatically," Garcia said. He adjusted something on one of his panels, and the voices became clearer. "I'm getting bounce from one of the rear windows—a kitchen, I think. They're having something to eat."

"You'd need the help of the drug cartels along the

border," McGarvey was saying. "That might create a problem."

"Not at all," María said. "Tell me one segment of your society where someone doesn't at least smoke pot, or better yet, snort cocaine? And who better to spy for us than the boots on the ground, small-time dealers?"

"In exchange for what?" Louise asked.

"Safe haven when it's needed and transportation from Colombia to more than a dozen airstrips, some within fifty miles of the U.S. border. Which is how we'll get the gold out, using the cartels' own aircraft but with protection once they enter our airspace."

"Does anyone on Campus know about this?" McGarvey asked.

Otto answered. "I didn't."

"The CIA doesn't have a lock on intelligence operations," María said. "Sometimes the DI stages its own little coups."

"Big coups," Louise said. "We've been monitoring the air activity for the past three years, but we figured the flights from Cuba were smuggling Cubans who could get across our border into Texas, New Mexico, or Arizona, easier than across the strait into Florida. And we catch a few of them every now and then. Mostly convicted felons."

"It's background noise. You're supposed to catch them."

"Still leaves you two problems," McGarvey said. "First you have to convince the cartels not to simply take the gold away from you when they get it across the border from New Mexico."

"You know where it is?" María asked.

Fuentes held the earphones closer, barely able to contain his excitement. He'd hit the jackpot. Maybe even something bigger for him than the Operations Directorate.

"Yes."

"Even if we managed to take a lot of gold out of there, those guys won't risk an ongoing business that nets them in excess of forty billion dollars per year. They'll let us keep our gold, and continue to spy for us, because we'll continue to work as their state-sponsored support mechanism."

"An arrangement that even your own directorate wouldn't interfere with, no matter how high a priority bringing you down is for them," McGarvey said.

"Something like that," María said. "You said two problems."

"Where do they usually land once they reach Cuba?"

"They're coming back empty most of the time, so they land wherever their next drug pickup is scheduled, which can be just about anywhere for security reasons, but usually somewhere in the southwest. It's a thousand kilometers from there to Columbia's north shore west of Riohacha, and about eight hundred if they use the route through Nicaragua. No reason for the DI to suspect the inbound aircraft aren't empty."

"We're talking about several hundred tons of gold that the U.S. is going to want back—assuming you manage to get it across the border," Otto said. "Means you're not going to have a lot of time before the Mexican army drops in to find out what's going on. You'll have to send an armada of aircraft to get in, load the gold, and get out all in one night."

"And if the army does show up in force, it won't make your cartel pals very happy," Louise added. "Have you figured out how you're going to handle that issue?"

"We'll assemble the planes at a half dozen airstrips a few at a time over a period of several days, before we grab the gold and bring it across. We can have it distributed and loaded in twenty-four hours or less."

"It would be cutting it close," McGarvey said.

"Even if we get only half of it out, I'd win."

"I'd win?" Louise asked.

"I meant we."

"What happens after you get the gold back to Cuba? Have you figured out how to distribute it?"

"I'll need your government's help."

"You've already said that," McGarvey said. "But exactly what help? Physically, what are we supposed to do?"

"First we need to get the gold to your base at Guantánamo Bay, and from there it can be auctioned for hard currencies, which can be distributed to the people."

"Naïve," Louise muttered. "What about the political fallout? Or do you expect your government will sit on its hands? And even if you could pull off this stunt, and actually get some of the money to the people, what would stop your military from simply confiscating it?"

"From a population of ten million?" María asked.

"Put it in any bank, and it would be gone in a heartbeat."

María sounded frustrated. "Fly over and drop it from

the air like propaganda leaflets. Send it ashore in bales. Distribute it with the marijuana and coke. I don't have all of the answers."

"Why should we cooperate?" McGarvey asked.

But Fuentes knew what the answer would have to be, and he had to admire the woman. Like her father, she was just as devious as she was ruthless.

"Think about what that kind of money would do in Cuba. Certainly Raúl's government would fall. When the army moved in to try to grab whatever it could, the people would fight back. And the army is made up of ordinary Cubans who would themselves share the wealth, so I think mass desertions would speed up the overthrow. And it wouldn't cost the U.S. a centavo. Maybe even make a profit by brokering the auction."

"Revolution," Fuentes whispered.

"Revolution," Otto said. "Just like in Egypt."

"What Washington has tried and failed to do ever since the Bay of Pigs fifty years ago," María said. "No reason for your government *not* to cooperate."

Fuentes pulled the headphones away and called the two people López had sent. They were waiting in a Potomac Electric Power Company maintenance van two blocks away. Bruno Murillo answered on the first ring.

"*Sí.*"

"Move in now," Fuentes said.

"Give us ten minutes."

"When you're finished, I want you to stand by for backup."

"As you wish," Murillo replied.

He and José Cobiella were highly trained to hack

into and disrupt any sort of electronic signals, fiber-optics or ordinary copper phone lines, cell phone towers, and in this case, electrical service to individual buildings or entire blocks or neighborhoods. López had guaranteed that, in addition, they were both more than competent marksmen.

Fuentes donned the headset again in time to hear Louise Horn speaking.

". . . where the gold is buried in New Mexico, and getting to it are two different things. How in the world do you expect to bring in the trucks you'd need to get it across the border without detection?"

The room fell silent and it was nearly a full minute before María answered, and when she did, Fuentes could do nothing more than laugh. The *coronel* was devious and ruthless, and even brilliant, but she was crazy—certifiable.

"The Mexican people are going to invade the United States, and your government is going to allow it to happen."

FIFTY-SEVEN

The lights went out, pitching the kitchen in near absolute darkness. The refrigerator motor stopped working, but all the alarms, motion sensors, and antisurveillance gear switched over to emergency battery power, and they were once again safe from eavesdropping.

Otto switched on a small penlight, but directed its beam at the floor, which made it less likely to be seen outside through the blinds. "Just what you figured, kemo sabe."

McGarvey went to the hallway, which ran the length of the house, and cocked an ear to listen before he went to the front door and carefully peered out one of the flanking narrow windows in time to see one man in dark coveralls and a hard hat jump out of a Pepco utility van and enter an apartment building across the street. He carried a nylon bag slung over his shoulder. The van parked a few yards away, and the driver in the same type of uniform got out and hid behind it.

Otto stood at the kitchen doorway. "Company?"

"A Pepco van twenty yards away. Two men in coveralls. One just went into the building across the street, probably heading for the roof. The other is behind the van."

"The guy you spotted earlier wasn't wearing coveralls, was he?"

"No," McGarvey said. "So there's at least three, and probably more. Is there a basement exit to the rear?"

"West corner. What do you have in mind?"

"I'm taking the fight to them as soon as you and Louise and María are out of here. But stay low on the roof, because the guy across the street was carrying a bag, probably a sniper rifle. He's most likely covering the front door and windows, but if he spots you, he'll let the others know and you'll be stuck."

"I'll call for backup," Otto said, pulling out his cell phone.

"Not unless you absolutely need it," McGarvey said.

He wanted at least one of them to get away and get the message back to Havana, and he could see that Otto understood the reason why. "Just get out of here. I'll give you five minutes."

"My life's on the line," María said at Otto's shoulder. "Give me a gun, I'm going with you."

"Not a chance," McGarvey said.

But María pushed past Otto, her features barely visible in the dim penlight. She seemed driven. "I know how they operate. Fuentes is out there, but he's almost certainly got the help of Carlos López. He's our Washington station chief. Good man. Conservative. Won't waste his assets on a short-term operation."

"His people kidnapped Louise."

"Wasn't him. He didn't want to jeopardize the long-term mission here, so we had to use a team from Miami," María said. "I'm telling you that these guys aren't going to stick around if there's any chance that the cops are going to show up." He turned back to Otto. "Use your cell phone and call nine-one-one."

Otto shook his head. "I'm getting no signal."

"Whatever," María said. "You want to take the fight to them, fine. Give me a pistol and I'll go with you. If we make enough noise, they'll cut and run. If that's what you want."

"Fuentes, too?"

"Especially him. The *flojito* has no stomach for a standup fight."

McGarvey considered what she was saying. In order for his plan to work, someone needed to get word back to Cuba. If the DI had monitored their conversation over the past several minutes, which Mac was sure they had, María had become expendable as far as they were concerned. DI operations under her chief of staff's direction could conceivably take care of the situation in Mexico with the drug cartels, including the invasion of New Mexico, as completely crazy as that concept was.

And maybe she knew it or felt it. The timing of the team's move immediately after she'd stated her plan was way too coincidental. She had to expect surveillance equipment had picked up at least some of it. Her only option at this point was to take them out, or at least take Fuentes down.

"Give her your gun," he told Otto.

Otto handed over the Glock, which María expertly checked, and then the silencer and two spare magazines, which she pocketed. "How do you want to play this?" she asked.

"You're going up on the roof."

"I'm coming with you—"

"You're going to do as you're told for a change," McGarvey said. "My friends are going into harm's way for the second time because of you. And now you're going to make yourself useful by taking out the sniper on the roof across the street. Or at the very least, keep him busy. And make all the noise you want."

María said something under her breath, but then glanced over her shoulder at Louise right behind her. "Show me the way," she said.

"Careful where you aim," Louise told McGarvey. "We have a lot of innocent neighbors."

"Give me the keys to the Toyota," McGarvey said.

"What have you got in mind?" Otto asked.

"A diversion."

Louise fetched her car keys. "Think they'll buy it?"

"Might make them wonder about what's going on. Just keep your heads down," McGarvey told them as they headed upstairs.

"I'll be seeing you in a few minutes, so don't shoot me when I show up," María called back.

"Don't tempt me," McGarvey muttered.

He waited until they had disappeared, then went to the window and checked out the street again, but nothing had changed. So far as Fuentes's people were concerned, the front of the brownstone was covered from street level as well as from above.

Which left the rear courtyard, where Louise's Toyota SUV and Otto's battered old Mercedes sedan were parked. The only way out was the driveway around the east side of the house to the gate that opened to the street. Or over the tall brick wall to the narrow alley.

The stairs to the basement were off the back pantry in the kitchen, but before he went down, he checked out a window, but nothing moved yet in the courtyard, though he was pretty sure that Fuentes had to have placed at least one shooter, maybe more at the rear. The problem was his intention.

By now he knew María's plan—the timing of the power cut was not coincidental—so it was almost certain that he wanted her dead. But he would also understand that the only ones who knew where the treasure was buried were McGarvey and Otto and possibly Louise. So at all costs, one of them would have to be taken alive. And if it were McGarvey's choice, he would pick Louise again.

A dim light showed through a narrow, dusty window high on the rear wall just beneath the ceiling joists. Except for the oil furnace, water heater, and washer and dryer, plus a workbench in one corner and what had probably served as a wine rack along the opposite wall, the basement was empty. No crates or boxes or old furniture. Everything of interest to Otto and Louise, including each other, was upstairs.

The door to one of the bedrooms on the third floor had been open when McGarvey passed and looked in earlier. A tiny bed with side rails and a bright pink elephant spread that matched the curtains were waiting for their adopted daughter, Audrey, when this business was all over and she could come back home.

Pretty much most of his adult life, he had moved from one crisis—like this one, in which his friends and family had been put in harm's way because of him—to another, in a seemingly never-ending stream. Sometimes, like just then looking at his granddaughter's bed, he got the feeling that he'd had enough of it. Yet a number of years ago, he told someone who'd asked why he just didn't turn his back and walk away that he did what he did simply because it was who he was.

But then and now, he was brought up against a question he'd asked himself from the beginning: Had he made a difference?

He hoped so.

But even if he hadn't, it was impossible for him to walk away from this situation.

The exit out of the basement was tucked in the west corner. The steel door lifted upward at an angle, and McGarvey, expecting that Fuentes or at least one or more of his people would be either coming up the driveway or most likely over the wall from the alley, switched the Walther's safety lever off and eased the door open far enough so that he had a clear angle on the back wall.

But as before, nothing moved. Fuentes was either very slow, or he was very smart and had laid a trap.

McGarvey opened the door the rest of the way, hesitated for just a moment—expecting to take incoming fire—but nothing happened so he slipped outside and, keeping low and in the deeper shadows next to the house, hurried to the east side, where he checked the driveway.

The electrically operated gate was unlatched, but still closed. A Yellow Cab passed slowly as if the driver were looking for an address. No one was in the backseat.

McGarvey started to turn away when he caught two muzzle flashes from the roof of the brownstone across the street, and he was in time to see the silhouette of the shooter falling back, a rifle pitching over the edge of the roof and landing with a clatter on the curb, just missing a parked car.

It had to be María's doing. Exposing herself to draw the two shots, and then taking the sniper down. Twenty-five yards with a silenced pistol. A damned near impossible shot unless it had been a setup, but for the life of him, he couldn't understand why, or what the arrangement with Fuentes could be.

He went back to the basement door and waited for her to show up, all his senses heightened. The woman was the head of the DI's Directorate of Operations, and by all accounts plus what he'd witnessed firsthand, she was bright, devious, and extremely driven to secure her own survival in the new Cuba. Most telling was the fact she'd used the silencer.

"Kirk," she called softly from inside the basement.

McGarvey raised his pistol. "Come."

FIFTY-EIGHT

Fuentes, standing in the shadows at the opening of the alley from where he had a clear sight line to the wall behind the brownstone, answered his cell phone on the first ring. "*Sí.*"

It was Vásquez, who'd just made a pass in his Yellow Cab. "José is down."

"What do you mean, down?"

"They have a shooter on the roof. Looks like José took a couple of shots, and the last I saw as I made the corner was him falling back. And I think he dropped his rifle on the street."

"Turn around right now," Fuentes ordered. "I think they're trying to get out from the front."

"On my way."

"*Rápido,*" Fuentes said. He speed-dialed Murillo's number, and the agent hiding behind the Pepco van answered on the first ring.

"They have a shooter on the roof," he said. "José is down. And the *imbécil* dropped his rifle on the sidewalk. What do you want me to do?"

"Vásquez is on his way to back you up. Has anyone taken notice?"

"Not yet."

"Stay where you are. I think there's a good chance they're going to come out the front way."

"They'd be fools."

"Don't underestimate these people, especially Colonel León."

"What about you?"

"I'm at the alley, in case they come this way," Fuentes said.

"That's a comfort," Murillo said, and before Fuentes could respond, the agent broke the connection.

Garcia called. "I saw gunfire from the roof across the street."

"Start the van and get ready to go," Fuentes said. "I think they're going to try to leave the front way."

"They'd be fools."

"I've heard that before. Just start the van and stand by."

"*Sí.*"

Holding his pistol tightly, Fuentes started down the alley toward the brownstone, his stomach sour, his mouth dry. His ace in the hole had been the sniper on the roof across the street, who was supposed to keep them bottled up, leaving them only one way out. Right into his arms, where he would have been waiting at the corner to take them out one at a time as they came over the wall.

But Cobiella had made a mistake and they'd taken him down, and Fuentes was seething with rage. He knew the colonel's plan, and as insane as it was, he thought that with Ortega-Cowan's help, they might be able to pull it off. But not before learning where the treasure was hidden. Somewhere in southern New Mexico, they knew that much, but they needed the exact location. It was the one piece of information apparently known only to McGarvey, Rencke, and Louise Horn.

No matter what, then, McGarvey and the colonel had to be eliminated—priority one, because they were too dangerous. Which would leave only Rencke and his wife—an egghead and a woman.

FIFTY-NINE

María took her time coming up the stairs from the basement, and when her head and shoulders emerged, she looked up directly into the muzzle of McGarvey's pistol and reared back, her eyes wide in the darkness. "Are you going to shoot me?" she asked, keeping her voice low.

McGarvey was having a hard time reading her. Right now she was cautious but not fearful. And the corners of her mouth turned up in a half smile. Triumph? "The thought occurred," McGarvey said, lowering his gun.

"May I come up?"

"Yes. What about Otto and Louise?"

"Out of danger for the moment," María said. "I took out the sniper. Do you mean to take the fight to them, or will you wait until they come over the wall?"

"A little of both," McGarvey said. He still didn't know if he could trust her, which on the face of it was stupid. She might be running for her life, but she was Castro's daughter, and following her father's deathbed request. For Cuba's salvation, or for her own personal rescue. She had to figure that if she actually pulled this off, actually got at least some of the treasure across the border and back to Cuba, she could return to Havana on a white charger, a hero of the state.

"What do you want me to do?"

"Cover the rear wall," McGarvey said. "I'll be right back."

He headed to the driveway and, keeping low and as much as possible in the shadows, reached the gate. The Pepco van hadn't moved from its spot about thirty yards on a diagonal across the street, nor did the shooter hiding behind it show himself.

After screwing the silencer on the end of the Walther's barrel, he yanked the gate open as he fired two shots, aiming for a spot on the pavement beneath the van just behind the front tire. But if the ricochet shots found their mark as he thought was only an off chance, the Cuban agent didn't cry out, nor did he return fire.

He hurried back to the house. "It's me," he called softly around the corner.

"Clear," María replied.

She was watching the top of the wall from where she crouched in the shadows behind Otto's car when McGarvey came around the corner and went to Louise's Toyota SUV and opened the driver's-side door.

"Get ready to move," he told her. "We're going over the wall in about one minute."

"We're not driving out?"

"No," McGarvey said. Pocketing the pistol in the waistband of his jeans, he got behind the wheel, started the engine, backed out from where the car was parked nose in to the wall, and when he got it turned around, dropped it into drive and headed toward the open gate, jumping out only at the last minute just before the nose of the vehicle cleared the opening.

Several silenced shots hit the windshield as the SUV slowly moved across the street, where it came up against a parked Chevy Impala and stopped.

McGarvey raced back to where María was still crouched. "We're going over the wall now."

"Me first?" she asked.

"Together," he said. "Before they figure out the Toyota was a bluff."

SIXTY

Fuentes ran to the end of the alley and, making sure no traffic was coming up the street, hurried around the corner, past the van where Garcia was waiting with the engine running.

He was still connected with Murillo across the street from the brownstone.

"Bruno. What's going on? Talk to me."

"I've been hit in the leg," Murillo came back.

"Did they get past you?" Fuentes demanded. "Are they gone?"

"No, no, it was a trick. They opened the gate, someone fired a couple of shots, and a minute later the SUV came out of the driveway and I started shooting at the driver. But there was no one behind the wheel. The bastard just came across the street and crashed into a parked car."

"Have you attracted any notice yet? Anyone come snooping to find out what's going on?"

"Not yet," Murillo said, and he sounded steady, but in pain.

Fuentes ducked behind a parked car three down from the florist van and looked back to check the shadows toward the alley. But so far, there was no movement. "Stand by," he told Murillo.

"What do you want to do, Captain? This situation will not last more than a few minutes."

"Stand by," Fuentes repeated, and he speed-dialed Garcia. "Have the police been notified?"

"I'm picking up nothing yet," Garcia came back. He, too, sounded steady. "Where are you?"

"Behind a car about twenty meters to your south. I think they might be coming from the back after all. Are you getting anything from the house?"

"Nothing. But listen, Captain, I think we need to get out of here."

"Hold your position, you bastard, until I say we head out!" Fuentes shouted.

He speed-dialed Vásquez in the Yellow Cab. "Where the hell are you, Hector?"

"At the end of the street from Bruno's position, still covering the front of the house. What do you want to do, Captain?"

"Just hold where you are until I give the order to move out. This is still my operation."

"The hell it is—"

"*Hijo de puta,* do as you're told or I'll have you in front of a firing squad in Havana for dereliction of duty, failure to obey the direct order of a superior, and for cowardice in the middle of an operation vital to the state."

Murillo made no reply.

Fuentes turned again to watch where the alley opened to the street, but still saw no one coming out. It was possible that they had crashed the SUV to get someone's attention, figuring that they would call the police. Time was running out and he was frustrated and fast losing his patience. Everything was falling apart.

"Do you understand what I'm saying?" he sputtered. "Answer me!"

"I'm calling López."

"Hold your position!" Fuentes shouted, when the muzzle of a pistol was placed against the back of his head.

"Tell him and the others to leave," McGarvey said. "Or I'll put a bullet in your brain."

Fuentes froze for a moment. "We have a development," he told Vásquez. "Leave right now, and tell the others to pull out."

McGarvey grabbed the cell phone out of his hands, tossed it across the street, and stepped back. "Your man in the florist van?"

"*Sí*," Fuentes said, and he looked over his shoulder at McGarvey, whose face he'd only ever seen in photographs. But he'd not been prepared for the man's bulk, or the look of confidence and even contempt in the American's eyes. And instantly, he realized that he had made a very large mistake underestimating the man.

"You were in Mexico City and then Miami—why did you come here?"

Fuentes hesitated.

"Give me one good reason not to blow you away."

"We came for Colonel León. She's a traitor to the state."

"To arrest her or kill her?"

Fuentes came down a little. Evidently, McGarvey was more interested in information than anything else. "It didn't matter which, though we would have preferred to take her back to Cuba to stand trial."

"Because she no longer has her father's protection?"

"*Qué?*"

"She's Castro's daughter."

Fuentes laughed. "She is simply a traitor to the DI, and to the state. She's been stealing and extorting money from a wide range of low- and midlevel government officials for years. Trading on her father's name, threatening them with arrest and even torture if they refused to cooperate. What story did she try to sell you?"

"That's not a matter for the U.S. court system, whoever the hell you are and what your real purpose here is, but the murder of three people in Miami is."

"Traitors," Fuentes said, but then he glanced across the street and saw María standing between two parked cars. She was holding something in her right hand.

"She wants to kill you," McGarvey said. "She told us some story about a treasure of gold somewhere just across our border with Mexico. She claims that you've come here to kidnap her and force her to tell you where it is."

"And you believe that?"

"We're looking into it," McGarvey said. "Which leaves you two choices. And two only. Leave now, return to Cuba immediately, and you'll have your freedom, because at this point my government is not involved nor should it be."

"What about the people in Miami you claim I shot to death?"

"I didn't say anything about how they were killed."

"What's my second choice?"

"Die."

PART
FOUR

SIXTY-ONE

First thing in the morning, the CIA's Deputy Director of Operations Marty Bambridge powered down the rear window of his chauffeured black Cadillac limousine and showed his credentials to the guard at the White House's West Gate, who waved him through. The driver let him off at the West Entrance, where he was met by Doris Sampson, who was the secretary to Frank Shapiro, special adviser to the president on National Security Affairs, and she took him back to the NSA's office.

Shapiro, a husky man in his mid-fifties with thick dark hair and childhood acne scars, was just finishing a telephone call and he hung up. He seemed harried and moody. "What brings you across the river this morning?" he asked.

"We have a developing issue that I think you need to know about," Bambridge said. He and Shapiro were not on a first-name basis, but they knew each other from a number of security briefing sessions here in the West Wing at which the DDO had made presentations.

"Walt Page send you?"

"No."

Shapiro looked at him for a moment, but then

nodded. "Close the door," he said, and he phoned his secretary to tell her he was not to be disturbed for the next few minutes.

"I'm not going behind anyone's back. But it's a situation involving Kirk McGarvey for which I—the agency—could use a little guidance."

"He's been of some service to the CIA and to this country. The president has a great deal of respect for him."

It's not the reaction Bambridge had expected, and he nodded. "Perhaps it would be better if I fully briefed the director."

Shapiro waved him off. "You've come this far—tell me what's bothering you."

"I'm not sure this is the correct time."

"I am," Shapiro said coolly.

"There've been five shooting deaths—one in Georgetown last night, three in Miami the night before last, and one of a museum curator in Mexico City—all of them involving McGarvey and Colonel María León, who heads the Cuban intelligence services Directorate of Operations."

Shapiro was definitely interested. "This have anything to do with the kidnapping of the wife of one your officers?"

"We've learned that it was ordered by the DI in order to force her husband, our Special Projects officer Otto Rencke, to fly to Cuba with the State Department delegation that attended Castro's funeral."

"Jesus Christ, why weren't we briefed?"

"We didn't know all of the details ourselves until yesterday, and then there was a shooting last night in

Georgetown. The victim has been tentatively identified as a Cuban national who we think works for a DI cell here in Washington."

"Precisely how is McGarvey involved?"

"By his own admission, he's actually working with Colonel León. In fact, he flew clandestinely to Cuba to rescue Mr. Rencke, where he met with the colonel, who apparently arranged for the two of them to escape."

Shapiro shook his head. "Do you realize just how crazy this sounds?"

"Yes, but it's even worse."

"Page knows all of this?"

"Yes, he and I were briefed by McGarvey and Rencke yesterday."

"And?"

"The director gave them forty-eight hours to finish what they'd started," Bambridge said. "But since the incident last night, I don't think we can afford to wait."

"What did McGarvey have to say about it?"

"He and the colonel plus Mr. Rencke and his wife have disappeared. Again."

"Okay, Martin, tell me the worst."

And he did, leaving nothing out, including everything that was said in the meeting with Page after McGarvey and Rencke returned from Spain.

Shapiro was silent for several beats, until he shook his head. "If McGarvey wasn't involved, I would have to say that you're talking utter rubbish. But why did he want the forty-eight-hour delay before he talked to the Bureau?"

"He expected the DI to trace Colonel León to

Washington, and I think that he wanted to see what they would do."

"They tried to kill her, which you think validates her story in McGarvey's mind?"

"Exactly, as does the fact that he and the others disappeared sometime before the police showed up to investigate the shooting."

"How do you know McGarvey was in the middle of it? Were there witnesses?"

"No, but a SUV was involved, probably as a distraction, and we traced it to Louise Rencke. From there we gained entrance to a brownstone across the street from where the DI shooter's body was found. The place was filled with sophisticated computer and countersurveillance equipment. A lot of it CIA gear. Along with some personal effects belonging to Rencke and his wife. We think it's where they were hiding the colonel. Somehow the DI found out and apparently tried to smoke them out by cutting the electrical power to the house."

Shapiro was thoughtful. "So now what?"

"I think that McGarvey means to help Colonel León find the treasure and somehow get at least some of it to Cuba."

"That makes the least sense of all. McGarvey may be many things, some of them contrary and certainly not pleasant, but he's never betrayed his country, at least not in the long run."

"I'd like to ask him to explain himself, but as I said, he's disappeared again."

"That would be up to your people," Shapiro said. "But you did the right thing coming to see me."

"What would you like me to say to the director?"

Shapiro smiled. "That's up to you, Martin."

And Bambridge smiled inwardly, because he had gotten exactly what he wanted. A friend in the White House who would help bring McGarvey down off his high horse. It was a first step.

When Bambridge was gone, Shapiro walked down to the Oval Office, where President Joseph Langdon standing behind his desk was talking with John McKevitt, his chief of staff, and Howard Pursley, his chief speechwriter.

"I need a couple minutes whenever you have the time," Shapiro said.

"Anything earth shattering?" the president asked. The press had dubbed him the Dapper Dan when he ran successfully for the Colorado governorship ten years earlier, because he habitually wore three-piece suits, the ties always proper, the bottom buttons of the vests always undone, the same as this morning.

"No, sir, but interesting."

"Okay, let's take this up later," he told his speechwriter. "Anything John needs to stay for?"

Shapiro shrugged. "That's up to you, Mr. President." It was a code that he wanted some one-on-one time.

"Give us a couple of minutes," Langdon said, and his chief of staff and speechwriter left, closing the door behind them.

"We have a developing situation involving Kirk McGarvey and the colonel in the Cuban DI that frankly beats the hell out of me," Shapiro said.

"John said that he saw Marty Bambridge entering your office."

"Yes, sir. He came to talk to me without Walt Page's knowledge."

Langdon's expression darkened. "I don't like it."

"Neither do I, Mr. President. But you might want to know what he told me. At the very least it's interesting."

"And at the very worst?"

"Could very well either solve the Cuban problem once and for all, or escalate it almost to the point of another Bay of Pigs."

Langdon sighed in resignation. "What are the bastards up to now?"

And Shapiro recapped everything that the CIA's Deputy of Operations had told him, including the apparent fact that McGarvey and Otto Rencke had disappeared with the colonel.

Langdon took just a moment to come to his decision. "First of all, we're not sure that any of it is true. So the first order of business is to find McGarvey. But quietly. I'm told that he's a man who does not like to be sneaked up upon."

"I'll have Nick put someone on it," Shapiro said. Nicholas Wheeler was director of the U.S. Secret Service. They worked directly for the president and would make a lot less noise in such an investigation than would the FBI.

"When you find him, find the colonel and take her into custody. She ordered the kidnapping. Let's hear what she has to say for herself, after which I might telephone Raúl Castro to find out what he thinks he's up to."

"You might want to hold off before making that call," Shapiro said. "Because there is the matter of a possible Spanish treasure buried somewhere in southern New Mexico."

"I've read some of those stories, which hold about as much weight as alien abductions, or the Bermuda Triangle."

"Yes, Mr. President, but this time there may be some validity to the claim. The colonel is an illegitimate daughter of Fidel, who on his death made her promise to find the treasure and bring it back to Cuba, where he felt it rightly belonged."

Langdon laughed without humor. "If there is such a treasure—which you admit is more than far-fetched—it won't be going anywhere except Fort Knox. And just maybe Castro's daughter will be shot to death trying to escape."

"I'll see what should and can be done," Shapiro said.

"Yes, do that," the president said.

SIXTY-TWO

A half hour later, an aide ushered Kirk McGarvey into Walt Page's office on the seventh floor of the CIA's Old Headquarters Building, where the DCI was waiting with Gavin Litwiller, the director of the FBI.

"From what I gather reading the overnights, you've already struck a nerve, if that was you," Page said.

"It was me," McGarvey said. "We set a trap and they took it."

"You know Gavin, I'm sure," Page said.

Litwiller was a tall, senatorial-looking man in his late sixties with white hair and wide, expressive eyes that made it seem as if he was seeing absolutely everything for exactly what it was. Actually, it was a skill he had perfected as a lawyer in military intelligence, from where he'd been elected to the bench in Denver. The president had picked him to head the Bureau three years ago, and by all accounts he'd done an outstanding job. He and McGarvey shook hands.

"Only by reputation," McGarvey said.

Litwiller smiled faintly. "I'd have to say the same," he said. "Walt told me that you wanted this meeting, just the three of us, and here I am. My people still want to interview you about the kidnapping of Louise Horn, and then of course this business last night in Georgetown. And you have our attention because we've tentatively identified the dead man as DI. Makes us curious about what's going on between you and Cuban intelligence."

"It has to do with a deathbed request by Fidel Castro that could involve a substantial dollar amount in a Spanish treasure from the sixteenth, seventeen, and eighteenth centuries buried somewhere in New Mexico. The Cuban government wants a piece of it, but a DI colonel who's apparently defected claims she wants the money for the people."

"Good Lord," Litwiller said. "That's quite story to swallow in one bite. Who is the colonel, and where is she?"

"María León, and she's right here in Washington. In

fact, it was she who the DI came for last night. And it was to her that Castro made his deathbed request."

"The obvious question is why her?"

"She's one of his illegitimate children."

Litwiller and Page exchanged a glance.

"As my oldest son used to say when he was a teen-ager, this is rad, or fringe, or something like that," the FBI director said. "Do you believe her?"

"We've established that a cache or caches of gold and silver and perhaps other things of historical value might have been buried in southern New Mexico. Some of it could still be there—we haven't established all of that yet."

"Yes, but do you believe her motivations? Or has she merely involved you in some elaborate scheme to get your help?"

McGarvey shrugged. "I honestly don't know, or least I'm not sure. The DI had traced her to Miami, where they killed three people and very nearly got to her. Then they traced her here to Georgetown, where they nearly got to her again. But it was she who took down the DI officer whose body you found on the roof across from where we were staying."

"Rather convenient of them to have traced her so easily," Litwiller said. "Any chance she was leaving a trail of bread crumbs?"

"It would have been easy for her to do in Miami, but here in D.C., it would have been tough."

"But not out of the question?"

Louise had picked her up from Andrews, and the two of them had been alone together for most of the day. "Not out of the question."

"From what I understand, the DI managed to cut the power to the house. How many of them were there, besides the one on the roof who we took to be a sniper?"

"Four, maybe five," McGarvey said.

"And they just turned around and cleared out when you took down one of their people?"

"I created a diversion on the street in front of the house and went over the back wall, where I managed to come up behind the guy I took to be their point man and told him he had two choices: go or die."

"So you let them go," Litwiller said.

"I wanted at least one of them to report back to Havana that the Spanish treasure did exist in New Mexico and that the colonel and I knew where it was."

"Do you honestly think that once whoever came here to arrest or kill this colonel of yours gets back to Havana and tells their bosses about the treasure, the DI will actually mount an operation to grab it?"

"It's going to get a little more complicated than that, Mr. Director, but yes, that's essentially what I think will happen."

Litwilller sat back and eyed McGarvey for a long beat. "I received a call from Nick Wheeler in my car on the way over here. He's director of the Secret Service. The White House had just asked him to find you and this Cuban colonel. I won't say who made the suggestion, but they thought it wouldn't be a bad thing if the colonel were shot to death trying to escape."

This one took McGarvey by surprise, and he turned to Page. "Did you give the president or anyone from his staff the heads-up on what Otto and I discussed after we got back from Spain?"

"No," the DCI said. He went to the phone on his desk and asked his secretary to reach Mr. Bambridge. After a moment, he thanked her and hung up.

"He's at the White House?" McGarvey asked.

"On his way back," Page said. "But my secretary didn't know from where. So where does it leave us, Mac?"

"I want the Cubans to go after the treasure in New Mexico, and I want our government to cooperate."

Litwiller almost laughed. "You're talking about an invasion?"

"Yes, but if you'll let me explain at least that part of it, we just might be able to put a big dent in two of the problems we have down there."

"Which are?"

"The massive amounts of drug smuggling across the border, and the drug cartel violence in northern Mexico."

Again, Litwiller held his peace for a beat or two, until finally he shook his head. "I knew that coming here to meet with you this morning was going to prove interesting at the very least, but just not this sensational. And I suppose it would be foolish of me to ask that you and Colonel León voluntarily submit to interviews, under the Bureau's protection. The Secret Service is quite good at everything it does. If they have a White House directive to find you and the colonel, someone might get hurt in the process."

"We're leaving Washington tonight, or no later than tomorrow morning."

"The first places they'll stake out are the airports and train stations."

"But not Andrews," McGarvey said. "We're flying out on a CIA aircraft. Miami first, then Mexico City, and finally Holloman Air Force Base."

"New Mexico," Litwiller said. "To the treasure."

"You'll have one of the jets, but first I'll have to know what you're up to," Page said.

"I know where the gold is buried, or at least I have a pretty good idea, and I have an idea how get to it so that no one innocent should get hurt."

"You don't seriously believe that if such a treasure exists—on U.S. soil—and if you find it, that any of it will actually be sent to Cuba," Litwiller said.

"The Cubans could make a pretty good case based on historical facts that one third of it belongs to them, but not one ounce of it will ever make it to Havana. And that I'm willing to guarantee."

"Okay, you've got the aircraft and crew," Page said. "But you have to tell us how you're going to pull this off and, even more important, why. After all, it was nothing more than the deathbed request from a dictator to his daughter, herself a spymaster who's been responsible for dozens of deaths, probably hundreds or more in her career. Why are you helping her?"

"First the how, and then the why," McGarvey said. And he told them.

SIXTY-THREE

Just before noon, Román Ortega-Cowan was admitted into the office of the President of Cuba, where he stopped directly in front of the desk and raised a crisp salute. Raúl Castro—seated behind his wide desk strewn this morning with dozens of files, documents, international newspapers, and magazines—finished jotting something on a notepad before he looked up, his eyes narrow, the expression on his face not pleasant.

The room, not changed much since Fidel had turned over the government to his brother, felt more like the study of a college professor with a lot of books on built-in shelves than a government office: a studious place of intellectual work.

"I received two disturbing reports this morning," Raúl said. "One from Washington and the other from Miami that should have come to me directly from your office. Can you tell me why I had to go to the effort to find out for myself what you should have brought to my personal attention?"

Ortega-Cowan lowered his salute, knowing exactly what two reports the president was talking about, though he had no idea who'd sent them over. "I'm sorry, sir, but routine operational reports aren't usually sent to you—otherwise, it would be necessary for you to spend every waking hour reading them."

"Don't toy with me, Major," Raúl warned. "You know what I'm talking about, unless the department you are presently overseeing is even more inept and inefficient than I'm coming to believe it is."

"I'm sorry, Mr. President, I'm at a loss—"

"Miami is in an uproar. The traitors there are close to a revolution, which has caught the attention of Washington."

"There is always some sort of trouble in the Calle Ocho."

"Not like this, or truly has your intelligence apparatus there not made a report?"

Ortega-Cowan really was at a loss, and worried that something else was going on that he didn't know about, something involving the funneling of information like this directly to the president's office. "There was a disturbance a few days ago, perhaps three deaths that may have involved the dissidents' crude intelligence apparatus."

"Were you also not aware that Colonel León was traced to Washington, and that a DI operation to arrest her last night not only failed but resulted in the death of one of our people as well, and focused attention on our intelligence-gathering unit?"

"One of my overnight staff received a brief call from Carlos López, who heads our Washington operation, that a minor disturbance may have taken place, and that as soon as he had all the facts, he would send me a report."

"I've read it," Raúl said. He picked up a file and handed it across the desk to Ortega-Cowan. "Both incidents are there. And can you guess who the two common denominators are?"

"I'm assuming Colonel León and Captain Fuentes,

who was sent to Mexico City to find her. He traced her to Miami and yesterday to Washington. His orders—my orders—were to bring her home, where she could be charged with espionage and high treason. It's possible that his and the colonel's presence in both cities created the problems you speak of."

"Indeed," Raúl said.

Ortega-Cowan had learned early in his career that when a lie was necessary, make it a very large lie that was laced with just enough verifiable truth to make the entire thing believable, at least in the short run.

"Captain Fuentes has become something of a problem," he said. "Since El Comandante's death, he's talked about becoming Minister of Foreign Affairs. In my estimation, he'd become expendable, which is why I sent him after Colonel León. I thought at the very least he might flush her out where the dissidents in Miami might kill her, and the same in Washington, where Major López could take her in. Apparently neither happened."

"Where is Captain Fuentes at this moment?"

"If not still in Washington, where he might have gone to ground, then on his way here."

"If he shows up here, arrest him," Raúl ordered. "And tell me what further plans you have to find and arrest Colonel León."

"That depends on what is in these reports, Mr. President, and what Captain Fuentes will tell us when we have him in custody. Much will depend on why the colonel defected. She was up to something before she escaped, but she wouldn't share it with me."

"Something involving the CIA officer or officers whom she allowed to leave from her compound?"

"Presumably," Ortega-Cowan said.

"I want this matter to be resolved, Major. Soon."

"Of course Señor Presidente," Ortega-Cowan said. He saluted, which Raúl returned, then turned and headed for the door.

"Your career depends on this," Raúl said. "Maybe even your life."

Over the past few years, Ortega-Cowan had developed the habit of taking a cab up to the Malecón whenever he was bothered and had something to work out in his mind. He would walk along the waterfront and sometimes stop for a coffee in the horribly run-down Hotel Deauville, which still evoked something of the old, grander Havana.

The day was pleasantly warm, the streets comfortably anonymous, and deep in thought about what he would have to do to keep Raúl at bay, he was unaware that he had picked up a tail, until Fuentes came up behind him.

"Good afternoon, Román."

Ortega-Cowan almost stumbled, but he recovered smoothly. "Your name just came up no more than fifteen minutes ago."

"Let me guess, in the office of El Presidente, who wants both of our heads on a platter for allowing the colonel to simply fly away like a little bird."

"Mostly your head for the debacles in Miami and Washington. Apparently, you had her in your sights and you lost her both times."

"Where's he getting his information?"

"I don't know," Ortega-Cowan said, and he held up the file Raúl had given him. "Only this matters."

"I have something much better," Fuentes said.

"I hope for your sake you do, because El Presidente wants you arrested and interrogated vigorously, and I have to agree with him. If you were to be taken down, most of my problems would go away."

Fuentes stopped and faced the older, much larger man. "Román, what do you want? What's in your wildest dreams?"

Ortega-Cowan considered Fuentes for a long moment. Castro's former chief of security seemed more confident than ever before, even excited and happy. "Raúl off my back, and then the directorship of the DI. For starts."

"Well, you'll have all of that and more. And I'm going to give it to you."

"The treasure exists, and you know how to find it," Ortega-Cowan said, keeping his suddenly raging emotions in check.

"El Comandante's gold exists, and I know exactly how to find it and bring it back here. But I'll need your help, and we'll have to act fast."

They found a small *paladar* with a few tables on the broken sidewalk a few doors down from the Deauville. After they ordered coffees, Fuentes explained everything that had happened in Miami, and then the operation in Georgetown. "We managed to penetrate the computer freak's security systems and listen to the conversation they had with the colonel, and it was nothing less than illuminating."

"Any chance they knew you were snooping?"

"Doesn't matter, the treasure does exist in southern New Mexico—McGarvey and his pals know exactly where—and the bitch told him how she planned to grab it and get it back here. Only we're going to beat her to the punch."

"How?" Ortega-Cowan asked, and after Fuentes explained everything, he began to think that they might just have a chance of pulling off the biggest coup for Cuba since the Bay of Pigs, or even the revolution. But he also came to the realization that he now had all the information he needed; Fuentes was just about superfluous.

"One more thing," the captain said sitting back, grinning. "I have another piece of information for you. Something I learned from El Comandante's files. Something I decided not to share with you until the time was right. Until now."

Ortega-Cowan could imagine what Fuentes was talking about, but he felt the first stirrings of unease. "I'm listening."

"Do you know your mother?"

The question was startling, and Ortega-Cowan almost didn't answer. But he was intrigued. "She died in a car wreck when I was five, but I remember her telling me that my father had been a hero of the revolution and would one day come for me."

"But he never did."

"No."

"Nor did he ever come for the *coronel*, your half sister."

SIXTY—FOUR

They had rented a couple of cars, including a plain Ford Taurus and a Chevrolet Impala from Hertz at Dulles, and had taken up residence at a small two-story colonial in McLean that Otto had purchased almost two years ago. The house at the end of a cul-de-sac backed to a stand of trees that would provide cover if they needed to make a run for it. And although the neighborhood was quiet, the four of them kept out of sight so far as it was possible.

After his meeting with Page, McGarvey had spent most of the rest of the day on the phone with a number of contacts, including, and especially, Martínez in Miami, who fed him up-to-the-minute reports on not only what the DI was up to, but also what the mood of the exile community was.

"*Caliente* and growing," Martínez said.

"And you're fanning the flames."

"Of course. But you might have to come here soon and talk with a few key people before they'll commit as a mob. You understand?"

"Do you have a leak in your organization?"

"There're DI spooks all over the place. We work around them."

"The word is out about the treasure?"

"Yes," Martínez said.

"We'll be down first thing in the morning."

"Not sooner? They need to know what this is really all about, and what their chances will be."

"I still need to make sure of one more thing."

"The *coronel*?"

"*Sí.*"

"There, you do speak Spanish."

"*Claro que sí.*" Of course I do, McGarvey said. "Tomorrow. Early."

By late afternoon, he'd taken his plans about as far as he could from Washington, and he went into the kitchen and opened a Pils Urquell beer and sat at the counter drinking and looking out the window at the woods and darkening evening and thinking that Katy would have liked it here, at this hour with a glass of nice merlot.

"A centavo," María said at the doorway.

McGarvey looked up. "Actually it's a penny for your thoughts. Are you ready to leave?"

"Louise and Otto have pinpointed at least one site near Victorio that looks very promising. I assume we're going to take a look before I go to Ciudad Juárez to start everything in motion." She looked bright, fresh, even animated.

And naïve despite her hard experiences, McGarvey thought. "First Miami, we need to put out a few fires. Your Captain Fuentes evidently assassinated three key people. The entire Calle Ocho is in an uproar."

"It's not part of the operation—"

"It is now, because you're the cause of it," McGarvey said coolly. "You're here, and you'll do as I tell you to do. *Comprende, Señora Coronel?*"

She turned and stalked down the hall as Louise and Otto came back to the kitchen.

"Tantrums?" Louise asked.

McGarvey laughed. "Just the start, I think. What'd you two find out?"

Louise glanced over her shoulder to make sure María had gone upstairs. "Victorio Peak was all but hollowed out sometime back in the sixties. If there was any treasure buried in the caves, it's long gone by now."

"Hollowed out by who?"

"The military, of course. It's what you expected, wasn't it?"

"Counted on, actually," McGarvey said. "She doesn't know?"

"Probably does, but there're a dozen conflicting accounts," Otto said. "Take your pick."

"What about the topographic maps of the vicinity? Did you find anything promising?"

"Oh, yeah," Louise said. She'd brought her laptop with her, and she opened it on the counter in front of McGarvey, and pulled up a satellite view of the southern New Mexico desert just northeast of the border. "Fort Bliss Military Reservation land about fifty miles south of Victorio Peak. Looks really promising."

"We'll need permission for what we want to do."

"I spoke to Walt Page fifteen minutes ago," Otto said. "He's going to the president with it first thing in the morning."

McGarvey sat back. "Castro's gold," he said. "I would never have believed it actually existed."

"Oh, but it does, kemo sabe," Otto said, and he began hopping from foot to foot.

. . .

They were leaving for Andrews around four in the morning, and after an early dinner of Cuban pork roast with rice and plantains—the ingredients for which Louise and María managed to find in a small bodega in Alexandria and which María cooked for them— McGarvey turned in early.

Being on the hunt and with friends like this, he'd turned a little morose; he missed his old life with Katy and Liz and Todd. Standing now in jeans but no shirt at the window in his second-floor bedroom around midnight with a snifter of brandy, one part of him was engaged with his memories, while the other professional part was going over his plan, and everything that could go wrong—which was just about everything.

Dealing with thousands, perhaps tens of thousands of people was unpredictable. Anything could, and probably would, happen. But it was going to come together very soon now, and he honestly had no feeling for how it would turn out. Too many variables, most of which were out of his control, he told himself, and yet for the first time in a long time, he thought that he had a shot of changing something important—not just the elimination of some expediter or even some cabal, but something even more important, more fundamental for a lot of innocent people whose only misfortune was being born in the wrong place.

Someone came to his door, and he resisted the automatic urge to reach for his pistol lying on the nightstand a couple of feet away. This place was a safe haven.

"I didn't know if you were asleep," María said.

"It's late and we have an early start. Get some sleep."

"I can't. I'm frightened."

"You should be—after Miami, you're going back to Havana sooner or later."

"Don't be a fool. They'll arrest me the moment I step off the plane, and I would just disappear as if I'd never existed."

"You should have thought about it before you started this thing," McGarvey said.

"Goddamnit—"

McGarvey turned. "Shut up before you wake up the house," he said. "What the hell do you want? Who the fuck do you think you are? How many people have to kiss your ass while you send them to be tortured or murdered? How much is enough for people like you and your father and all the other insane bastards who think that the only way to lead a country is to put it in chains? Bullies, all of you, even worse than the Taliban. They only want to take away women's rights—you want to take away everyone's."

"I want to make amends," María said in a small voice. She came closer. "I want it to stop. Honest to God. Finally. I need your help."

McGarvey turned away. "And you're getting it."

She came to him and laid her head on the back of his shoulder. Just that and no more.

He could feel her heat and smell her scent. "As long as they're convinced that you know how to retrieve the treasure, they won't touch you," he said. "But we're dropping you off in Mexico City, and from there it'll be up to you."

"Where will you be?"

"In New Mexico, waiting for you."

SIXTY—FIVE

Ortega-Cowan picked up his bedside telephone at the same time he glanced at the clock. It was a little past four in the morning, the sun not yet up. *"Quien es?"*

"Ernesto," a man said softly. "I have news."

"Sí," Ortega-Cowan said. He got out of bed, glanced at his eighteen-year-old ballet dancer, Giselle, lying curled into a ball tangled with the damp bedsheets, and padded nude out to the balcony of the eighth-floor penthouse looking out over Havana harbor to the northeast and the wooded Maestranza Park that paralleled the Avenida del Puerto, formally known as the Avenida Carlos Manuel de Céspedes.

Ernesto Cura had lived in Miami as an exile, where he owned a small coffee shop just off Southwest Eighth Street (Calle Ocho itself) and Ponce de León Boulevard, and was a reasonably trusted if somewhat fringe observer of the local power structure. He heard things. "There is a development."

"I'm listening."

"Colonel León is on her way back with her CIA friends. Should be touching down at Homestead in the next hour or so. I thought that you might be interested."

It wasn't quite what Ortega-Cowan expected, at least not if Fuentes's report about the conversation he'd surveilled in Georgetown was true. But he was very interested. "How do you know this?"

"CK Alpha's people were at my shop and they were

talking." CK Alpha was the DI's designator for Raúl Martínez. "Still talking. The entire district is in an uproar."

"Because she's on her way back?"

"That and something else."

María returning to Miami, where she was a woman marked for assassination, made no sense—unless Kirk McGarvey had somehow convinced Martínez that she knew where the treasure was and had a plan to retrieve it, and she meant to include the dissidents. But if that were the case, it might mean that she had something else up her devious sleeve. Another misdirection for which she was an expert, well trained by her Russian instructors.

"What else?" Ortega-Cowan demanded.

"The whole place is practically going crazy. Trash fires in the streets, people singing and marching. No vandalism yet, but it almost feels like a religious festival, except—"

"Except what?"

"It's crazy."

"*Madre de Dios,*" Mother of God, Ortega-Cowan said. "You're not making any sense!"

"They're chanting the number seven over and over. Seven cities. And they're all happy."

Ortega-Cowan's heart began to race. Cíbola and the Seven Cities of Gold. "Are they getting ready to take a trip?"

"What?"

"Are they getting ready to leave Miami? Maybe ordering buses, or getting their cars ready, or buying train or bus tickets?"

"I don't know," Ernesto said.

"Find out," Ortega-Cowan said.

Giselle didn't stir when he went back into the bedroom and got dressed for the day in his plain olive drab military fatigues. They'd both done too many lines of coke last night with Maximo Extra Añejo rum chasers, but she had a lot less body mass than he had and she was still zoned out, whereas his own head was crystal clear.

Outside, he got in his old Chevrolet Impala, kept in good running condition by one of his operational planners who happened to be a master mechanic on the side, and headed to his office in Plaza Havana. If María was on the move, he had a lot of work to do before the distraction of regular hours. And he would need to set Fuentes to the hunt.

His cell phone vibrated. "*Sí,*" he answered.

It was Ernesto in Miami, and in the background, the crowd noises were loud. "You were right, they're getting set to leave in the next twenty-four hours. A convoy."

"To where, exactly?"

"I haven't been able to find out. I don't think most of them know where themselves."

That final detail actually didn't matter, because Ortega-Cowan knew exactly where they were going— New Mexico. But he was a man of completeness, of elegant endings just like the operas he so loved. "Find out. And let me know when Colonel León arrives, and especially where she goes, who she talks to and what reaction she causes."

"I think that if she shows her face here, the mood of the crowd, they'll tear her limb from limb."

"Keep your eyes and ears open," Ortega-Cowan said, and he phoned Fuentes, who was staying at the same DI safe house on the Malecón where María had stayed before she made her run for Camagüey.

"*Sí,*" Fuentes answered on the first ring all out of breath, as if he'd been waiting for the call.

"Can't sleep, either?" Ortega-Cowan asked.

"Has something happened?"

"María should be touching down in Homestead in an hour or so with McGarvey and Rencke."

"That doesn't make any sense."

"It might, but listen. All of Calle Ocho is in an uproar. People in the streets, chanting about seven cities, singing, partying."

"What's that supposed to mean?"

"Cíbola. The Seven Cities of Gold. They've been told about the treasure and apparently they're getting ready to go after it."

"That doesn't make any sense, either. The only way they'd know about it is if the bitch somehow got McGarvey to convince Martínez that the traitors and defectors could go directly to New Mexico to grab the gold themselves. No need to involve the Mexican cartels or try to bring it to Guantánamo."

"It'll take them time to get organized, and at least two days to get across country," Ortega-Cowan said.

"We'll need to beat them to the punch," Fuentes said.

"Exactly. And I'll tell you how we're going to do it."

SIXTY-SIX

The CIA's Gulfstream G650 biz jet touched down at Homestead Air Force Base twenty miles south of Miami just before the sun began to rise, and the pilot was directed to immediately taxi to a hangar across the field from flight operations. Louise remained in McLean to backstop them, so it was just McGarvey, Rencke, and a highly agitated María aboard.

Martínez was leaning against his car inside the hangar, his arms crossed, an unlit cigar at the corner of his mouth. He looked dangerous this morning.

"I can understand going back to Havana to pull this off," María said. "I still have enough clout in the DI to at least make my chief of staff listen long enough to put everything in place. After all, the only way I could have found out what I needed was by supposedly defecting. But why this now?"

It was the same thing she'd been saying since early this morning. But in fact, McGarvey thought that she'd agreed way too easily. It was nearly impossible to read anything usable from her eyes, yet he was almost certain he detected something there, maybe something disingenuous.

"You're going to explain to Raúl just how you mean to keep the treasure away from your government and make sure that it gets to the people."

"You know," she said.

"But he doesn't, and the explanation will have to come from you," McGarvey told her. He glanced out the window as they came to a stop and the jet's engines began to spool down. "And by the looks of his mood, I suggest you tell the truth. It was because of you that three of his people were gunned down."

The young male flight attendant in a crisp white shirt and dark blue blazer opened the hatch and lowered the stairs, then got something from a forward galley and brought it back to Otto.

"Will this do, Mr. Rencke?" he asked.

It was a small digital video camera, and Otto quickly checked it over and nodded. "Just fine," he said.

And María understood the real purpose for this stop, and realized there was nothing she could do about it. "Blackmail," she said.

"Maybe you'll turn the gold over to the navy at Guantánamo, and do exactly as you said you wanted to do—get the money to the people. But then again, maybe you'll change your mind. Maybe a video of your cooperation with the DI's most wanted man might show up on Castro's desk, or better yet broadcast over TV Cubana or Cubavision on the Internet so that the people could see what had been promised and been taken away from them—by you."

Martínez pushed away from his car, pocketed his cigar, and started for the aircraft stairs.

"I've told you want I want to do and why I'm doing it, but what about you?" María asked. "If you know where the gold is, why not just tell the military and grab it for yourselves?"

"We're going to take most of it, but you'll get away with at least a third. A lot of money by any account, but for Cubans a king's ransom."

"If the money gets to the people, there'll be a real incentive to topple the government."

"And you'll be the one who did it for them."

"Along with the help of your government."

"Something like that," McGarvey said.

María glanced over at Otto, who'd already begun recording. "How much of that do you want me to tell Martínez?"

"He knows most of it already, so don't hold anything back. This is just a stage drama that we may never have to use."

"Colonel León, back so soon?" Martínez said from the open hatch.

The attendant had gone into the cockpit with the flight crew and closed the door.

"She has something to tell you before she goes back to Havana," McGarvey said.

"Better not try to get her out through MIA, the mood up there just now is ugly," Martínez said, and he sat down across the aisle from her.

"We're flying her to Mexico City soon as we're finished here."

Martínez nodded. "I'm all ears, Colonel. And believe me, I do wish you the best of luck when you get home."

"Mr. McGarvey tells me that you've been told everything, so I won't go into the details—"

"Ah, but by all means, please do."

"*Bastardo*," she said, but she told him the same things she'd laid out for McGarvey in Georgetown, including the use of the Gulf Cartel based in Matamoros, the Sinaloas who used to be Gulf's main opposition, Los Zetas, all of them ex-military and their main allies the

Beltrán-Leyvas, to gather ordinary Mexicans and herd them en masse across the border. "No guns," she said. "No one will get hurt."

"And you think that your ordinary Mexicans—as you call them—will actually do it? I mean why?"

"Fear."

"What's in it for the cartels?"

"Without us, a major link in their supply chain would suddenly disappear. They'll want to protect it."

"Have you talked it over with any of them?" Martínez asked.

"With all of them," María said.

"And you think you can pull this off right under the noses of your chief of staff and that little prick Captain Fuentes?"

"That'll be easy part. The rest will be up to Washington."

Martínez seemed to consider her words for a moment, then looked at McGarvey. "What happens after you drop her off?"

"We're going to Holloman. The main cache of the treasure is to the south, we think somewhere on Fort Bliss. Not too far from the border. We've got it pinpointed to two or three spots within a mile or so of each other. Should take us less than twenty-four hours to check out all three."

"So you find this treasure, then what?"

"Dig it up."

"You sure of this, *comp*?"

"Sure enough about what it means to us and to Cuba," McGarvey said.

Martínez got to his feet. "Then I truly do wish you

the best of luck, *Coronel*," he said. He nodded to McGarvey and Otto and left the aircraft.

Four hours later, they were allowed to taxi to an empty slot at Benito Juárez International Airport's Terminal 2, which serviced international flights. A pair of nervous customs agents came aboard to check everyone's passport, and they visibly relaxed when they learned that only María, under a work name, was getting off and would be flying to Havana on the next available commercial flight. The aircraft did not have CIA written on its tail, but the number came with diplomatic immunity from an unspecified agency that was not affiliated with the U.S. Department of State. Nothing was said about the warrant for McGarvey's arrest because Otto had temporarily blocked it from the Mexican police computer system.

"Do you wish for us to stamp your passport, Señora Delgado?" one of the uniformed agents asked.

"As a courtesy, no," María said.

"*Sí, señora*," the agent said, and he returned her passport.

"How long do you wish to remain in Mexico?" the other agent asked McGarvey.

"We'll leave as soon as we refuel and have clearance to take off."

"Have you filed a flight plan?"

"Yes, for Albuquerque, New Mexico."

María gathered her purse and bag, and before she followed the customs officers off the aircraft, she turned back to McGarvey. "I want this to work."

"So do I."

"I have your sat phone number—I'll call you in a day or two to see what you've found. And maybe I'll see you in New Mexico in a few days, maybe sooner."

"Can your Mexican contacts round up enough people to storm the border in that short a time?"

"They guarantee that they could do it even faster. Do you think you can find the treasure and convince your government not only to dig it up, but allow us to cart it off as well?"

"I'm working on it."

"To bring down my government."

McGarvey didn't bother to answer, and at the open hatch, María hesitated again and looked back.

"This is crazy, you know?"

"Certifiable," McGarvey said.

In the air again, heading northwest, with Bloody Marys as they waited for the attendant to rustle up some breakfast, McGarvey phoned Page in his office at CIA headquarters.

"Everything is just about in place now. Time for you to see the president."

"The colonel is on her way back to Havana?" Page asked.

"We dropped her off in Mexico City a couple hours ago."

"Where are you now?"

"About two hours from Holloman, Mr. Director, so you'll have to hustle—because these guys aren't going to go along on my word alone. And we'll need the New

Mexico Army National Guard and probably the border patrol."

"And someone who can assume overall command," Page said. "This is insanity—you do realize it, I hope."

"Convince the president, because if we can pull this off, it just might solve our problem with Cuba once and for all."

Page was silent for several beats. "I'll do my best, Mac. But give me three hours."

"You got it," McGarvey said. Using the aircraft interphone unit, he called the flight deck. "Can you slow us down a little? I don't want to get to Holloman for another three hours."

"No problem, Mr. McGarvey," the captain said. "In fact, I'll let air traffic control know that we've run into an unexpected head wind."

"Good man," McGarvey said, and he put the phone down.

Otto was staring at him, obviously troubled.

"Do you think this is a mistake?" McGarvey asked.

"Tons of stuff could go wrong, kemo sabe," Otto said. "I mean, why not just dig up the treasure and somehow convince the president to share it with the Cubans? Wouldn't have to involve Colonel León—she was lying back there, by the way."

"Yeah, I know. There's no way she could have struck some kind of a deal with the Mexican cartels that fast. She was on the run."

"She's got help, and I'm betting it's her chief of staff, because she didn't seem overly worried about going back to Havana."

"Which leaves Captain Fuentes," McGarvey said. "I

have a feeling he has his own agenda. Probably part of the internal struggles going on ever since Fidel died."

"So, back to my original question," Otto said. "Why not just dig up the treasure and convince the president to share it?"

"In the first place, it wouldn't be likely the president would be convinced, leastways not right now, not with pressure from the Mexicans or from Havana."

"And in the second?" Otto asked.

"There is no treasure in New Mexico. At least not on Holloman or Fort Bliss."

SIXTY-SEVEN

María's credentials under the work name Ines Delgado raised no eyebrows at Havana's José Martí International Airport passport control nor had she expected they would, though it seemed a little strange to be coming home like this. As anonymously as she had left just a few days ago.

She had only her carry-on bag, which was given a cursory check by customs, and then she was outside—where Ortega-Cowan, in tan slacks and a crisp white guayabera shirt, was waiting with his Chevy, the top down.

"Your call from the airplane came as a surprise," he said. "Welcome home."

"Intrigued?" she asked. She dumped her bag in the

backseat and got in the car as Ortega-Cowan slipped behind the wheel and they took off. The traffic was light and the weather fabulous, warm, the air silken and the breeze light.

"Somewhat. But I thought you'd defected—we all did. Though I couldn't fathom why."

"I did defect," she said. "It was the only way to maintain the illusion for McGarvey and Rencke."

Ortega-Cowan glanced at her. "Illusion?"

"I needed to seem sincere."

"By flying to Miami and putting your life in danger?"

"Exactly. Just as I've returned and put my life in danger again. I'm sure that El Presidente was quick to issue orders for my arrest for treason, which right now puts you in his crosshairs."

"You were never one to mince words, Comrade Colonel," Ortega-Cowan said. "You're back, which means you believe that there's something to this business with a treasure somewhere in New Mexico."

And she had him, as she knew she would. No one, especially not a man of Ortega-Cowan's appetites and ambitions, could resist a good treasure story. "It's there all right, Román, and the Americans are going to help us get part of it."

"Does it have anything to do with the agitation going on in Miami right now?"

"Sí, they're also going to help us."

They drove in silence for a time, but Ortega-Cowan kept glancing at her. "You've changed," he said.

It surprised her. "What do you mean?"

"Your father's death, and then the attack on your

compound and McGarvey and your defection and now the gold. Manuel said that you truly were a traitor."

"How would that little bastard know?"

"He recorded your conversation with McGarvey and Rencke and the man's wife you had kidnapped."

"Impossible," María said. Louise had showed her the antisurveillance systems, promising that they were perfectly safe from eavesdropping.

"Nevertheless, it's true. He's back and we're going to him right now so we can figure out what comes next."

"The bastard tried to kill me," María flared. "He's not a part of this. I want him behind bars."

"It's too late for that," Ortega-Cowan said mildly. "He knows about the deals you made with the Mexican drug cartels, and he's spent every waking hour since he got back cementing those deals for you. All we need now are the precise location across the border and the time you want the invasion to start."

"Listen to me, Román. If need be, I'll tell the president everything and recommend that both Manuel and you be placed under arrest."

"As I said, sister, it's too late for that."

It took a moment for what he had called her to sink in, and she looked at him, really looked at him. He was smiling, and he glanced over at her and nodded.

"It's true. Manuel told me about it, and showed me the records. Actually we're half siblings. Different mothers, same father. It explains why we've worked so well together over the past few years since you got back from Moscow."

She wanted to argue, but looking into her own feelings, she realized the truth of it. They had too many similarities in tastes and ambitions. And she remembered staring at him every now and then, wanting to say something or ask him something; it was always on the tip of her tongue, but she'd never been able to give voice to it.

"Papá was a very busy man," she said at last. "Five sons and a daughter, plus you and me."

"Who knows, maybe there's more of us," Ortega-Cowan said. "In the end, what it comes down to is that you and I have to trust each other."

María chuckled. "What trust?" she asked. "We're Castro Ruz's. We have the genes for intrigue and scheming and double-crossing."

And Ortega-Cowan laughed again. "Well, I promise not to try to stab you in the back, at least not until we actually get our hands on the gold. And I agree with you about Manuel. But for now he knows too much—or thinks he does—so we might as well use him."

"And if something goes wrong, we can always lay the blame on his doorstep. Or is he also related to us?"

"I very much doubt it. But he said that you planned on giving the treasure to the Americans at Guantánamo. You weren't serious, were you?"

"What do you think, brother?"

Ortega-Cowan nodded. "I think that this will turn out to be an interesting operation, no matter what happens. At the very least, if we come back empty-handed, we'll give the international lawyers something to do, suing in The Hague for our share."

María turned over in her mind what else her half

brother and the little prick Fuentes knew and what they might be planning. "Where are we going?"

"The Malecón safe house."

Fuentes, in jeans and a T-shirt, was talking on the phone when María and Ortega-Cowan walked in. A Russian-made 5.45 mm PSM semi-automatic pistol was lying on the coffee table in front of him. He looked up. "I'll call you later," he said, and closed the cell phone.

María's anger spiked, and before he could move, she snatched the pistol, checked to make sure that a round was in the firing chamber, and pointed the gun at his face.

"This came from my office safe," she said. "How did you get it?"

Fuentes blanched.

"I brought it here," Ortega-Cowan said. "It was necessary for me to clean out your safe to find out what documents and credit cards you had taken so that you could be traced, and to keep anything incriminating out of El Presidente's hands, in case he sent someone over to make an independent check."

"I thought that I was marked as a traitor."

"One can never be certain of everything."

María had the almost overwhelming urge to shoot both of them. But getting out of the country with them dead would be difficult, maybe even impossible, depending upon what safeguards Román might have put in place. Something she would have done, were she in is shoes.

"Would you mind pointing that gun someplace else?" Fuentes asked.

"Yes, señora, please do before there's an unfortunate accident," an older man with neatly trimmed gray hair said, coming from the kitchen. He was impeccably dressed in a white linen suit and open-collar white shirt.

María's hand shook, but she lowered the pistol. "Who the hell are you?"

"Julio Rosales," Ortega-Cowan said. "He is the Ministry of Justice's chief counsel for international law. He knows everything, or at least as much and Manuel and I know."

María tried to figure out what Ortega-Cowan and Fuentes had been busy doing while she was gone. But this was starting to get seriously out of hand, and yet she'd known almost from the beginning that she needed McGarvey and Rencke—especially McGarvey—to make the operation work in New Mexico, and that she would need at least Román's best efforts here.

"Please, señora, put the gun down," Rosales said. "And let me tell you the only way in which this project of yours will have any chance whatsoever of success."

SIXTY—EIGHT

Holloman Air Force Base is located about sixty miles
north of Ciudad Juárez on the Mexican side of the Rio
Grande and El Paso on the north, which straddles the
Texas–New Mexico border. And when McGarvey and
Otto arrived in the CIA's Gulfstream, the day was hot,
dry, and dusty.

Captain John Whitelaw, the base public affairs officer met them as they got off the plane that had pulled
into an empty hangar, and they shook hands. He was
in his late twenties or early thirties and acted nervous.
"Gentlemen, welcome to Holloman. Have you eaten
lunch yet?"

"We had something on the plane," McGarvey said,
and he and Otto followed the captain to a large table
set up near the rear of the hangar.

"Our base CO, Lieutenant Colonel Ron Endicott, is
on his way, and so is Brigadier General Melvin Gunther, the CO of Fort Bliss, and I have to warn you that
neither of them is in a particularly receptive mood."

A topographic map of the desert and narrow mountain ranges that also included Alamogordo to the east,
White Sands Missile Range to the north and south, and
the army's vast Fort Bliss Military Reservation that
stretched from New Mexico to Texas was spread out
on the table. Overlaid on the map was a transparency
that showed the roads—including unpaved tracks—
towns, bases, and a dozen other military facilities scattered here and there, and even the few abandoned

cattle ranches, most of them bought or seized by the government during or after WWII.

"We're not equipped to handle what Colonel Endicott says you want," the captain continued.

Studying the map, McGarvey could see that the major problem they were faced with was the distance. If the Mexicans, and presumably a fair number of Cubans, were to cross the border west of El Paso, they would have a twenty-mile trek across the desert just to reach the Rio Grande, and another sixty to Holloman. Impossible without some sort of transportation. However, if they crossed the Rio Grande into Texas well southeast of El Paso, they could be on Fort Bliss in well under ten miles.

"What's down here?" McGarvey asked, pointing to the area on the military reservation between the museums and study center and the National Cemetery.

Whitelaw studied the chart. "Desert, mostly scrubland."

"Anything like a hill?"

"Lots of them, but no real mountains, unless you go farther east and north."

McGarvey looked up. "All I need is a hill."

Otto set up his laptop at one corner of the big table, powered it up, and got online.

Whitelaw watched him. "Sir, this is a secured area, you're not authorized to use our Wi-Fi connection."

"I'm connected via satellite with my own server in Washington," Rencke said without looking up. "It's a whole bunch more secure for some things, you know."

"Anything yet?" McGarvey asked.

"No. But Page has his BlackBerry on, and I've located him at the White House. West Wing."

"Good," McGarvey said.

A Hummer with air force markings pulled up outside, and a lieutenant colonel in desert BDUs jumped out and strode into the hangar. He was an athletic-looking man with a long, narrow face, and he was mad as hell. His name tag read ENDICOTT.

Whitelaw saluted. "Colonel, these are the gentlemen from the CIA."

Endicott returned the salute without looking at the captain. He glanced at the map and at Rencke and the laptop, and finally at McGarvey. "I suppose you'll tell me what the hell you're doing on my installation, and what sort of sheer bullshit you're trying to pull off."

McGarvey didn't have the patience to put up with the man's bluster. "Turns out, I probably won't need your installation, Colonel. I'll probably have to commandeer some Fort Bliss real estate on the Texas side."

Endicott thought it out for a second, then turned to Rencke. "Turn that goddamned machine off, mister," he ordered.

Rencke looked up with a mild expression. "Sorry, I can't do that. The president will be wanting to talk to us shortly, and in any event, I think that General Gunther is about to land."

At that moment, they all heard the sound of an incoming helicopter and a half a minute later, a UH-60 Blackhawk with army markings sharply flared and touched down just in front of the Hummer. Almost immediately, a one star also in desert BDUs jumped down from the open hatch and marched into the hangar, where Whitelaw and Endicott came to attention and saluted.

Gunther was a large man about forty-five years old

with a pleasant look and slight smile. He could have been a younger brother to Colin Powell. "Kirk McGarvey?" he asked.

"Yes, General," McGarvey said, and they shook hands.

"I gave you a briefing on a new satellite hardening system when you were the DCI, no reason for you to remember." He glanced at the map. "So what brings you down here, you need something from Ron?"

"Actually from you, General," McGarvey said. "I need to borrow one of your hills for a day or two, plus some earthmoving equipment and the crews who know what they're doing, along with a video and audio system, and five hundred armed troops led by someone who knows what he's doing when he's under the gun, especially how to follow orders that might not seem to make a lot of sense."

Gunther didn't blink. "The hill, the earthmovers, and the audio/visual system are no problem. As for the rest, I'm going to need to get some orders. Damn specific orders."

"Otto?" McGarvey said.

"Not yet, but he's still in the West Wing, I'm guessing the Oval Office."

Gunther and the other two officers were taken up short when Otto mentioned the Oval Office, and they were suddenly very interested.

"You'll get your orders, General, but first let me explain what's going to happen and why and how you can help," McGarvey said.

"You have my attention, Mr. Director," Gunther said.

"Everything I'm about to tell you is not strictly speaking classified yet, but I'm sure that when the president talks to you, it'll be mentioned. At the very least, what I'm about to share with you is diplomatically highly sensitive, and totally crazy."

"Ron mentioned something about some people coming across the Mexican border. But that will be handled by the CBP, not us." CPB was the U.S. Customs and Border Protection service, which was an agency of Homeland Security.

"Not some people, more than a thousand—and very possibly a lot more," McGarvey said. "Most of them will be ordinary Mexican citizens, but there'll probably be some Cubans in the mix, and I want the confrontations to be kept to a minimum, and no arrests if possible unless I give the word."

"What the hell are you talking about?" Gunther demanded. "What do these people want? Can't be immigration status. We'll round them up for you and ship their asses right back across the border."

"You won't have to do that, because within twenty-four hours, probably less, they'll turn around and leave of their own accord. All I want you to do is contain them."

"If they make it across."

"They will because you'll let them," McGarvey said.

Otto turned the laptop around so that they could all see the image of President Langdon seated behind his desk in the Oval Office.

"Good afternoon, Mr. President," McGarvey said. "Has Mr. Page briefed you on what I want to do with your help and why?"

"Yes, he has, and he's here now with Frank Shapiro," Langdon said. "I understand that you and Mr. Rencke are at Holloman. Who is with you at this moment?"

"General Gunther who runs Fort Bliss, along with Colonel Endicott who is the CO here and Holloman's public affairs officer, Captain Whitelaw."

"Can they all see and hear me?"

"Yes, Mr. President," Gunther said, stepping into view so that the laptop's camera could see him.

"Has Mr. McGarvey explained what he wants to do?"

"Yes, sir, and I think there is a very great possibility for any number of things to go wrong."

Langdon didn't hesitate. "I completely agree with you, nevertheless you and Colonel Endicott are going to give Mr. McGarvey every assistance within your power, short of starting an all-out shooting war. Do you understand?"

"Frankly no, Mr. President. But we will do as we're ordered."

"Good. And until you hear otherwise—from me personally—this mission is classified top secret."

"What about the media, Mr. President?"

"That'll be up to McGarvey, how close they're allowed to come, but under no circumstances will they be briefed by your people."

"Yes, sir," Gunther said.

"Very well. Wherever you are, I want you to clear out for a minute or two. What I have to say next is for McGarvey's ears only."

SIXTY-NINE

The Cubana de Aviación Yakovlev-40 refueled at Mexico City's International Airport at three in the afternoon local and made the eight hundred miles up to Ciudad Juárez's Abraham González International Airport a little under two hours later.

María, dressed in jeans, Nikes, and a light New York Yankees jersey against what she figured would be a relatively cold desert evening, got up from her seat in the front row as most of the other thirty passengers who'd flown up from Havana with her and Fuentes shuffled past. They would be taken to a staging area closer to the border to wait for the word to pull out. The four who remained in their seats were DI field officers, handpicked by Ortega-Cowan, well trained, dedicated to the mission and the state, all of them expert shooters and hand-to-hand combat killers.

"No telling what that bastard McGarvey and his CIA pals will have waiting for you," Ortega-Cowan had told her.

"You're sending bodyguards to protect me?"

He'd shrugged and smiled, and she thought at that moment that she'd never trusted anyone less in her life. Power corrupted and absolute power corrupted absolutely, and he wanted the whole enchilada.

It was ballsy flying one of the VIP jets that her father, El Comandante, had used for diplomatic trips around the Caribbean and South and Central America, but again she'd agreed with Ortega-Cowan, who suggested that not only didn't Raúl and his people suspect that she was back, they would never dream that she was flying out again on a supposedly government-sanctioned trip.

"Listen up, *compadres,* the mission will begin in the next eighteen hours or so, but I want you to remain alert because we could get orders to move out at a moment's notice," she told them.

Most of them were young, in their early to mid-twenties, and this afternoon they were dressed in ordinary civilian clothes, mostly jeans or khakis, dark jackets to cover the holstered or pocketed pistols, and sneakers or boots.

"We understand, *Coronel,* but can we finally be told our mission?" a young lieutenant by the name of Ruiz asked.

"We're ready to kick ass, señora, just tell us whose and where," someone else added, and they all laughed.

"You'll have plenty of opportunity," she told them. If it came down to it, they would be her rearguard getting back across the border. "Two hints: We're heading a few kilometers north of here, and the opposition's headquarters is at a place called Langley just outside of Washington."

"About time," someone said.

María turned, and she and Fuentes went up the aisle to the main hatch where the pilot and copilot where waiting on the flight deck.

"You and my people will stay at the DoubleTree Hotel downtown," María told them. "But be ready to return here within a one-hour notice."

"How long do you contemplate our time on the

ground will be?" the captain, a former air force major, asked.

"I don't know," María said, and she turned to the open hatch, but then came back, her tone softening. "I really don't know. But I suspect it'll be at least twenty-four hours, but very probably less than forty-eight. I just need you to look sharp twenty-four/seven."

"*Sí, Señora Coronel.*"

A gray Hummer was waiting for them at the arrivals area outside, a driver and another man riding shotgun in front, but neither of them said a word when María and Fuentes climbed in the backseat. Nor did they speak or even look over their shoulders for the fifty-mile drive southwest, the last few miles of it on a dirt track to a palatial compound on the shores of Laguna Guzman, which was a fair-sized lake in the middle of the desert.

The place was well lit up from inside, and armed guards in pairs continuously patrolled the perimeter all the way out to five hundred yards. Infrared and motion detectors monitored every square inch of ground out to one mile, and active radar based at the five-thousand-foot paved runway a half mile to the west watched the sky out to fifty miles. The compound had its own cell phone tower, and two secure microwave links via satellite with advanced surveillance units hidden in the deserts, hills, and mountains of California, Arizona, New Mexico, and Texas. Tens of millions of dollars had been invested for security here; money well spent, considering the multibillion-dollar-per-year return.

María had been here twice over the past six years, setting up the drug routes in Cuba, along with coastal waters and airspace for promises not of any significant money, but for intelligence the cartels' various dealers and distributors across the border could supply about U.S. federal, state, and local law enforcement authorities as well as military installations along the southern tier of states.

It had been something of an uneasy truce, but neither the DI nor the cartels wanted to break it. The money and intel were simply too good.

They were passed through a tall iron gate in the razor wire–topped concrete walls only after they surrendered their weapons and were expertly patted down. Even the Hummer was searched with dogs for explosives and electronically for bugging devices.

Fuentes was impressed and he started to say something when they finally pulled up in front of the main house, but María squeezed his knee, and he bit it off. They got out of the car and walked up to the house, where a short, slightly built man in his mid-forties, with dark hair, thick eyebrows, and thin mustache was waiting for them.

"So good to see you again, señora," he said, and they embraced. He was Juan Callardo, leader of the Los Zetas cartel, whose compound this was, and son of Miguel Angel Félix Gallardo, the godfather of all Mexican drug lords.

"You're looking fit, Juan," she said.

"And you more beautiful than ever. And still devious."

They laughed and María introduced Fuentes, to whom Gallardo only nodded before they were led inside to a windowless conference room in the center of the sprawling one-story Spanish hacienda-style house. Three other men, all of them dark and serious looking, were seated around an ornately carved stone conference table that had once served as an Aztec altar, bloodstains epoxied over but not removed.

Gallardo introduced them, only by single names and the cartels they represented: Muñoz-Torres of the Sinaloas, Gonzáles of the Beltrans Leyvas, and Sigfredo of the Cartel Golfo. Only Gallardo's name was real, because María had dealt directly with him from the beginning. The others chose to remain anonymous.

María went to a sideboard and poured a small glass of what she took to be tequila from an unlabeled decanter. Ignoring the pitcher of water, plate of limes, and a small dish of sea salt, she knocked the drink back, smiled, poured another, and sat down at the table across from the others, with Fuentes on her right.

She sipped delicately this time. "Añejo, without a doubt," she said, and she sipped again. "Herradura Suprema?"

Gallardo threw his head back and laughed loudly, while the others smiled. "Exactly right, of course," he said. "I wish I had the same sensitivity and discerning tastes for your excellent rums."

"I'll send you a few mixed cases of our best, when we are finished."

The humor left the room. "So tell us exactly what you want us to do and what's in it for us?"

María finished her drink and set the glass down on the table. "Over the next twenty-four hours, I want your help to mass at least one thousand people, hopefully

five or ten times that many, along the New Mexico–
Texas border. Some of them will be ordinary Cuban
citizens whom you will fly up from your distribution
airstrips in my country."

"For what reason?"

"We are going to invade the United States."

No one laughed.

"Why?" Gallardo asked.

"For a Spanish treasure of gold and silver," Fuentes
blurted, but María waved him off.

"There may be no gold where we will be going," she
said. "Though almost certainly gold does exist somewhere in New Mexico."

"Then why the operation?" Gallardo asked.

And María told him.

SEVENTY

The hill about a mile and a half southwest of the Fort
Bliss National Cemetery rose barely two hundred feet
above the general elevation of the desert scrub. Bull-
dozers had been working all through the night since
late afternoon, and a little before dawn, McGarvey sat
nursing a cup of coffee on the tailgate of an army
pickup truck, watching the activity.

He'd given General Gunther twenty-four hours to
complete the job of carving three intersecting trenches
in the hill, and building two large mounds of dirt ten

feet apart straddling the main trench. At this point, it looked as if his engineers were ahead of schedule.

Anyone approaching from the south would be funneled into the narrow opening between the hills in order to reach the trenches. Lights and large projection screens were to be set up on top of each mound, which would rise to at least twenty-five feet.

McGarvey put his coffee down and stood up on the bed of the truck. A couple of miles to the east, El Paso's International Airport, its rotating white and green beacon flashing in the sky, was well protected by tall fences. Sometime later this morning, the manager would be informed what was going to happen in the next twenty-four hours so that he would have time to beef up his security in case some of the crowd spilled over from here.

Spread out to the south of Fort Bliss, the city of El Paso was brightly lit from the University of Texas and Centennial Museum to the west, and the zoo and the Coliseum to the east, cut through by Interstate 10, which even at this hour had traffic. But across the Rio Grande, which the locals called the Río Bravo del Norte, dividing Mexico from the United States, the city of Ciudad Juárez, with more than twice the population of El Paso, was relatively dark. And very often from even this far, the sounds of gunfire wafted across the river on a chance breeze.

Northern Mexico was at war with itself, mostly over the drug cartels' desire to control the entire border from Tijuana to Matamoros, and the army's inability to stop them.

The general had been out here a few hours ago to

check the progress his people were making, and he'd shaken his head when McGarvey gave a couple more pieces of the puzzle.

"The border people aren't going to like it, and El Paso's cops sure the hell aren't going to welcome five or ten thousand people walking across the Bridge of the Americas and strolling up the middle of Highway 54 to get here. That's four, maybe five miles, and it's going to take them several hours to make it that far. Traffic will be disrupted."

"Tomorrow's Sunday."

"Doesn't matter, because the first time someone pulls out a gun and takes a shot, all hell will break loose."

"I don't think they'll be coming across with guns," McGarvey said.

"I'm not talking about the Mexicans."

"This is going to be nothing more than a march across the border by ordinary people, who are coming here to stage a nonviolent sit-in."

"For what?"

"For something they think rightfully belongs to them."

"Cut the bullshit, McGarvey," Gunther said. "You commandeer my base, you talk in private with the president, who orders me to do whatever the hell you want, and that's apparently going to involve Homeland Security, the local and state cops, and National Guard, and have my people dig up a hill and set up a drive-in movie. Then you tell me five or ten thousand people are going to come here for something they believe is theirs. Which is what?"

"Gold," McGarvey said. "Spanish treasure from the seventeenth and eighteen centuries."

Gunther was taken aback for a moment. "There's no gold here. Never was."

"Was up on Holloman."

"Victorio Peak. A legend."

"There was gold there—that much we know for sure."

"Then why are they coming here?" the general demanded. "You've set up an elaborate ruse, why?"

"I can't tell you that part. You'll just have to trust me for the next twenty-four hours or so."

The general shrugged after a bit and he turned away, but then turned back. "Are you armed? Are you carrying a weapon?"

"Yes."

"If you're not expecting trouble, then why?"

"Because there're probably going to be two people, maybe a few more, who are not going to like what they find, and they're going to want to take it out on me."

"Do you want some backup?"

"Nope," McGarvey said, and now looking in the direction of Ciudad Juárez, he clearly remembered the general's last words.

"An angry mob is a whole lot more than the simple sum of its parts. Best you remember it."

But the rewards, he'd decided as early as Spain, were worth the risks. And if they could pull it off with a minimum of damage and casualties, nothing in Cuba would ever be the same again—not for the government, not for the people, and not for the exiles in Miami who only wanted to go home.

He telephoned Otto, who was set up in a suite at the Radisson Airport Hotel, and his old friend answered on the first ring.

"It's started."

"Tell me," McGarvey said.

"Lots of private air traffic across the Gulf, landing at airstrips within a hundred fifty miles of Ciudad Juárez. At this point, Mexican air traffic control is only just beginning to take notice. But it'll be at least twenty-four hours, probably longer before the army is sent up to investigate. I've tried to task a bird to look for infra-red signatures across the area, but Louise says there won't be anything in position until at least noon, and by then, we should start getting visuals. But my guess is they're putting it together and are heading this way."

"Stick it out until noon, three at the latest, and then take the jet and get out of here."

"I still haven't got a lock," Otto said. "But I'll keep trying. Have you talked to Raúl this morning?"

"Not yet."

Otto hesitated for a moment. "Take care of yourself, kemo sabe."

"You, too."

Like Otto, Raúl Martínez also answered on the first ring, as if he'd been holding his cell phone waiting for the call, but unlike Otto, he sounded wound up. And in the background McGarvey could hear a lot of noise, a chanting crowd, a lot of people shouting all at once, and someone on a bullhorn, the voices distorted.

"Are you just about ready?" Martínez asked.

"Within the next twelve hours," McGarvey said.

"Are you getting any hassles yet from the cops or anyone else?"

"The locals are keeping clear, and so far the *federales* have not interfered, thanks to you, but the situation here is nearly at the breaking point. I can't hold it together much longer."

"How about the DI?"

"There've been a couple of incidents, but nothing we can't handle," Martínez said. "Give me the word, Mac."

"How many people do you think you'll be able to move?"

"Between the trains, buses, and private cars and vans, at least two thousand, probably more once we actually get started. A lot of people down here have heard this kind of shit almost from the beginning. They're skeptical. They want to see something concrete for a change, and I can't blame them."

"I want them in place in twenty-four hours," McGarvey said. "Can you manage it?"

"You're damned right, *comp*!"

"No guns."

"I can't guarantee that."

"Goddamnit, Raúl, this isn't going to work if there's even a hint of violence. This has to be a peaceful demonstration."

"I'll do my best," Martínez said. "But they're fired up. What about Otto?"

"He's still working on it."

"This is goddamned tight."

"Tell me about it," McGarvey said. "I'll see you sometime tomorrow."

"Where will you be? Exactly."

"Around."

"Good luck."

"You, too," McGarvey said, and he phoned María. She, too, answered on the first ring. "Is it time?"

"Twenty-four hours. Where are you?"

"Just outside Ciudad Juárez. Have you actually found it?"

"It's not in New Mexico, it's a lot closer than I thought," McGarvey said.

"Is it fabulous?"

"More than you'd think," McGarvey said. "How many people will you have?"

"At this point, it looks like at least five thousand, possibly more."

"No guns, no violence. This is going to be a peaceful sit-in. It's the only way it'll work."

"I understand."

"I shit you not," McGarvey said. "The first shot fired, and all bets are off."

"I told you that I understood," María said sharply. "You said closer. Where do you want us?"

"You're to cross the Bridge of Americas on foot. And from there, it's a little less than five miles to Fort Bliss. I'll send a map to your cell phone."

"It's actually there?" María asked, and she sounded breathless.

"Twenty-four hours," McGarvey said.

SEVENTY-ONE

Waiting on the Mexican side of the Bridge of Americas across the Río Bravo del Norte a little past three in the afternoon, María sat in one of the four Hummers blocking the northbound lanes to all but foot traffic as thousands of people, most of them Mexicans, but more than one thousand of them Cubans flown in by the cartels, walked by. And she couldn't help but think of the colossal chance she was taking.

She had lied to Ortega-Cowan about her intentions from the beginning, and of course she had lied to Captain Fuentes and to Raúl Castro and to McGarvey and his geeky computer freak friend Otto Rencke. Getting the gold to the people had never really mattered to her, nor had McGarvey's efforts to find the treasure, going so far as to Spain and to track it down.

All along her goal had actually been a simple one: Ever since she'd learned as a child who she was, she'd wanted power. Not the same as her father or uncle, but real power and especially wealth that she could hide from the people and yet still enjoy.

For that to happen, she'd always figured that she would need a cause célèbre, something so big that it would attract the attention of not only the government, but the people as well and propel her to a seat on the Council of Ministers—even a seat as one of the vice presidents on the Council of State just a few ranks beneath the president himself. But the years had passed with nothing on the horizon until her father died and set her on a quest to find Cuba's salvation with the help of Kirk McGarvey.

And her time was now, yet she was uneasy, unsatisfied.

The pock-faced driver glanced at her. "Are you going to walk with your people, señora?" he asked, and he laughed roughly. He was one of the Los Zetas, a Glock pistol holstered on his chest, a Kalashnikov assault rifle in the rack between the seats.

In the end, the cartels had agreed to take on the job of getting the crowd to the border and across for the continued cooperation of the Cuban government, but so they could get more of their own people across the border in relative anonymity, so that they could slip away and filter north to manage to drug pipelines within the United States. Too many interruptions in the distribution network were happening, and a new order needed to be put in place.

"Of course I am," she said. "But you're staying here."

The driver turned away. This wasn't his battle.

"Doesn't matter if you actually find any gold," the lawyer Rosales had explained to her and Ortega-Cowan and Fuentes at the safe house. "Even though you're certain such a treasure actually exists, and you can enlist Mr. McGarvey's aid."

"It's there," she'd said.

"Be that as it may. But if a sufficient number of Cuban citizens can be somehow gotten across the border into the U.S. to stage a peaceful demonstration on the site of one of your treasure caches, the U.S. military will move in, as will Homeland Security, the FBI, and certainly the local authorities. And as long as no Cuban raises his or her hand—and there should be some mothers with children in arms, and old women—this will have a chance of working. Of course, it would be infinitely better if the U.S. authorities were pushed into firing on the crowd, with luck killing someone—a mother and child, an old woman."

"You mean to get this into the international courts," Ortega-Cowan had said.

"It's the only way," Rosales said. "If there is gold there, none of you can certainly believe that the crowd would be allowed to stuff their pockets and simply return home."

"You're talking about a three-way split—us, Spain, and the U.S.," María said.

"It'd probably be more complicated than that. The treasure has been on U.S. soil for several centuries now, and much of what was hidden by the monks, if the stories are true, was bound for the Vatican."

"Doesn't matter, most of the gold that was lost at sea went through Cuba. There's a treasure off the U.S. East Coast, a portion of which also belongs to us."

Rosales had nodded patronizingly. "Your job, *Señora Coronel*, is not exploration and mining, it's simply making a claim loudly enough that the international press will sit up and take notice."

But the gold could be there after all, and she had given her DI operatives one simple instruction: "No matter what happens, you'll make your way under cover of darkness to wherever the treasure exists and simply take any samples you can find. Doesn't matter how much, just bring back something that we can use for proof."

"Are you sure it's there, *Coronel*?" Lieutenant Ruiz asked.

"*Sí.*"

"What if we run into opposition?"

"Get the samples out and meld back into the crowd," María said, and before the lieutenant could speak, she answered his next question. "Whatever it takes, but quietly."

At that moment, Ruiz passed by but didn't look over to see who was parked in the Hummer, and within minutes he was lost in the crowd on the bridge.

She got out as Fuentes walked up. Like most of the others choking the roadway, he was dressed in jeans and a loose shirt.

"Any trouble from the other side?" María asked.

Fuentes was in cell phone contact with one of the DI operators near the lead. "The cops and Texas National Guard are there, just like you said they would be, but they're not blocking the roads, just directing the parade through downtown toward Highway 54."

"Any sign of the media?"

"They're all over the place, also just like you said they would be."

María had phoned Ortega-Cowan and given him the word to start calling the media in the States immediately after she'd talked to McGarvey. *The New York Times, Washington Post, Los Angeles Times*, plus all the wire services, including the AP and Reuters, online sites such as AOL Latino, and the television networks

CBS, ABC, NBC, CNN, Fox, and the local television, radio, and newspapers.

"Treasure march for the people." The catchphrase had grown overnight, as Ortega-Cowan promised it would, because the average non-Cuban American was frankly sick of what seemed to be a senseless embargo against an island just ninety miles south of Key West. Cubans were pleasant, if desperately poor, the tropical nights were fantastic, the rum even better. And who really remembered Batista, the revolution, even the Bay of Pigs or the missile crisis? If some Spanish treasure could be shared, why not?

None of this ever really had a chance of success, not from the beginning. And yet what else was there? María figured that if she made it to the treasure cache, whether it was there or not, and then made it back across the border, she would have won. In the end, Rosales would make it right.

And yet María had a gut feeling that she had lied not only to everyone else but to herself as well. Lied all her life, because as corny as it sounded even to her inner voice, all she ever really wanted was to fit in somewhere, to love and be loved, to be appreciated for—as a lover had once said—her inner beauty.

But she had always denied it.

"Shall we take a walk?" she said to Fuentes, and she joined the crowd moving slowly across the bridge, a mother with a crying infant in her arms, and two others hanging on to the hem of her dress just ahead.

The power of a mother and child, indeed.

SEVENTY-TWO

McGarvey stood just below the crest of the hastily bulldozed mound on the east side of the first trench, binoculars raised as the first of the crowd estimated at seven thousand people began to appear on Highway 54. The sun had set fifteen minutes ago, and many of the people carried flashlights or torches, but they made no noise. The panorama was nearly surreal, other-worldly, or from another time; Egyptian workers marching in protest on the pyramids.

"What do you want to do?" General Gunther called up from the base of the mound, where he was waiting next to a Hummer.

"Let them come ahead," McGarvey said, lowering the binoculars.

"Sure you don't want backup?"

"It's okay, General. They'll be gone by first light. Some even before that."

"What about the media? They're all over the place."

"Don't interfere with them," McGarvey said absently. It was just as he figured it would turn out. Gunther had given his people strict orders not to contact the press or television networks. It meant that María or someone directed by her had leaked the word to the media.

"How about when the marchers get here," Gunther shouted. "Do you want me to set up a perimeter?"

María was out there; he could practically feel her presence. And she had almost certainly brought muscle with her. For just an instant, he caught an image of her face as she had emerged from the basement of the brownstone in Georgetown. She'd been wide eyed, her lips pursed, excited, maybe even a little frightened. And vulnerable. She was in a place that for her was badland with some serious people gunning for her.

McGarvey lowered the binoculars. "No," he called down. "Just keep them from spreading out, especially east toward the airport."

"How long do we keep the highway closed?"

"Until they clear out."

Gunther turned away, then looked back up. "There're a lot of them."

"I'd hoped there might be."

"Some of them are probably armed."

"Almost certainly," McGarvey said.

The general shook his head, got back in his Hummer, and his driver took off.

McGarvey phoned Martínez. "Where are you?"

"Close. A few hours."

"How many people?"

"Maybe three or four thousand. I didn't stop to count."

"It'll have to do," McGarvey said. "Good luck, Raúl."

"You, too, *comp*."

Otto called almost immediately. "I'm in."

"Did you find it?" McGarvey asked.

"Looks like it."

SEVENTY-THREE

Except for the four-man swing shift crew in the operations center, Ortega-Cowan was alone on the fifth floor in his office watching the events unfolding in Texas as reported by CNN. So far, everything was going exactly as planned. The American authorities were doing nothing to block the marchers who were beginning to enter Fort Bliss along a narrow road south of the National Cemetery, which was just as incredible and unprecedented to him as the correspondent was terming it.

". . . nothing short of a so far peaceful invasion of the United States, for what purpose no one is saying yet."

The only difference in his sister's plan was the ultimate outcome for her. At some point in the confusion tonight, Fuentes would shoot her to death. An unfortunate accident, but one with some poetic justice. Colonel León had become unstable over the past weeks. She'd even been called before El Presidente to explain herself.

Of course, it was the unfortunate passing of her father that had sent her over the edge, caused her to defect to the United States, and led to her current delusion that by somehow staging some mass demonstration in Texas, she would find the salvation she'd preached she was seeking.

"But salvation from whom or what?" Ortega-Cowan had written in his daybook. It was an answer she couldn't or wouldn't give to him, at which time, he wrote, he'd become deeply concerned for her sanity and loyalty to the state.

He happened to glance up when the elevator, which had been on the ground floor, stopped on the fifth and two very large men, wearing khaki slacks and plain white guayabera shirts, got off and marched down the hall to his office.

He got to his feet. "This is a restricted area," he said. "Who are you and what are you doing here?" But he knew.

Both of them were dark, with the solid build of rugby players. One held up an SDE identification booklet with the name ERNESTO NUÑEZ. It was the Seguridad del Estado—the state police under Raúl Castro's direct control. "Major Román Ortega-Cowan, you are under arrest."

"On what charge?"

"Treason."

"Don't be ridiculous," Ortega-Cowan said, but his heart froze. The incredible bitch had done it to him.

"Are you armed at this time, Major?"

Ortega-Cowan, who was dressed in plain olive drab fatigues, spread his arms. "No."

He was handcuffed and taken downstairs past the evening security officer, who looked away when they passed, and outside was handed into the backseat of a Gazik with military markings.

Not really paying much attention to where he was being driven, Ortega-Cowan tried to work out his next moves, because there was no way he was going to face a firing squad on such a charge, although it did have some truth to it. It could be proved that he had helped with María's scheme, but he could and would argue that everything he had done was to prove that she—not he—was the traitor. And it was she and Captain Fuentes who were at this moment marching on a military installation in Texas, while he was still here in Havana at his desk doing his job.

But before this was allowed to go much further, and definitely before he was locked up in some cell, he needed to speak to the president, and he started to tell that to the officers when he realized that they were on the Malecón, evening traffic just beginning to pick up.

"Where are you taking me?"

"You know where," Nuñez said without looking over his shoulder.

Two minutes later, they pulled over and parked in front of the apartment building where he'd last spoken with María and Manuel and the attorney Rosales, and he was hustled out of the jeep and taken upstairs to the safe house, a very sour taste in his mouth.

The place was in a shambles: the furniture was cut apart, the tables and chairs and appliances in the kitchen and even the fixtures in the bathroom had been dismantled, the wallpaper stripped, holes punched in the walls.

Raúl Castro stood in the middle of the mess and he turned around. "Here you are at last."

Ortega-Cowan's heart soared. He still had a chance. "I'm glad that you're here, *Señor Presidente*, I have so much to tell you."

"*Sí,*" Castro said. "But first I will tell you what I have

learned about you and your plotters of treason, including Colonel León, Captain Fuentes, and two spies who have worked for you from their *paladar* downstairs in this very building. Fidel and Margarita de la Paz, I believe their names are." Raúl brushed it aside. "But they have already confessed and have been taken care of, along with Julio Rosales—a personal friend and an exceedingly sad surprise."

This was even worse than Ortega-Cowan had feared. "If you will let me explain—"

"I will explain to you about the plot you hatched with Colonel León to kidnap the wife of a senior CIA official to lure her husband here, who in turn was used as bait to lure a former director of the CIA. All of it culminating in a march of innocent Cuban citizens, most of them simple farmers and shopkeepers, some of them old women, others women with their children, across the Mexican border into Texas." Castro's voice steadily rose. "For what?" he shouted. "Some mythical Spanish treasure that even if it ever existed, would only deepen the embargo against us if we tried to steal it?"

Ortega-Cowan said nothing. There was nothing he could say.

Castro turned away and looked out the window toward the water. "What to do," he muttered. "How to repair the damage you have caused us?"

"May I speak in my defense?" Ortega-Cowan asked.

"No," Castro said. He turned back, stared at Ortega-Cowan for a long moment, then walked out, not bothering to close the door.

Ortega-Cowan could hear the president's footsteps

down the hall at the same time he realized that Nuñez was pointing a pistol with a silencer on the end of its barrel directly at his head from just a few feet away.

He started to raise his hand, but a thunderclap burst inside his skull.

SEVENTY-FOUR

President Langdon and a half dozen of his staff, including his National Security Adviser Frank Shapiro, his Chief of Staff John McKevit, and the Director of the FBI Gavin Litwiller, were in the Oval Office watching the CNN reports on the events unfolding in northwest Texas when Mrs. Stubbs, his private secretary, appeared at the door.

"Mr. President," she said. "Raúl Castro wishes to speak with you."

Everyone except Langdon looked up in surprise. McGarvey had predicted this.

"You might want to hold off taking his call until we know how this shakes out, and until we can get someone who speaks Spanish in here," Shapiro said.

Langdon had been leaning against his desk. He motioned for someone to mute the sound on the television, and when it was off, he punched the number for the line that was lit and hit the speakerphone. "Good evening, Mr. President," he said.

"Good evening to you, Mr. President," Castro said

in English, no translator. "Undoubtedly you are monitoring the events that are taking place outside of El Paso, Texas."

McGarvey had not only raised the possibility that Castro might call and why, but how to respond. Nonetheless, just now it was extraordinary to Langdon.

"Yes, we are, with great interest. From what we've been able to gather, some of the marchers may be Cuban citizens."

"They are," Castro said with no effort at diplomacy. "Which is why I have made this call to personally give you my word that neither I nor anyone in my government allowed such an operation. In fact, it just came to complete light a couple of hours ago. Before this evening, my only knowledge was of the kidnapping of the wife of one of your CIA officers and the interrogation outside of Havana of that officer and another at the hands of my director of intelligence operations."

"Which would be Colonel María León."

"Yes, Mr. President. You also may know that she was my late brother's daughter. Unhinged, I fear, by her father's death."

"Are you telling me that she is leading this march across my border?"

"Yes."

"With the help of President Calderón?"

"No. It is my understanding that Colonel León and others in her ring of traitors enlisted the help of a number of drug cartels to not only transport Cuban citizens to Mexico, but to force ordinary Mexican citizens to participate."

"To what end, Mr. President?" Langdon asked.

Castro was silent for several beats, and for a moment Langdon thought the call had been disconnected. But then the Cuban president was back.

"I hesitate to tell you what I have learned. The story is almost too fantastic to believe. But it involves the quest for a Spanish treasure of gold and silver that may have been buried in the deserts of southern New Mexico and perhaps northwestern Texas."

"Yes, I, too, have heard something of the same fantastic story," Langdon said. "But it isn't true."

"No, Mr. President," Castro said. "But it brings us now to the problem at hand. We wish no harm to come to any of our citizens, nor any to yours in El Paso or on your Fort Bliss. I'm told that the demonstration will be peaceful, and by morning the marchers will return across the border."

It was almost exactly word-for-word what McGarvey had said might happen. "You are asking for restraint."

"Yes. Mr. President, I'm asking for exactly that. And you have my personal word that once the situation has calmed down that I will discover all the facts, and report them to you."

"You say that this Colonel León may be among the marchers?"

"Yes, along with a Captain Manuel Fuentes, who is her coconspirator."

"If we find them, they would be subject to arrest and prosecution," Langdon said.

"Of course, Mr. President. But if they manage to return here, they will be harshly dealt with as traitors."

"I understand," Langdon said. "Thank you for this call, Mr. President."

Again Castro hesitated for a few beats. "Perhaps this could be the beginning of a useful dialogue between us."

Langdon didn't hesitate. "Certain difficulties would have to be overcome first."

"Naturally."

"In the meantime, there is something that you can do to help resolve the situation in Texas."

"Anything within my power, Mr. President," Castro said without hesitation.

And Langdon explained what he wanted.

"Extraordinary," Litwiller said when Langdon had hung up.

"I spoke with Kirk McGarvey, who predicted something like this might happen, and if it did how he suggested I handle it," Langdon said. "And he was right."

Shapiro looked a little uncomfortable. "Mr. President, I should have said something earlier, but I wasn't aware of all the facts when Marty Bambridge came to me two days ago with a story about McGarvey and the Cuban Colonel León and the Spanish treasure in New Mexico. Marty thought it likely that McGarvey was actually going to somehow help the Cubans recover some of the gold."

Litwiller had walked away to receive a cell phone call, and before Langdon could respond to Shapiro's admission, the FBI director interrupted.

"I'm sorry, Mr. President, but we have another situation developing. This one in Kentucky."

SEVENTY-FIVE

The mob had been gathering for several hours, and now that it was finally dark and only a few last stragglers were coming in, McGarvey was ready to make his move. He'd been waiting in the deeper shadows between the two mounds, watching the people gathering, almost all of them obviously nervous and uncertain. Crossing the border, they'd not been hassled by the police or National Guard, and here on the base, General Gunther's people were at least one hundred yards out around the perimeter, but the marchers had come across the border illegally, and there were cops and soldiers everywhere.

María was just ten yards from where McGarvey was standing. She said something into a cell phone, then started to raise a bullhorn when he stepped out of the shadows.

"I have a much better sound system set up for you," he called to her.

She turned around, surprised at first, but then relieved when she saw who it was, and she put the bullhorn down and came back to him. "I didn't know if you would be here."

"I told you I would," McGarvey said. "Do you want to talk to your people?"

"I was just about to," she said.

"Come with me," McGarvey told her, and they went to the rear of the east mound, where they scrambled up a ramp that had been bulldozed then stabilized with a light wire mesh.

At the top, McGarvey took out a remote control that Otto had set up, pushed a button, and suddenly the bases and front slopes of both mounds were softly illuminated. He handed María a microphone, stepped back out of camera range, pushed another button, and María's image was projected on the big screens. A collective sigh swept across the crowd.

"Is it here?" she asked. "Did you find it?"

"They're waiting," McGarvey said, and for just a moment, María hesitated, but then she turned back to the people and keyed the microphone.

"My name is María León, and I am a Cuban who with your help wants to save her people from poverty. And I have a story to tell you how. It has to do with a fabulous treasure of Spanish gold and silver buried right here. A treasure that in part belongs to us."

McGarvey went down the base of the mound and phoned Otto. "Are you in place?"

"Yes. How about you?"

"It's just started. But before I showed myself, she called someone on her cell phone."

"Stand by," Otto said. He came back ten seconds later. "Looks like some sort of a network call. One number for maybe four or more phones."

"Who'd she talk to?"

"Unknown. But she said only two words: 'Go! Go!'"

"Son of a bitch," McGarvey said when someone jammed the muzzle of a silenced weapon into the base of his neck.

"Mac?" Otto asked.

"The mission's a go, but I have company," McGarvey said. He broke the connection and pocketed the phone.

"Unless I miss my guess, Captain Fuentes has decided to cooperate with Colonel León after all."

The crowd out front suddenly cheered.

"She's a convincing woman," Fuentes said. "But she'd have to be to get you to cooperate like this. The problem is that none of us can understand your motive. What's in it for you?"

"Justice."

Fuentes laughed. "That's the one thing your government knows nothing about. You've kept Cuba in the dark ages for half a century. Before that, you supported that *hijo de puta* Batista."

"I meant for kidnapping the wife of a friend of mine," McGarvey said.

"Not my doing."

The crowd cheered again. María had said something about gold and silver in Havana.

"Let her talk," Fuentes said. "Right now, we have something more important to do."

"What's that? Why'd you come here?"

"The gold, of course. And you're going to take me to it."

"There's no gold here," McGarvey said. "Never was."

Fuentes jammed the silencer harder into the back of McGarvey's neck. "You're lying."

"I'm telling you the truth."

"No!" Fuentes shouted.

At that moment, María's voice was replaced by that of Raúl Castro, whose image would now be on the big screens. President Langdon had evidently managed to convince the Cuban president to do this to try to defuse the situation, and Otto had set it up.

"What's happening?" Fuentes demanded.

"You have been duped," Castro's voice rolled over the crowd. "Traitors in my government have used you to help smuggle a large number of drug runners across the border into the United States. Without America's insatiable appetite for cocaine and marijuana, the Mexican cartels would not exist, and the killing of innocent Mexicans would come to an end.

"What I do care about are the traitors who have used you for their own financial gain. The only treasure there tonight is the money the cartels are willing to pay to get their people across. And now that it has happened the way they planned it, it is time for you to come home."

The crowd was ominously silent, and at this point, María's microphone and the camera were locked out so she could not interfere.

"The woman who is leading this traitor's act is María León, a colonel in the Dirección de Inteligencia, who along with coconspirator Captain Manuel Fuentes, is there now, and will be arrested the moment they return to Cuba. The others—Román Ortega-Cowan, a major in the DI, and Julio Rosales, who was a trusted man in our Ministry of Justice and, I am sad to say, a personal friend of mine—have already been arrested and have confessed to their crimes."

"I'd tell you to put your gun down and go home," McGarvey said. "But you might want to consider asking for asylum here. You were Fidel's chief of security—you might be able to trade information for safety."

"I'll make a deal, but it'll be with El Presidente, when we bring back samples of the treasure. Enough to convince him that we were not traitors after all."

"She lied to you."

"No," Fuentes said. "There was no reason for it. Besides, I heard everything you talked about in Georgetown."

"I know," McGarvey said. "We set it up so you would."

SEVENTY-SIX

Raúl Martínez stood smoking a cigarette next to his Caddy not two hundred yards from the U.S. Bullion Depository on Fort Knox, a series of razor wire fences protecting it from intruders.

Otto had set up his laptop on the hood of the car, his fingers flying over the keyboard. Apache gunship helicopters from nearby Godman Army Airfield were incoming, along with more than one thousand soldiers from the Third Brigade Combat Team of the First Infantry Division, and fifty officers from the U.S. Mint Police force. But they were late to respond because Otto had interfered with their initial security alert system.

It was early evening, but the squat, prisonlike concrete structure and the open grounds around it were lit up like day, as were the roads that surrounded it, including Gold Vault Road and Bullion Boulevard, now completely choked by buses and cars and vans and pickup trucks and even a number of motorcycles, some with sidecars, that had streamed up from Miami and more than a dozen other communities in Florida, among them Sweetwater, Palm Springs, and Coral Gables, plus West New York, in New Jersey, and even some by plane from Houston, where they'd rented cars in Louisville for the short drive down.

And Martínez and several of his organizers had been clever enough to bring the four thousand Cuban exiles and their families to Fort Knox from all different directions, a lot of them up I-75, where they spread out along I-64 and a bunch of secondary highways; others as far west as I-65, from where they used other secondary highways to approach from the west. Everyone stuck to the speed limits, stopping only for bathroom breaks or to switch drivers. They were on a mission; they were dedicated.

Most of them were out of their vehicles, a lot of them singing some old Cuban folk songs, a lot of them with guitars and even some trumpets and other instruments. But no one littered or created any disturbance.

The first police had arrived only ten minutes ago, but generally everyone in the crowd politely ignored them, offering only their driver's licenses, registration, and proof of insurance.

But now the military was on its way in force.

Otto looked up. "Okay, you have three choices," he said, handing Martínez a cell phone. "Press one for Ronald Campagnoli, who is the Director of the U.S. Mint, Fort Knox; two for Colonel Leonard Chalmers, who runs the U.S. Mint Police here; or three for Brigadier General Thomas Bogan, who is in overall command of all Fort Knox operations."

"What about Mac?"

"I'll try to reach him again."

Martínez pressed three, and after one ring, General Bogan came on. "Who's on this secure number?"

"My name is of no importance for the moment, General," Martínez said. "But if you want to avoid a blood-bath tonight in which a lot of innocent civilians will be hurt or killed, listen to what I have to say. I won't take up much of your time."

The general was silent for several long seconds, but there was a lot of noise in the background. Martínez figured the general was in a helicopter somewhere near, surveying the situation on the ground.

"I'm listening," he said at last.

"We are Cuban exiles, mostly from Miami, here to stage a peaceful demonstration. None of us is armed, none of us mean any harm to the facility."

"A demonstration to what end?" the general demanded.

"We believe that a portion of the gold and silver bullion that has been stored in either vault B or C since the late fifties belongs to the Cuban people."

"Start making some sense, whoever the hell you are, or I will order your people to be removed, by force if necessary."

"Don't turn this into another Tiananmen Square, please."

"You have five minutes."

"For three hundred years, the Spanish in Mexico, Cuba, and throughout the Caribbean and South America collected huge amounts of gold and silver—stealing it from the natives, then forcing them to work in the mines as slave laborers. This treasure was sent back to

Spain, most of it through Havana, where very little of it was given to the people who produced it. Maybe as much as four to five hundred tons were stolen from the Spanish in Mexico City and buried in several locations mostly in southern New Mexico. One such place was inside a small mountain on what's now Holloman Air Force Base. It's the treasure from Holloman that was excavated and brought here."

The general was silent for a long time, and when he came back, he sounded somewhat subdued. "Approach the fence or the front gate and you will be shot."

"You have my word," Martínez said, but the connection dropped.

He tried Campagnoli, who was director of the Depository, and then Colonel Chalmers, who was chief of the Mint Police, but neither number answered after five rings.

The dozen or more helicopters that had been incoming minutes ago took up station, hovering two hundred feet above the perimeter of the mob.

"Looks like we're okay for now," Otto said. He'd brought up a Google Earth image of the Depository and the crowd surrounding it. Tanks blocked every road out, and soldiers were deploying from Hummers and APCs, completely surrounding the open fields all the way to the edge of the woods. No one else was getting in, and for the moment, no one was getting out.

"I think I threw the general a curve," Martínez said, looking over Otto's shoulder.

"Just like Mac said they would take it. But it won't last long. We'll have to be out of here by morning."

"So far, so good—but we're going to need him here

long before then, because there's no way in hell the general or anyone else is going to do much more talking other than order us to get out."

Otto looked up from his computer. "Contact your unit leaders and let them know we need to hunker down for now. Meanwhile, I'll try to reach Mac."

The crowd had been roughly divided into a half dozen sections, and Martínez had picked six lieutenants in Miami to ride herd on them. He phoned them now and brought them up to date.

"It's party time, but nobody even thinks about getting anywhere near the fence line or even *looking* like they're thinking about it."

"How long do we need to hold them here?" all of them wanted to know.

"Until first light, and no matter what's happened or not happened by then, we're going home."

"A lot of these *gente* aren't going to like it, Raúl. They've come a long way on a promise, and the road home is going to be ten times as long as it was getting here."

"It's not over for us even if we go home empty-handed," Martínez said. "This is just the start. And remind everybody that the road home leads not just to Miami, but all the way to La Habana."

Within five minutes, Martínez could hear the chant rolling through the crowd, echoing off the depository building: "*Viva la liberación! Viva la liberación!*"

SEVENTY-SEVEN

The president had moved his staff into the situation room down the hall from the Oval Office, where it was easier to monitor the two developing situations—the one he'd expected in Texas and the other, at Fort Knox, which had blindsided them all.

Audio and visual feeds were displayed split screen, on the flat-panel monitors, and actually seeing the two crowds, listening to them chant and sing, did nothing to dispel Langdon's sour mood even though there was apparently no violence.

"Unless this is handled with a delicate touch, and not a sledgehammer, the situation could go south in a blink of the eye," McGarvey had warned. But that was for Texas; he'd not mentioned Kentucky. And just now he was missing.

In Langdon's estimation, Raúl Castro's speech had been short and to the point, effective. And yet the crowd on Fort Bliss had made no move to disperse. They seemed to be waiting—watching the two big screens blank now atop the twin mounds, waiting for someone to tell them exactly what they were supposed to do.

Shapiro picked up an incoming on one of the phone lines, had a short conversation, and then caught Langdon's attention. "Mr. President, we have General Bogan." The general was in overall command of all army units at Fort Knox, including Godman Army Airfield.

"Put him on the speakerphone," Langdon said. When the call was switched, there was a lot of background noise. "General Bogan, Joseph Langdon. What's your situation?"

"Good evening, Mr. President, but I'm sorry to report that I don't really know except that I have about five thousand civilians who've surrounded the depository and are demanding their share of some Spanish treasure that was supposedly moved here in the sixties from Holloman Air Force Base in New Mexico. My people checked, and apparently there was such a cache out there—or at least there were legends about it, but nothing concrete."

Langdon's anger began to rise. McGarvey had lied to him. "Did these people identify themselves, do they have a spokesman?"

"They claim to be Cuban exiles, and one of them somehow managed to hack into my tactical comms system. Said they were mostly from Miami, and they were here because some of the gold belonged to them."

"Did you get a name?"

"No, sir," the general said. "But he claimed theirs was a peaceful demonstration. Told me he didn't want another Tiananmen Square. I can remove them, but people are bound to get hurt, and I certainly don't want to open fire unless they actually try to storm the depository. Their spokesman said that they were unarmed, but I have no way of verifying it."

"Can you contain them, can you keep them there for the time being?"

"We're in control of the perimeter, but by morning the situation will almost certainly began to deteriorate. Unless they brought their own food and water, it's bound to get a little dicey around here. At the very least, there are no sanitary facilities."

"Stand by, General," Langdon said, and Shapiro put the speakerphone on mute.

"If they can't get out of there, we need to set up portable toilets and water stations," John McKevitt, the president's chief of staff, who'd come out from Cincinnati after the campaign, said. "Bad PR otherwise."

"Has the media become involved?"

"Not yet, but they're all over it in Texas."

"McGarvey lied to me."

"I think he might have felt that it was necessary, Mr. President," the CIA's director Walter Page said, and Langdon glared at him.

"Care to explain that to me, in one easy sentence, Walt?"

"A dialogue has finally been opened between us and Cuba. I think that counts for something."

Langdon held back a sharp retort because in his gut he had a feeling that Page might be right. But presidents were not to be manipulated. "What about this nonsense with the Spanish treasure?"

"I don't think it matters if it ever did exist outside of legends, local folktales," Page said.

"Get me McGarvey," the president said, and he motioned for Shapiro to unmute the sound. "Are you still there, General?"

"Yes, sir."

"You're to open fire only in self-defense or if an attack that seems to have some chance of success is made on the depository. In the meantime, I want portable comfort stations and drinking water delivered."

"Yes, Mr. President," General Bogan said with only the briefest of hesitations.

"I'll have further orders for you before the night is over."

"Yes, sir."

Langdon nodded and Shapiro tried to reach McGarvey in Texas.

"I think I might have an idea who's at Fort Knox," Page said.

"Who?"

"The general said someone hacked into his tactical communications system, could be Otto Rencke."

"Your computer expert and a close personal friend of McGarvey's," the president said.

"Yes, sir. And if it is him, it means McGarvey probably had this planned from the beginning. Texas was just a diversion mostly to get Castro to cooperate. It also means that the spokesman for the Cuban exiles at Fort Knox will be Raúl Martínez, who runs our counter-DI operations in Miami."

"Another friend of McGarvey's?" Langdon asked. And he was beginning to boil. Presidents definitely did not like to be manipulated.

"Yes, sir," Page said.

Shapiro was holding the phone. "Still can't reach McGarvey."

Page gave him another number. "Try this one."

Langdon nodded, and Shapiro made the call, which Otto answered on the first ring.

"Oh, wow, you're calling from the White House situation room. Is that you, Mr. President?"

"Mr. Rencke, I presume?" Langdon said.

"Yes, sir," Otto said.

"Is Mr. McGarvey with you?"

"No, he's still in Texas, but one of our aircraft is standing by at Fort Bliss and I expect him to show up here sometime tonight."

Langdon looked at his advisers, who seemed just as mystified as he was, just not as angry. "Then I want you to explain what the hell is going on. Because I spoke with the commanding general, who has you surrounded and is ready to disperse you by force if he's given the slightest provocation. And I gave my authorization to do so."

"Believe me, Mr. President, this is a peaceful demonstration."

"I hope for your sake that it remains so."

"You've been briefed about the Spanish gold in New Mexico, sir?"

"Yes. It was supposedly found at a place called Victorio Peak on Holloman Air Force Base. But it was either never there or it was looted a long time ago."

"Yes, Mr. President, excavated by the air force, possibly by presidential order, and transported in secret here to Fort Knox, where it's been stored in either vault B or C."

"I have no knowledge of any such thing."

"I've found pretty convincing evidence, sir."

"For the sake of argument, then, let's say that you're right and the gold is there, and the demonstration in Texas was just a diversion to force Raúl Castro to speak to his people—what are five thousand Cuban exiles doing at Fort Knox? What do they hope to accomplish? Do they actually believe that we'll open the vault and let them stuff their pockets?"

"No, sir. What Mac wanted to accomplish was to get Raúl Castro to make a public statement, and to give the Cuban exiles here the possibility of eventually getting a share of something they believe was stolen from them."

"McGarvey has turned them into treasure hunters. To what end?"

"If a court can be convinced to release even a small amount of the treasure, and if it could be converted to U.S. dollars and if the money could find its way into the hands of ordinary people in Cuba, it's very possible the regime could change. Solve our problem."

"You're talking about a long court battle, because I'm sure that Spain and Mexico will make their claims."

"A few hundred million dollars would do it, Mr. President. And it wouldn't cost us one cent."

"Far-fetched," Langdon said. "Exactly what do you and McGarvey want?"

"Nothing more than confirmation that the treasure actually exists."

"And then what?"

"Then the people will return to their homes and wait for the courts to decide," Rencke said. "What it will give them is hope, Mr. President."

"How did they find out that the gold might be there?"

"Mac and I told them."

"As soon as McGarvey shows up, I want to talk to him," Langdon said. "And whatever happens, no violence there. Not even a hint of it."

"I can guarantee it," Otto said.

But then everyone in the situation room heard the gunfire, a few shots at first, and then what sounded like controlled bursts from automatic weapons, and the call was terminated.

SEVENTY-EIGHT

At the bottom of the first trench, which was about two hundred feet back into the hill and about thirty feet below the level of the field where the mob was spread out, only dimly illuminated from the lights outside, Fuentes grabbed the collar of McGarvey's jacket and pulled him up short. Two men, armed with U.S.-made Ingram MAC 10 ultra-compact submachine guns slung over their shoulders, were just coming out of the intersecting trench to the right—and they, too, pulled up short.

"What did you find?" Fuentes asked in Spanish.

McGarvey understood only a couple of the words, but the meaning was clear.

"*Nada,*" the taller of the two said. "What's going on out there? It sounded like El Presidente."

"It's nothing," Fuentes said. "Just a recording that Colonel León brought with her."

The DI operatives were skeptical.

"Where is the gold?" Fuentes demanded in English, jamming the muzzle of his weapon in McGarvey's neck.

"It's not here."

"Bastardo!" Fuentes raged, and he slammed the handle of his weapon into McGarvey's skull.

Bright stars flashed in front of McGarvey's eyes as he was driven to a knee. His head cleared almost immediately, but he stayed down as if he were still out of it.

Fuentes kicked him in the ribs, and he went with the blow, rolling over on his side.

"Where is it?"

McGarvey didn't respond.

"Pick him up! Get him to his feet!"

The two DI officers came over, grabbed McGarvey by the upper arms, and dragged him to his feet, but at the last second, McGarvey lurched to the left, pulling them momentarily off balance.

It was time enough for him to draw his pistol from the holster at the small of his back beneath his jacket, get off one shot into the side of the head of the officer to his left then pull the other man around as a shield, jamming the muzzle of his pistol in the back of the officer's head.

"No one else needs to get hurt here tonight," McGarvey said.

Fuentes had his silenced MAC 10 pointed directly at his own officer. He was breathing hard and his weapon hand shook badly. Any moment, he was going to open fire.

"You don't have to go back to Havana," McGarvey said.

"Fuck you."

"Something can be worked out."

"I want my gold. Just one bar. Anything to bring back."

"It's not your gold."

"Don't tell me that!" Fuentes screamed. "Don't lie to me, you bastard!" He was waving his gun all over the place.

"Captain, you don't want to die here tonight," McGarvey said, trying to calm the man down.

"Listen to him, Captain," the officer McGarvey was holding at gunpoint said. "We can go home."

"Not without proof."

"It isn't here," McGarvey said.

"One third of it belongs to Cuba!" Fuentes screamed. "Colonel León promised. So did Román."

"You may be right," McGarvey said. "But the gold is not here."

"Where, then?"

"Fort Knox, in Kentucky, and the Cuban people are there right now, making their claim."

Fuentes digested this thing slowly as if he had been fed something strange and totally inedible, and yet something that he knew he was going to have to digest. And when the taste of it finally hit him, he was physically rocked back on his heels and he went ballistic, lurching forward and opening fire, the 9 mm slugs slamming into the body of the DI officer.

McGarvey shoved the man away as he feinted to the left and fired one shot on the move, catching the captain high in his left cheekbone, just below his eye.

Fuentes fell back, dead before he hit the ground.

Two more DI officers came around the corner in a

run, their silenced MAC 10s in hand, and they pulled up short.

McGarvey let the pistol fall from his hand, no way possible for him to outshoot a pair of submachine guns. "This is as far as it goes tonight."

They looked like professionals, not so excitable as Fuentes had been. "What has happened here?" one of them demanded in heavily accented English.

"There is no gold."

"Yes, we know that. What happened?"

"Captain Fuentes did not believe me, so he opened fire, killing one of his own men, and I was forced to shoot him."

"What about Lieutenant Jiménez?"

"The situation is what it is. I was defending myself."

One of them said something in Spanish to the other, which McGarvey didn't catch.

"What about the colonel?"

"If we can resolve this situation, I'm going to offer her amnesty. She can't return to Cuba now."

"And us? Will you have us arrested?"

"The crowd is going to disperse sometime tonight. You're free to go back across the border with them. No one will be stopped."

"There are soldiers out there."

"You're on a military reservation, but they have been instructed not to interfere with anyone so long as the demonstration remains peaceful."

Both men looked pointedly at the three bodies.

"Leave your weapons and get out of here," McGarvey said. "Go home."

The men exchanged a glance, then slowly laid their

weapons on the ground and disappeared back down the trench to the north side.

McGarvey picked up his pistol and holstered it, then speed-dialed Otto's cell phone, which wasn't answered until three rings.

"We've got big trouble here, Mac!" Otto shouted, all out of breath.

And in the background, McGarvey could hear the sounds of sporadic gunfire. "I'm on my way!" he said, his gut tied in a knot, but the connection was terminated. And when he tried to call again, he could not get through.

SEVENTY-NINE

María had brought a subcompact Glock 36 Slimline .45 Auto across the border this afternoon. It held only a six-shot magazine, but even with the silencer attached, it was very small and deadly at close range. Walking away from the crowd in the darkness, she checked the action by feel, then took out her DI credentials booklet as she approached an unmarked Ford Taurus with plain hubcaps and government plates about one hundred yards out.

A slender young man in a business suit was leaning against the car, and when he spotted her coming out of the darkness, holding up her credentials, he straightened up and tossed his cigarette away.

"Federal District Chihuahua Police," she said from ten feet away, and the cop—she took him to probably be FBI—relaxed.

"Looks like it's about over."

"FBI?"

"Don Schmidt from Albuquerque," he said, and he reached for his credentials.

María brought the pistol round from behind her right hip, and before the agent could react, she pointed the pistol at his head. "Throw your gun to the ground, along with your cell phone and your badge, and walk away or I will shoot you."

No one from the crowd still gathered in front of the two mounds waiting for something to happen, maybe someone else to talk to them from the big screens, could see what was happening here, and as far as she could tell, the nearest Fort Bliss soldiers were at least one hundred yards away in the opposite direction, and the cops had stopped at the military reservation limits. Only a few FBI agents had come in closer. No one wanted to spook the crowd.

"Who the hell are you?" the agent demanded, but he was nervous.

María motioned toward the crowd that was already beginning to head back to the highway. "You're going to join them."

The agent held for a moment, like a deer caught in headlights, but then he pulled out his pistol and dropped it to the ground along with his identification wallet and his cell phone, and turned and headed toward the crowd.

Shoving the pistol in her purse, she picked up the agent's badge, pistol, and cell phone.

Checking one last time that no one was coming her way, she got behind the wheel and headed for the west checkpoint on the narrow two-lane Forrest Road that ran straight across the base from Airport Road to Highway 54, which in turn would take her a few miles south to I-10 and from there only three miles farther to El Paso's international airport.

Even if McGarvey came looking for her, no one would suspect she'd used the local airport to make good her escape instead of returning across the border to Mexico.

She had been standing in the shadows at the bottom of the trench, just a few feet from where Fuentes had taken McGarvey, and she'd heard everything. The gold was at Fort Knox, not here, and the traitors from Miami had gone there to claim it. It all had been a gigantic ruse that had claimed the freedom and probably the lives of Román and the attorney Rosales. Fuentes was dead, by McGarvey's hand, and there was a good chance that she would be assassinated if she ever returned to Cuba, unless she could make another end run. God, how it rankled, how it hurt, how it was so stupidly embarrassing. She'd reached high—El Comandante's daughter had—and she was on the verge of failure. No going back for her. Not now, not like this. No settling in with the traitors in Miami, either. They would kill her the moment they saw her.

Unless she could make one final deal. A desperation move, but she figured it was her only avenue.

A Hummer was parked on the side of the road, and María held the FBI badge out the window, and the soldiers waved her through.

As soon as she hit Highway 54, she used her Black-Berry to connect with an airline booking agency for any flight direct to Atlanta, and she got a first-class seat on Delta flight leaving at nine this evening. She paid for it with her Ines Delgado credit card, which she thought would raise no red flags anywhere except Mexico City and Havana. With luck, the FBI agent would not be believed by the army units without identification long enough for her to get away, and his car wouldn't be discovered in the airport parking garage until morning, by which time she would be long gone.

Her father had made her promise: for salvation. He'd meant Cuba's salvation, or at least that's what she thought he'd meant. But now it was for her own salvation, and maybe her personal retribution, because she was angry that she had been so easily used.

Her grip tightened on the steering wheel as she made the connection with I-10 and headed east. She had been angry for as long as she could remember, and for just a few beats now, she wondered if it had been worth it. If she'd ever accomplished anything worthwhile because of it.

And another thought crossed her mind—so sudden, so compelling, and so alien to everything that she believed in, it almost took her breath away.

She realized, just then, that she had fallen in love, which in a way made her even more angry than she'd ever been. It was a weakness that she despised.

EIGHTY

The gunfire had been reduced to sporadic shots around the nearly three-quarter-mile perimeter just outside the depository's fence line. Raúl was hunkered down behind his Cadillac with Otto, who was trying to establish contact with someone, anyone, via computer.

"Anything yet?" Raúl asked.

"Cell phones have been blocked."

"I know, I can't contact my lieutenants to find out what the hell is going on. But I think the goddamn DI infiltrated us in Miami. What about your sat phone?"

"I'm searching who on Fort Bliss has one. Maybe I can get patched through to Bogan."

Minutes after the first shots had been fired, the tanks blocking access to the roads leading off the base had rumbled closer, and the one on Bullion Boulevard to the east had moved to within twenty or thirty yards of the line of cars and buses that stretched along Gold Vault Road.

"Whatever it is, do it fast," Raúl said. He pulled out his 9 mm Beretta, checked the load, and got up.

Otto looked up from his computer and blinked furiously. "Where are you going?"

"The DI has infiltrated us, and someone has to take care of it, because most of these people aren't armed."

"What about your lieutenants?"

"I told them no shooting unless their lives depended on it."

Otto cocked an ear. "Well, it's calmed down for now,

but if you go out there and get into some kind of a gun battle with the bad guys, the general is likely to send his troops in, and then we'll have a big mess on our hands."

"We've already got a big mess," Raúl said.

"Mac said that he was on his way before we were cut off."

"That's a thousand miles or more to Louisville and twenty miles by road here. So even if he's already in the air, I don't think we can hold out that long—maybe until two this morning—unless we do something right now."

Martínez was a lot like McGarvey: almost impossible to argue with once his mind was made up.

"Don't get yourself shot to death," Otto said. "Mac would never let me forget it. Besides, you've got a lot of work to do after you get back to Miami."

"Try to reach Bogan," Raúl said, and keeping low, he scrambled to the two dozen people flat on the ground behind the bus that had brought them north. Many of them were women with a few children. But most were men and they were angry.

"You said there would be no gunfire!" one of them shouted.

"Keep it down," Raúl said. "Did you see anything?"

The man, who was at least in his mid-seventies, noticed the pistol in Raúl's hand. "Muzzle flashes about fifty yards maybe a little closer to the west, but that was fifteen minutes ago."

"I maybe saw something on the other side of the depository," another man said. "But it's quiet now."

"What about the military?" the old man asked. "Are they going to try to arrest us, or move us out?"

"They will if this shit keeps up."

"Is it the DI *bastardos?*"

"I don't know who else," Raúl said.

"Where is he going?" one of the other men said, pointing down the road.

Raúl turned in time to see Otto marching along the line of cars, past where people were huddling, directly toward where the tank had taken up position.

"Dios mío!" Raúl shouted. He jumped up and raced back, catching up to Otto who was just coming abreast of the last bus before the intersection with Gold Vault Road which went left.

Otto had his hands up and Raúl grabbed his arm and tried to stop him, but Otto pulled away. "Get your pistol out of sight, and stay right here. I might have a chance to buy us some time."

"You're going to surrender to the tank commander?"

"What do you think he's going to do, order his crew to shoot me?"

"He just might," Raúl said. But he stuck his pistol in his belt beneath his jacket. "I'm coming with you."

"Stay here," Otto said, but Raúl shook his head.

"If I let you get shot to death, Mac would for sure never forgive me."

"Let me do the talking," Otto said, and keeping his hands up, marched past the bus and across the intersection, Raúl right behind him, the people behind the bus watching them as if they were *muy loco.*

The tank's turret swiveled so that the main gun was pointed right at them, and they stopped about ten yards away.

"Either shoot me, or pop out of there so that we can talk!" Otto shouted.

The Abrams M1A2 battle tank's engine rumbled softly, and in the distance they could hear other engines, but most of the helicopters had landed in the field near the woods to the east, only one in the air at least a half mile south.

"I don't think they know what to do with us," Raúl said at Otto's shoulder.

The tank's top hatch opened, and a man with lieutenant's bars, a tank commander's helmet, and headset appeared. "Gentlemen, state your names and business."

"I'm Otto Rencke, and I work for the Central Intelligence Agency. Please relay to General Bogan that I was the one who hacked your communications system and unless you pull your heavy hardware back, we could have a serious situation here."

"Yes, sir, stand by," the tank commander said. He spoke into his headset for a bit. "Who is the other man?"

"My associate," Rencke said. "Kirk McGarvey should be here in two or three hours, at which time the entire situation will be explained."

The lieutenant was relaying Otto's words. "General Bogan asks that you immediately disperse, return the way you have come."

"That's not possible at this time."

"You will be subject to arrest and prosecution."

"I think that General Bogan has other orders from President Langdon."

In this instance, the delay between the time the lieutenant relayed Otto's words and the general's response was longer. Almost a full minute.

"There has been gunfire from your group."

"We believe that several Cuban intelligence officers

have embedded themselves within the exiles. So far as we understand, none of it has been directed at your people or at the depository."

"Why are they here?"

"To stop us," Otto said. "Mr. McGarvey will explain everything as soon as he arrives. He's flying up from Fort Bliss aboard a CIA Gulfstream, and he'll want clearance to land at the nearest airstrip. I would expect Godman."

"That's not possible."

"Tell the general that the president will in all certainty direct otherwise."

"I'm sorry, Mr. Rencke, but the general again orders that you immediately disperse."

Otto took two steps forward, when he was flung face-down onto the pavement, and seconds later, the sound of a rifle shot whip-cracked from somewhere behind.

EIGHTY-ONE

In the air, McGarvey tried twice again to reach Otto's cell phone with no response, and he was beginning to get seriously worried. It was a little after nine in the evening Mountain Standard, and the pilot had given him an ETA at Godman Air Field of 12:45 A.M. Eastern, two hours plus, during which a lot of bad things could happen.

"We still don't have clearance to land at Godman," the pilot, Roger Darling, told him.

"They give a reason why?"

"No, sir. But from what I'm reading between the lines, something big is happening out there, and they've got the entire complex on lockdown."

"Who'd you talk to?"

"I managed to get a relay from Cincinnati Center direct to Godman's chief air traffic controller."

"Can you get him back?"

"Yes, sir, but he won't talk to you," Darling said.

There'd been resistance—it was the only explanation McGarvey could think of. He and Martínez had discussed the possibility that the DI might embed agents in the crowd and once at Fort Knox might try to start some trouble. The real problems were how Martínez and his lieutenants would handle it and what the military response would be.

"Get me the president," McGarvey said. "I'll take it in the back."

He went aft and sat down at the communications console, and waited until the call came through a couple of minutes later. The flight attendant had made himself scarce.

"Good evening, Mr. President. I think we may have a developing situation at Fort Knox."

"We certainly have. There's been gunfire and casualties, including Otto Rencke, a friend of yours, I believe. The army is on the verge of moving in and breaking up the crowd by force."

For several long beats, McGarvey could feel his sanity slipping away, and he didn't know how he could possibly bear another loss, and what would it do to Louise and to the baby they'd adopted? Or how he could keep from going on a killing rampage?

But then the aircraft's interior came back in focus and he loosened his iron grip on the phone. "What's his condition, sir?"

"I'm told a bullet grazed the side of his head, but other than headaches and some blurred vision for a day or two, he'll be fine," Langdon said. "Where are you?"

"In the air about two hours from Godman Air Field for which we've been denied clearance to land," McGarvey said. The relief was sweet. "And apparently cell phone traffic has been blocked."

"On General Bogan's orders, he didn't want the dissidents to coordinate any sort of an attack."

"Exiles, sir," McGarvey said. "I'd like to talk to him, three-way with you, Mr. President."

"Would you mind explaining what the hell you have in mind?" Langdon demanded.

"It'll be easier if I explain it to both of you at the same time, sir."

"Just a minute," the president said, and it was obvious he didn't like being talked to this way.

A minute and a half later, the president was back. "General Bogan?"

"Yes, Mr. President," the general said. He sounded tense, and there was a lot of noise in the background— what sounded like radio traffic.

"Kirk McGarvey is on the line with us. He's incoming in about two hours aboard a CIA aircraft, and he will be given clearance to land at Godman."

· "Sir, I can't guarantee that he won't receive ground fire."

"Mr. McGarvey?" the president prompted.

"We'll take our chances," McGarvey said. "I'll instruct my pilot. In the meantime, there're a number of things that I need you to do for me, so that we can get through this night with no further casualties."

The general started to object, but Langdon cut him off. "Mr. McGarvey is operating under my orders."

"Yes, sir."

"Is there any gunfire from the crowd at this moment?" McGarvey asked.

"Not for the past ten or fifteen minutes, and then only a single shot here and there."

"Then it's not an all-out assault."

"No," the general said.

"You will order your troops to stand by but not to open fire for any reason—any reason—other than to defend their own lives."

"What if they storm the fence?"

"I'm hoping they'll do something to get inside—in fact, I'm counting on it. But even if they actually reached the depository, there's no chance they could get inside. At some point in the next two hours, I want all the lights cut, and under cover of darkness, I want the gate opened and the Mint Police manning it to go to the depository and wait inside."

"Mr. President?" Bogan asked.

"You have your orders," Langdon said tightly.

"And I want the cell phone network restored. The leader of the exile group has arranged lieutenants to keep the peace. Without communications, they cannot coordinate any effort to take out the embedded DI operatives."

"Is there anything else, sir?" General Bogan asked briskly.

"The next part will be up to you, Mr. President," McGarvey said.

"I'm listening."

"You understand what's at stake, so I want two things. From what I understand, it takes ten members of the depository staff to dial separate combinations to actually get into the vault area."

"I don't know that for a fact at the moment, but providing you are correct, what is it that you want?"

"Access to vault C at first light for me and one representative from the exiles."

Bogan started to protest, but again the president cut him off. "For what purpose? What do you want?"

"Just to look, nothing more."

"I'll consider it."

"And I want the media to be allowed access to the crowd immediately after we've seen the vault."

"And then what?" Langdon asked.

"What we talked about will have a chance," McGarvey said.

The area cell phone service was resorted ten minutes later, and McGarvey was able to reach Otto at the hospital near Fort Knox Headquarters.

"Oh, wow, I think I got lucky."

"Sounds like you did. How do you feel?"

"Like a computer with a badass virus," Otto said. "Are you close?"

"Less than two hours. Langdon's going along with everything, so we'll know by dawn."

"I hope it's there."

"So do I," McGarvey said. "Take care."

He phoned Martínez, who answered on the second ring, all out of breath. "I hope this is Mac."

"Two hours out with Langdon's blessings. What's your situation?"

"We just got cell phones back, and my guys are working the problem. We might have a half dozen live ones left. That many have already met with unfortunate accidents."

"How about your people?"

"Our people," Martínez corrected. "We've taken a few serious hits, but we've been at war long enough to understand casualties. And we brought a couple of doctors and several nurses with us, so we're okay for now."

"Listen up, because you're going to stop being hunter killers, to hunter herders." McGarvey said. "And this is what I have in mind."

EIGHTY-TWO

General Bogan, a man with a very large, gruff voice and manner, turned out to be in his early forties, slightly built, mild looking, with thinning sand-colored hair and pale blue friendly eyes. He was standing on the tarmac dressed in sand-colorerd BDUs with two body-guards beside a Hummer when the CIA Gulfstream pulled up to a halt, and the engines spooled down.

He came forward when the stairs opened and Mc-Garvey thanked the crew and stepped down.

"McGarvey, you've for sure put our tits in a ringer."

They shook hands. "Didn't say this was going to be easy, General. What's the situation?"

They headed to the Hummer, the bodyguards' heads on swivels. "The media started descending right after your call," Bogan said. "We've managed to hold them back with a little creative bullshit, but it won't last."

"I don't expect it will," McGarvey said. "What about gunfire?"

"About twenty minutes of it after we restored cell phone service, but since then it's been quiet."

When Mac had been coming in from the air, the lights surrounding the depository were like a necklace around a black hole. "Have the Mint Police at the gate gotten back to the building okay?"

"That's the part that has us the most nervous," Bogan said. "The guards got out of there okay, but less than ten minutes later, we spotted the infrared images of two men running down the access roads right up to the open gates."

"Did they go inside?"

"No, they stopped at the guard post, and it looks as if they're waiting for something or someone."

"Me," McGarvey said.

The Hummer headed to the depository.

"We can verify that at least one of them is armed."

"They'll both be carrying," McGarvey said, checking the load and the silencer on his own pistol. When he looked up, the general was watching him. "They're Cuban intelligence agents sent here to either disrupt the demonstration or somehow make their own claim. It's what I was counting on."

"Are there others in the crowd?"

"They're all dead."

"You're sure?"

"Yes," McGarvey said. "Now I want you to get me as close as you can, I'll go the rest of the way on foot."

"I'll take you where your friend was shot," Bogan said. "From inside the crowd. Wasn't us."

"I understand," McGarvey said. "How about the depository officials with the combinations?"

"Four were inside the building when this started, five are standing by in an armored Hummer, and the tenth is being choppered down from Louisville International. Should be here within twenty minutes."

"Hold them until I give the word."

"You can reach my tactical cell phone," Bogan said.

"Yes," McGarvey said, and he phoned Martínez. "I'm in the Hummer approaching your position, is one of your docs standing by?"

"At the end of the access road, along with a couple of escorts. You sure you don't want some backup?"

"They have to be twitchy by now, so this isn't going to have much of a chance if I bring help."

The Hummer pulled up beside the lead tank where Otto had been shot. "Once I give you the all clear, have the guys with the combinations sent in, but keep the media out until afterwards," McGarvey told the general.

"Then what?"

"Then we'll make an announcement, and the people will go home."

"I meant the two at the gate. They're going to kill you."

"I just want to talk to them, and when the dust finally settles, I want them flown down to Guantánamo, where're they'll be released."

"Jesus," Bogan said, but then something came across his face as he finally caught a glimmering of what was actually going on. "Jesus," he said again.

McGarvey got out of the Hummer and walked across the road to where Martínez was waiting for him by the bus at the edge of the crowd. The people had been told who he was and why he had come here, and they were happy now and smiling.

"You wearing a vest?" Martínez asked as they headed through the crowd toward the access road.

McGarvey shook his head. "They're pros, so if it comes to that, they'll go for head shots. It'll be at nearly point-blank range, because I'm going to have to crowd them. It's the only way I'll have a chance of pulling it off."

"Doesn't have much of a chance anyway," Martínez said. "You do know that."

"We can't live forever."

"That's supposed to be my line, *comp*. This is for Cuba. Should be me going in there, why you?"

"For Cuba," McGarvey said. "Anyway, I want you guys to get the hell out of Miami and go home."

Martínez laughed. "Where would the tourists go for go for a good cup of coffee?" he asked, and McGarvey laughed with him.

"Havana. I've always wanted to smoke a good cigar. Legally."

They stopped at the access road. "Seriously, Mac, watch your ass. Those guys won't hesitate to pull the trigger."

"Neither will I," McGarvey said. He took out his pistol and, holding it out of sight just behind his right leg, headed to the open gate and the guard post the length of a football field away.

About fifty feet from the inner fence, a DI operative stepped out from behind one of the concrete structures flanking the gate. He was holding what looked like a compact automatic weapon of some sort.

"Do you speak English?" McGarvey called out, not stopping.

"Yes."

"The shooting is over, your associates are all dead. I'm here to talk."

"We'll talk to the newspapers and television."

"First you have to talk to me. Do you know what happened in Texas?"

The Cuban was dark, with thick black hair, dressed

in jeans and a denim jacket over a dark shirt, making him nearly invisible. "We heard."

"The gold is here, not in Texas or New Mexico."

"That is our understanding, señor," the DI operative said. "Please stop where you are."

McGarvey took a couple more steps before he stopped less than ten feet away from the man. "You're here on behalf of your government to stake a claim. Which you have done. Now it's time to go home."

"We want to see it with our own eyes."

"I've arranged for you and your partner, still hiding like a pansy, to have safe passage through the crowd to the army officer in charge of this installation." He needed the second agent in plain view; otherwise, if there was a shoot-out he'd be at a sharp disadvantage.

The other operative, also armed with what McGarvey recognized was a silenced MAC 10, the same as the weapon the DI had been equipped with at Fort Bliss, stepped into view. "Never happen, you *bastardo.*"

"Nevertheless, it's the only way you'll get out of here alive."

"*Hijo de puta!*" the man shouted, and he raised his weapon.

McGarvey shot him in the forehead, driving his body backwards, bouncing off the concrete structure, dead before he hit the pavement.

The other operative raised his weapon at the same moment McGarvey switched aim to him. But the man hesitated.

"Believe me, I do not want to kill you, but if I must I will," McGarvey said. "*Comprende?*"

The Cuban said nothing. He was tense but not out of control.

"I want you to return to Havana to make your report that the gold has been found. The Cuban government can make its claim, just as the people here tonight are making theirs."

The agent looked beyond McGarvey to the crowd. "They'll never let me pass."

"The military will escort you to their airstrip here, from where you'll be flown to Cuba."

"You're lying."

"I'm not," McGarvey said, but he was close enough to see the tightening muscles around the man's eyes and mouth.

The operative shouted something in Spanish, but an instant before he pulled the trigger, McGarvey fired one shot, catching him in the right kneecap, knocking him down, the MAC 10 firing into the sky, the thirty-round magazine empty in under two seconds.

McGarvey was on him in three steps, kicking the empty gun away, and immediately the Cuban understood that he had lost, and though he was in pain, he laid his head back. *"Qué?"*

"You're going home, a cripple, but probably a hero. Mission accomplished. But if you return, for any reason at all, I'll kill you. Understand?"

"Sí."

"Medic!" McGarvey shouted, and he got on the phone to General Bogan.

EIGHTY-THREE

Unlike the other vaults, which were compartmentalized almost like hardened cubicles in a very large office, vault C was a big room behind a massive door that swung ponderously outward, a metal ramp sliding into place over the thirty-inch gap in the concrete floor.

The ten combination holders, four of them women, all of them fifty or older, most of them dressed in ordinary business clothes even though it was the middle of the night on a weekend, and all of them anonymous, had entered their personnel data into the computer system on the ground floor. To reach the actual vault, they went through the same procedure three more times, and were subjected to hand and retinal scans.

More than gold was and had been stored here at one time or another, including the original Declaration of Independence and Constitution during WWII, the reserves of several European countries, jewels given to American soldiers to keep them out of Soviet hands, one of four known copies of the Magna Carta, and before the invention of synthetic painkillers a vast supply of processed morphine and opium, in case our supplies of raw opium were to be interrupted.

When the door was fully opened, the two Mint cops who had accompanied the group stepped aside to let McGarvey and Martínez cross the ramp.

The room, a box actually of reinforced concrete and steel brightly lit with fluorescent fixtures recessed in the ceiling, measuring about twenty feet on a side, was totally empty and spotlessly clean except for a light coating of dust on the floor.

Martínez had gone first and left footprints. There was no treasure here, and nothing had been in this room for a long time, at least twenty or thirty years.

McGarvey started to laugh, and Martínez turned back to him.

"Where is it?"

"Your guess is as good as mine," McGarvey said.

Martínez looked again at the empty space. "Did it ever exist?"

"The gold and other stuff they found in Victorio Peak existed. Otto established that much. And it was moved."

"But not here."

McGarvey turned and looked at the Mint cops, whose expressions were neutral, and then to the combination holders, none of whom seemed the least bit surprised.

"Are you satisfied, Mr. McGarvey?" one of the women asked.

"Where is it?"

"If you're talking about our gold reserves, some of it is here in the depository while a slightly larger amount—about five thousand metric tonnes—is stored in a vault beneath the Federal Reserve Bank of New York. But if you mean some mythical Spanish treasure dug up somewhere in New Mexico, it does not exist here."

"We could look inside the other vaults."

"Yes, you could," the woman said reasonably. "But still you would not find your treasure."

"What do I tell the crowd?" Martínez asked.

"The truth, that it's not here."

"Or the truth, that it doesn't exist, or never did?"

"Oh, it's somewhere, tell them that," McGarvey said. "And tell them that we'll just have to keep looking."

"It could have been good," Martínez said before he went to talk to the people and to the media.

When McGarvey got to the dispensary, Otto was already out of bed and getting dressed, a thick bandage on the side of his head. He was worried.

"Louise doesn't answer her cell phone, and no one in the Building can reach her."

"Call security," McGarvey said, but Otto shook his head.

"María León disappeared, and a passenger by the name of Ines Delgado flew to Atlanta last night, and caught the last flight to Washington, which landed just before one this morning. Delgado is the name she used to get out of Cuba."

"There's no reason to her to go to the McLean house."

"I'm not so sure about that," Otto said. "Anyway, this is something you and I have to handle. We get security or the Bureau involved, it could end up in a shoot-out. I'm counting on you, big-time, Kirk."

"Call our pilot," McGarvey said.

"Already have."

EIGHTY–FOUR

It was nine in the morning by the time they touched down at Andrews Air Force Base, borrowed a plain blue Ford Taurus motor pool car and, McGarvey driving, headed the thirty miles on the Capital Beltway to McLean. Otto hadn't said much on the flight, except to try Louise twice without luck before they touched down.

"Keep trying," McGarvey said when they crossed the river to Alexandria.

"I'm afraid," Otto said. "She's the only woman in my entire life who ever loved me for who I was. All the warts and dirty sweatshirts, even my Twinkies and heavy cream."

"You're not going to lose her, because the colonel wants the gold so that she can go home a redeemed apparatchik, and she knows that won't happen if she does something to Louise," McGarvey said. "And she knows that I would hunt her down and kill her, priority one. Try again."

Louise answered on the first ring, and relief and joy spread across Otto's face. He put the call on speakerphone. "We were worried about you. Are you okay?"

"Just dandy," Louise answered, her voice obviously strained. "Where are you?"

"On the Beltway, maybe twenty minutes away."

"Is Mac with you?"

"He's driving, and you're on speakerphone."

"Just a minute," Louise said, and the sound changed.

"You're on speakerphone, too. Mac, someone wants to talk to you."

"Colonel León, I expect," McGarvey said.

"We've been watching CNN," María said. "No gold in Texas and none in Kentucky. Where is it?"

"I don't know, but we're still looking."

"I want answers." María's voice rose a little. She sounded ragged. "I've come too far to go home empty-handed."

"I think that we need to talk about that, figure out what's best for all of us—because making it a DI mission to keep kidnapping the same woman won't work."

"Got your attention. It's all I want."

"Stand by, Louise, we're almost there," McGarvey said.

"We're in the kitchen having some of your cognac—" Louise said, but the connection was broken.

"What do you think?" Otto asked.

"She's running scared. If she goes home empty-handed, she'll face a firing squad. If she stays here, she'll spend the rest of her life in prison."

"What're her options?"

"She only has one," McGarvey said. "Talk to us."

It was Monday morning, and McLean's residential streets were quiet, everyone was either at work or in school. Nothing moved on the cul-de-sac that backed into Bryn Mawr Park, and McGarvey pulled into the driveway of the Renckes' secondary safe house and after a moment or two switched off the engine.

"Concentrate on Louise," he told Otto. "Let me do

the talking, and if you see an opening just bug out of the line of fire with her."

"I'm not leaving you."

McGarvey turned on him. "You'll goddamn follow orders for once," he said harshly. "I'm not losing any more people I care about. *Capisce?*"

Chastised, Otto nodded, and the two of them got out of the car and walked up to the house. The front door was unlocked, and McGarvey pushed it open with the toe of his shoe as he drew his pistol.

The place was deathly still.

"We're here," McGarvey called out.

"In the kitchen," Louise responded.

"What's your situation?"

"Pistol on the table. I think it's a compact Glock."

"Coming in," McGarvey said, and taking the lead, his pistol pointed down at his side, he moved down the hall, where he stopped at the open doorway.

"Good morning, Kirk," María said, making no move for the pistol on the table in front of her. She looked disheveled, as if she hadn't slept in a couple of days, which she probably hadn't.

"Pick up the gun, Louise," McGarvey said, but María snatched it up first and switched the safety off.

"I can't allow that," she said. Her pistol was pointed a little to the left, not at Louise or at McGarvey, but she was wired.

"Will you allow Louise to leave the kitchen?"

"No. For the moment, she's my only bargaining chip."

The kitchen was large, with a lot of big windows

that overlooked an expansive backyard with a swing set and elaborate-looking children's play station, or gym, with slides and bars and even a tree house of sorts. McGarvey could see Audie playing here, and he could hear her laughter. And he was finally beginning to see himself back in the picture.

He stepped the rest of the way into the kitchen, and María stiffened when she saw he was holding a gun. But moving slowly, he holstered the Walther under his jacket at the small of his back and then sat down at the table across from her. Otto came in a moment later and sat down next to his wife, and put an arm around her shoulder.

"Okay?" he asked.

Louise was looking at his bandage. "They were a lousy shot, thank God."

"You came here to get my attention," McGarvey said. "What's next?"

"Where's the treasure?"

"I don't know if we'll ever find out."

"But it exists."

"I'm almost certain of it," McGarvey said. "But none of it will ever get to Havana, at least not to the government."

"Which you think you can bring down."

"Not me alone," McGarvey said.

María nodded. "You are a man at once formidable and *pavoroso*."

"What?"

"She means fearful," Louise said, and she looked at María. "You can't imagine the half of it."

"Yes, I can."

"So I'll ask again, what's next?" McGarvey said.

"If you don't know where the treasure lies, or are unwilling reveal it, then there is nothing left for me."

"Nothing in Havana, but if you agree to be extensively debriefed on DI operations and long-range planning, something might be worked out. Maybe a plea bargain."

But María was shaking her head, a sudden infinite sadness in her large dark eyes. "I could never do such a thing, never stay here for the rest of my life in or out of jail." She looked out the windows at the swing set. "I am what I am. A product of my genes and my upbringing, my training. I'm a Cuban, and the only man who ever wrote that he loved me was my father."

For a long time her statement seemed to hold in the air, but then she turned again and smiled wistfully.

"You are a formidable and *pavoroso* man among men, Kirk McGarvey. In another time and place, under different circumstances, I could have loved you more than my country. More than my life itself."

"Whatever you do next, just no more killing, no more blood," McGarvey said. "Something can be worked out."

María got to her feet. "Give me the keys to your car."

"They're in the ignition."

"If you try to follow me, or send the police after me, I'll defend myself. And I am a very good shot."

"I'm sure you are."

She gave him another long, searching look and then,

keeping her pistol trained in their general direction, backed out of the kitchen and disappeared down the front hall and out the door.

"Aren't you going after her?" Otto demanded.

McGarvey shook his head, and it seemed to him that he hadn't slept in days, maybe not in years, maybe not since his first kill in Santiago when he was nothing more than a very young husband with a baby daughter at home. Now they were all dead and buried, just as so many others who'd become close to him were.

"We're just going to let her go?"

"She has nowhere to run," McGarvey said.

And maybe he'd finally had his fill of it all. Maybe if he thought hard enough about it, his life had been pretty much a waste.

Otto and Louise were watching him. And after a beat, Louise reached across the table and put her hands on his.

"Think about Audie," she said.

"I do all the time."

"Then it should be enough."

"I'm not following you."

"You're feeling sorry for yourself—I can see it in your eyes from a mile away."

Coming from Louise just now it stung. "You're probably right. And it's why I let her go. I'm tired of the blood. Up to my neck in it, and it's time for me to back off."

"Go back to your Greek island to lick your wounds?"

"Something like that."

"And then what?"

McGarvey wanted to look away, but he couldn't. "I don't know. I haven't thought that far ahead."

"There'll be something else for you," Louise said. "You do know that much at least."

"I'm getting out."

"No," Louise blurted.

"It's over."

"What about the rest of us, what are we supposed to do? Me and Otto?"

McGarvey held his silence.

"You have a gift, Kirk. Rare and terrible as it is, we need you."

"All the killing."

"All the lives you've saved. What about them, or don't they count?"

"My wife and daughter were murdered because of my gift, as you call it," McGarvey shot back. His anger was rising. "I'm done."

"What about your grandchild? Are you going to just walk away from whatever comes her way?"

"That's not fair, goddamnit."

"No it's not," Louise said. "But it's the hand you were dealt."

She was right, of course. He knew it in his heart of hearts, just as he knew that he would have to go back to Serifos at least for a little while. A month or two, before he could work up the courage to come back to Casey Key, reopen the house he'd shared with Katy, and pick up the threads of his life. If he had the courage.

But Louise was smiling gently now, sadly. "Anyway, Happy Birthday, kemo sabe," she said.

McGarvey looked at her. "What?"

"It's your birthday today, Kirk. Otto and I were hoping that this business would be done soon enough, because I planned a party. With Audie. Turns out she likes chocolate cake, with chocolate frosting, chocolate ice cream, and chocolate milk."

EPILOGUE

It was five of a bright, sunny afternoon in Havana, when María, dressed in starched and crisply pressed olive drab fatigues and bloused highly polished boots, entered Raúl Castro's office. She marched across the room, came to attention in front of his desk, and saluted.

"*Señor Presidente,* Colonel León reporting as ordered, sir."

Castro returned her salute, then picked up the telephone to his secretary. "I am not to be disturbed for the next hour."

Exciting new things were happening in Cuba because of her uncle. Private businesses were beginning to thrive, the formerly government-controlled private property market had been newly opened—apartments and houses could be legally bought and sold, which meant a lot of money was starting to flow into the country and the strict restriction on tourism from the States that had been in place for fifty years was finally beginning to relax with the promise of even more foreign capital.

But in María's estimation, it was not nearly enough. They—the island—needed much more.

Castro motioned for her to have a seat. "Your mission was not a success," he said, but his tone was not harsh.

"But not a failure, either," María said.

"Tell me."

"I spoke with my friend in Seville, Dr. Adriana Vergílio, who has come up with fresh evidence. Something new. On the second Spanish expedition to New Mexico, one of the enlisted men who survived was actually a spy for the Vatican. His name was Jacob Parella, and he kept a diary."

"Your friend has this diary?"

"No, but she thinks she knows where it might be found. Parella may have made it back to Rome, but he never reached safety in the Vatican. Instead he was murdered and robbed, supposedly by a street gang. But Dr. Vergílio thinks it was the Voltaire Society."

"What's next?" Castro asked.

"I'm going to find it, of course," María said. "Jacob's diary is the key to the treasure."

"You'll need help."

"Yes. Kirk McGarvey."